The Mitt Man

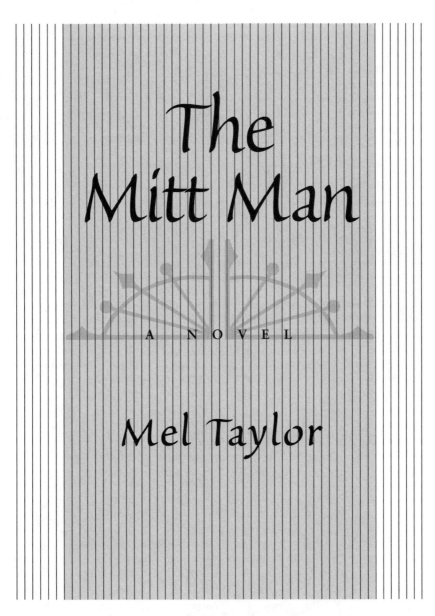

The Mitt Man

A NOVEL

Mel Taylor

WILLIAM MORROW AND COMPANY, INC. ✴ NEW YORK

It is the policy of William Morrow and Company, Inc., and its imprints
and affiliates, recognizing the importance of preserving what has been written,
to print the books we publish on acid-free paper,
and we exert our best efforts to that end.

Library of Congress Cataloging-in-Publication Data
Taylor, Mel, 1939–
The mitt man / by Mel Taylor.
        p.   cm
ISBN 0-688-16094-8 (alk. paper)
1. Afro-Americans—Louisiana—New Orleans—History—20th century—
Fiction. I. Title.
PS3570.A9462M58 1999
813'.54—dc21   98-38984
CIP

Printed in the United States of America

First Edition

1 2 3 4 5 6 7 8 9 10

BOOK DESIGN BY OKSANA KUSHNIR

www.williammorrow.com

FOR HANK

Rest in peace, gentle warrior
No more mountains now
No more demons to slay
Tomorrow, you fly with the wind
See the face of God
He knows your heart
And so do I

Acknowledgments

A big thanks to my super agent, Pam Bernstein, who took a chance on me, and Donna Downing, her assistant, who always gave me confidence. To Claire Wachtel, my editor, who knows everything there is to know about writing a novel and guided me gently through my first one, and Jessica Baumgardner whose warm reception was important in those unfamiliar waters. To my friends Danny Brown and Carol Johanson both of whom believed in the "Mint Man" from the very first page. To my brother, Tony, who first gave me the idea to write and my sister, Vanessa, my biggest cheerleader. To Norma Ibironke, thanks for the year. Another thanks to Joyce Dorsey, who has believed in me forever. To my friend Doris and her daughter Alice who worked with me early on. To my angel, Cheryl Taylor, who has never let me down. Thanks to C. E. Kimber Hopson for a wonderful suggestion. To my children: André, my son who can quote from the Bible on request and who at times became like my father. To my son Ché, stay strong, young man. To my son Darren, there's still time. Thanks to my daughter Tiffany, one of the brightest people I know, and my daughter Jeanette, who also has talent as a writer. Thanks to *all my friends and relatives who have wished me well in this work.*

BOOK ONE

King Fish

New Orleans, 1926

The sweet, pungent, odor of jasmine crept through the windows of the New Orleans Charity Hospital, permeating the air and mingling slowly with the harsh chemical stench of the third-floor operating room. Doctors and nurses in full operating gear floated back and forth like spirits in a séance. King Fish, a thirty-six-year-old black man, lay very close to death. In New Orleans the ninth ward district was hard, filled with hot tempers and violent exchanges. King Fish was the victim of one such exchange. Two bullets had penetrated his chest and now his breath came in short, unchoreographed bursts, giving way to hopeless gurgling sounds. All around him the white images began to fade in and out of his vision, dancing and shimmering, like silhouettes done up in alabaster. Somewhere in the deep recesses of his mind King Fish heard the siren again, first far away and low, then increasing in volume, ever-building, soaring to a crescendo that seemed to explode in his head . . . then a sudden eerie calm claimed the room, the faint wisp of jasmine, the nausea of his own blood, and again, the calm, the calm, the calm. . . .

It could have happened to any man, at any time, over any woman, if he lived in the "Bottoms" and gambled too much, drank too much, and wore his ego on his chest like a medal of valor. Sue

Ellen knew this as well as anyone; she had witnessed it firsthand over and over again. She had been introduced by King Fish to this subculture within a subculture, to this untamed world where every man carried a gun, and every woman a razor in her stocking, where conscience was an enemy and perspective as rare as virtue, a place where people lived dangerously—just for the thrill of it. She wondered if King Fish understood that. If he lived through this he wanted to ask him "if it was worth it." Maybe it was cold having these thoughts, with him fighting for his life, but he had taught her that life was cold, especially the truth. As for tears, she had cried bucketsful. From the moment he had fallen to the floor with blood bubbling from his mouth, she had cried, in the ambulance, and all the way to the emergency room, where she now sat waiting for a miracle.

Suddenly she seemed to be drained of feelings and of tears. It had been fun in the beginning when love was sure and springtime fresh, when she was too young to think, too young to be afraid or to care, ten years ago when she had been only fifteen and glad to be considered grown-up, proud to be known as King Fish's woman. Life was not complicated then; it was just one unrelenting adventure. She had seen him many times before he had ever noticed her. He stayed in her thoughts, in her daydreams, and in her night dreams. On weekends she would come alive with excitement and anticipation, which made her body go all warm and moist—even between her legs and under her arms—because she knew that she would at least see him. He'll want me one day, she would think to herself. It didn't matter that her hair was not straight, or that she was not light-skinned like those high-yellow women who were always in his company. She was young and unused, the way she knew a man wanted his woman to be, and she would be devoted. Her grandmother had taught her these things and God was her grandmother's teacher. It was a shame He hadn't been able to teach her mother. "The best gift a woman can give a man is a body what ain't been touched," her grandmother would say, and Sue Ellen would smile as she cleaned the two-room shotgun shack before preparing her grandmother's breakfast.

Afterward she would drag the old number-ten washtub in from the back porch, boil some water in the big black kettle, and scrub herself fresh with Castile soap. In the cracked glass that stood against the wall and served as a mirror, she would watch her reflection as she polished her body with olive oil and applied baking soda to her underarms. It was a flawless body, shiny and muscular, with full pointed breasts that seemed to have appeared there overnight. Her teeth were perfectly straight and pearly white in her smooth black face, her smile quick and disarming. She always wore an old dress on Saturdays, one she had outgrown, to better show off this newly discovered body that her grandmother had warned her about. "You smell'n yo' pee, ain'tcha? Better watch yo' step and don't be messin' wit' dem nasty little boys, else you gonna git sup'n ya don't want." Sometimes she felt her grandmother was too old-fashioned, and sometimes she didn't give her credit for the knowledge of her years, but she loved this strong proud woman with silver hair and arthritic hands, who smelled of liniment, and of snuff, who was grumpy and opinionated. Her grandmother was and had always been her protector, her mother, and her friend, the one who rubbed her chest with Vicks, forced her, with love, to drink castor oil, and stayed up with her all night when she was sick. She loved her but had begun to hate the way they lived. She hated the run-down house, the smell of the kerosene lamp, and the stench of the slop bucket she had to empty each day. Most of all she hated the trips to the outhouse in back. She wanted something better for her and her grandmother and she was determined to get it, even if she didn't quite know how. She only knew that being cooped up there was not the way.

On Saturday, when her grandmother would fall asleep in the old rocking chair with her Bible in her hand, as she always did, Sue Ellen would tiptoe past the potbelly stove that stood boldly in the living room, sidestep the quilted couch she slept on, and ease out of the door into the bright summer sunlight. She loved the summer. The summer meant freedom, it meant birds and flowers and wonderful aromas. It was a time to dream, to wish, to fly. She would trot barefoot down the dirt road that snaked from her house to the one-room school the colored kids attended (*when it was not summer vacation, as it was then*), and make her way across the creek on a wooden makeshift bridge built years ago by prisoners on a chain gang. Her heart would pound when she came into view of the Bucket-of-Blood. Then she would put on what she imagined was the walk of a lady.

The Bucket-of-Blood was a faded run-down bar that leaned drunkenly on a plot of land fifteen miles outside of New Orleans. A large hand-painted sign boasted a dare to all those who walked through its doors: buy my moonshine whiskey, shoot dice at my table, or if you really want a thrill spend a *sweaty* ten minutes upstairs with one of Big Lil's fancy whores. The Bucket-of-Blood was the only thing in Gator Creek that had ever produced any excitement, even if it was considered by church people to be a den of iniquity. Of course she was too young to go inside, but she could watch as the hustlers paraded in and out wearing the finest fashions she had ever seen.

She finally met King Fish on the day of the monthly Kotch Ball, which was a deceptive name in that it suggested a posh affair where giddy virgin girls sipped punch and made small talk with promising young boys. Instead, a Kotch Ball was a jubilant, festive gathering of colored hustlers from near and far who arrived in fine carriages with their silk-clad ladies. They came to witness or participate in a high-stakes card game called "Kotch." A group of farmers gathered around every month to gawk at this spectacle; this time Sue Ellen had gotten a bucket and stood tall in the midst of them as King Fish strode inside with two light-complexioned women, one on each arm. He was big and strong looking, dark like herself, which made him even more impressive in his white suit and derby hat. She liked his big laugh and gold tooth, and was a little jealous of the two women in his company, women she wanted to be like: beautiful and self-assured, with wonderful clothes and red lipstick; but she would never sell her body, as she suspected they did, nor would she have casual sex with different men and lose her respect, the way her grandmother told her her mother had. She would never be like this woman who had brought her into this world then abandoned her, a woman referred to by all as the town tramp, who didn't know who the father of her child was.

One man was enough for Sue Ellen. She was determined to have the one she wanted and determined to have him all to herself. The fact that she was bright would help her in this quest, and bright she was, so bright that Miss Brown, her teacher, had taken her on as a kind of protégée, introducing her to a world of classical reading that Sue Ellen had been convinced was reserved for whites only. Much to the delight of Miss Brown, she excelled in reading comprehension even beyond the teacher's expectations. Sue Ellen's young mind raced with delight as she encountered each adventure. With each romantic interlude she saw herself as the heroine, dressed in extravagant costumes, traveling at will all over Europe. In essence, books became a wonderful escape from the lackluster existence she led.

In the classroom Sue Ellen reigned at the top, excelling in all subjects, far outdistancing her closest rival. The challenges that frightened other kids seemed to inspire her, and her eyes would become bright and shiny, anticipating the successful outcome of each engagement. The true marvel, however, was that this fifteen-year-old had such insight into human behavior. This was a quality greatly overshadowed by her reluctance to use proper grammar, which made her appear, to learned people, to be less intelligent. To Sue Ellen proper grammar used by colored folks was a betrayal by white people, just another tool to emphasize their superiority and estrangement. On the one hand, this refusal to comply with what the status quo considered the foundation of scholastic achievement worked against her in social encounters, but on the other, the surprise and underestimation it led to often gave her an advantage, as, for example, when the so-called white do-gooders took their annual tour of the colored community to satisfy their consciences and pay lip service to the idea of ameliorating the deplorable conditions that existed there. When they came to the school Sue Ellen heard no sincerity in their words of praise, nothing heartfelt in their voices of concern, and responded by dramatizing her own pitiful state; as a result, without actually asking for them, she acquired funds for candy cakes and sweet water. Needless to say, Miss Brown didn't approve, trying as she did to foster an appearance of self-reliance in her people, but having no real grounds for protest, she resorted to sharp looks which Sue Ellen tactfully avoided. There were other looks Sue Ellen avoided as well. These were the unclean glints in the eyes of more than a few older black and white males who managed to find themselves in her company. These were sickening experiences that made her somehow hate her mother's behavior more and maybe even her mother.

If her mother was dead, the way it had been rumored after her disappearance, that might be better. No one could hate the dead. There existed in Sue Ellen's heart no emotional experience or visual image of her mother to love. True, her brilliant mind and tenacious spirit made her a formidable young lady; but that Saturday, in the presence of King Fish, she was reduced to a mere country girl who was indecisive and confused, who resorted to hostility to mask her vulnerability.

"I'm gonna make him pay 'tention to me," she said, under her breath, as King Fish and the two women walked into the Bucket-of-Blood. She even considered running up to King Fish and making herself known, but thought better of it. "Girl, you sho' is silly," she said, again under her breath. There was nothing to do now but wait. In resignation, she peered at him through the window, and to her surprise he, too, was looking at her. Even more to her astonishment, he left the women and walked out the door headed in her direction. It was a slow, deliberate walk, accompanied by a constant stare that held her spellbound. Even the farmers noticed and made a path for King Fish as if he were visiting royalty. In a way they were somewhat honored that he was interested in one of their own. For they were as different from him as night and day, as squares are different from hustlers; them with their bib overalls and tattered straw hats, and King Fish in a fine, gabardine suit. The farmers smelled of hard labor and the mules they worked with; they concerned themselves with the meager living they made off the land, but King Fish's only concern was the next mark he would swindle in a card or dice game. His aftershave lotion floated toward them like a slow, heavenly scented wind, causing some to question his manhood. When he asked her name, he and Sue Ellen were eye to eye.

"My name is Sue Ellen," she said, hopping nonchalantly to the ground.

"How ol' are ya?"

"Why? I'm ol' enough."

King Fish smiled. "What ya ol' enough fo'?"

"Fo' anything I wanna be ol' enough fo'."

She placed her hands on her hips and tried to look him in the eyes, but for a split second avoided his gaze, giving away her uneasiness. King Fish baited her.

"You ain't ol' enough to mess wit' me."

"I ain't said I wanna mess wit' ya no how, what you think anyhow?"

Her feistiness made him like her more.

"I think I wanna buy you a dress and some shoes to go wit' it."

Sue Ellen looked at her bare feet in embarrassment, but quickly recovered. "You think I ain't got no shoes? I got plenty shoes!"

King Fish moved closer and whispered, "Bet you ain't got no high heels. And bet you ain't got no red silk dress."

"You buy dem dresses fo' dem women you wit'?"

"Dat ain't yo' business."

"I ain't said it was my business. I was just askin'. Anyway, I thank I gotta go."

Clearly she was upset and started to walk away. He blocked her path with a step and an outstretched arm.

"Wait, li'l mama!"

"Fo' what? You ain't gonna buy me no dress and no shoes, no how." She placed her hands on her hips again and postured. " 'Cuz I ain't yo' business."

"I said, I was—"

"When?"

"Lighten up on ol' Fish, li'l mama. I do what I say."

She softened.

He said, "Let me trim these marks inside first, okay?"

He wrote his address on a piece of paper and handed it to her, along with two one-dollar bills. "Meet me at my roost in two hours, okay?"

She hesitated.

"C'mon, li'l mama!"

She relented. He gave her his best smile and walked back to the club.

"King Fish sho' like you," a voice said from behind her. He was a little old man, she noticed, wearing large brogan shoes that he walked on the heels of. His jaws were sunken where his teeth had previously been and his breath carried with it the smell of stale tobacco. Gus was his name and he introduced himself as King Fish's man.

"Tell you one thang, he always do what he say."

Sue Ellen thought him comical at first and resented his invasion of her privacy, but she wanted to hear more about King Fish.

"How ya know he like me?"

"Girl, I knowed 'im since he was a young boy. Knowed his uncle Ed Cook who raised 'im, after his folks got burnt up in that fiya."

"His mama and daddy got kilt in a fiya?"

Sue Ellen gasped.

"Brother and sister too. Don't tell 'im I tol' ya, 'cuz he don't talk 'bout it."

Sue Ellen tried hard to imagine King Fish as a boy, but the picture wouldn't come. She could only see him in fancy clothes and jewelry, even if she condensed him in her mind to the size of a child.

"Now he done gon' and giv' ya two dollars. Now dat's sumpin'." Gus spit a straight line of tobacco juice. "And you ain't done nuthin' fo' it, eetha."

She raised her eyebrows. "He want me to do sumpin' fo' this two dollars?"

"I ain't sayin' dat. I'm sayin', I know he like ya, 'cuz dem gals upstairs at Big Lil's do's ever' thang fo' jest one dollar. Sump'n else too. He ain't never give no woman no clothes right off befo' either."

The shadow of a smile danced around Sue Ellen's cheeks. She loved the thought of being special, the intoxicating feeling of being desired by a man like King Fish. She stretched her arms with confidence and a broad smile that she turned away from Gus's eyes. She had taken a stand, unwittingly as it had been, she stood up to King Fish, and this had been her first social exchange with a real man. There was an irony here too. Although she empathized with him for his childhood tragedy, he had somehow, because of that tragedy, become less of an icon, and in her mind, more accessible.

Sue Ellen was moving on stable ground when she walked the one-half mile with Gus to King Fish's house, as Gus had insisted, promising it would be all right, because he lived there as well and had somewhat the run of the place, especially when King Fish was in New Orleans, as he often was. Cheerfully, they walked down the dirt road past One-eyed John's blacksmith shop, the only business on the street which divided the rich farmland, with only a scattering of houses on either side. Big John, it was said by the townspeople, had done time in the state pen for beating a man to death with a red-hot poker. But you would have never been able to tell, given his friendly demeanor and hearty hello to Gus.

King Fish's house was the only one that sat on the dirt road, or rather slightly back from it at the end of a long bend. It was a small, neat two-bedroom place, almost military in its orderliness, with a couch covered in army brown and two olive-colored square chairs adjacent to it. The hardwood floors shone glossy like a spit-polished boot, challenging the luster of the tall, shiny, brass lamp with its yellow-and-amber shade, which seemed to have been plucked from the den of the most fashionable whorehouse in New Orleans. Sue Ellen smiled with delight when she entered the house, pausing to inhale what she thought was a most beautiful sight, before Gus ushered her to the bathroom, which had hot-and-cold running water. Sue Ellen thought, He must be rich! She had a powerful urge to fill the tub with warm water and lie in it for hours; only the music emerging from a Victrola she had not noticed in the living room pulled her away. It was the blues, funky and slow. She walked back to the living room in time with the beat as it moved her body and spirit, swaying back and forth, snapping her fingers and rocking her head. Gus explained, with considerable pride, his familiarity with each singer before they had become popular. She had grown very comfortable with Gus now, sitting at ease on the floor of a strange man's home. It was fun.

When King Fish walked through the door, Sue Ellen was so engrossed in the music she hardly noticed.

"Like dem blues, huh, li'l mama?" he asked with a smile.

"Yeah, I like 'um, 'cuz I can feel what they sayin'," she replied, never missing a beat.

"Sho' ya do, you got to. It's part of you. The blues is the tears of colored folks."

These words got her attention. He was right. She had never thought of it that way. King Fish began again.

"The blues is the greatest music in the wurl'! We dun been mistreated all our life, been slaves, built this here country with our tears and our blood and nuthin' ta hep us but our music."

Now Sue Ellen was looking at him in a new light, with a different kind of respect, and she noticed in his eyes the pain and the anger this knowledge brought him, and his struggle to balance that anger against the reality of the times he lived in. In that moment, as he stood there so proud and so angry, almost majestic, her realization of the oppression suffered by her people uncovered her own suppressed pain, and there existed, in her, too, a mounting rage that was replaced by sadness and a most awful longing that made her think of a father she had never known and the feel of his arms around her. King Fish changed the mood.

"Got sump'n fo' ya, li'l mama," he said, and walked toward the back.

She glanced at Gus, who wore his I-told-you-so smile boldly on his face; but her mind was filled with other thoughts, deeper and wider ranging ones. She had to address the rage she had just experienced. The lessons her grandmother and Miss Brown had taught had been well received. She had become a well-mannered young lady. She was clean, neat, and kind, but she suddenly realized it didn't mean anything in white America. No matter what she did or how well she did it, she could not rise above the color of her skin. Miss Brown was proof of that. Look at how smart she was and white people did not respect her, not really. There was something more—her anger. They had never addressed her anger, as if she had no right to it, no right, still, to condemn those who were responsible for it.

They had touched each other, she and King Fish, in a way she would have never imagined. They had shared pain and anger and were both more determined, stronger for it; at least she had gained strength from witnessing his resolve. Yes, she liked this man and she could feel he liked her, but now what? She knew what a grown man wanted from a woman. She also knew it was too soon for her, yet she didn't want to appear immature. King Fish surprised her again. When she looked up he was standing there holding a very pretty pair of red shoes and a beautiful red dress that she simply stared at. He read her face for a response.

"Dem some pretty shoes and a pretty dress," she said.

"Well?" he asked.

She hesitated.

"Ain't no strings, li'l mama. I jest like ya." He placed them in her hands. "Go on in the bathroom and try 'em on."

She rose up slowly and started in the direction of the bathroom, then turned back around.

"You don't want nuthin' fo' dese things, do ya?"

"Nuthin'," he replied, convincingly.

Satisfied, she walked to the bathroom. After she slipped the dress on over her own, she smiled.

Girl, you sho' look good in red! she thought, rotating her body to glimpse every angle in the mirror.

The shoes were too large, but that was okay, she'd simply stuff newspaper in the toes. She sure wasn't going to give them back. Sue Ellen quickly took off the dress and hurried back into the living room, wondering how to get out of there with her virginity and her ego intact. King Fish solved that problem for her. After asking if the items fit, he engaged her in a brief conversation about family, school, and her aspirations in life; then he suggested she head back home before darkness fell. King Fish would have told Gus to drive her in his buckboard, but didn't think her grandmother would like that. Maybe that was when she realized she might fall in love with him and what that really meant for a woman. She began to understand that love was more than just the fantasy of a young girl, that it carried with it responsibility for the other person. As Sue Ellen's mind began to ponder the subject, she imagined herself catering to King Fish's needs, washing his clothes, cooking his food, and maybe, someday, having his children. She was sure she wanted to fulfill his desires, but her grandmother's words were haunting.

"Where you been, chile?" her grandmother asked, when Sue Ellen finally made it home, hugging her new dress and shoes. "And where'd you git dem things?"

"A nice man give 'em to me, Gran'maw."

Her grandmother's stare was sharp.

"I ain't don' nuthin' wrong, Gran'maw, I swear."

"What I tell ya 'bout swearin'. People swear when they ain't got no mo' lies to tell."

"I ain't lying, Gran'maw. He give 'em to me fo' nuthin'. He just talked to me 'bout the blues and how white folks dun dun us—"

"Shut yo' mouf 'bout some blues. Dat's the devil's music and you been in the devil's den doin' Lawd knows what or fixin' to. Now you listen, little Miss Pissant. You too young and too dumb to be sashaying 'round wit' grown men. Ya know they only wants one thang."

"But, Gran—"

"Shut up, shut up. Ain't hearin' no mo'. You go clean off that back porch or sumpin' and don't forget to empty that slop bucket."

Sue Ellen knew her anger was less a condemnation and more a fear for her granddaughter's spiritual well-being. She also knew to stay in her grandmother's good graces, as she did for the better part of the next week.

Sue Ellen did not go to the Bucket-of-Blood that next Saturday, but King Fish was always in her thoughts, and apparently, she was in his. The knock on the door that Monday morning and his broad smile confirmed that. But this was not the slick, snappy dresser she had always observed, that commanding figure whose flashing style held everyone's attention. This was a common man in bib overalls wearing a straw hat much like the farmers in Gator Creek. He had even somehow adopted their slouching posture. Under his arm, she noticed with great surprise, was lodged a Bible, and on her porch, beside him, lay an array of vegetables next to a shoulder of ham.

"Who dat out there, chile?" inquired Gran'maw.

King Fish stepped past Sue Ellen into view. "Mornin', ma'am, bought sumpin' you and Sue Ellen might could use."

He began moving the food into the house as if it were the most natural thing in the world.

"Who are you and what you up to, young man?"

"He da one I tol' ya 'bout, Gran'maw, da one who—"

"I ain't ast you. I ast him."

"My name James Cook, ma'am. I came ta ast to court Sue Ellen."

Sue Ellen was taken aback, but said nothing.

"Befo' ya say no, ma'am, I know I'm older than her, but I got me a good business and some money saved. I'm a Christian man and I believe in dis hea Bible that I'm studyin' for when the good Lawd call me to preach the Gospel."

"Ain't ya da one what lissen to dat devil's music?"

"It ain't him, Gran'maw."

Sue Ellen had lied before she realized it.

"Well, it's his house, ain't hit?" her grandmother countered.

"That ain't altogether so, ma'am." King Fish said, defending himself. "I mean, it's my house all right, I own it and every thang, but I lives mostly in New Orleans. Gus, that's the ol' man she talkin' 'bout, he kinda rents from me."

Little did Sue Ellen know that day, but that lie was the beginning of her entry into the world of streetwise people. King Fish had to struggle to hold back a smile.

"What kind of business ya say ya in?" Gran'maw asked suspiciously.

"I'm what they calls a produce agent, which means I buy from the farmers here and sells to the stores in New Orleans."

Gran'maw's silence was an approval of sorts and King Fish knew it. The reality was, in spite of the age difference between him and Sue Ellen, he was the best catch in town, a fact not lost on this old woman with failing health who wanted the very best for her granddaughter, who she believed had received one of the most devastating blows life could deal to a child born into this world—the loss of a mother and a father. But if he all he cracked up to be, Gran'maw thought, dat ought not make no difference. For sure she was no match for this accomplished con man who played a "lame" as well as anyone and told her exactly what she wanted to hear. King Fish quoted from the Bible to her with total confidence, prayed over the lunch he had invited himself to, and bid her to tell him the story of her life, while listening patiently to the advice she had to give. It was not that King Fish, at this time, was a religious man; this was not the case. Although, as a child, the opposite was true. As a child he had been filled with that goodwill and purity of thought possessed by all true Christians. His mother and father had seen to that, especially his father, a church deacon who had introduced him to all the wonderful stories in the Bible, which were much more engaging than the stories in any other book he had attempted to read. King Fish had been drawn to the rhythm of the biblical passages, their poetry, their music, and their profundity. He stored them in his mind like literary treasures. Being a "saved" young man had brought him rewards as well. Because of a talent for reading the written Word aloud and a beautiful bass singing voice, he was held in high esteem by church people, even considered by most a gifted child, clearly destined for the ministry. He had believed this, too, before the tragedy that befell his family had cost him his faith. King Fish had then grown up the hard way, the street way, around pimps, gamblers, and con men, hustlers who had a much different view of life, men who believed the strong would always dominate the world, men like his uncle Ed, King Fish's father's younger brother, who would say with a crooked smile, "If the meek ever inherits this earth, it's gonna be 'cuz the strong give it up fo' a better planet." King Fish had patterned himself after this accomplished hustler with his sharp clothes and painted ladies, who was dubbed "Easy Ed" because of the nonchalant way he went about life's business. Under his uncle's tutelage King Fish quickly became a true "slickster," a skilled pickpocket and cardsharp. His knowledge of the Scriptures became, now, an instrument to be used in disarming his victims in petty con games and a device by which to make preachers look small whenever he could corner them in a debate. His singing voice, too, was now used to another advantage, mostly for self-aggrandizement, and when he grew older, as a means to lure women into his bed. By then he had dismissed his spirit-moving gospel songs in favor of the more sensual blues ballad. He did, however, sing the Lord's music for Gran'maw; and this may have been what finally won her over. No older Christian could think badly of any young man who quoted the Bible and sang spirituals as well as King Fish did.

The courtship, insisted Gran'maw, had to take place under her supervision, which meant under her roof. King Fish came, without fail, every day of that week to entertain Sue Ellen and her grandmother, bringing with him small gifts that delighted them both: a knit shawl for Gran'maw, and for Sue Ellen her first handbag; there were gospel songs, too, and they sang them together. These quaint moments reminded King Fish of his family, a bittersweet remembrance that sometimes brought him close to tears. More than anything, the retreat from the fast life was good for him and so was Sue Ellen, and in fact, he had grown considerably fond of both women in a very short time—fonder than he had anticipated. When Gran'maw began to fail he was genuinely concerned; he became even more attentive, and that was not his nature. Denial had been the defense he had used to maintain his sanity when he lost his family. In later years this denial, with the aid of his uncle

Ed, transformed itself into a chilling detachment from ordinary human emotions; but the gradual decline of this grand old lady struck a different chord, stirred up emotions King Fish thought had long since been laid to rest.

It was on a Sunday, a month after she and King Fish had met, and Gran'maw had just taken a turn for the worse when King Fish finally persuaded her to let Gus drive her in the buckboard to the colored hospital in New Orleans, the same hospital King Fish would find himself in ten years later. Sue Ellen remembered her words of warning as if they had been spoken only yesterday, and her eyes, with that strange distant glow that searched her face, and King Fish's, to measure their sincerity. Then there was a bright smile, as if she knew something they didn't.

"Listen," she demanded in a very strong and clear voice. "Ain't but one thang in dis here wurl' what make it worth livin'." She paused to look at them both again. "Love."

And, as if she had suddenly fallen asleep, she lay slowly back on her pillow and passed quietly and peacefully from this world.

Sue Ellen took the money with such ease she surprised herself. King Fish would be proud of her and his other two women soooo jealous! She smiled when she counted the three ten-dollar bills she had peeled from the bankroll of this white man who had stumbled into Bill Black's all-night blues club in New Orleans, as white men often did, in search of some colored "poontang." She had led the man into a corner of this smokyblue haze that was filled with loud music and intoxicated people and had picked his pocket. The going rate for sex was one dollar. The price of a drink ten cents. The thirty dollars Sue Ellen had stolen represented more than three months' rent in Gator Creek. She had been nervous at first, before a cool, calm aura had come over her from out of nowhere, making her hand in the man's pocket as steady as a surgeon's. Hopelessly drunk and without a clue as to the amount of money that remained after an evening on the town, he was the perfect mark for Sue Ellen's first shot move. When she saw her chance she eased away, promising to bring them both back a drink, leaving him prey to a real prostitute, instead of a girl impersonating one, as she had been.

Sue Ellen's life had changed drastically in the three weeks since her grandmother's death. For starters she had lost her virginity in the first week of her considerable grief. In one volcanic moment her pain and her passion had married, and with gratitude as her guide, she had moved easily into King Fish's arms. This was understandable, because aside from Miss Brown, who was very sympathetic and helpful, it was King Fish who stood steadfastly by her side, even to the point of opening up his house to her. Gus offered his bedroom temporarily. He would simply move into Sabria's house, one of King Fish's two women, who lived in New Orleans. This was not a problem, as Gus frequently moved back and forth between the two houses doing handyman work. He was, in fact, a friend to Sabria, and indeed, made a point of being friendly toward any woman who became involved with King Fish. Sue Ellen had offered little resistance to this arrangement for several reasons: she loved the house, she trusted the man, and she had convinced herself that her grandmother somehow might have approved. Lastly, she was still very young and had never been alone. King Fish's strong arms made her feel safe, just as the cover of a blanket gives a feeling of security to a child. The joy of lovemaking for the first time was even more wonderful than she had imagined, mostly because she was devastated by grief, and in that state of mind the act of love is always more poignant than at any other time. From that moment on she was totally his, and in spite of the presence of the other women, she considered him totally hers. However, her introduction to Sabria, the second week of her stay with King Fish, somewhat shattered her illusion, brought her face-to-face with a certain reality. She was in a competitive situation. And Sabria was competitive to say the least. A fast-talking Creole from New Orleans, she was a fiery-eyed, black-haired beauty who expressed herself with foul language and aggressive postures, a dangerous woman who carried a razor and wouldn't hesitate to use it. It was Sabria, along with another woman, whom Sue Ellen had seen with King Fish on that day of their first meeting. It was Sabria she had been jealous of; now it was Sabria who intimidated her, speaking about her as if she were a child. Sabria was seasoned—a hustler extraordinaire: a prostitute, a pickpocket, and a "booster" of clothes that King Fish fenced for her. She was a fiercely independent woman who managed her own money and helped King Fish on occasion, as he did her. She had come to Gator Creek that day to inform King Fish about a poker game to be held at Bill Black's club the following weekend. Jean Paul, a wealthy Frenchman who loved to play cards with colored slicks, as he called them, would be there. He almost always lost and didn't seem to care.

A loud knock on the door awoke them that morning, and when King Fish opened it Sue Ellen heard Sabria's New Orleans accent.

"Let me in! I'm 'bout to pee on myself!"

Then there was the rapid *click, click, click* her heels made across the floor on her way to the bathroom. When she returned, she explained the upcoming poker game to King Fish and then asked him about the new little whore he was fucking. Sue Ellen was outraged. King Fish was the only man she had ever been with. When King Fish tried to defend her, Sabria became loud, called her a nothing little bitch, who probably had the clap, which she hoped the fuck he didn't pass on to her. Sue Ellen quickly put on her clothes. Her anger demanded that she assault this women for her insults, but her good sense told her she couldn't win this kind of encounter. The verbal exchange between King Fish and Sabria became more heated—threatening to erupt into violence. King Fish had to restrain himself from striking her, but he knew that to strike one woman because of another would be an unforgivable sin. A different tactic was in order.

"You make me wanna fuck you when you git mad," he whispered to Sabria, grabbing her in the crotch.

She slapped his hands away. "Don't you be touchin' me, no!" she said, in a singsong Cajun accent.

But King Fish knew that sex was her weakness. Sex was one of the two bonds that held them together. The second was the respect she had for him. He was, in her opinion, the best hustler in New Orleans. Sabria's objection to Sue Ellen was not so much to him having other women—that was a part of his life she had accepted and understood. It was simply that she had grilled Gus about Sue Ellen and learned that she was pretty and very young. Youth was the only quality in another woman that intimidated Sabria, with the possible exception of innocence.

"Well, you scared to let me meet yo' new woman?" she challenged, with her hands on her hips.

King Fish called to Sue Ellen. "Li'l mama, put on somethin' and come out here."

Sue Ellen appeared nervously in the doorway. "Hello, Miss Sabria," she said, taking on a submissive posture and adopting an expression of hero-worship.

This took Sabria by surprise. "This ain't nuthin' but a baby," she said to King Fish. "What you gonna do with a dumb little girl?"

She spoke as if Sue Ellen wasn't there. Sue Ellen said nothing, but sensed a softening beneath this woman's tough exterior. And it was true. Sue Ellen's bright shining eyes reminded Sabria of her younger sister, a simple and innocent girl she had protected and cared for all her life. Sabria turned her anger to King Fish.

"You a dog!" she concluded, and stormed out of the house.

No one saw Sue Ellen's quick smile.

The third week, Sue Ellen received a crash course in street hustling. Her introduction to the life was expertly contrived, a methodical assault on her intelligence and her emotions. Love was the overriding theme. They were locked in each other's arms that evening, King Fish and her, listening to their own thoughts, when King Fish rose up suddenly and walked across the room to the window.

"What ya doin'?" she asked, her voice filled with concern.

"It ain't gonna work, li'l mama," he stated, without turning around.

She was out of the bed in an instant, rushing to where he stood.

"It ain't gonna work! What you mean, it ain't gonna work?" Her eyes and her voice began to fill up with tears. "What you *mean*?" She turned him around.

His face was pained. "It ain't that I don't want you, li'l mama. It's just that we from two different places in our minds."

"What you talkin' 'bout? We from the same place. We both colored, ain't we? White people hate us both the same!"

"That ain't what I mean, li'l mama. I know we both colored,

but you been brought up to be a good colored girl, to obey white folks' rules and laws, and I ain't stuttin' 'um. I gotta do what I gotta do the best way I know how to do it."

"I ain't nevuh said nuthin' 'bout whatcha do, King Fish. I don't care."

"Listen to what I'm trying ta tell ya, li'l mama. In my wurl' a woman do what her man do, if she really with 'im. See what I mean, now? I'm a hustler and you ain't."

She began to cry and whimper like a little girl lost. "I don't know how to be no hustler. I just know I love you. I don't wanna sell myself like Sabria and them. I don't wanna be wit' no other man. I just wanna be wit' you."

She clung to him in desperation.

"I ain't telling ya ta sell ya'self, Mama. It's mo' to hustlin' than that. There's con players, pickpockets, boosters, a lotta thangs."

She looked up into his face. "Can you teach me?"

"I don't know, baby."

"I can learn real fast!" she said quickly.

She pleaded and pleaded until he agreed.

3 Sue Ellen smiled to herself. Had it really been that easy? Had she really been that lame to swallow such a stale line; but then she had been overwhelmed by love, and of course, "love is blind." Ten years of her life had sped rapidly by. High living with a gifted player had been her passion. Now it had all become a bore, a meaningless and redundant bore. She saw the doctors out of the corner of her eye chatting casually as they entered the waiting room. Sue Ellen drew in her breath. She wanted to rush toward them, extract a quick answer, but remained fixed in her seat, as she had done all night, with the exception of one short break she had taken when she was forced to visit the ladies' room. Even then, she had promptly returned to resume her vigil, as if the outcome of the operation would be altered by her absence. The doctors were upon her now and she looked into the smiling blue eyes of the head surgeon. She knew the answer before he uttered a word.

"He'll be fine," the surgeon assured her, and then there was something about rest and quiet she barely heard.

Before she realized it, she had embraced the doctor and just as quickly disengaged herself from this white man. What was she thinking; this was the South. The doctors smiled and nodded their heads in understanding. For a brief moment a kind of kinship, one that transcends race, passed between them, hung briefly in space, then suddenly died. They each went their separate ways; the doctors, smiling confidently, hurried to their families. Their obvious delight was not necessarily connected to the man whose life they had saved during the night; rather, their smiles reflected the reaffirmation of their own abilities as surgeons. Sue Ellen didn't care. She was glad her man was alive.

The room she walked into was cold and impersonal, the way he had taught her the world was, she remembered. He lay very still, this man who had been all things to her, weak and helpless, playing an unconscious host to his own mortality and to her, a mere shadow of the strong, robust, and unyielding warrior she was accustomed to. Sue Ellen pulled up the chair beside the bed and sat very still and rigid in the presence of her fallen idol, feeling somewhat betrayed that two gunshot rounds could have reduced him to such a state. Suddenly things that she would have overlooked before came into sharp focus: the mucus that inhibited his breathing, the spittle that hung from the corner of his mouth, and that awful smell that sickness produces, which hung constantly in the room like a veil.

She began to cry, not tears of sorrow because he had been mortally wounded, or tears of joy because he had escaped death's clutches. These were tears of loneliness, not the tears of loneliness you shed when you graduate from high school or leave home for the first time, but the loneliness that grips you when you say goodbye to a long relationship. She had become aware of a growing unrest over the past several years, but had avoided or set it aside in a determined effort to retrieve that first glowing excellence. It was not that King Fish had been mean to her, unless, of course, his dominating demeanor or the way he ordered her around was mean. Everyone knew this was just his way, that King Fish was what they called "a take-charge niggah." He was even that way with men. It was also true he sometimes treated her like a child, but she knew he loved her, and in a way she had been his child. In the beginning his unfaithfulness had bothered her. She had been for a while threatened by those slick moneymaking yellow whores, but had bested them in the end. She had laughed to herself when the last one had left in a rage, promising to get even. Sue Ellen had that natural talent all women who are part of a great relationship possess, the talent for making herself indispensable to her man; and because she was so young, women fell victim unsuspectingly to her game, the oldest female game in existence. Sue Ellen had simply pretended to befriend them, gained their confidence, then leaked their secrets of romantic betrayal to King Fish. When King Fish discovered this ploy, he hadn't been angry. He respected her cunning, as a hustler would, and they actually became closer for it. "I got me the baddest little heifer in the Bottoms," he would say. Now she was remembering their exploits and him at his best, his witty remarks that always made her laugh, the way he cocked his hat to one side when he was trimming a mark in a card game, and his grand manner. They had ridden the wind together, danced with danger, courted death, and they had laughed all the while. At the fair they dressed as carnies and sold phony gold watches to white men, and the love potion they made from corn whiskey, molasses, and herbs, which "sho' would keep a man hard for an hour," so they said. Sometimes they disguised themselves as servants and went to the French Quarter and picked pockets, but most of all they sold guaranteed good-luck charms. "Rub my head, boss; you sho' gonna win at the cockfight tonight." Then King Fish would do a little dance, and they would laugh, oh, how they would laugh. They were amazed at how dumb white folks were, and just to think they runs the hol wurl'. In a small twisted way they had struck a blow for the colored race, proved colored folks were smart after all. A wave of despair surged through Sue Ellen's body and caused her to tremble. There were more tears and some doubts: maybe she should have questioned more, demanded more, even rocked the boat a little. She, too, needed a life. She didn't want to live only in his shadow. Couldn't he see that there were other things to life that didn't include playing con? This was a rhetorical question. She knew he would never change, could never change. Hustling was all the life he knew. He never wanted children or pets. He was very bright, for sure, but there was nothing profound in his future, nothing unselfish in his present, and she resented this most of all. No, he would never understand her wanting more out of life, maybe to go back to school, and maybe even, someday, become a teacher. *Dammit!* She wanted some kids, too, lots and lots of screaming kids running all over the place with dogs barking at their heels. He would be mad when he woke up and couldn't find her anywhere at all. He might even become violent, but she could not explain her thoughts to him. Sometimes she was a little unsure of them herself. Maybe they were more feelings than reason, or a young colored woman's dream of becoming more than she really could be, a misguided ambition, or maybe, it was just a woman's thing. She took one long look at him and managed a smile from another time; then she leaned over and kissed him on the forehead, touched his hand softly, and hurried out into the warm Southern night.

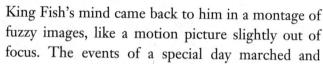 King Fish's mind came back to him in a montage of fuzzy images, like a motion picture slightly out of focus. The events of a special day marched and leaped across his mind: Crowds of colored folks, watching, laughing; gamblers, Pullman porters, waiters, chauffeurs, pimps, and whores were there, even one well-known singer. He was recalling, in part, the Kotch Ball. King Fish could visualize the last hand in the game, a game where three cards were dealt from the bottom of half a deck of cards, a game the white gamblers called "Nigger Poker." King Fish was a master player with his tiny mirror glued under the long nail of his baby finger allowing him to read every card he dealt.

Ultimately the Kotch Game was not the picture that came into focus with crystal clarity in his mind. It was the unassuming figure of a young girl who in worn but clean clothes stood outside the club on a bucket in the midst of a crowd of farmers, looking directly into his eyes. There was something about the intensity of her manner that drew him to her. She stood almost defiant in the gentle Southern breeze as it brushed her flimsy dress against the sculptured outline of her young body. He knew she was just a "chick," but an air of maturity about her reached far beyond her years. She seemed sure of who she was and what she could be. He moved forward and asked her name. "Sue Ellen," she responded quickly. The name echoed resoundingly in his ear, it screamed over and over in his mind, and then became louder . . . "SUUUUUE . . . ELLLLLLLEN," and he bolted wide-awake to the sound of someone screaming her name only to find that the screams he had heard were his own. A throbbing pain ripped through his chest and continued upward along his neck, pounding in his temples. Perspiration covered his face and he leaned slowly back on the bed, half moaning half calling Sue Ellen's name.

"Mister?"

The gentle voice of the young colored nurse was soothing.

"Please take it easy, sir. She was here all night; she'll be back; you need rest now."

Sue Ellen did not come back, not that day or that night or anytime during the two weeks of his stay. His first feelings had been of disbelief. Everyone knew Sue Ellen was his woman; ten dedicated years had proven that. Then disbelief turned to concern and finally panic. Maybe she had been hurt, or worse, even dead. These thoughts shook him day and night and caused him great grief. In his heart he knew the true answer. He had sensed it long ago. It occurred to him now that he might have spared himself this moment if he had been more considerate and not brushed her hopes and dreams aside. But he was a man, not some weak-minded sissy who let a woman run the show. It was his show or no show at all. He had to stand by his convictions lest he be emasculated.

Late one night something he had never experienced happened. He was awakened by a kind of empty terror and a longing so intense it turned his stomach and teared his eyes. Her face was everywhere. It floated across the room, glowing in the steel moonlight. Her smile beckoned from every corner; it moved in and out of his mind with such vividness he thought he was going mad.

Being in love, he believed, was something he had never experienced. For the most part he had always scoffed at love, said it was "jus' two fools puttin' a spell on theyselves." He refused to accept the obvious and his denial caused him to suffer more. King Fish began to remember the small things, special things: like the way she stumbled and wobbled in that first pair of heels he had bought her, that shy smile on "lovers" first night, and the childlike whimper when he was inside of her—the excitement of her young healthy scent. He remembered them snickering together and running when they recognized a mark they had played, or her trying to sing like Bessie Smith. There were the cold, rainy nights when she was sad for no reason and cried the way young girls sometimes do; but his fondest remembrance was of the night when she had picked his pocket. King Fish smiled to himself. They had returned to Gator Creek from a party in New Orleans. They had wanted to be far away from the crowd, alone with each other. She quickly put on his favorite blues record and danced close to him, grinding her young body into his until she could feel his manhood. "You want some of this good stuff?" Her question in a husky voice was a whispered invitation. She began to massage his member with one hand while sliding her other into his pocket to lift with ease his bankroll. "I'll call you when I'm ready, baby," she said in voice laced with sex, and was off to the bedroom. Moments later he had discovered his loss and pushed open the door in mock anger. There she was completely nude, sitting with her legs spread wide in the middle of the bed counting his money, smiling that infectious smile. He had undressed hurriedly, he remembered, and was on top of her with one pant leg clinging to his foot. He could hear her giggling and teasing, "You can't wait for this young stuff, can you?" Even now he could feel her nipples bursting forth with each passage of his circling tongue, her body arching under his exploring hand, the deep entry, the silent scream. Their lovemaking was wild and wet with sweat-drenched backs. The money clung to them like green leeches. Over and over they tumbled, pausing only to assume different positions, him behind or her on top. When their chimes rang in harmony they had both gone limp, like two marionettes who had been deserted by their master. Then, with her muscles rippling like a crouching black leopard, she half crawled, half slid close to him to kiss his mouth before turning on her back to lie still in the crook of his arm. The room became vacant and silent, except for the sound of their breathing and the thick alluring scent that told you love and passion had visited there for an hour.

Gus came early that morning to fetch him from the hospital. King Fish had been lucky; lucky, first, that no vital organs had been damaged; second, to have had two fine young interns in attendance. No complications had set in and he would be released sooner than had been expected, Carolyn Green, the young colored nurse, had told him with a warm smile that extended beyond professionalism, he observed. It occurred to him now how she had stood by him through his foggy state, his sadness, and his pain. She had always been there, and she was there now, extending well-wishes, telling Gus to take care of her special patient. She called to King Fish by his real name when he and Gus were on their way out the door.

"Take care of yourself, Mr. Cook!"

King Fish responded with a wave over his head. A nice little chick, he thought, but Sue Ellen was foremost in his mind.

Gus read it. "She sho' was broke up when she come in the club that day. She loves ya, Fish."

"You dun tol' me 'bout that crying shit she dun, niggah! Is ya seen her anymo' or ain'tcha?"

"Nobody ain't, Fish," Gus replied, bowing his head.

The ride home on the buckboard was awkward and silent. King Fish hadn't meant to hurt his feelings. It wasn't Gus's fault. It was just that the mental and physical pain had proven too much at the moment and he had to lash out at something or someone for relief. The horses stepped up their pace and King Fish felt the force of the wind against his face and the anxiety of an unknown conclusion approaching. He almost hated himself for hoping. He was a hustler, not a mark! He was not a man who put all his money in a poker pot to draw to an inside straight. In his mind he knew it was wise to fold and accept what the percentages said would be a loss, but affairs of the heart were much more engaging than a poker game and his experience more limited. He held out hope that she had changed her mind, that she would be there smiling that smile of hers. That's what broken hearts do . . . they hope when there is none. Gus pulled the horses to a halt in front of the house and King Fish was aware how much the neighborhood had changed since she had moved in with him.

The scattering of houses had now become a cluster—where the high-pitched laughter and sounds of children playing kick-the-can could be heard. The town seemed to have grown up with her. King Fish took his time climbing down from the buckboard and waved his hand to Gus, never once looking back at him and the horses galloping away in the distance. A neighborhood dog raced toward him, dancing and licking his hand as he walked to the door. He shooed the dog away, turned the key in the lock, and strode directly to the bedroom. King Fish froze in the doorway. The room seemed to tilt, or was it his head? A great throbbing from somewhere filled his ears and he bit down on his lip to keep from smashing the wall. Her closet stood open and bare like the mouth of a dead man. The blues hit him full force, sparing nothing, and he slid down in the big chair, arms dangling freely at their sides, emotionally exhausted (*my baby dun left me and I know she gone fo' good*). For a long while King Fish sat staring at nothing, numb to the past and the present, with no thought of the future. When he rose to walk to the kitchen cabinet, where he always kept a jar of moonshine, he had already convinced himself he didn't care; but what he really didn't care about was his own life, and that first drink launched him on his mission of self-destruction. Some nights King Fish could be seen taking drunken walks on some lone and dusty road. On weekends he gambled recklessly, betting too fast and too much, and he called dangerous men out too often. He used and discarded women like the chain of cigars he had begun to smoke and bragged excessively about his sexual prowess. But the answer did not lie in excesses or playing the cavalier womanizer, in hard drinking or violent behavior. It surely, for him, did not lie in the Bible, where he retreated in his last desperate attempt for refuge. To King Fish the Bible was merely a means by which to engage in one of his favorite pastimes, the art of sophistry, and he was pushed deeper into the abyss because he did not believe in the premise on which this sophistry was founded. Maybe love is simply identifying with an object or person so strongly they become eternally connected to you, or maybe it's a kind of self-hypnosis where subject and master become the same. Believe what you wish about the mystery and power of love, there is one truth concerning the remedy for its pain which cannot be argued—*time*.

That night when King Fish walked into the Bucket-of-Blood time was on his side. Almost a year had passed since he had been home to Gator Creek, since he had almost lost his life, since she had walked out on him. He had spent the last eleven months fleecing marks in New Orleans and in the surrounding cities. But in the back of his mind he had been hoping to find Sue Ellen, whom he still considered to be his woman, and bring her back by force if necessary, even if he had to kill another man to do it. He had also been looking to settle the score with Bill Black: neither was to happen. Sue Ellen was nowhere to be found and Bill Black's club had been closed down. Rumor had it that Bill Black had moved to Houston, where he had opened another club.

Nothing changes, he thought. The same odors greeted him at the door, perfumed bodies drenched in sweat and Utty Pellon's lonesome voice crying the blues from the far end of the room, where he sat dressed all in white on his piano stool. To King Fish's left sat Big O, fat and greasy, as usual, and, as usual, wearing the same old sun visor and the red garters that were his trademark on his sleeves. Poker was his game and he played it as well as anyone in the Bottoms, black or white, and he played it on the square. Of course, Big Lil was there, loud and commanding, wearing one of her many red dresses. Big Lil always wore red. Wherever she went became a red-light district, she would say, roaring with laughter. There was also in her company, wherever she went, no fewer than two pretty young girls. The two that were with her this night looked to be hardly more than nineteen, but he knew they were already seasoned pros by the way they moved around the men. The last time he'd been there he was in a drunken rage. The thought of Sue Ellen with another man had proved too much and he'd vowed to find her wherever she was. He accused his friends of conspiring with her against him, even hiding her out; he'd shot up the place, and told everyone to "fuck themselves." Luckily, no one had been hurt.

"What you motherfuckas lookin' at? You ain't nevuh saw a crazy niggah befo'?" King Fish said with a big smile.

The club broke out in laughter. He walked to the bar and told Smitty, the one-armed bartender who managed the place, to "run 'um," in his biggest voice, then ordered a Coca-Cola for himself. He wanted them to know he was all right now, that he was through with drinking, which meant, also, that he had gotten over Sue El-len. He drank a toast to all of those with the courage to take what they wanted from life, and he drank a toast to women. "May the next filly be a rich, white one like Society Red got," he said, and they all laughed, everyone that is, except Gus, who sat hidden in a corner feeling sorry for himself because he knew King Fish had plans to go to New York, as King Fish was announcing at that very moment in a loud voice:

"Goin' up there wit' ol' Red, Fish?" Big O asked.

"Ya got it," King Fish replied, turning up the Coca-Cola.

Big O said, "Don't you and Red fo'git 'bout Big O stuck down here in the Bottoms."

King Fish finished off the drink and let out a loud belch. "We ain't gonna forget you down here, you can bet on that."

This statement invited more laughter. King Fish noticed Gus and walked over to him. Through the years Gus had been his main man, had been loyal, had always done his bidding, but King Fish knew he had to go to New York alone, that he had to put the

South behind him for a while. Maybe after he was settled in good and tight he would send for Gus, but now he could only give him money and ask him to take care of his house, which King Fish realized was his only possession. Then, surrounded by well-wishers, and feeling sorry for Gus, he said his good-byes and left the Bucket-of-Blood and old friends for what he believed would be a very long time, to voyage to a new land, which perhaps separated the superior hustler from the mere impostors.

He stepped into the cool December night with echoes of laughter from the years following close behind. A sharp wind egged him on, even issued a simple warning: he must move forward. King Fish agreed in thought; still, he would miss the Bottoms. He would make things simple, pack tonight, and go to New Orleans in the morning. Po' Sam would drive him. Then a train would take him to New York City. He patted Society Red's letter on the inside of his coat pocket and for the fourth time read it over in his mind. He laughed out loud, whispering with glee, "That niggah dun dun it. He dun really turned hisself white now." If the truth were told, Society Red had always passed when it suited his purpose. Even as a boy, when he and King Fish had sometimes come in contact with each other while putting down their hustle on some New Orleans street corner, Red had used his striking good looks and Caucasian features to his advantage. When Society Red grew up he could have doubled for Douglas Fairbanks, which helped him when he wanted to trim some white man in a pool parlor where Negroes were not permitted. It seems that during one such fleecing a big-time gambler had noticed Red's talent and had taken him to New York to play in a high-stakes pool game. After Red had won the match and a considerable amount of money for the gambler, the man introduced him to New York's upper middle class, where Red had met and married a white divorcée of some means. Longing to be around his own people, Red had opened an after-hours club in Harlem and wanted King Fish to run it.

The letter inflated his spirits, filled him with confidence. Red had made it in New York and so could he. King Fish began to walk with a different rhythm. He was in a hurry to meet his future.

Now he felt daring and bold. He was only slightly troubled when he passed One-eyed John's place, which stood deserted now—a harsh reminder of a man gone mad over a no-account woman. She had two-timed John and it cost her her life. Poor John, who in his painful rage had killed her and her lover, now lay in some prison graveyard, the victim of an inmate's knife attack. Tonight there was only a whisper left of One-eyed John's spirit. Maybe what alarmed King Fish most was knowing that the same fate could have been his. "A no-account woman," he mumbled under his breath.

He was approaching his house now. He saw a light. King Fish shook his head, bet that Gus would learn to turn off the lights when he had to pay the bill hisself or be in the damn dark. Well, that was Gus, his main man. He would miss him too. Most of all he would miss his house, its smell, its warmth, the sense of accomplishment it brought him. His father had said a man couldn't be a complete man until he owned a piece of earth. King Fish opened the door and rushed inside to start packing. He turned on the Victrola to hear Bessie and walked to the bedroom. He froze, the way he had done once before. She sat like a statue in the middle of his bed, completely naked, just the way he remembered her. She didn't make a movement or flutter a lash. There was only that impetuous smile that had always warmed his heart. He was almost afraid to move toward her. Mirages vanish when one gets too familiar. In a second all the painful images of a love lost passed before his eyes and in another instant he reached for his anger, his revenge, his violence, but his overwhelming joy suppressed them all. Sue Ellen had come home. "Happy holidays, baby." She smiled and held out her arms.

In the morning she whispered "I'm sorry" to his sleeping head. After a night of unspeakable bliss she believed their love alone could overcome any problem. Sue Ellen had done what true love demands one do and taken a second look at a decision she had made a hundred times before. She was glad. Even when she had left him in the hospital that night, she knew she still loved him. Even then only the determination she had learned from him kept her going. Before she knew it she'd been in New Orleans, missing him terribly, doing what she'd come to hate and had vowed not to do again—stealing. But fast living had not taught her to be careful with money and she was broke. A slick pickpocket was what she was and she'd resorted to her survival skills. The pickings were so good in New Orleans she overstayed her time, something King Fish always warned her against. Maybe defiance was the reason she went against the rules. In any case she worked in the quarter two days and took them going and coming. She barely made it out of the city before the complaints came in and her description was given to the police. Sue Ellen wisely threw away her maid's uniform and caught the first train to Houston. That's where she met Robert Gaines, an ordinary-looking man, a poet and teacher who had lived in New York and had actually been a part of the new artistic movement in Harlem. If she hadn't been so fat with money, he would surely have been added to the list of victims. She summed him up quickly: a mark, a lame, a spruce. He was all the names hustlers use to describe someone outside of their circle. She saw him watching her the moment she boarded the train. He was harmless—she knew that for sure, and she had time to kill. After she was seated she smiled. King Fish would think she was crazy, flirting with a mark she wasn't trying to beat. Suddenly a rash of loneliness came over her, almost moved her to tears. She struggled to maintain her composure. Not on this train, she thought, she wasn't breakin' down on this train, and King Fish couldn't tell her what to do no mo'. She was on her own. She spoke to this man with her eyes.

There was no excitement to Robert Gaines, no flair, nothing slick. But there was something settling about him, something wise in a different way. Very quickly she found herself back in a world she had almost forgotten, a world of books and poetry and ideals. They talked about everything, music, art, religion, and Jim Crow, but most of all they talked about Harlem's avant-garde, musicians, poets, muses, artistic revolutionaries. They talked about a young woman, Zora Neale Hurston, a student of anthropology and a brilliant young writer. Sue Ellen wanted to be like her. By the time they'd reached Houston he had convinced her to rent a room from his mother, who owned a rooming house for respectable coloreds, and take a small-paying job as a tutor in the little schoolhouse he was to run for Negro children. So that was how she had met Robert Gaines, the smartest person she had ever known—a man of vision, commitment, and principles—a wonderful man who wanted to marry her. It was all perfect and in a short time she had grown very close to him, but King Fish was in her blood, like a virus. He took her over slowly, broke down her resistance, overcame her will. Her days were filled with thoughts of him. But her nights were the worst; then she was haunted by his passion, the feel of his touch, his breath on her naked body, the comfort of his arms, but most of all there was the overwhelming guilt for having walked out on him.

King Fish opened his eyes with one question on his lips.

"Who you been with, Sue Ellen?"

Everything depended on her answer, she believed—their relationship, maybe even her life. This was the world that love had thrust upon her. His eyes were intimidating.

"I ain't seen nuthin' but marks in Texas since I got there."

Judging from her expression, his question was absurd.

"I been teaching little kids in school, baby, somethin' I think I wanna keep doin'. You gonna let me, huh?"

"What part of Texas?"

"Houston, baby, I lived in Mama Gaines's rooming house. I'm gonna miss them little kids, but I guess I missed you mo' "

Then she used her body to smother his suspicion and any thought she had of Robert Gaines. No other man could match King Fish's smooth stride or that explosion he caused in her loins. Her single encounter with Robert hadn't come close. Yes, it was King Fish who moved her to passion's end. Yet that morning it was more than just the magic of two people desperately in love that drove them. It was a concentrated effort to erase any ill will that remained because of the action she had taken. Without thought or design they engaged themselves to banish it forever from their lives. For theirs was a true love, but love, in and of itself, cannot sustain a relationship; only truth and understanding can. They missed it that morning, the only chance they had to fully repair the damage. He placed jealousy and ego in front of understanding and she exchanged a lie for womanhood. It could have been that they were already doomed, that he was content to be who he was and that she was rapidly becoming who she would be. These, however, were possibilities hidden for the time being well beneath layers of unconscious denials. And, for the moment at least, they pulled it off. Nothing would stand in the way of the love they had recreated. They stroked and petted each other and cooed and were overly considerate. Now smiling and fully satisfied, she lay back in his arms.

"I wanna have me some babies." She turned to face him. "First a boy then a girl for him to look after. She'll have a big brother like I always wanted. Then maybe I'll have twins!"

She laughed and nudged him.

"Why don'tcha just gather up a buncha them little nigguhs in New Orleans and take 'em in?" he asked.

"No, baby, not New Orleans, right here we could do that, have like a boarding school where I could teach 'em!"

But she had misinterpreted King Fish's facetious statement.

"Sue Ellen, you dun gone crazy. What else ya want since you tellin' me now?"

She was silent for a moment. "And I want a husband."

"Hold up, you carryin' me too fast now." King Fish laughed. "Which one a' these things you want first, the li'l nigguhs or the husband?"

She laughed, too, to cover up the hurt, but mostly to prevent any damage to their newfound old love.

Later, after dinner, they dressed and went to the Bucket-of-Blood. She wore her favorite long dress and wide-brim hat with feathers. They walked that evening the way they had done so many nights. Even in this cool winter reunion they remembered the summers. She had been so young then, so silly in love, and everything was wonderful. She was in love now, too, but being very young and in love was special. Maybe remembering is the reward we receive for growing older. She did remember the very first time she had walked this path with Gus. Tonight she admitted to King Fish how nervous she had been, how frightened she was of One-eyed John when she had learned about his past, how terrified of Sabria. Then, for the sake of love, she would willingly have endured anything. Now, ten years later, love was not so simple, so selfless.

When they entered the club it was like the first time, all those years ago on Christmas Eve, when she was accepted as one of them, and in spite of her youth was permitted inside. She wore a raccoon wrap King Fish had given her and was the envy of every woman there. Everything she wanted in this world was hers. Never would she have suspected that someday she would need more and that more would bear no resemblance to this life. She learned many things during those years. Three stood out in her mind: greed is the greatest compromiser of character, change is unpreventable, and King Fish was not perfect. Tonight she was greeted with the same enthusiasm and King Fish with the same respect. Gus was ecstatic. The old gang converged on her and she was moved. It was good to be liked and respected, to have choices. Big Lil pulled her aside and in the midst of the noise spoke her admiration. "Girl, you sho' know how ta come back an' pick up where you left off!" Her laughter roared above the crowd. And in the pale yellow light Sue Ellen spotted Utty Pellon in the corner, decked out in his white, playing her favorite song on the piano. Much to everyone's surprise, King Fish's big voice rang out. They all moved to the piano wearing warm smiles. No one there except her and Gus had ever heard him sing, and she watched as everyone gave themselves over to the joys of this different world. From the outside she saw his complete happiness, his total unity with who he was, and she was sad.

The next day was one of remembrance, a time to pay another tribute to the grand old lady who was her grandmother—a tribute she had made every year since her death. Even King Fish had commented on Gran'maw's wisdom, which seemed to have increased as she had gotten older. They borrowed Gus's buckboard and drove out to the small Negro cemetery on the outskirts of town. From time to time King Fish would smile and take Sue Ellen's hand in his. He could be gentle and kind, she thought, and he had been good to her. It was peaceful and still that day, except for a gust of wind that fanned her dress and spun two leaves into a miniature whirlwind. Gran'maw's spirit was strong, she thought, her words even stronger. "Some people think the wurl' owes 'um, but it's the peoples what owes the wurl'." And there were those last words she had spoken to them that sang the praises of love. Sue Ellen's happiness in love had been her wish, and Sue Ellen was bound to honor that wish. It was she who owed so very much to her grandmother. They placed flowers around the stone that read WE LOVE YOU GRANDMA. After reflecting a moment, they left this place, where even the lonely who come to visit leave lonelier. "I gotta go to Slidell," King Fish said quietly, as if to himself, as they were driving home. Sue Ellen understood. Slidell was where he was born and where "they" had all died, Slidell was where his guilt was, where he had abandoned God. All of those years and he had never gone back. To her his words were a good sign. Maybe there he would discover that part of himself tragedy had stolen. She needed him now.

Two weeks later he asked her to go to the quarter with him. She was quick to tell him how she'd disregarded his teachings and overstayed her welcome in New Orleans. He was so furious he trembled, but never said a word. In his heart he knew she had broken with him in the most crucial place, in her mind. The flesh from time to time may bow to weakness and be overcome, but it was in the mind that a man really laid claim to his woman.

Sue Ellen was devastated. After promising her children, he wanted their mother and teacher to be a thief. After promising her a husband, he wanted his wife to be a criminal. The pain of this discovery followed her everywhere they went. He hadn't even heard her, didn't know who she had become. Hope began to wane. At the gambling table, what she had once thought was stylish now seemed silly. The way he set his cap and his witty remarks impressed her no longer. King Fish was intelligent, she knew that, but he just wouldn't grow. A new movement for the Negro was under way, a striving for equity through artistic achievement, headed by people like Langston Hughes, Mary Johnston, and Zora Neale Hurston, who were ready to challenge the very conscience and humanity of white people. Their voices might determine the future of the colored race. She wanted to be counted among them.

One week before Christmas she walked out, leaving with only the clothes on her back. King Fish had been in a major Kotch Game and had won big. He entered his house calling her name. After the third time he could feel it in his gut. That's where the truth hits you and the pain. The funny thing was he had felt it coming. He had even tried to change it, but he couldn't. He couldn't make himself want a dull life with wild little children driving him crazy. He liked the smell of a gambling joint, the loud noise, the excitement, the danger. He liked having money and spending it. He liked being a player.

King Fish hired Po' Sam to drive him to New Orleans, where he would eventually catch his train to New York. Sam was the only colored man in Gator Creek who owned both a truck and an automobile, machines that had once been only wrecks, for sure, but Sam could repair anything broken and his wife, a two-hundred-fifty-pound shrew, who treated Sam more like a son than a husband, had a remedy for any illness. Now, there was a pair to beat a full house, King Fish thought. Sam was also the hardest-working man King Fish had ever seen—a farmer, a repairman, and a pickup-and-delivery man. He even functioned as a cabdriver on occasion, as he was doing this evening. It was known by colored folks that this little, bug-eyed man, with a mouth filled with gold, who wore coveralls every day of his life, was one of the richest men in the Bottoms, but was smart enough to play down his wealth around white folks and was content to stay in his so-called place. What most people didn't know, however, was that he owned the Bucket-of-Blood, and received a cut from every illegal activity promoted there; but no one had ever seen him inside. Smitty, the one-armed bartender, was his front man.

"Fixin' to snow," Sam commented, looking up at a winter cloud formation, as they drove along. "Be the first time in ten years."

King Fish smiled. I'm fixin' to have some fun, he thought to himself. "You know what people sayin', don'tcha, Sam?"

" 'Bout Po' Sam?" Sam's voice was already pitched high with concern.

"Yeah, 'bout you, Sam. Sayin' you the richest niggah in the Bottoms. Even richer than most rich crackers."

Sam drew up as if someone had doused him with a bucket of cold water.

"What you sayin', Fish? You know how white folks is, 'specially when they thinks a colored man got money. You fixin' ta mess me up! I ain't got no money, Fish!"

King Fish couldn't resist one more dig. "That ain't all, Sam. They say ya got ya'self a white woman hid back a' dat ol' shack a' yourn you keep up in the hills."

Sam screamed like a banshee. "Lawd, lawd! He tryin' to git Po' Sam hung!"

Sam clasped his head with both hands, causing King Fish to grab the steering wheel. King Fish was still laughing when they rolled into New Orleans.

After King Fish had rented a room for the night, Sam helped him with his two suitcases and a chest. There was a single handshake and a brief pause that said, after all, they would miss each other. They were not what you would call great friends and they had, maybe, only one thing in common, the ability to make money, but these men were the two major ingredients in Gator Creek's Negro community. It was men like them who gave this small town of farmers a sense of importance. It was from this knowledge that King Fish's and Po' Sam's mutual respect was born.

The room was cold as usual, but King Fish had always stayed there when he came to New Orleans. He could see Bill Black's old club from his window, alive again, under new ownership, but he was sure there had been no major changes. Everything in the Bottoms stayed the same. An unforeseen thought flashed quickly across his mind—a feeling of guilt or regret, he didn't know which, only that he should have listened to her that night. She had a sixth sense about such things. Her woman's intuition had saved them many times before, but strong drink and arrogance can be a deadly mix. That night arrogance had demanded that he override her protest and make at least a brief appearance at Bill Black's club. It was true that Charlene, the "high-yeller" beauty from Lake Charles, had been the reason for the bad blood between him and Bill Black. Sue Ellen had warned him about her from the beginning, that she was a flirt, an attention getter, and a dick teaser. Even though Charlene had never been intimate with King Fish, she had been seen in his company and there were promises that she had made, promises that reached far beyond just the physical. She had played the giant egos of him and Bill Black off against each other until there had been an explosion.

The saxophone of Big Buck Taylor's all-night blues band was wailing that night when he walked into the club. He could see Charlene melting over Bill Black's shoulder as he sat operating his card game, his teeth perfect and white, flashing that self-assured smile. He and Bill Black had once been friends. They had trimmed marks together, chased women. Now he wanted to teach this mothafuckah a lesson with his own cards in his own club. It didn't take long for the night to turn into near tragedy. The argument with Sue Ellen, who didn't want him to gamble, the fast-betting Kotch Game, and the disagreement with Bill Black, the quick flashes, the thundering sound of his gun (*that came from nowhere*), and two dull thuds like successive swings from a sledgehammer that knocked him backward on the floor. The last thing he had remembered was Sue Ellen's scream and the scent of her perfume before he closed his eyes. These thoughts of her were only a brief intrusion . . . only the last frantic efforts of the ghost of a dead love trying to reclaim his soul. Not this time, he thought to himself. The New Year had almost arrived and he had made a resolution. King Fish was putting his past behind him, giving himself a fresh start. Life is about new beginnings, and there are no yesterdays. There are only present memories that, with each recall, turn themselves into an eternal now. He had grown wiser over the past year, discovered some things that in an uneventful year would never have been revealed to him. Adversity has a way of drawing attention to itself and a habit of demanding profound responses to unanswered whys. He had come to the understanding that an untamed ego had been at the root of his problems. Ego and arrogance are merely toys in the hands of men parading as children. The tools of accomplished men are those of purpose and direction. He was astounded at the ease with which he had forfeited his relationship and almost his life in the pursuit of such an empty ideal as self-adulation; still, he had come out of it all undaunted, secure in his discovery that out of adversity grows the strength and knowledge that greatness demands.

King Fish looked at his watch. It was eleven P.M. At the stroke of midnight the New Year would come in and white folks would be so drunk a man with five thumbs could pick their pockets. He intended to be in the French Quarter by then. He quickly changed into his chauffeur's uniform, then looked into the mirror for approval; satisfied, he picked up his bankroll, his hook-blade knife, and walked down the stairs past two hookers with their johns. He could hear one woman's Creole accent before he made it to the street. "We gon' have some good fun tonight—yeah." King Fish smiled. The two johns would be dead broke in fifteen minutes. Those Creole girls could steal. He was just in time to catch the Desire streetcar, which could land him in the French Quarter in less than thirty minutes. He boarded the car and took one of the seats with a wooden board marked COLORED nailed to the back of it, next to a fat black man who smelled more like fish than human. This was the last seat available to colored folks, and it was in the rear. There were empty seats in the front, with the exception of two that were occupied by a tipsy white couple. King Fish knew the proportions would reverse themselves by the time he reached his destination. Quickly, they were in motion, wobbling through the ninth ward past the nightclubs and dives that would soon be busting full with the cheerful sounds that welcomed the incoming year. Outside, as if on cue, the clouds delivered on their promise in a sudden flurry of drifting snowflakes which skillfully dodged the outstretched hands of each gleeful person before disappearing into the ground. It was a time for feeling good and he indulged

himself with thoughts of New York, mostly with visions of those
fine chicks in Harlem he had heard too much about. Yeah, New
York was the place for him.

At Canal Street, when the car made one of its many stops, King
Fish bumped a drunk about to board and lifted his wallet before
hurrying with the crowd in the direction of Bourbon Street. There
existed in the air the same festive mood the ninth ward offered on
holidays, but somewhat subdued. The laughter here was polite and
controlled and occurred in measured outbursts. Like the music, the
laughter seemed to have been rehearsed to perfection, with no in-
novation, no daring, nothing that moved the spirit. They did not
see him, these people moving easily around in evening clothes,
oblivious to the lives of the darker people in the world. They
looked right through him as if he didn't exist, and this made him
angry.

King Fish saw his mark coming out of a club, walking very stiff
and too straight, like someone struggling to hold his whiskey. He
was the Reverend Malcolm Cage, a man of massive size, with bushy
red hair and a mustache to match, a gun-totin' Bible-carrying
preacher of fire and brimstone who drank rum and chased women
all week but preached hell and damnation on Sunday. Something
about this mark troubled King Fish. He even seemed vaguely familiar, but King Fish pushed the feeling aside and continued on.
It was colder now and King Fish pulled his jacket together against
a sudden gust of wind. The snow crunched beneath his feet as he
neared the man whose breath leaped from his mouth like steam
from a locomotive and hung briefly in the air like tiny clouds before disappearing over his head. King Fish put on a broad smile.
"Hep ya, suh?" He was already steadying the man with one hand.
In an instant his other hand was inside Malcolm Cage's pocket.
The thick wad made his heart pound. Then he felt an iron grasp
pin his hand to Malcolm's leg. The world stopped, lending a frightening stillness to the moment. King Fish felt a nudge just above
his rib cage. He looked slowly down to see a stacked-barrel der-
ringer pointed at his heart. Cautiously and nervously, King Fish
looked up into two stone-cold-sober green eyes set in an implac-

able face that was flushed red. The silence, as loud as a factory whistle, charged the night, then was broken by the low gravel voice of Malcolm Cage.

"Boy, you got more gall than a nigger at a Klan barbecue, putting yo' hand in my pocket. Now get it out, boy! Git it out reeeeal sloooow!"

King Fish trembled, carefully removing his hand. Malcolm's next words were chilling.

" 'Behold, all souls are mine, as the soul of the father, so also, the soul of the son is mine. The soul that sinneth it shall die.' Ezekiel 18:4."

King Fish stood petrified, waiting for the thunder and the pain he remembered. Instead, the words came to him in a flash.

"But, suh, it's wrote also: 'Because he considereth and turneth away from his wickedness that he hath committed he shall surely live, he shall not die.' Ezekiel 18:28."

The tension eased and the dead-cold expression on Malcolm Cage's face turned to one of astonishment. King Fish's next line was easy and his con so smooth.

"I dun sinned against you, suh, and I'm sorry, but most of all I dun sinned against da Lawd." King Fish's tone was soft and majestic. He raised his head to the sky. " 'Let him who is without sin cast the first stone.' "

He paused and glanced out at Malcolm Cage from the corner of his eye. "Suh, I dun been called to preach the Gospel."

The night exploded with the resounding laughter of Malcolm Cage; it bounced off lampposts and buildings, causing people to stare; it was uncontrollable even for him. Malcolm Cage, still laughing, slipped his gun inside his coat pocket, stepped back, slapped his knee, and pointed at King Fish.

"Boy," he began, wiping his eyes with his fingers. "Boy," he began again. "You the cunningest nigger I ever seen. I don't believe a gawd-durn word of what you sayin', but I sho do like the way you say it, else I'da dun blowed your heart out aw'ready. C'mon, boy. You take a ride with me."

It was said in a less-than-demanding way. Malcolm Cage believed he had found his man.

King Fish followed him cautiously, wondering if Malcolm was making a citizen's arrest, as white men sometimes did with Negroes. He began to look for an avenue of escape, but something told him to wait for a better opportunity.

"Right here," Malcolm said, and stopped in front of a gold-monogrammed Model T Ford. "Git in!"

It was a command this time. King Fish obeyed, but he had made up his mind. This white man was not taking him to jail. He would jump him in the car somewhere along the way and then just split to New York. Malcolm Cage walked around the other side of the car, retrieved a crank, and began to crank up the engine.

"Don't allow nobody to fool with my automobile, nobody but me," he said, when he got in the car. "Let me introduce myself," Malcolm said, lighting a cigar. "I'm the Reverend Malcolm Cage."

He looked over to King Fish with raised eyebrows.

"Fish, they call me King Fish."

Malcolm nodded and pulled away from the curb. He studied King Fish before he again began to speak.

"I see somethin' in ya, boy." He blew a perfect smoke ring. "I don't know just what, but somethin'."

King Fish listened close, his head slightly turned from the man's face.

"Now, I'm gonna try and talk some sense into that woolly head of yourn. You gotta respect white folks. You see, the way I got it figured is this. The good Lord made it, the wurl' I mean, and everything in it the way He wanted. You and me, He made us like He wanted. Let me put it this way. Dogs and horses can't talk, can they?"

"No." King Fish knew exactly where this was going.

" 'Cuz that's the way God wanted it," Malcolm repeated. "Now, I'm a white man and you's a colored man. It so happens the white folks is on the top and the coloreds on the bottom. 'Cuz that's the way God intended it. Got it? So we gotta be glad, boy, to be alive, glad for what we have; we gotta make the best of what we got; see what I mean?"

King Fish nodded. He didn't buy this, but debating it would serve no purpose. By now he doubted if Malcolm Cage was taking him to jail, unless, of course, he had lost the way, because he was traveling in the opposite direction.

"You ever go ta school, boy?"

"A little."

"Where'd you learn the Bible?"

"Just read it over and over till I learned it."

Malcolm Cage chewed on his cigar. "How many times, would ya say?"

"Lots and lots of times, suh, took me a long time."

"And ya unnerstan' it, do ya?"

"Pretty much, I think so, suh."

"Ya know this verse?" Malcolm tested. " 'And when the Sabbath was past, Mary Magdalene and Mary, the Mother of James and . . .' "

King Fish joined in, " 'Had bought sweet spices that they might come and anoint him.' " Then he added, "You want the verse, suh?"

Malcolm said nothing and they rode in silence. He looked at King Fish several times, placing his cigar in his mouth and taking it out. Then it came to him as if in a great discovery.

"Ya right, ya been called, boy! I didn't know it till just now. It just come ta me, else why'd God give ya a white man's mind. Ya been called to raise up yo' people, and by God, He dun called me to hep ya. It's clear to me now. Ha, ha!"

He laughed loud and clapped his hands together. He almost had a head-on collision with an approaching car. They could see the driver showing his fist and moving his lips as he passed them. The sounds of the New Year celebration could be heard along with gunshots and firecrackers. Malcolm laughed again, louder this time, and grabbed the wheel.

"Boy!" he shouted in a hearty voice. "Let's get ta my place!"

God had sent him the man He had promised. Someone intelligent enough to accept Malcolm's teachings and lead his own people down the path of righteousness.

The road they finally turned in to led to a mansion with large white pillars that rested on forty-five hundred acres of land in a small farm town just outside of the city. Cypress trees stood tall and silent like royal British guards near the entrance of the palace. The air was cool and fresh when they walked to the door.

"Well, there she is, boy. I'm gonna show ya what the Lawd done for me."

King Fish hadn't expected this much extravagance. A colored maid answered the door and eyed him suspiciously from head to toe. Then he was led from a marble hallway to a drawing room so huge it seemed to have no ending. Crystal lamps and chandeliers winked their rainbow brilliance from every corner and from above. The ice-blue carpet hosted an array of Louis XIV satin couches, love seats, and chairs in alternating colors of blue and pale pink, clearly a woman's touch.

There she was—tall and majestic in a light blue dressing gown with pale blue ribbons. She blended perfectly with the carpet she took long, even-paced strides across. The black ringlets that fell from her bouffant hair kissed white cheeks that had been gently tanned by a touch of Spanish blood. She was beautiful, like a priceless artifact in motion, and she moved to Malcolm's side, ignoring King Fish completely, or so it seemed. Malcolm's manner, King Fish noticed, softened in her presence. He wondered how Malcolm had captured this angel.

"You are late, my darling. The New Year has already arrived." There was nothing hostile in her voice, just a matter-of-fact statement. Malcolm, rather than make excuses, quickly introduced King Fish, but placed the word "reverend" in front of his name. This surprised King Fish.

"Pleased to meet you, Reverend King Fish. My name is Lorene."

Lorene had rolled over the syllables with simple grace, her voice musical, like the sound of a waltz. She wanted to know if King Fish's ministry was in New Orleans. Malcolm cut in, explaining that King Fish would be spending some time with them, all the while staring King Fish down. King Fish understood. His mind began a race to comprehend the total meaning behind Malcolm's statement.

"He's the sign we been waiting for," Malcolm said.

"Are you sure?" she asked.

Malcolm assured her he was. The only person in the dark now was King Fish himself.

The first thought that entered his mind was the tragic story of Junior Holmes, a young colored boy who lived and worked on a farm owned by a middle-aged white couple. Junior Holmes had been coerced by both into having sex with the wife while the husband looked on. This practice had continued for several months until the couple's son, on a surprise visit home from college, had discovered what to him was an unbearable scene. He responded by retrieving a shotgun and killing Junior Holmes, also wounding his own mother in the process. King Fish's senses became alerted to any possibility, even the slightest chance that he might, somehow, leave their place with the bankroll he had gone to the French Quarter to obtain. Then Malcolm Cage did something that flabbergasted him. King Fish jumped back when he reached into his pocket, but instead of a gun, Malcolm's hand came out holding a wad of money. And as if he had read King Fish's mind, he said, "This is what you want, boy? Take it!" He grabbed one of King Fish's hands and thrust the money into it. Lorene stood silently by, perfectly still and unblinking, with a slight smile on her face.

"This ain't no money, boy. Look around you. This is only a down payment on the blessings God got in store for you!"

Still holding tightly to King Fish's hand, Malcolm's eyes bored into his and King Fish felt the dynamism of this man.

"God dun sent ya here fo' me to teach you the ministry, to help you build a church fo' yo' people. That's yo' destiny, boy, and it's mine too. Now, you listen real close ta what I'm about to say and ya lissen good. You can walk out this door with this money and be a small-time thief the rest of yo' life, or you can keep this money and stay here, learn the ministry, and in a couple of months have more money than you ever had a chance to count."

King Fish didn't believe half of this, but he suspected Malcolm did. What King Fish understood most was the difference between a winner and a loser. Even if this crackuh was half-crazy, he was a winner, and King Fish wanted his game. Then he would simply cut him loose.

"Boy, your choice!" Malcolm demanded unflinchingly.

"I'll stay," King Fish said even before he realized it.

Malcolm's face lit up.

"Knowed ya was the one all right, knowed it almost from the start."

He had been holding King Fish's hand all the while, which he released with a smile. "Time for us men of the cloth to go to a man's room," Malcolm said in the same hearty voice King Fish remembered. Lorene stood by, both amused and a little irritated by her husband's abruptness. This, in a way, was his selfish side. He tended to hoard briefly any new adventure like a giant bear guards his food before sharing it with its family. Lorene smiled to herself. The bedroom was where she was most comfortable and that's where she headed. Lorene loved her bedroom more than any place in her mansion. It reminded her of her childhood, all frilly and pink like a nursery. She had had her large bed with the canopy brought in from Montgomery, along with the two marble-based antique lamps her mother had loved so much. Sometimes she felt a little guilty forcing a man like Malcolm Cage to live in her private world of silk and satins. Well, at least he had his den, a place she loathed, with all those dead animals looking at her from the walls, making her feel guilty. She had never understood how a man who was basically as kind as Malcolm could kill animals for the fun of it. But she knew he had killed men too. In fact, there were so many sides to this man it was difficult for her to keep up with them. But that was just fine with her. She would have been miserable married to one of those so-called Southern gentlemen who had inherited his wealth, some spineless weakling who had earned nothing, dared nothing, and pranced around all day pretending to be important. Maybe her husband wasn't of genteel bearing, but in his veins ran the blood of a true explorer, a man who allowed himself to dream any dream and dared to make it come true.

Lorene had come to believe in him totally because everything he had ever accomplished was unbelievable, from surviving his plight as a child, gaining her father's permission for their marriage, and in just ten years becoming one of the most powerful men in New Orleans. Malcolm had promised God that this year he would set in motion a plan to bring to salvation all the Negroes in the South so that they may appear before God's throne spiritually ready, holy enough to receive God's gift of everlasting life. Meeting this Negro with the amazing memory was the beginning of the realization of that dream, he believed—and because he believed it, she believed it too. Her husband was no ordinary man. She had known this on that very first day she heard him speak. His eyes had told her so. On the podium he had been commanding, larger than life, sometimes even frightening. Then suddenly, to emphasize a point, and to punctuate the seriousness of that point with a touch of humor, he would tiptoe across the stage like a ballerina, imitating the Willy-Nillies of the world who were not strong in their faith. But Lorene had been watching his eyes. A man's true essence is revealed in his eyes. Malcolm's eyes were all-encompassing, piercingly wild and determined. They were the eyes of man unsoiled, almost prehistoric.

The first time she saw him and heard the thunder in his voice was at his huge church in New Orleans. A professor at the university in Montgomery Lorene attended had taken the anthropology majors on an extended field trip. Of course the professor could have saved money by attending a revival in Alabama, but both he and the class had agreed New Orleans would be more fun. She had been drawn to Malcolm that first day and talked to him much longer than any other student, even flirted a little, something she never did. Strangely, they didn't talk about her class project. He delighted her with stories of his African safaris. That reminded Lorene of her father. The class debate had been centered in part

on Africa, but less about wildlife and more about religious prac-
tices. It was asked if there was a correlation between the rise of
civilization and the rise of Christianity? Since the United States
and Europe were mostly white and Christian, and seemingly much
more civilized, it appeared to be so. This was a theory that escaped
Lorene, as a great many things concerning culture did, mostly the
ideal of white supremacy, which again seemed to be supported by
the much superior status of the white race; however, on closer
observation and with the nonbias and unaltered findings of an-
thropologists, the story changed drastically. Before there had ever
been any mention of Europe, there was Egypt to consider, the
ancient civilization of Cush, Nubia, and Ethiopia. Why did Na-
poleon blow the nose off the Sphinx? Possibly because the features
on the oldest known edifice in the world were Negroid. The presentation of these facts to her classmates and to the professor caused
eyebrows to be raised. It rendered the professor mute and it caused
hostilities to be voiced. This was not new to Lorene. She had always been at odds with her peers. She believed she had always seen
life in a more mature light than they.

As a teenager she was never coquettish with boys and she never
participated in gossip or any meaningless conversations. Lorene
had always been older than her years. Perhaps the real change in
her had begun at age seven, when her mother died giving birth to
the son her father had so hoped for. It had been a dual tragedy,
with the baby being born dead as well, a tragedy that was com-
pounded by the devastating effect it had on her and her father,
Lorene because her little-girl life had been patterned after this
beautiful woman whom she had worshiped, and her father because
his sorrow was heightened by the guilt he felt for having robbed
his only child of a complete family.

Lorene's father had attempted to ease this guilt by submitting
to her every whim. The gifts were many and always extravagant—
fine ponies, carriages, and so many clothes it would take her
months to wear them all. He began to use Lorene as a replacement
for his wife in all things (*except sex*), even conferring with her on
every important issue as if she were an adult. By age fifteen she

had, in fact, become the lady of the house. She ran the huge plan-tation and its seventy-five workers with precision and fairness. The workers, each and every one, willingly gave their all to her and in turn she attended to them and their children's needs. As a result, her father was free to travel abroad and pursue his business ven-tures. Lorene's father was the descendant of three generations of males who had amassed great fortunes in imports and exports, the slave trade not to be excluded. He, the most enterprising of the three, became the wealthiest. Whenever her father returned from one of his many trips or adventures (*as she called them*), she would corner him and they would sometimes talk for hours, she wide-eyed, taking in every detail, hanging on every word. Even then her views were unbiased. She looked at everybody and everything ob-jectively. Lorene even understood how the racists came to be the way they were (*racism was not inherent in people; it was the result of conditioning*). In her eyes there were no lesser or greater people, only lesser or greater status, and even that was debatable. The status syndrome mirrored the values of the culture that enjoyed it. It was more than plain to her that the world, left to exist on its own devices, without one group trying to impose its will on the other, would do just fine. The amazing thing was that nobody else, her father included, seemed to understand this. Sometimes she would become so enraged by what she called "the premeditated stupidity of the people of Alabama" that she would tremble.

By the time Lorene saw Malcolm Cage again she had graduated fourth in her class from the university, had a master's degree, and had taken up her residence in a lavish home her father had reluc-tantly purchased for her outside of New Orleans. This had been two years later, and by now she was thoroughly convinced the Western world was so entrenched in arrogance that no viable so-lution was possible (*at least not in her lifetime*). America, as great as she was, had imprisoned herself in her own contradictions. America had fought for freedom, equality, and justice, but now denied oth-ers these same rights on the basis of race, religion, and social status; alas, these were facts she had to accept (*even though she would never be governed by them*). She was not a crusader, so a compromise was in order if she was to get along at all in this crazy world. Attending the luncheon of the Southern Ladies' Auxiliary was part of that compromise, and seeing the Reverend Malcolm Cage, their guest speaker, her reward. They were married three months later. Maybe he wasn't young like the sons of those wealthy planters who continually pursued her. Maybe he wasn't always attired in the latest fashions or cutting the fancy steps at a ball. She didn't care and neither did her father. Malcolm was like her father, a man of vision and action.

She had been a twenty-four-year-old virgin on their wedding night. He had been twenty years her senior and she was at a complete loss for the first time since her mother's death; then, she couldn't handle the fact of death, and this night she did not know how to handle the act that created life. She had read about sex and had heard different stories in the parlor, but now, in her nervousness, she couldn't remember, or at least she couldn't remember them in sequence. Lorene wanted to make her husband happy; this was her wish and her duty, but the size of him made her cringe in fear. She thought he would tear her insides; but he was gentle and easy in his manner and she relaxed. He removed her gown slowly and kissed her plum-colored nipples until they stood on point; then he tasted the honey on his fingers, after massaging her gently between her legs. Her mouth was slightly parted and all her feminine instincts opened to receive him and then she screamed and bolted from the bed. "*No!* I won't die like my mother!" She had pushed him aside in a superhuman effort and then had run into the bathroom.

After that night she had become the perfect wife and more. She brought to the marriage her expertise in management and communication. She convinced Malcolm to sell his much smaller place and move in with her. She then transformed their plantation into one of the most beautiful and efficient estates in Louisiana.

Lorene smiled to herself again. That had been twelve years ago. It had taken him a whole week to seduce her and then only after he had promised to practice withdrawal so she would never have children.

The room Malcolm and King Fish entered was a mahogany affair decorated with his hunting trophies. The pinewood walls supported a series of photographs of Malcolm's African safaris.

"King Fish; that your real name, boy?"

"No, suh," King Fish replied, smiling. "My name's James Cook."

Malcolm laughed. "Reverend James Cook. Now, that's a name for a preacher if there ever was one."

Malcolm's mood became serious again. He walked across the room and placed his hand on a bronze statue of George Washington standing in a boat directing his men across the Delaware.

"Wish I'd been there," he said, and lit a cigar.

King Fish studied the man, wondering what he would say next. Malcolm began to speak.

"This here's a great country, boy, great country. Maybe you don't think so, 'cuz you colored, but it's a great country for coloreds too; better'n 'em jungles back there in Africa."

He looked to King Fish for a response and got none. If King Fish had dared, there was little he could have said. In spite of the Negro's condition in this country he was ultimately more American than African, but in the eyes of white America, less American than a newly arrived immigrant. This was a paradox that was depressing and psychologically defeating as well. Malcolm continued.

"Like I said, sometimes we gotta make the best of what we got. Take me, I started out in life with nothin'. My pappy was just a poor farmer, worked all his life and got hisself nothin'—nothin' but tired, so tired, mind you, he just laid down and died. My maw, she'd died too, from overwork, if I hadn't started being a man 'fore my time. I was twelve years old when I took off to New Orleans. I learned to rob, learned to steal, and I learned how ta pick pockets, too, boy."

He looked King Fish straight in the eye and smiled.

"I dun it all, boy, dun it all till the good Lord called me to preach. The Lord blessed me with a small farm and a small church, which I turned into a bigger farm, and a bigger church. I kept on gettin' blessed, boy, 'cuz that's the way the good Lord is."

King Fish didn't care; he didn't give a damn about this crackuh's life history. White folks was always doing this, trying to make colored folks look small or feel better 'cuz they had some hard times theyselves. But if they had them same hard times and a whole wurl' on their back 'cuz they's white, they couldn't stand it. He tuned Malcolm Cage out and thought of his own family and the love his mother and father shared for each other and their children. He remembered the look of love in his mother's eyes when his father playfully tossed his younger brother and sister in the air one by one. They had felt safe and secure with this tall gentle man who had sacrificed his youth to twelve-hour days of backbreaking work in the fields. He remembered most of all the day when, through no fault of his father's, the family's respect for his father had slightly dwindled and their sense of security had been broken altogether. That day was the first time he had seen his father cry. He had hated the red-faced sheriff who made a pass at his mother and he was proud when his father had physically thrown the man out. For a short while his father had been the champion of his family, even a small champion of the colored race. He had made the sheriff run to his car in fright, but James had caught a look in his father's eyes he did not understand, a kind of grave concern that had no reason, was the way he read it. Then there was the pounding on the door. The entire family froze in fear. And he remembered how the sheriff and three brutish white men had kicked in the door and beat his father down. He had felt shame, fear, and hate when his mother fell on her knees and begged for his father's life. He remembered the savage kick to his father's face as the men were leaving. The blood had gushed from his father's flattened nose and hung like thick strings of mucus from his chin. He saw his brother and sister huddled together, screaming, their eyes wide with fear and horror. Seeing their father's pride broken had scarred his memory even more than the battered face and blood-soaked undershirt his father wore. Never once had his father bowed his head or slumped his shoulder to a white man. He had been taught self-pride as a child by his slave master, a young handsome Easterner, who had inherited the plantation and had ultimately set all the slaves free. His father had grown up believing that hard work and faith could overcome anything. He had been a proud man with an unwavering faith in God and family. In a last desperate effort to give them hope the words had come. They rushed out through broken teeth and grotesque lips along with a flood of tears that streamed from his eyes and mingled with the blood on his face. His body was racked with pain and he choked, spitting up still more blood. "In this here country a po' colored man can't protect his family. He can just die fo 'um." Then he looked to the sky while James's mother sponged his face with a wet rag. He held up his hand and he said, "God's gonna lay His heavy hand on 'um; you wait and see." Little James Cook had wondered why, if God was on their side, did He let them white men do that to his father? Why didn't He just strike 'um dead right then? Maybe there weren't no God after all. Maybe his mother and father was just lying to make him act good, or maybe they's just plain dumb. For a while he had somehow hated his father for being weak. If it was him he'd got the shotgun and went and killed 'um all. So James had run away from home to show his parents, to make 'um pay for the lies they had told him and for making him black like them. In less than three weeks they were all dead. Then he was sorry and he cried and cried and wished he was dead too.

"Something wrong, boy?" Malcolm asked.

"What . . . No!" King Fish answered. "Just thinking how you got from where you was to where you is now."

Malcolm stared questioningly at King Fish then asked him again if something was wrong, this time more demanding. King Fish felt a hot surge of hostility spread across his face and a brief flickering of desire to cut this man's heart out. After all, pulling a gun on a man and not using it was an unforgivable sin in King Fish's world; but there was no advantage in this kind of confrontation. Con men looked for an edge and King Fish was almost always a con man.

"I'm thinkin' what a jump it is from who I am to a preacher," he said.

Malcolm laughed. "Ain't no jump a'tall. You just sell salvation the way you sell whatever else it is you been sellin'."

He patted King Fish on the back. "You gonna be just fine," he said.

Malcolm looked at his watch. "Well, Reverend James Cook, we better hit the hay. Even men with a destiny need to sleep."

He pulled on a cord hanging from the wall next to the drapes, and before he could light up his cigar, a sleepy-eyed, light-complexioned Negro appeared in the doorway. Malcolm ordered him to show King Fish to his sleeping quarters, a house in the rear of the main house which was once used by the overseer when there were slaves on the plantation. Malcolm also told King Fish to give the servant the address where his belongings were so the servant could fetch them the next morning. The place he and the servant walked in silence to was a small, unattractive, but clean wooden structure with a bathroom, a kitchen, and a bedroom. King Fish thanked the servant and tipped him generously, much to the servant's surprise. This generosity would help King Fish obtain any information he wanted about the plantation and about Malcolm Cage and his wife.

Sleep did not come easy for King Fish that night. Plagued by a guilty conscience because of his broken word to his friend and a nightmare about the story of Junior Holmes with himself as the lead character, he sat upright in bed listening to the sounds of crickets all around him. What was he doing? This white man had redirected the course of his life? The disturbing thing was that even beyond the promise of money, something compelled him to follow this course. King Fish liked the word "destiny" being associated with him. It made him feel important, and maybe he did have one. He did fall asleep just before dawn, a deep, black sleep that brought with it a hint of eternity—no dreams, no thoughts—only oblivion.

King Fish was awakened by a light tapping on the door. He found his pants crumpled on the floor next to the bed, stepped inside of them, and dragged himself to the door. The servant and another man stood there with his trunk and suitcases. King Fish opened the door wider, motioned for them to put the things in the corner, and he crawled back into the bed. He was asleep again in an instant, clothes and all. The next time there was a knock on the door it was followed by the voice of a young girl calling for "Reben Cook." She stood there wide-eyed, no more than eleven or twelve years of age, holding a tray of breakfast food in both hands.

"My name Nettie Bean. Reben Cage says to feed you."

She handed King Fish the tray and he thanked her.

"Reben Cage say iff'n you want to donate some money to the church, you can."

King Fish smiled at her, set the tray on a wooden table next to the window, and fished into his pocket for a dime along with the five-dollar bill he peeled off his bankroll.

"The five dollars is fo' the church; the dime fo' you," he said.

Her smile was bright and quick, not unlike another smile he remembered. King Fish stood there and watched her skip happily across the road in the direction of the big house.

King Fish had finished his meal, washed up, and was fully dressed in his regular clothes when Malcolm Cage opened the door and walked in wearing a big smile.

"You just had your first lesson in the ministry, Reverend Cook."

King Fish was puzzled.

"The little gal," Malcolm said. "I'm talkin' 'bout Nettie Bean, the little gal. Gave her a donation for the church, didn't you? Women and children, that's what makes a church. Women is what a church is built on. You see, Reverend Cook, it's the women that bring the men or they bring the men's money. The children, now, they warm the hearts of cold men, or they embarrass them till they reach inside their pockets."

Even King Fish thought using children was going a little too far, and it showed in his face.

"A thief with principles!" Malcolm exclaimed. "Now, ain't that a refreshing thought, Reverend Cook. Now I'm gonna teach you somethin' you never wanna forget. You fight for the good Lord the same way you fight for the devil, with all your might. You fight to win, and to win the war of salvation you gotta have money. Most people can't understand that, can't understand that folks ain't paying much attention to what a broke man got to say. It's the church with the most money that saves the most souls, or has the most souls to save."

King Fish conceded Malcolm's point with a smile.

"Wanna show you somethin'," Malcolm said, and handed King Fish a minister's collar. "Try it on and follow me."

King Fish questioned briefly with his eyes, but obeyed. As they walked out the door, Malcolm asked, "Somethin' been on my mind, I'm wonderin' 'bout. What was it you was doin' in that chauffeur's uniform?"

Before King Fish could lie, Malcolm was roaring with laughter, which King Fish took up as well.

King Fish followed him across the dirt road until they reached an old hastily built barn. It was smaller than most barns and in need of much repair, completely vacant of grain, hay, or farming tools. It showed no evidence of being used. Malcolm directed King Fish to follow him up an old rickety ladder to a loft, where they were both suddenly bathed in golden rays of sunlight that streamed through the roof like signals from heaven. Malcolm stretched out his arm and threw back his head.

"God is here," he whispered emotionally. "Here is where I come to talk with God. Every morning I come here to give thanks." He knelt and motioned to King Fish, who did the same. After a moment of silence to honor "His" presence, Malcolm got up. He looked down at King Fish with sincerity and said, "Except for my wife, you're the only other person who's seen this sign."

King Fish didn't believe in signs. He didn't believe in God, but he was impressed by this racist white man's actions toward him, even beyond what he understood to be Malcolm's reasons. The fact was that in less than twenty-four hours a total stranger had given him more money than he could have stolen that day and permitted him alone to view what Malcolm considered to be no less than a sign from God. Malcolm Cage, in King Fish's opinion, was as sharp as they came. There was a compliment somewhere to King Fish in all of this.

After they had climbed back down the ladder, Malcolm told King Fish how he had built the barn himself in remembrance of Jesus' humble beginning and his own, thus keeping a kind of kinship with the have-nots. These were admirable thoughts, but the contradictions in this man, King Fish would learn, were severe, as they almost always are with anyone possessing a hint of madness and genius. The first example was demonstrated shortly after they made it back to the big house, where Lorene joined them on the huge half-moon-shaped enclosed side porch for coffee. King Fish sat a few respectable spaces away on a lawn chair near the steps so as not to give the impression that Malcolm Cage and his wife were doing exactly what they were doing—having coffee with a colored man.

Lorene thought Malcolm's notions concerning the proper placement of colored folks in a setting with whites—excusing, of course, the bedroom, a place she was much too much of a lady to mention—seemed absurd, even silly to her; more important, they were the height of hypocrisy. Negro women had even nursed white children and these children had sometimes grown up side by side with the colored ones. Lorene's sly smile was not lost on Malcolm, who by now took it as the condescending expression she always leveled against those less intelligent than herself. Then there was that quick burst of light laughter that followed; this made him goddamned angry. Today this anger distracted the light-skinned Negro, who overpoured Malcolm's drink. In a sudden rage Malcolm sent the coffeepot flying, with the back of his hand, across the yard along with the obscenities he hurled at the man, until the magic touch of Lorene's hand on his shoulder stayed his anger. Then, as if nothing happened, it was over. Lorene waved the servant away with her free hand just as little Nettie Bean wandered curiously out on the porch. Nettie's mother rushed out in a desperate effort to retrieve her child, but Malcolm Cage was already moving quickly toward the girl. Her mother stopped still in her tracks. King Fish felt his jaw tighten. The young girl's unblinking eyes never left the face of this giant man coming toward her. Suddenly his right arm shot out and reached behind her ear. Then slowly, and with considerable style, Malcolm pulled back his hand to reveal a twenty-five-cent piece walking between his fingertips. Nettie Bean's eyes lit up the porch. "The ol' red bear scared you a little, did he?" Malcolm asked. She shook her head. "If the ol' red bear gives you this quarter will you say a prayer for him that he won't lose his temper so much?" This time she nodded her head. Malcolm Cage placed the quarter in her hand, instructing her to put it into her bank. She was off with a big smile, holding her quarter high over her head until she reached her mother, who then ushered her into the house.

What was known by everyone present, with the exception of King Fish, was that Malcolm Cage would have never harmed little Nettie Bean. They had all seen the red bear—as Malcolm had nicknamed himself, much to the delight of the then-four-year old with the bright eyes—humbled by the smile of this child. Notwithstanding the natural charm of this beautiful young girl, the Good Book had spoken in no uncertain terms on the matter (*and a small child shall lead the way*). At the insistence of the adults, Malcolm was to be referred to, in the presence of visitors and strangers, as Reverend Cage. In the children's world, however, he became the lead character in a mystical story Malcolm himself had created about a good-natured red bear who was always on hand to rescue children in danger.

It had been eight years ago when Willa Mae Bean, then in her late thirties, brought Nettie Bean, her tired and hungry only child, to the Cages' plantation in search of food and lodging following the untimely death of her husband, who had been killed by a mule in a freak accident while working as a sharecropper in Alabama. Lorene had been sympathetic and, despite the fact that no positions were available, had hired her on the spot, taking Willa Mae and her daughter in without hesitation. Almost as swiftly, Nettie Bean had become Malcolm Cage's favorite, giving rise to the argument that Malcolm would have adopted her as his own if not for the color of her skin. There may have been some truth to this, but Malcolm Cage's affection and generosity toward children of all colors was well documented. His highly publicized Easter, Thanksgiving, and Christmas dinners were the most lavish in the city, with the possible exception of the ones sponsored by St. Louis Cathedral, of the large Catholic diocese in the French Quarter. There were also the gift-bearing impromptu trips to the houses of the poor, the picnics he arranged, and the annual Kids' Day outings he promoted when the circus came to town. The playground, segregated as it was, which bore the name New Zion, the same as his church, was further testament to Malcolm's involvement and concern for children and their development. Still, as much as he loved children, the church above all else was the focus of his existence. To him, the church should be sustained at all costs; because it was through the church that all blessings from God should flow. He believed this with such fervor that he devised additional means by which to ensure the longevity of his house of worship. Some were controversial tactics for sure, but effective ones all the same, which subjected the participants to a kind of religious blackmail. Any endeavor he undertook, whether it had to do with the church or not, required the other person or business to pay, in the form of a donation, a levy, seemingly for the pleasure of doing business with the Reverend Cage. If you purchased goods from Malcolm Cage's huge farm, which were, indeed, very well priced, you paid in accordance with the amount of that purchase a percentage to the church. If the reverse was true and you were selling goods to Malcolm, a percentage of your profits were taxed, again, for the church. Such was Malcolm Cage's influence at city hall, so close was his friendship with Walter Stone, the state congressman, it was considered suicide in the business world to fall into disfavor with him.

After Nettie Bean and her mother disappeared from the front porch, Malcolm smiled, but his comments drew a cool silence from King Fish.

"They're all like children, ain't they, young and ol' ones, just like children," Malcolm said.

Lorene cut in. "Darling, as usual you are being much too general."

He turned to look into King Fish's eyes, which were steadfast; also, within that brief look was revealed a sharp challenge. But more troubling to Malcolm than the quick defiance, there was the depth of the intelligence he found.

"You're different, ain't you? Ain't like no niggah I ever met. Shows in your eyes."

Anger began to overtake Malcolm because he sensed he had underestimated King Fish.

"Oh, don't you go thinking I was at all fooled by that Uncle Tom talk you been doing since I found your hand in my pocket. Ain't been fooled one bit by it."

Lorene moved to Malcolm's side and hooked her arm inside of his. "Darling, you have to know that colored people are only permitted to relate to white people from a position of intimidation."

"Ain't the same with this'n here. This'n ain't intimidated by white folks one bit. Matter of fact, thinks he's equal to any white man!"

Lorene's eyes locked briefly with King Fish's, begging for understanding.

"Come on, old grouchy red bear, you must be hungry," she said to Malcolm, and, ignoring his feeble protest, led him into the house.

King Fish was angry and he might have left right then. He could have gotten a ride into town, hired a cab, come back, picked up his belongings, and still caught a train to New York; but he didn't. Two things made this only a momentary temptation. His uncle Ed's teachings was one. His uncle Ed had told him that "having a word" was the thing that separated squares and small-time hustlers from big-timers. The latter always kept their word, and that principle alone could make him a giant, could make him accessible to people who could do him the most good. Having a word was top game, he told King Fish, and had nothing to do with morality, character, or honesty. King Fish's uncle had somehow always had the ear and even the trust of some person of power in "The City." King Fish's second reason for staying was simple. He still believed this crazy cracker could show him the way to big money.

After cautioning himself about his own temper, King Fish began walking toward his living quarters in the back. Over his right shoulder, and for miles, all his imagination would let him see were black figures carrying white cotton sacks, young and old alike, Malcolm Cage's children, breaking their backs so a minister of the Gospel could live like a king. The irony of it all caused King Fish to laugh out loud. He sure was glad he was a hustler. Before he made it to the door he heard the sound of happy feet behind him. Nettie Bean blurted out her message before she came to a complete halt.

"Reben Cage say ta tell you I'll bring you some food." She hesitated and said quickly, "You got some pretty clothes," and giggling shyly, sprang away with that special exuberance only children can command.

An hour later, when King Fish was settled back on his bed thinking about New York, the excitement he could have found in Harlem, and what he should tell Society Red, Nettie Bean brought him dinner, as she promised. One hour after that he was asleep, with just a hint in his subconscious that someone had entered the room and quickly left.

The next morning, as King Fish lay half-awake, Malcolm again barged into his room—bursting with excitement, loquacious, basking in the afterglow of the night before. He had just recently come from the hayloft where he had given thanks to the good Lord for another blessing that he believed had come to him a year before in the form of a rowdy black prostitute he referred to as his concubine, named "Sassy." Last night she had even outdone herself, he told King Fish, and went on to explain it in intimate detail. King Fish's eyes widened with discovery. It suddenly came to him why this man had somehow seemed familiar that first night. There had been a scandal of sorts, featuring a redheaded white preacher whom King Fish had glimpsed on occasion in the ninth ward. The preacher had killed another white man over his beating of a colored whore. Sassy had been the woman.

"I'm the one you thinking about," Malcolm confirmed almost proudly. "Had it coming to him. Some people ain't no better than a mad dog, running and tear'n at the world, spreadin' their poison all over, givin' nothing back, givin' nothing to God. Ain't no place on God's earth for 'um."

King Fish witnessed a physical transformation in Malcolm greater than any he had ever seen in any man before. The red in his skin deepened, and the veins in his temples and neck began to protrude. Like the roar of a great furnace about to explode, Malcolm Cage's voice rose up from the depth of his stomach.

"He beat her bloody for no reason at all!" he thundered, trembling uncontrollably.

The green in his eyes grew dark and their focus retreated from the present. For a moment Malcolm Cage lost himself, gave himself away to the passion of this great revenge he was remembering, and he rose above his mortal station as if he were the Almighty Himself sitting in judgment. Malcolm's words became musical, colored with the flavor of his Baptist ministry.

" 'But whosoever shall offend one of these little ones which believe in me, it were better for him that a millstone were hanged about his neck, and that he were drowned in the depth of the sea.' Matthew 18:6."

He paused and faced King Fish squarely.

"I took out my gun and for the good Lord, in defense of his children, put a bullet in this devil's brain. We're soldiers, Reverend Cook, soldiers in the Lord's army, like David, Samson, and Joshua. They all killed; it was God's work they was doing, following God's order!"

In that moment King Fish realized the true power and madness he had come face-to-face with. He experienced a kind of fear with which he was unfamiliar—and King Fish was not usually intimidated by other men. After all, he had stood unflinching in the deadly glare of Bill Black's eyes, had been unwavering, still, when he had glimpsed the flash of steel and heard the explosion that stole his consciousness and almost his life. But this man's actions were born from something more than the conventional emotions of hate, rage, or revenge. His actions were far more chilling because they contained within them his belief that a mandate from

God to do murder was his. To make matters worse, he seemed exempt from the long arm of the law. No lawman ever confronted Malcolm for his drunkenness or occasional brawling.

"Can I hep you home, suh?" were the words he heard from the police during these times.

Maybe eyebrows had been raised because of the killing of a white man, but no serious inquiry was ever made into Malcolm's guilt concerning it. In the ninth ward he had even been celebrated as a kind of defender of Negro womanhood. In a weird sort of way, some of what they believed was correct. Closer to the truth, however, was King Fish's observation: Malcolm Cage was as crazy as a road lizard, just like some a' them crazy nigguhs in the Bottoms, a white supremacist who owned an enormous ego. King Fish, therefore, a man who in the past had relied on words to help earn his livelihood, was forced to adopt a new strategy to forward his ambitions—the strategy of silence. Malcolm Cage noticed.

"Cat got you tongue now, Reverend Cook?"

"Reven Cage, you make a man do a lot of thinkin'. "

Malcolm laughed. "You come with me, now; we're gonna see if I can outdo myself."

King Fish rushed to the bathroom, sponged himself off, and dressed quickly.

A bright Saturday morning greeted King Fish when they stepped outside, a strange quiet with no one in sight. Malcolm led the way, walking quickly across the yard in the direction of the barn, occasionally smiling back at King Fish, who followed in close pursuit. Malcolm's smile was sly. They reached the barn together and Malcolm, almost unable to contain himself, insisted King Fish open the door. King Fish saw them everywhere—sitting on the floor, on old benches and chairs, standing against the walls. The room smelled of them, not an unclean odor, but the kind that hangs thick in a room filled to capacity. The field hands had come with their children to what Malcolm Cage had told them was a special service. There at the head of the room near the hayloft sat a freshly polished pulpit with a Bible butterflied on top of it. To the right of the pulpit sat Lorene, talking to little Nettie Bean.

"This here's your congregation," Malcolm said, stretching out his hand.

King Fish was flabbergasted. "You want me to preach—just like that? You want me to *preach*? It ain't even Sunday."

"Every day's a day for uplifting souls, Reven Cook. You ought to know that."

Malcolm walked casually over to the pulpit and introduced a stunned King Fish to his workers as their pastor. He praised King Fish for his knowledge of the Bible then quietly took a seat beside Lorene. King Fish hesitated only a moment before moving to the pulpit and gripping the sides firmly for support. His legs had felt heavy during the brief walk, and he had been a little nervous, but surprisingly, his hands were comfortable there. As he watched the God-loving faces, hopeful in their curiosity, filled with anticipation, and somewhat awed, King Fish was struck with a realization that brought with it a feeling of power. It had been he who had commanded the attention of others, not the reverse. Adulation and recognition were the rewards bestowed on those who dared everything, rewards endorsed by ordinary people, who dared nothing. He had known this feeling of exaltation and respect most of his adult life; he had elicited it by his grand manner, by being the most colorful at what he did. And what he did was to be: the best all-around hustler, the best talker, the best dresser, with always the prettiest women on his arm. If that was not enough, he presented to those who already adored him a unique and wonderful singing voice. King Fish had not before asserted himself in this arena, but now confidence was his and he began to welcome the new challenge. He looked down at the Scriptures, which were open to the Book of Job, and he thought with a nod to himself that Job was a good book to begin with. Now he was ready. He was ready to preach and teach the Gospel.

"Hallelujah!" he shouted in almost startling fashion, and received little response.

He turned sideways, showing his profile, leaning his head in toward his audience and shouted again. "I said Hallelujah!"

He received a resounding echo and he raised his voice in an old spiritual song known by everyone. He began slowly, with his rich bass voice vibrating off the walls in bold mellow tones, sending a warm sensation over the whole of the crowd, causing even Malcolm Cage and Lorene to tingle with spiritual excitement. King Fish, always in perfect voice, began to move among the people, extending a hand here and there to the men, giving a nod of introduction to the women. He got to know them quickly that way; and he quickly began to touch them inside: their bodies swayed with the slow rhythm of the song. The women raised their hands over their heads. The old men said "Amen." Then King Fish lifted them higher. He threw back his head and screamed the lyrics in perfect falsetto. The women rose to their feet. The men drummed their feet on the ground. The Spirit massed heavy in the room and in their heart, conjured up by a man who didn't believe in God. King Fish made it back to the pulpit and there he released them from the hypnosis of his song. Then he preached the word as he had always felt it should be preached. He compared them to Job and Job's faithfulness, signaling them out individually at times, and at times overwhelming the whole of them with grand gestures and the enormity of his presence. He concluded by asking them to join hands and in a final prayer he made them promise to live with Jesus in their hearts every day of their life.

With smiling faces fixed on King Fish, they came forward to offer congratulations and to drop money into a basket provided by a beaming Malcolm Cage. Old women touched his shoulder and old men nodded their approval. Even Willa Mae Bean, who had been so suspicious of him at first, moved with her daughter, Nettie, following close behind, to the front to show her support for their new minister. Blessings went out to him from her and every other female. Nettie Bean's fluttering eyes and bashful smile revealed the crush she pretended to hide. King Fish quickened the pace of Nettie Bean's rapid heartbeat by complimenting her on her pretty dress and the pretty smile she wore that matched it. The occasion also was not without tears, which Malcolm Cage shed abundantly as he placed an envelope with a large donation into the basket.

"God is real!" he repeated over and over with clasped hands in front of his chest.

Lorene, standing next to him like a queen in some European state overlooking her subjects, offered a reassuring smile to the farmhands as they filed by. It never occurred to her that this was a con game in progress, no more than she suspected any other ministry that took in large sums of money of fleecing its congregation, her husband's included. It was written in the Word that the church is responsible for God's messenger. The saving of souls was the important thing. Malcolm, on the other hand, knew who King Fish was, but was sure his salvation was in God's plan, and that he, Malcolm, was the instrument of that salvation. It was all working just fine. He believed you couldn't preach the Gospel and not be affected by it. The power and inspiration of King Fish's sermon served to support Lorene's argument that the Negro was, in fact, an intelligent being and not merely some less-than-human specimen who was base, degenerate, and only slightly more literate than a moron. This dynamic colored man who, her husband told her, much like himself, had no formal education, was living proof she was right. No doubt the cream of Southern society would hasten to conclude that this Negro was simply an exception to the rule, as there always is, and not indicative of the race as a whole. Still, meeting the Reverend Cook in a somewhat social setting would cause some questions concerning such a position on the matter to be raised, and that would be satisfaction enough—for now. A dinner should be arranged to introduce her husband's protégé to Christian society, she thought, a simple well-orchestrated affair where Reverend Cook, from a minister's perspective, could mingle, discuss the Scriptures and, in general, showcase his intelligence. She wished her father were still alive. She missed him very much, but more than that, she had a need to prove to him she was right. Well, at least one of the two men she loved could bear witness to the simple but effective articulation of Reverend Cook. To make the evening more interesting she could ask him to sing.

As for King Fish, he was more surprised than anyone. Never

before had his self-esteem been lifted as it had been today. At this moment he almost believed in God, but came instead to believe more in himself.

After the congregation had gone, leaving only the three of them, Malcolm Cage emptied the money from the basket into a small burlap sack he retrieved from the hayloft.

"This is for you, Reverend Cook," he said in his proud voice and handed the bag to King Fish.

The three of them left together, each savoring secretly an individual victory, but bound in spirit one to the other, inextricably connected by an emotion that held no regard for color, gender, or the dictates of the times. This is how they moved—in sync with each other, like soldiers led by some unseen officer. King Fish felt almost noble in his exaltation, like a man on the brink of setting off on an honorable quest. For the moment he almost forgot he was merely a hustler after a hustler's buck. Undeniably he had had fantasies of being more in his thirty-seven years. There had been times when he imagined himself a righteous minister who preached the true Gospel from his heart, but he had learned that all things that looked pure and good were only the magic of misdirection conjured by the hands of some gifted con man. Malcolm Cage, too, felt exalted, but unlike King Fish, the credit for everything he was blessed with went to the Almighty and "everything," he believed, was what he had: good health, wealth, position, and power. He had a beautiful wife who loved and stood by him, even, he suspected, tolerated his involvement with other women, some of questionable virtue. Most of all he was on his way to fulfilling the promise he had made to his God.

Lorene felt like a college girl again: young, independent, and defiant, a woman who had reclaimed her spirit. She was a little angry to have succumbed so readily to the unfair rules a female in married life was expected to follow. However, today her passion for debate and controversy had been rekindled. When they reached the big house, Willa Mae Bean, who had rushed home ahead of them, and had now spotted the trio from the kitchen window, was there at the door with a smile to greet them. It was significant that

King Fish had been invited to the house a second time. She felt good that one of her own had reached this status. King Fish's eyes read even more. He saw the hopes and dreams of his people being transferred to his shoulders, along with a whisper that begged him, "Do us proud!" In the fraction of a second she had communicated this plea and then she was gone. King Fish watched her move gingerly back to the kitchen, which was her undisputed domain, to finish preparing the brunch her experience told her would be expected. He and Malcolm, on Lorene's suggestion, followed her as far as the dining nook, where they seated themselves around an antique table covered with fine linen and imported china, a small portion of Lorene's inheritance. Malcolm began quickly to speak of plans to enlarge the barn, build a pulpit and a vestry, just as his own church had. He even intended to have stained-glass windows placed inside and a cross on top. King Fish sat in silent amazement as his ministry was planned without once consulting him. Even Lorene, with her eyes shining, joined in, and soon began to dominate the table, hastily putting together as she talked, the details of her dinner party. Suddenly Willa Mae Bean was there with thick slices of bacon, ham, and eggs scrambled to a fluff. There were also hot biscuits with butter and blueberry jam, potatoes smothered with green onions, piping-hot coffee, and orange juice. For the first time since he had arrived at Malcolm Cage's house King Fish broke his silence, uttering a prayer that asked God to bless Malcolm and his wife for leading him in the direction of this "Divine Calling." This is how King Fish would play the game. He knew Malcom believed he could change him, and Lorene didn't know who he was. He would use Malcolm's ego and Lorene's blind faith to his own advantage. King Fish gave thanks for the good health the three of them enjoyed, and for life itself. Lastly, he thanked the good Lord for the food that lay before them and even for Willa Mae Bean, who was such a great cook. King Fish's prayer touched them and he knew it. Malcolm again was moved to tears. Lorene was moved as well, but she understood something neither of them did: these tears were the beginning of a bond between her husband and King Fish, one she intended to fully exploit, to prove to her

friends that coloreds and whites could coexist equally. For these
tears revealed feelings that reached far beyond those that were expressed. They spoke of a new acceptance on the part of Malcolm
Cage for King Fish—and, yes, maybe even a kind of love. This
fact was not lost on King Fish, Lorene observed, whose eyes responded ever so slightly in kind. Maybe this was indeed the true
beginning of a relationship, and the balance that came with it.

The next day, before the crack of dawn, as Malcolm Cage had
promised, he came to fetch King Fish. The old Ford truck, one of
six used to carry cotton and sugarcane to market, jostled them
around like cowboys on a bucking horse as they traveled over
most of the plantation. That morning King Fish learned something more about Malcolm Cage—that he was a wonderful storyteller. Malcolm Cage placed a delighted King Fish on a safari in
the remote jungles of Africa along with himself and Congressman
Walter Stone—warding off an attack by wild animals and escaping
by a hair at least one encounter with a hostile native tribe. King
Fish suspected a great many of these stories were exaggerated, but
like a child he was engrossed in them all the same. There was, of
course, proof, in the form of the animal heads lined along the
walls of Malcolm's study, that he had hunted the black rhino, elephants, and leopards. There was proof again in the form of the
photograph that featured Malcolm and the congressman standing
with guns in hand beside a huge beast they had just slaughtered.
These tales were sometimes interrupted by a sudden stop. They
would get out of the truck and Malcolm Cage would converse
with a field hand, occasionally joking with the man about his sex
life. To the young boys he quipped about their lack of one. King
Fish could tell that Malcolm Cage had a true affection for his
workers; indeed, he conveyed the feeling that he would always
protect them, with his life if need be. He even said as much, then
went on to complain how lazy and dumb they were. He seemed to
be expressing a kind of mock dissatisfaction with them, like a parent does with a child he or she is actually proud of. What seemed
a little paradoxical to King Fish was that despite Malcolm's de-
meaning opinion of Negroes, he had only Negroes in his employ.

As for the Negro women, he said they were all abrupt, raw, and the lot of them not to be trusted. Still, Malcolm Cage spent as much time in bed with women of color as he spent with his own wife.

By noon, they had visited the livestock, the cows, pigs, chickens, and the stables where the horses were kept. There was not one white face. Two weeks passed quickly and two more of King Fish's sermons, each more successful than the last, fourteen days of hearing Malcolm Cage boast of his sexual prowess with Negro women, one half of a month of simultaneously hating and respecting him, and all the while the three of them—Malcolm, Lorene, and King Fish—seemed to grow closer. Suddenly it was the evening of the dinner and King Fish found himself standing in front of the round mirror the houseboys had provided for him. Then he was walking nervously through the side entrance of the big house and Lorene was leading him into the huge drawing room where he met Congressman Stone, Malcolm Cage's friend, and his freckle-faced, red-headed wife, who, because of their close friendship with the Cages, had arrived early. They were standing next to Malcolm Cage, drinks in hand, having a hearty laugh. They turned to King Fish and Lorene immediately, Walter Stone's steel-blue eyes making a quick appraisal of King Fish. They were the prettiest blue he had ever seen, unsettling for sure, but a perfect complement to the congressman's wavy, very prematurely silver hair.

"So you're the boy of the hour?" the congressman said before Lorene could made an introduction.

"Yes, suh, that's what Mrs. Cage told me, sorta," King Fish replied with a slight nod.

"Congressman Stone, meet the Reverend James Cook," Malcolm Cage said, giving King Fish a pat on the back.

"Reverend Cage, here, says a little devil in a preacher makes him more honest," Congressman Stone stated, then asked with a smile, "Got any devil in you, Reverend Cook?"

"Just enough to make me a good Christian," King Fish replied.

They all laughed, except Congressman Stone's wife, who remained uncomfortably silent. Quickly it came to King Fish that she did not approve of him or of his presence in this social setting. The disappointment registered in Lorene's face. She realized she had made a mistake. Time had not changed a thing. Time and her secluded lifestyle had only served as a mask that hid what she did not want to believe. The truth was even present in the condescending way Walter Stone had addressed Reverend Cook. Most white people had an inherent dislike for Negroes or a built-in disrespect for them. She knew that her guests would not give Reverend Cook a chance. It was Malcolm Cage who solved the immediate problem by suggesting to Congressman Stone that the three of them retire to the study and leave Lorene and his wife to the other guests, who were just beginning to arrive. Everyone followed that suggestion but not before Congressman Stone's wife took time out to reaffirm her hatred for Negroes with one hot stare, which she darted at everyone present. King Fish felt her hatred penetrate his skin and settle heavy in his stomach. Her feelings about the Negro were far more severe than those myths of inferiority expressed by most white men, like her husband and Malcolm Cage. Hers was a hatred that was pure, uncompromising, where no quarter was given to kinder feelings. King Fish knew there were three kinds of white people in the world. The ones who promoted hatred into violence, the ones who acted out that violence, and the ones who stood silently by and did nothing to stop it. This woman belonged to the first class. He knew well the second kind; he had seen them one night in his youth.

Following Malcolm Cage's lead, he and the congressman walked to the study. Even then, King Fish could feel the woman's eyes burning in his back. Inside the study, the congressman's silent whistle and head shake to Malcolm Cage told King Fish he did not share his wife's passionate hatred of Negroes. Malcolm Cage quickly walked to a handsome cabinet of mahogany where the spirits were kept and poured himself and the congressman a brandy. King Fish stood silent, intimidated by the power and riches of this white world, the control these men had over other men, even over his life, if they wished. The room smelled of success, of expensive leather and of mahogany wood. The trophy heads of dead animals made it a room of conquest. The photographs on the walls depicting Congressman Stone and Malcolm Cage's big-game-hunting kills gave further proof of their power.

"Want a drink, Reverend Cook?" Malcolm Cage offered.

King Fish quickly searched the congressman's face for approval.

"Have one, boy, have one!" the congressman said.

Malcolm told King Fish to help himself and handed his friend a drink. Thinking fast, King Fish made a bid to include himself in the two men's conversation.

"Can I make a toast, suh?" he asked.

At first the two men hesitated. Then Congressman Stone's blue eyes smiled.

"Make your toast, boy," he encouraged.

"To Storyville," King Fish shouted, "and the whores that lived there!"

They all smiled at each other. With the joy of remembrance on their faces, they lifted their glasses high, enthusiastically toasting a red-light district that had long since faded into the past, taking younger and less responsible days with it.

"To Storyville!" they all cried, and clicked their glasses.

"This city ain't been the same since Storyville closed," King Fish said.

"Don't say that too loud, but I couldn't agree with you more," the congressman confided, giving Malcolm Cage a look married men understand. They had another drink and Congressman Stone in a lowered voice began to tell about his experiences at Madam La Ru's House. His stories brought images of fine crystal and china imported from Europe, exquisite furnishings, and fine Creole ladies with lace panties who smelled of perfume that Madam La Ru ordered from Paris. And, of Madam La Ru herself, totally French in her refinement, in her accent, and in her manner, a grand older woman who brought great style to the world's oldest profession. Congressman Stone had been a high-spirited boy of fifteen when his father had first taken him to her establishment. He was tall and red-faced with curly blond hair, a well-endowed young man whom nature chose to embarrass with an erection much too often for his father's comfort. The kindness of Madam La Ru and the girls who worked for her endeared the whores to him for the rest of his life. His first time had been a wonderful experience of clever hands, moist lips, and a warm body whose mysterious opening reached to the stars. Once a month he was allowed a trip to Madam La Ru's, without the knowledge of his mother, of course. This was a practice that was continued even after he had grown up and was married. That bond between him and his father was never broken. Their secret was never revealed to his mother. In fact, on his deathbed, his father had weakly flashed him the okay sign, which, a moment later, he returned. This had been their only communication that first day as he had emerged from Madam La Ru's place. It was a rainy night in December, just before Christmas, when his dealings with the House of La Ru came to a sudden halt, dealings that, had they become known, would have halted his young political career as well in any city except New Orleans. Just as he had finished passing out gifts to all the girls who had serviced him that year, his wife appeared at the door with two un-uniformed policemen and demanded to see her husband. The newspaper had a field day, but nothing ever came of it, except a minor embarrassment. To this day, a twinkle was visible in the congressman's eyes at the mere mention of Storyville.

Malcolm Cage, of course, too, had experienced the pleasures of Storyville, but he had chosen a less-than-glamorous part of the district for his visits. In this section illusions were not promoted. No silks and satin sheets graced the beds, no exotic paintings hung on the walls, and the scent that greeted you was the faint odor of lye soap. This was where the Negro girls plied their trade, for less money and in less time. This was where Malcolm Cage had taken up the task of saving the soul of one comely young woman with an innocent smile who worked for herself in her own house and seemed very interested in his ministry, especially when his tips were large, Malcolm confessed with a laugh that almost shook the room. It had been she who had almost taken him to hell rather than he bringing her to salvation. King Fish and the congressman got bellyaches from laughing. King Fish doubled over and Congressman

Stone went red-faced and teary-eyed. This had occurred before Malcolm had met and married Lorene. Now the two white men were looking to King Fish, a man who knew Storyville from the inside, they were willing to venture. King Fish did not deny this. He had wanted to sing with Buddy Bolden, one of the architects of that then-new and exciting music called "jazz" that had gotten its start in the whorehouses. King Fish told them he had been a young man then, in his late teens, working on the riverboat as a waiter and, on his off days, steering johns to the different houses in Storyville for tips from the men and kickbacks from the madams who ran the upscale houses where the jazz bands played, and where he, from time to time, got a chance to hear Buddy Bolden. He never did sing with Buddy Bolden, but because of his considerable skills with a deck of cards was soon elected to run the poker games that had become popular in a few of the Negro houses. There existed in all of the houses the standard story of a prostitute who ran away with a wealthy john and was living happily on a ranch in Iowa, or someplace such as that, with her two kids. There was also the story of the middle-aged housewife who went to work in the upscale house of Saint Clara in order to win a bet with her husband. She eventually got religion and became a crusader against prostitution. And the story of Gold Nugget Pete, the old greasy prospector who got lucky in California and squandered his good fortune in the houses of Storyville.

The funniest story King Fish could remember, however, happened because of a he-she by the name of Satin, who this certain madam kept in her employ for men (*of which there were more than just a few*) with different tastes. As the story went, and King Fish himself bore witness to, a young man from Oklahoma who was unfamiliar with the term "he-she," and most other things any boy his age who lived in the city would be familiar with, engaged Satin, over the mild protest of a couple of girls anxious for a laugh, only to discover that Satin had a member larger than this own. Believing that Satin was still a female, only afflicted by demons, this hick bolted from the bedroom, fully nude, broke down the front door on his way out, and was never seen again. Malcolm and the congressman had to seat themselves to keep from falling over. They were all still laughing when Lorene knocked on the door just before peering inside. She informed her husband and the congressman that many of the guests had arrived. And with a somewhat pained expression, she told King Fish that her plans had changed, that she wouldn't be needing him after all. Even though King Fish had known her only a short while, he thought of her as a different kind of white person. He knew it, without words between them. Just as he could feel Congressman Stone's wife's hatred without her speaking to it, he could feel Lorene's compassion. It was in the uninhibited and friendly way she moved around him, or sometimes that quick look or smile that said they both agreed or understood. But the phrase "won't be needing you" struck a wrong chord in him. It wasn't that he cared about not being part of her little experiment. He had only agreed to that because he liked and respected her. It was simply, it seemed, that colored folks had heard these words from white folks all their lives and he hated it, hated the image of some po' niggah standing in front of some white person, hat in hand, future in hand, only to hear in a matter-of-fact tone that nobody gave a good goddamn about him or his family. King Fish said his good-byes to Congressman Stone and Malcolm Cage, and walked out as gracefully as he could.

It was one of those special nights, balmy and fresh, with a gentle breeze and stars overhead that seemed to follow him as he walked back to his quarters. The night was mysterious and lovely the way it had been on many other star-filled nights, but he had not been alone then. The scent of her came from nowhere, flaring his nostrils in a great rush. Suddenly Sue Ellen was full beside him in his mind, and he could again hear that bright laughter and maybe even her whisper of love to him. Then, just as quickly as she had come, she was gone, and King Fish realized that he was very lonely.

King Fish hadn't expected the knock on the door, and he hadn't expected Lorene to be there, but somehow he still wasn't surprised. Her face was flushed and her eyes looked eerie and undecided, as if she was unsure of which emotion to reveal—her anger or her sadness. She apologized, then in an attempt to make him feel better, tried to explain away the actions of her friends. But King Fish saw them in a different light, through different eyes. He saw only their evil and mean-spiritedness. It didn't matter to him about their charitable work, or their love of children, or even their professed love of the Good Book. To him they were still evil, and he told Lorene as much, something he had never told any white person. Surprisingly enough, Lorene agreed with him. He went on to tell her about his father, and was surprised again, this time by his own tears. Through the telling of his father's story, something else he had never told to anyone, he had to face, completely, for the first time in his life, his father's courage and his own awareness that he had let his father down. King Fish began to make comparisons between his father and his uncle Ed, and as he did so, the difference between them became clear. Ultimately, his uncle Ed cared for no one but himself, while his father had cared for everyone but himself. This was the reason why, despite all things his father lacked— the smarts, the charm, and the knowledge to deal with white folks—King Fish could never measure up to him. Also, the elusiveness of this thing that his father always talked about that couldn't be seen, felt, or tasted, and was more important than fame or money. King Fish was beginning to understand it now. It was the reason he had to speak out. He would be silent no more, for Malcolm Cage or anyone else. He was going to be more like his father. The story touched Lorene deeply. It also pointed her mistakes out to her. She should have never abandoned her stance against racism, neither then, after her marriage to Malcolm Cage, nor now, as she had done less than thirty minutes ago. It was clear to her that this was a cause that validated her existence. Lorene realized something else as well. She had not come to King Fish solely to apologize, but more out of a need to indict herself for yet another failure to herself.

Malcolm Cage walked in. His voice thundered with anger.

"What you doin' in here?"

King Fish felt for his hook-blade knife. He would be all over Malcolm Cage this time if he reached for his gun. Lorene did not budge or blink. Her stare ate her husband's anger like cotton candy and her words converged on him like an unsuspected army.

"I'm trying to reclaim my dignity." Her eyes narrowed. "I'm also trying to understand why I should stay married to a man who disrespects me with other women, overcomes me every night with the smell of whiskey, and stands by and lets a group of stupid people make jokes at my expense."

Malcolm Cage started to speak, but she overtalked him.

"Because I won't agree that Christians who profess to live a life of righteousness should hate an entire race of people who happen to have a different skin color. How could they be so dumb? How could you?"

Malcolm asked her to come on home. Lorene brushed his arm away and walked out ahead of him. It was the first time he had seen her that way, so hostile. He hadn't realized she felt so strongly about the coloreds. He liked them, too, in their place; but she was taking this too far. He thought he had gotten her out of that romantic notion, that all people were created equal. It just wasn't so. It was as plain as the nose on her face. The coloreds were little more than savages. It wasn't their fault, he knew that, it was the way God had intended it. He watched his wife walking across the grass to the big house, her face tight with anger and determination, her beauty leaping out at him. He had created her in his mind long before he had ever met her. She had even surpassed his dreams of a mate. He had wished for a beautiful and devoted wife, one who was tender and agreeable. Lorene was more; she was smart, aristocratic, and very rich. Now she was very angry. So many charges she had leveled against him. She didn't understand. Some of these things were just a man's way, but they weren't more important than her, only God was that important.

King Fish knew he had crossed the line where Malcolm was concerned. Lorene had been alone in a room with him, actually apologizing for the actions of white folks. He had been openly critical. It was not good for him to be around Malcolm now. He intended to be gone in the morning.

King Fish awoke to a knock on his door, and opened it to find Malcolm Cage standing there with the strangest look on his face. The fire that had once blazed through his eyes had somehow extinguished itself. The air about him was not fierce and determined, but docile and cautious, making the rhythm of his body look unsure. He stared at the packed suitcases King Fish had neatly placed in the corner, longer than he might have, and his words came out stumbling.

"I been use ta tellin' coloreds all my life, but I know I can't tell you."

He paused.

"I listened to my wife last night, maybe for the first time, 'cause I thought I was about to lose her. She was right about some thangs, about colored folks, even me. Now, I ain't sayin' I think coloreds is equal to whites. I don't know about that yet. Maybe that's for the Almighty to say. Truth is, you equal to any man I met and I take you as my friend."

He held out his hand and grasped King Fish's firmly.

"Like I said, I ain't used ta asking." He looked hopefully into King Fish's eyes. "Stay with us, for me and Lorene and for your destiny."

"I don' know, I—" King Fish began.

Malcolm cut in. "Nothing's changed. You gonna git the blessings same as I told you. You gonna have a real church too. If I have to build one myself."

King Fish knew what it had taken for Malcolm Cage to break with that fierce pride and ask him not to leave. That moved him.

Later that afternoon they took a walk in the cool air, because they felt like it. They walked past the big house over brown grass, that would turn a lush green come summer, down to the plantation's entrance, where a dirt road took up after the highway ran out.

"They say Lee and his troops come down this road one summer," Malcolm said. "Some say he spent a night in my house. Them was good times—the best. My granddaddy use ta tell me stories. The South was king then, great plantations, Southern ladies dressed in they best, making the young men's heart skip a beat. Lots of happy slaves, too, singing and dancing."

He looked at King Fish.

"I know you think all slavery was bad, but it just ain't so. Now, some of it was bad, I know that; but some slaves was better off."

King Fish stared at him a moment, then shook his head. Maybe white folks just don't know what better off is, he thought.

King Fish said, "Massa say to the slave come here, boy. You happy? Slave grin and say yes, suh, massa, I'm plenty happy. What he 'spose ta say? That ain't happy, Reven Cage, that's just scared. Happy fo' a man is being able to do what he want. The mo' you able to do what you want, the mo' happy you is."

For just a second anger showed in Malcolm Cage's face.

"Ain't nobody able to do what he want, most of all a ni— Well, I can't always do what I want."

"Yeah, but you don't git kilt fo' tryin'."

"You think the world's fair, do ya, Reven Cook? Coloreds ain't the only one. Some people born rich, others ain't, some cripple, some tall, some short."

"Being a slave is worse than all that," King Fish said.

But King Fish did stay, and over the next several weeks he and Malcolm Cage disagreed on many things, even about the most effective way to pick a pocket. More often they would debate the

Bible, but the more they disagreed, the more respect they gained for each other. They talked in detail about their passage from childhood into manhood and discovered how really similar their lives had been. In detail, King Fish told Malcolm Cage about the Bucket-of-Blood and its colorful characters, about the Kotch Balls and even about Sue Ellen.

One Sunday morning things changed, or rather Malcolm did. King Fish entered the barn to practice that day's sermon. He was distracted by a pitiful howling sound, like a wounded animal in pain. King Fish followed the sound cautiously, which led him up the ladder to the hayloft. Cringing in the corner and totally nude was Malcolm Cage, his head resting on his knees, begging God's forgiveness through his tears. King Fish stepped quietly back down the ladder and out of the barn.

King Fish did preach later that afternoon, his fourth sermon. Malcolm Cage preached, too, that Sunday. He and Lorene drove to New Orleans to his all-white congregation in the seventh ward, where he delivered a sermon on adultery. Maybe it was Lorene threatening to leave, or King Fish's position on being free, that caused Malcolm to undergo a change. Maybe he had heard the voice of God that morning. That evening, as King Fish sat lonely in his little house, feeling cut off from the world he knew, without a mark to trim or a woman to make love to, Nettie Bean knocked on the door. She stood there, looking skyward, trying to remember exactly what she had been told to say.

"Reben Cage and Mrs. Cage say . . . okay, they say if it pleases you, they would be honored if you accept their imbatation for late dinner."

From that evening on Malcolm treated King Fish as an equal and as a friend. From that evening on Malcolm Cage never took another drink or another trip to the ninth ward.

It was after a morning of prayer in the hayloft when Malcolm Cage woke Lorene and then sent for King Fish to tell them both the news together. After they had assembled in the kitchen and Willa Mae Bean had poured coffee, Malcolm spoke.

"I talked to the good Lord."

He looked at King Fish.

"About your ministry, Reven Cook. God is so good!" Malcolm said, clasping his hands together. "It come to me almost like a dream, but I was wide-awake. Like in a vision. God's solders came and tore down that den of sin you use to gamble in. Tore it down, mine you, and planted a cross in its place, not the cross of the Klan, but the cross of God! Where is God's house in Gator Creek?" he asked.

King Fish shook his head. The truth was, there was not a single place of worship there. There were gatherings held in one house or another, which were little more than Bible readings, but no real church service. King Fish knew what was coming next.

"So you want to build a church in Gator Creek?" he asked.

"In the same spot the devil's been operatin' in," Malcolm said.

"You mean the Bucket-of-Blood? Po' Sam ain't gonna give the Bucket-of-Blood up."

The look on Malcolm Cage's face told King Fish Sam just might. Then came the next shock.

"Told you, you was gonna have a real church." Malcolm was smiling.

King Fish was lost for words and glanced at Lorene, who gave him a smile of reassurance. "Now, Reverend Cook, all you need is a wife," she said. She had become aware of King Fish's almost nightly trips to New Orleans, his late-evening or early-morning returns. On more than one occasion she had heard the laughter of a female coming from his place. She had spoken to Malcolm about it. Fornication was no less a sin than racism. In some ways he and her husband had traded places, she told Malcolm.

Early one morning, a week later, Malcolm and King Fish drove to Gator Creek. For a few miles they rode in silence. King Fish didn't speak his mind, but he had thoughts: Po' Sam ain't gonna sell the Bucket-of-Blood to this white man and nobody else. Malcolm Cage looked at King Fish as if he had read his mind. He spoke with difficulty.

"Temptation's a mighty thang. It can turn you blind, make a

righteous man misinterpret the Word on account of his desire. What I'm sayin', Reverend Cook, is, a minister of the Gospel needs a wife."

King Fish smiled. "What else did Mrs. Cage tell you to tell me?"

"Now, you wait a minute—"

"What else, Reven Cage?"

Malcolm paused. "Okay, no more women at your place."

King Fish began to whistle "Dixie."

"Okay, okay, Reven Cook, it wasn't me."

They drove directly to Po' Sam's place, a large white house sitting on a hill hidden by trees, along with a pigpen and several broken-down wagons—also three cars, one of which Sam was working on when they pulled into his yard. Po' Sam was surprised to see them, to say the least. His eyes questioned King Fish on this strange white man's presence. Malcolm Cage did not wait for an introduction.

"I'm the Reverend Malcolm Cage and you're Sam," he said, holding out his hand.

Sam wiped his own hand on his coveralls and hesitantly shook Malcolm's.

"God sent me here to do His work. You believe in God?"

Sam slowly nodded his head.

"Then, Sam, we ain't gonna waste no time. God wants a church here. I'm gonna buy the Bucket-of-Blood, and I'm gonna give you twice what it's worth."

Sam looked at King Fish again then back at Malcolm Cage. "Twice what it's worth?"

Malcolm nodded.

"Gotta talk to my wife inside the house."

Sam hurried away.

"Tell her in cash!" King Fish called, looking at Malcolm Cage, who agreed with a nod as they followed Sam into the open door.

King Fish and Malcolm stood in a living room filled with lamps, vases, and whatnots that sat over a fireplace and filled every other space, it seemed. They were there only a few minutes before Sam's wife, all two hundred fifty pounds of her, preceded Sam down the stairs.

"Did y'all say cash?" she asked, before she introduced herself.

Malcolm produced a billfold filled with one-hundred-dollar bills. She quickly agreed to the offer.

After she counted the money, she introduced herself, then insisted they sit for coffee, and try out the cookies she had just baked. She was a large woman for sure, but her presence was larger, commanding. Po' Sam was dwarfed beside her.

"Don't just stand there, Sam, do sumpin' or sit yo'self down somewhere."

Sam hurried like a little boy to the nearest chair. Malcolm and King Fish smiled at each other. She was gone only a short time before returning with a tray, which she served the coffee and cookies from. The cookies actually were very tasty. She sat across from them smiling, waiting for a compliment. It came from Malcolm Cage, was reinforced by King Fish.

"You know," she began, "we got another piece of land we thinkin' 'bout sellin'?"

Malcolm held up his hand. "I think I had enough land for one day."

"Y'all got any aches and pains? I got sumpin' to stop pain," she said.

King Fish had to smile. Malcolm shook his head. Sam sat in the chair very quiet and still. The visitors quickly finished their coffee and cookies. They thanked her and got up to leave. "See yo' friends to the do', Sam." Sam was up instantly and shook Malcolm's and King Fish's hands vigorously before they left. As they were walking to the car, Sam's wife called to them from the doorway. "Y'all change yo' mine, just com' on back, hea?"

Malcolm Cage arranged over the next several weeks to have the Bucket-of-Blood torn down. Not too long after, a church and a parson's house were erected in its place.

8

In his loneliness King Fish understood it all now. There would always be traces of her. A smile, a look, that special scent she produced when passion was upon them. No, he had not gotten over her. Last night he had awakened from her image, his arms filled with emptiness. The dawn found him that way. This is what he learned. Love should never imprison you with self-pity or shame. Love should walk proudly through your life and rest quietly in your soul. Set you free with a gentle smile. This is what the dawn had taught him.

He breathed deeply as he stood in front of the church that had once been the Bucket-of-Blood. The heavy air was pungent with the smell of summer and moisture. He was reminded of his boyhood and carefree Negro children, their laughter rising sharp and clear, floating through the air, making summer music. He thought of his brother and sister, a fireplace, and the stories two former slaves, his parents, would tell. What would they be like now? Would his shy sister have become a beauty and brother the head of his own family? Maybe his mother's back would be bent from the years, her bright eyes clouded with age. And his father, would the fields have broken that strong frame? Would his hair be the color of snow?

The first drop of rain struck his shoulder with a light thud. He held out his hand to catch the second. On that early Sunday morning the clouds rained down on Gator Creek and on him. It was not an angry rain, but quiet and warm to his cheeks, one he didn't mind standing in, one that stopped as suddenly as it had begun, leaving the earth's perfume to occupy the air after it had gone.

THE REVEREND JAMES COOK
OFFERS SUNDAY SERVICE
FROM 11:00 A.M. TO 4:00 P.M.

King Fish almost laughed aloud. Just six months ago he'd had dreams of living the high life in New York. Now a turn of events, unimaginable dreams, had set him on a course that mystified even him. Reverend James Cook was a good name, one that commanded respect; but it still sounded a little strange to him. No one had called him "James," except Reverend Cage, since the fire twenty-six years ago that killed his family. After that tragedy, and because of his insatiable appetite for catfish, he had been dubbed "King Fish" by an old farmer who had taken him in. From there he had fled to the city to make his mark and was again taken in, this time by his father's younger brother, "Easy" Ed Cook, a slick hustler, who had taught him the ways of the streets. King Fish looked at the freshly painted church, white and pure, with its stained multicolored windows that bore images of Jesus and other holy men. The shiny cross stood as a beacon to all those who would change their lives and redeem their souls. For one brief moment a sense of something wonderful stirred in his heart. He thought of his father and his undying faith. He could see his mother's smile and the little flowered hat she wore so proudly to church. He could not help but wonder how his life would have turned out had his family survived. Just as quickly his mood changed. He thought of the old crowd, the smoke-filled club, the fat women who wore too much makeup and too few clothes, the sweet musky scent of perfume and sweat, Big Lil, smiling with gap teeth, and Society Red, tall and regal, with his thin mustache. Even the cold menacing eyes of Bill Black crossed his mind. King Fish had come early that

Sunday morning to preach his sermon and, in a way, to mourn the passing of another family. They had been a family, these less-than-worthless rogues, hookers, hustlers, gamblers, very cunning and selfish, but a family nonetheless. He knew he had to leave them now.

Then the faces of those with whom he had been so recently intertwined slowly began to fade from his mind like ink from an old writing pad. Only one name and one face lingered stubbornly in his thoughts. He wondered what she would think of him now. Would she regret that she had left? He answered his own question and a feeling of triumph and satisfaction warmed his face. He smiled smugly to himself. He was on the brink of something big, maybe even great. He would become the biggest preacher in the South, maybe even the whole country, and she would regret that she wasn't there.

He gazed down the road as people began arriving. They came in horse-drawn wagons, doubled up on horseback, and some walking. Po' Sam and his wife were in a new car (*something his wife had demanded*). King Fish shook their hand at the door. Gus came too.

"What you want me to do, Fish!"

King Fish glared. "Call me Reven Cook."

"Oh, okay, Fish."

King Fish shot him another look. Gus's hand flew up to his mouth and he rushed inside. Malcolm Cage and Lorene drove up next.

"Morning, Reverend Cook." They spoke in unison like school-children, and smiled.

"Great day for a sermon," Malcolm commented before he and Lorene walked inside.

The choir, which had gotten there early, began to sing. Next came a surprise. Big Lil in a car filled with whores, followed by two other cars with hustlers from the old Bucket-of-Blood converged on King Fish. Big Lil was laughing before she reached him.

"Lawd, Lawd, King Fish, if you don't beat all. Got somethin' new fo'um every time!"

King Fish didn't step out of character. "God bless you, sisters."

She laughed, louder this time. The girls laughed too. Big Lil was wearing a blue satin dress. It was the first time King Fish had seen her in anything other than red. Big O came with Utty, the piano player, and the rest. They were more in tune to King Fish's position and didn't make little asides. Big O did wink before they all went inside. King Fish remained stoic.

The inside of the church was beautiful, with a glossy podium draped with a white cloth. There were new wooden benches and a red carpet brightened the pulpit area. Malcolm and Lorene sat in this section.

"Hallelujah!" King Fish shouted, and the church echoed him. "It's a good day! I feel mighty good! Feel like singin'!"

He lifted his big voice and the choir joined him in song. When the song ended, King Fish spoke to them.

"Can I get a 'Amen' fo' Reven Cage and his wife. It was them what built this hea' church and everything in it!"

"Amen!" the congregation shouted.

"Glory to God, all the glory to God!" Malcolm shouted. "I built this church on God's orders."

"Amen!" the church said.

King Fish smiled. He began to tell the story of Paul and how God, when Paul was on his way to Damascus, knocked him from that big horse and turned Paul's life around.

"Paul used to do the devil's work—use to punish slaves, own slaves," King Fish told them.

He compared his life with Paul's and told how God sent Reverend Cage to turn his life around. He challenged those in the congregation still living in sin to do the same. King Fish walked down to the front of the pulpit and began to sing the old spiritual "Leaning on the Everlasting Arm." The choir sang with him. One by one he blessed those who came forward. One of Big Lil's girls was in the line.

After a final prayer to close, the old Bucket-of-Blood crowd, including Big Lil and all of her girls, left—uncertain of King Fish's position, taking second looks at him and each other before they walked outside.

It had become, in the Negro community in New Orleans and the smaller towns around, the most popular topic of conversation—this story of the white man who turned a thief and gambler into a preacher and built him a church. All the talk created a demand for King Fish as a visiting pastor. When Malcolm showed up with him, the demand increased. There were times when Malcolm stole the show, brought a kind of hope to an oppressed people. Because of the power and wealth of this positive white man who was sure a place in heaven awaited them, even a better life here on earth, they embraced him. Both Malcolm Cage and King Fish had assistant pastors glad to fill in for them at their respective churches while they did a kind of tour of the Negro communities. They appeared at schools, fund-raisers, and performed, each of them, two marriages. When the pastor of the largest Negro Baptist church in New Orleans absconded with a young girl and the church's funds, it was King Fish who they elected as the new minister. Malcolm Cage was elated even more than King Fish. To Malcolm the Word would be spread much faster with King Fish working from two churches. The contributions and dues were large at the big church and the congregation more sophisticated. To King Fish, this meant only one thing—more money. He alternated his Sundays between two churches. Still there was an empty space, a void only a woman could fill. He began to steal away for brief affairs with women from both churches, risking everything he and Malcolm Cage had accomplished. He could not resist this urge. He even thought of Sabria as a possible release. He also thought about what Malcolm had said: "Temptation can turn you blind."

King Fish saw her at the nurses' station of the New Orleans Charity Hospital. The floor was busy and she was standing alone, absorbed in reading her chart, carefully making notes. Just as he was approaching she looked up and they recognized each other immediately. She was Carolyn Green, the nurse who had attended him during his stay there. She was delightfully surprised. She smiled sweetly and extended her hand.

"How are you? You look wonderful!" she said, in her most professional voice. Then she noticed his collar. "It's Reverend Cook now, I see."

I was called," King Fish replied, gently taking her hand in both of his.

Then he explained to her that he was residing in Gator Creek, at the parsonage that had been built for him by Reverend Cage, that he had come to New Orleans as the new pastor of the Pleasant Green Baptist Church. A member of his church was very ill and had requested that he visit him in this very hospital.

"Well . . ." she stated, slowly withdrawing her hand, her eyes never once leaving his face.

"Walice Jones is his name," King Fish said quickly.

"What?" Then it came to her. "Oh! His name is Wallace Jones? That's the little old man down the hall, Room 13C."

She was more lovely somehow than he remembered. There was more honey in the tone of her skin, more luster, too, and the cleft in her chin was more pronounced. He hadn't noticed how nicely the natural waves of the hair that escaped from under her cap caressed her cheekbones, or how brightly her eyes shone. King Fish walked to Room 13C, looking back at her with her and two other nurses looking at him, then smiling to each other.

A week passed slowly before he was to preach in New Orleans again. Carolyn haunted him every day, so much so, he found that thinking of her made him nervous. Had he turned square because he was impersonating a preacher, or was it just that this time he had become aware of what a classy young woman she was. Certainly he could not hold his own with her in this arena, unless of course, she simply liked him for himself.

He showed up at the hospital on a Friday with no excuse, as Wallace Jones had been released two days before. He was prepared for rejection. It occurred to King Fish that once she seemed to be inviting him. Now he was pursuing her. He thought, maybe he should have brought flowers, but he didn't know how that would play for her on her job. He went to the nurses' station and asked the nurse on duty for her by the only name he knew: "Carolyn." The nurse smiled and pointed behind him. He turned around and there she stood, wearing that sweet smile.

"Can I help you again, Reverend Cook?"

King Fish smiled too.

"Well, you see . . ." He paused and looked at the other nurse. "Excuse me," he said to her, and walked Carolyn a few feet away. "Well, you see . . ."

"You said that already."

"You ain't gonna think it right, me being a preacher and everythang."

"Think what's right?"

"Me bettin' all that money."

She was getting a little impatient. "What in the world are you talking about?"

"Okay, don't get mad, I'll tell you. I bet Gus a hundred dollars you'd go to lunch with me," and he quickly added, "I'm going to hell for gambling, huh?"

"No, you're going to hell for lying. Why didn't you just ask me?"

"I did."

"The answer is no!"

"Hey, I was only—"

"But I will let you take me to early dinner. I get off in two hours."

She began to walk away.

"Three o'clock?"

"So nice to know you can count, Reverend Cook, but then I suppose counting is a prerequisite to gambling."

She held up three fingers and was on her way to do her business. It was a proud walk, proud and confident, with the fragrance of cinnamon filling the air behind her. King Fish had at least two hours to kill and decided to go to Bourbon Street Black, which was a kind of semicommunity within the black community inhabited by professional musicians, music teachers, people who either played music or loved to hear it played. He drove the used Model T he had rented from Po' Sam, as he did every other week, to Jack Stacey's, a club owned by a white jazz buff. This is where the cats hung out, especially the old-timers, and they jammed. Jack Stacey's was really a bar with an upstairs. In the evenings different jazz groups took turns playing in the part of the bar they called the "Loft." It had seating, provided you could get one. Otherwise, you were a patron in the bar waiting for the sound to filter down. In the early afternoon long before dark, the musicians sat around talking about one gig or another, sharing experiences, sometimes working out new numbers. King Fish walked through the bar, waved at the bartender, and made his way upstairs. Everybody seemed to be there: Creoles of color, blacks, and even a few white cats. This is what jazz had done, brought the Creoles of color together with the blacks. Outside of Bourbon Street Black there were still problems between blacks and the Creoles of color—at least the Creoles felt they were superior to blacks. It was well known by blacks that if you were darker than a brown paper bag and you had nappy hair, most Creoles would not associate with you. It was not that way in Bourbon Street Black. Bourbon Street Black was all about music. King Fish hadn't been in Jack Stacey's but once in almost two years, and that was when he was looking for Sue Ellen. Before then, he had been a regular. Twenty-some years ago, before his uncle Ed had been killed, King Fish had been allowed to go upstairs with him. Pop Creole, an old-timer who played trombone, saw him first.

"Hey, Fish, what wind blew you in? Where you been, my man; heard you was preachin' now. Hey, Freddie, look what the wind blew in!"

A tall dark man who loved musicians rushed over, his hand outstretched. "Say it ain't true, Fish. The best gambler in New Orleans ain't turned into a preacher?"

"Only on Sundays," King Fish said, and they all laughed.

"Fish, hang tight; want you to dig this new number we puttin' down," Pop Creole said, and went to join the rhythm section that was beginning to form.

King Fish stayed for a complete set that ended with a tune titled "Mellow," which featured a crying tenor saxophone solo; it had been his uncle Ed's favorite song. He was saying good-bye to the cats and promising to return soon when he heard her voice, loud and laced with whiskey.

"Well, if it ain't Mr. Pussy Whupped hisself, in person."

It was Sabria, with too many drinks, too much weight, and too few baths. She was ruddy looking, with only traces of her past beauty. Next to her was Short Note, a little man who played a mean sax, an older man, who once played with Louis Armstrong and had been in love with Sabria all of her adult life. He didn't like King Fish for that very reason. King Fish didn't like seeing Sabria like this. At least some of the blame was his. She spat her next words at him.

"Heard she lef' you in the hospital fo' dead; then you run all over the worl' lookin' fo' her. The hustlers laughin' at you, say she made you git religion." She put her face close to his. "Know what? Bill Black shoulda kilt yo' ass!"

King Fish looked at Short Note. "You oughta take bedda care of yo' woman," he said, and walked downstairs and out of the bar.

Carolyn Green was all smiles when he walked up to the nurses' station, a contagious smile that infected the other nurses there. He and Carolyn decided to walk the three blocks to the small colored restaurant around the corner. It was a nice day for walking, a full-blown summer day, but not hot and sticky. Vendors were out with pushcarts selling crab and poorboy sandwiches. And there were children, wild and wonderful children, dashing off to nowhere. She slipped her arm inside of his as if she had known him a much longer time, and maybe in her mind she had.

They sat at a table near the window and ordered gumbo with rice. Without her nurse's cap her hair was short and wavy, a chestnut brown that blended with her skin. She was the product of a good solid family, her mother being a successful beautician with a mostly white clientele. This was because her mother was a Creole, she explained. Her father, on the other hand, was a very dark-skinned Negro who was a shoemaker and owned a small shop that did mostly repairs. In a small way, she reminded King Fish of Lorene because of the fluid way she put her sentences together. She praised him for his remarkable transformation from a street hustler to a messenger of the Lord. The subject, then, came up that no woman interested in a man could ignore.

"You really loved her, didn't you? I don't believe I've ever witnessed anyone in so much emotional pain."

King Fish tried to appear unaffected. "She had to do what she had to do and so did I," he said rather nonchalantly.

"So, you never saw her again?"

"Never," he lied. "And what about you? How many hearts you dun broke?"

She laughed back in her throat. "Loads and loads of them, Reverend Cook, but I'm sorry to report they were all little boys. I'm afraid I've been too busy with school and my work to break any big boys' hearts."

"No boyfriends?"

She shook her head. "Just callers, but no one special."

"What kinda special man you lookin' fo'?"

"One like my father, I suppose."

"Somebody who goin' spoil you?"

She smiled. "How'd you know my father spoiled me?"

"It's wrote all over yo' face when you talk 'bout him."

"You're right, but it's not that. My mother and I, the two women in his life, adore him for his strength and for his knowledge. He's a Garveyite, you see."

"That niggah that's talkin' 'bout us goin' back to Africa?"

She smiled. "Don't git so excited. I know what you're going to say. I don't want to go back to Africa either. I was born here. I don't agree with my father on that. It's the knowledge that Marcus Garvey gives to colored people, that my father gave to me, that's important."

She caught herself. "I'm sorry! I just took over your job."

It was his turn to smile. He invited her to be his guest at a gospel jubilee on Sunday evening to be held at the Masonic Hall, which he had secured to raise funds for the treasury of his church in New Orleans. She accepted without hesitation. When they finished eating he offered to drive her home, but she was driving the family car, she explained. King Fish walked her back to the hospital where her car was parked and she promised to see him at the jubilee.

On his way to Malcolm Cage's house he thought again about Sabria, and remembered her once stunning beauty. They both had worked in Storyville for Hatty Briggs, an aggressive domineering woman who ran her house and girls like a drill sergeant. King Fish, who managed the poker game and was there two years before Sabria came, had once straightened Hatty out about speaking to him in a disrespectful way. Sabria had gone further than that. In her dispute with Hatty over money shortly after she had arrived, this black-haired Creole beauty with the gorgeous figure cursed Hatty like an angry sailor and threatened to whip her ass. Hatty backed down, which was good for her, as was evident by the outcome of the next scrape Sabria got into. A patron attempted to manhandle her and was taken from the house a bloody mess, with straight-razor cuts over a good portion of his upper body. The man was lucky to survive. Sabria was lucky he wasn't white. She stayed on because she was the biggest moneymaker Hatty Briggs had ever had. And Hatty loved money more than anything. To King Fish, Sabria was the sexiest woman he had ever seen. Even her foul language, in some strange way, complemented her, made her seem hot and exciting. But she didn't like King Fish, or anyone else, for that matter. She was all business. She didn't even fraternize with the other girls. Playing poker was her passion—something she did very well. But King Fish did it better. He always seemed to beat her. Even when she had known her aces-high full house was the best hand and had bet all her money. He bested her with four jacks. She never played cards against him again. Soon, however, she was in his bed. Sabria was the kind of woman who submitted only to a man who could outdo her.

A few years they went well together—they rented a small house in the ninth ward and both took the streetcar to Storyville. There were other women too; but she didn't mind as long as they gave him money and she could continue to care for her sickly mother and young sister. Then Storyville closed down—a bad day for the girls who worked in houses. King Fish and Sabria had no real problem with the closing of Storyville. Sabria had been a straight-razor-carrying street whore before she had come to work for Hatty Briggs. She was also a booster. King Fish, aside from being a gambler, was a pickpocket and con artist even then. Besides that, they had made loads of money and still had most of it. Their response to Storyville's closing was to throw a party. It was a major event in the ninth ward which drew most of the colored hookers in Storyville and their men. A few had husbands. Hatty Briggs was there with an older light-skinned man with straight gray hair who had come up from Lake Charles. Both the up- and downstairs of their house was packed. The music was loud, the whiskey free, and the drunks numerous. It was daybreak before the house cleared, leaving only three girls behind. That early-morning party, at Sabria's suggestion, turned into an orgy which included them all. King Fish learned something else about Sabria that morning. She was "interchangeable," equally at ease with male or female. All in all, Sabria had been a good woman for him until Sue Ellen entered the picture.

At the entrance to the plantation King Fish waved at two of Malcolm Cage's workers, who were also members of his church, walking down to the road. They didn't recognize him at first, but then, with smiles on their faces, waved their hands high over their heads. The place bustled with workers. In the distance he could see the white cotton sacks and barely make out the people in the fields. When he pulled into the front yard, Pike, a new worker, and some of his boys were entertaining Malcolm Cage, Lorene, and Congressman Stone, who were sitting on the front porch. Pike played a banjo and the other men sang and danced.

Nettie Bean was at the car door shouting his name before he could get out. King Fish embraced the girl quickly then walked to the porch to take the extended hand of Malcolm Cage. Next he shook the hand of Congressman Stone. Lorene nodded with a smile.

"My favorite storyteller," the congressman quipped.

"Suh, I hope you become president one day. Country needs a man what can laugh."

The congressman shot Malcolm Cage a look of approval.

Lorene said to the congressman, "I agree with Reverend Cook. Walter, I think it's a marvelous idea. You should consider it, not now, maybe, but in a few years, for sure."

The congressman held up his hands but was clearly enjoying the whole idea.

"Pretty good start, Walter. Got the women and the preachers on your side already," Malcolm Cage pointed out humorously.

"Still got enough devil in you to have a drink with a pretty down-to-earth politician, Reven Cook? Our friend Reverend Cage is still on the dry wagon, as you can see."

Malcolm Cage held up his glass of lemonade proudly.

"One won't hurt," King Fish answered.

Malcolm Cage called the light-skinned servant standing nearby and sent him for the drinks, warning him not to slip one for himself. Walter Stone's cordiality today was less a result of a change in his feelings about Negroes than a sign of the respect he had for Lorene, who had made it clear that Reverend Cook was a friend of theirs. Also, as powerful as he was, Congressman Walter Stone had been overwhelmed by the daring of Malcolm Cage from the beginning. He knew the significance of Reverend Cook in his friend's life. He had even promised to look after King Fish if he ever needed a favor and Malcolm Cage somehow was not around. The drinks came as Pike and the boys were finishing their last number. Malcolm Cage tipped them and they left smiling. King Fish and the congressman tossed the brandy hard and fast. The servant poured another.

"Tell me, my boy, what would you venture the two most important power bases in the world are?" the congressman asked King Fish.

"The banks and the police," King Fish replied.

"Wrong; the government and the church. Politics and religion, my boy, politics and religion. You can't go wrong there, Reverend Cook."

"Ain't much power if you can't vote, suh," King Fish pointed out.

"Being a Southern man, I shouldn't be sayin' this. Some of my friends would be real upset with me, but I'll say it anyway. Things change, times change—just like slavery changed. After all, it is the law of the land," Congressman Stone said.

"Them Klan ain't thinkin' 'bout no law, suh."

"I think I like him, Reverend Cage," the congressman said, planting his hand on King Fish's shoulder. "If I can ever do anything to help out Reverend Cook here, and you're not around,

Reverend Cage, he can call on me. Just remember what I told you—everything changes."

King Fish doubted if the white folks in the South would ever change. He finished his drink and said his good-byes to everyone, reminding Malcolm and Lorene about the jubilee before he got into his car. He gave Nettie Bean a nickel through the window and drove back to Gator Creek.

The jubilee was a complete day of gospel singing that lasted until late evening. Gospel quartets, choirs, and solo performers, both in and on the outskirts of New Orleans, came to showcase their talent for the passing of the collection plate and the free food that was served in the recreation room. Admission was paid at the door; part of this went to pay for the hall, the rest was pure profit for the church, considering that the food was provided by a women's church club at no cost to the church. King Fish hadn't expected to sing that evening; in fact, being the producer and the master of ceremonies, something he had never attempted, crowded his thoughts and had kept him jumping from place to place all day long. In the one rehearsal they had, he staged the jubilee in imitation of the various traveling minstrel shows that were popular throughout the South. There was only a slight difference between gospel music and the blues—the words "oh baby" and "oh Lord." The audiences, essentially, were alike; sometimes they were the very same.

King Fish was dressed all in white when he walked onto the stage that evening. He was also more than a little nervous when he spotted Carolyn Green.

"Good evening, brothers and sisters."

"Praise Him! Praise Him!" the audience echoed.

King Fish lifted his arms and his voice rose. "Praise God, they're here this evening! Brothers and sisters! The Spirits of Joy and the Golden Wing Singers!"

They came from the back of the hall, down separate aisles, two different choirs, beating tambourines and singing, "gospel stepping" onstage to their upbeat tempo. They did the lead-and-refrain routine to perfection and rocked the hall. The Golden Wings did the lead and the Spirits of Joy the refrain.

"Jesus is comin'... He's comin' soon ... Gonna tell all sinners ... He's comin' soon ... Wade in the water ... He's comin' soon ... Gonna take us to glory ... He's comin' soon."

When they had finished their songs, the stage was still charged with excitement. They were quickly followed by a series of the best gospel talent in the South: the young boy with the high tenor voice, the eighty-year-old man who played the spiritual guitar, the all-female quartet, and the three Blind Boys, who stole the show. They each, with their special talent, gave their all to their performance. They gave to the people, who filled this overcrowded and over-heated hall, a sweaty delight.

Malcolm and Lorene were seated in the section reserved for honored guests and they, too, were caught up in the spirit of the moment. Malcolm rose to his feet several times with the rest to give praise to his God and to egg on the performers. When King Fish called on him to say a few words, he shocked the room by reaffirming the unsegregated status of all Christians in God's heaven. Then, overcome with joy and filled with the Holy Spirit, Malcolm thought he was witnessing the beginning of his dreams of a united Christian world. He looked to the sky, eyes filled with tears, and shouted, "GOD IS REAL! GOD IS REAL!"

When the three Blind Boys had completed their rendition of "I'm Comin' Up, Lord," Carolyn, sitting in the front row, was visibly moved. Her sheer mint-green dress was damp now with perspiration. The ends of her hair were glued to her face; but she wasn't bothered by that. The best had come when King Fish was asked by the Blind Boys to join them in song. His thundering bass voice beautifully complemented the high-pitched harmony of the three talented tenors, who sang in three octaves, a dramatic change from the standard tenor, baritone, and bass harmony. This new, fresh sound vibrated through the hall with such a magnetic force that people seemed cemented in their seats, afraid to move, lest they miss a note or a chord change. The Blind Boys had worked out a showstopping routine, with one of them becoming overjoyed and straying very close to the stage's end, only to be prevented from falling at the last moment by the group's attendant and valet.

All this gave King Fish an idea. He would put a new group together and name it Reverend Cook and the Three Blind Boys. He would also ask Malcolm to manage them. He was so excited he had to rush and tell Carolyn before he mentioned it to either Malcolm Cage or the Blind Boys. Her eyes were shining like new pennies. He had given her even more than she had expected and she told him so. She also thought his idea of a group was a good one. King Fish took her hand and walked over to where Malcolm and Lorene stood smiling.

"She's lovely," Lorene said after the introduction. "And so young. Look at the color of your hair!"

Carolyn blushed. "Mrs. Cage, you are too beautiful and too kind."

"Thank you."

"We must be the two luckiest men in town," Malcolm stated.

"Just a minute," King Fish said. "We just met. I don't know if she even likes me."

"All you have to do is look into her eyes," Lorene said. "You must both come over for dinner."

King Fish told them his idea and they decided to celebrate. Now all King Fish needed to do was to ask the Blind Boys. He motioned for Johnny Boy, the valet, who brought them over. Then King Fish asked them. Johnny Boy and the Blind Boys were ecstatic. Malcolm Cage would have them for dinner at his house on Friday, along with King Fish and Carolyn, to work out the details. Everyone said their good-byes and King Fish found himself alone with Carolyn Green, walking her to her car.

"You got some voice, Reverend Cook."

"So do you."

She smiled. "I don't sing."

"Sound like ya singin' ta me when you talk."

"Oh, go on."

She pushed him playfully and he grabbed her and kissed her quickly. She pulled away and looked him in the eyes.

"You know I'm supposed to slap you, don't you? At least that's what would happen in the movies."

"This ain't no movie what we makin', baby. You dun got my nose open for real."

She didn't retreat one inch. "Why you saying that to me, Reverend Cook?" She was whispering now. "Don't you know a preacher isn't supposed to lie?"

"Would you help me? Feel like I'm in over my head."

She kissed him this time, very gently on the lips. When he tried for more, she pulled away. He was on fire.

"You can take me to the movie tomorrow."

She wrote down her address, got into her car, and drove away. King Fish could still feel her lips on his.

The next evening at seven o'clock, King Fish drove to her house on Lincoln Avenue, a middle-class mixed neighborhood of two-story Spanish-style homes with balconies draped in wrought iron. Carolyn's place was in the center of the block. King Fish's black suit and minister's collar drew respectful greetings from passersby. Carolyn opened the door immediately. Her hello was warm and her smile inviting. The house was cozy, felt lived in, with maybe too much furnishings and too many pictures. King Fish removed his derby hat and walked inside. Before he could sit, her mother walked in. She was fair-skinned, with long straight hair, but she was not pretty. Carolyn's father, who came in just behind her, was a hard-looking medium-built man with dark skin and bloodshot eyes. King Fish felt their disapproval—the mother because King Fish was too dark, and the father because he thought King Fish too old. After the introduction he came directly to the point.

"Don't you think you a little old for my daughter?"

Carolyn almost fainted. "Daddy?"

"I just asked Rever'n Cook a question, not you," he said.

"I don't know. I ain't no ol' man; I ain't even forty."

Carolyn couldn't contain herself. "Daddy, I'm twenty-three years old. Mama, tell Daddy."

"Carolyn, you know how your father is."

Her father interrupted. "There's nothing wrong with sayin' what you thinking. People should be more honest. That's what's wrong with black people, they rather hear a lie than the truth; they even believe in white folks' lies."

"Daddy, Reverend Cook came to take me to a movie."

"Well, I was just sayin'. Okay, Rever'n Cook, bring my daughter back the way she left with you, understand?"

There was a real threat behind his words. King Fish assured him that he understood. By now Carolyn was so embarrassed she was pulling King Fish to the door by his arm. Outside in the car, she couldn't stop apologizing.

"My mother's just as bad. She's so color conscious."

"I don't git it. Your ol' man's darker than me."

Carolyn explained. "I know it's crazy, but she says she doesn't want any little nappy-headed grandchildren running around calling her 'Grandmother.' To tell the truth, I don't know how she married my father. Well, maybe that's not altogether true. It was my father's strength. My mother would run over a weak man, even if he were white."

King Fish didn't care. He didn't care if her father liked him, if her mother, aunts, and cousins didn't. He just wanted her. Her eyes were glowing now, staring at him, distracting him while he drove.

"Some people think a preacher shouldn't go to the movies," she commented.

"Let 'um think. I do what I want."

"Really?"

"Really."

He kissed her quickly on the mouth. She didn't respond, not even a movement.

"See what I mean?" he bragged.

She smiled. "I can see you're such a tough one. What made you become a preacher?"

He had to consider this. "Reven Cage. He dun it mo' than any-thang."

"How is that?"

"Said it was my destiny."

She didn't speak, but the night did. It spoke of enchantment and romance and ordered the stars to go on parade. The moon was there, too, bold and low to the earth.

"How lovely this night is. Nights like this make you feel close to God."

He felt a little uncomfortable with this subject and changed it. "How long do I git ta keep ya out?"

"Don't be funny. I'm a grown woman. But I do have a job; and I go five days a week, unlike some people I know."

"Miss Green, saving souls's a job fo' every day."

"I don't suppose you are trying to save my soul. Is that your reason for asking me out?" she asked with a smothered smile.

He had to smile at that. "Naw, yo' soul's in good shape. I need to work on yo' heart."

She didn't respond. King Fish found a spot in front of the all-Negro theater and parked. It was a weeknight and not crowded. He opened the door, took her curved outstretched hand, and she sprang forward in one graceful move like a ballerina. Desire came quickly over him and he had to restrain himself from kissing her right then. She hooked her arm in his and they walked into the theater.

The next day King Fish made all the nurses on the floor, both colored and white, smile when he walked in with a dozen long-stemmed red roses and presented them to Carolyn.

"You have me blushing," she said, and she was. Her skin color even seemed to deepen and she smiled shyly. "You want to feed me too?"

"Fo' the rest of yo' life."

"I'm only hungry today. I think I can manage the rest of my life."

"I don't know 'bout that, yo' folks look like they ready to put you out ta me."

That made her chuckle.

"You do need a man in yo' life that ain't yo' father."

"You trying to get serious on me, Reverend Cook?"

"What we gonna eat today?" he asked.

She thought a moment. "Fried chicken and mashed potatoes."

"Let's go," he said.

She proudly carried her flowers as they walked around the corner. They sat at a table by the window, the same one they'd sat at before. The place was crowded today. A group of people visiting from back east with name badges on their lapels and dresses had filled the restaurant. They sounded like New Yorkers or New Englanders to King Fish. Not that he had ever been to either place, but a fair amount of Easterners came to New Orleans. He had picked a lot of their pockets when that was his line. He stared at Carolyn.

"Something wrong?"

"Girl, you got dem eyes. I like you, Carolyn Green."

"You hardly know me, Reverend Cook."

"How 'bout James?" he asked.

"You hardly know me, James. I might have some dark secret. I may not even be what I appear to be."

"Remember, I use ta be a gambler. I still ain't scared ta take a chance."

The waitress came, a very tall young girl who looked like the lady who owned the place. King Fish ordered for them both.

"If you could git one wish what would you take?" he then asked.

She thought for a moment. "I think I would wish that we, all colored people, were really free, that we were not despised all over the world. The American Negro is thought less of than any person on earth." Her eyes glared. "Think about it, it's really true. No one comes to America to befriend us. Every immigrant from any country joins right in with other white people to treat us badly. Even Africans avoid us."

"Now who's gittin' serious?"

"Sorry, sometimes I get angry when I think about the way they treat us. I suppose I get a little carried away like my father. Anyway, guess what? I start my vacation tomorrow."

That was Wednesday and he took her to Lincoln Beach, the all-colored amusement park. She wore a bright yellow dress, and next to it in the sunlight, her skin glowed a honey gold. On that day it was she the magazines should have photographed; it was she who personified youth and grace together, while still retaining that adventurous spirit of a child. She ate ice cream and cotton candy, and screamed like a teenager on the Ferris wheel. On the merry-go-round she pretended to be some royal princess riding sidesaddle next to her king. She tried the shooting gallery, but it was King Fish who won her a Kewpie doll. She caressed it as if it were a baby. The park was crowded with smiling faces and children running wild. There were people in costumes of dazzling colors, a pony for kids to ride, and, they said, a man who ate live snakes. She didn't want to see that, and cringed next to him. Even then her body sent a sensation through the whole of him. He knew there was no turning back now.

Thursday she wore lavender and packed a picnic basket. They went to Gator Creek over her father's objections, and found a spot not far from the church. She was even more beautiful then. The lavender seemed somehow to run into her skin and shade it with a touch of pastel. There was always about her just a hint of cinnamon. She brought crab cakes, jambalaya, and potato salad to show off her cooking skills. She also knew the name of every tree and every flower. After they had eaten, they lay on a knitted blanket with the sun warming their bodies and he kissed her passionately for the first time. When he tried to do more she gently pushed him away.

"I'm sorry, but I can't until it's my time."

King Fish knew what she meant and he respected her position. He had an urge to ask her to marry him right then, but feared, at that moment, she might not understand his reason.

"I'm really sorry," she said again. "You must think I'm a baby." Her face brightened. "I know, let's go see your church!"

He agreed and they put the blanket and basket in the car and walked hand in hand over the grass. Suddenly she broke away and began to run, and she shouted over her shoulder, "I'll race you!" laughing all the while. King Fish caught her before she reached the door.

"Now you owe me another kiss."

"Right here in the front of the church? What if someone sees us?"

"We git caught," he said, and kissed her.

"You are crazy," she said, but he knew she liked it. Inside the church he blurted out the question.

"Will you marry me?"

She was caught completely off guard. "But I'm a Catholic—"

"And can it be soon?"

"We've only just met, I—"

"I love you mo' than anyone or anything in this wurl'."

"What about my father, my family?"

"I'll adopt 'um."

She smiled. "You know what I mean."

"I'll talk ta 'um, but first you."

She looked long and hard into his eyes. "You know we are both crazy," she said.

"I gotta hear the word."

She kissed him this time.

"The word," he insisted.

"Yes."

Friday he gave her a ring. He brought it when he came to take her to dinner at the Cages'. Her father and mother were both working when he arrived and they weren't told that day. She wore a cool emerald-green dress that evening, which matched the small emerald-and-diamond earrings she had had to have and had gone into debt to buy.

When they reached the mansion and Willa Mae Bean opened the door, Carolyn's eyes sparkled like the diamonds in her ears. Willa Mae was overjoyed to see King Fish and delighted with Carolyn. They stepped inside and immediately heard familiar voices singing in another room. They smiled to each other. The Blind Boys had already arrived.

"Miss Lorene be right hea'," Willa Mae assured them, and left.

"James, it's beautiful! It's like something out of a magazine. Look at the crystal!"

Lorene came walking quickly across the room with her hand

extended. "You look absolutely stunning, my dear!" she told Carolyn, and lightly shook her hand.

Carolyn hid her ring hand behind her dress. She wanted King Fish to make the announcement himself.

Lorene noticed the action and realized what it meant. "This is wonderful! Reverend Cook, you are a very lucky man."

Carolyn smiled. "I would say the same to Reverend Cage. You are so chic and warm as well, a combination rarely found in women of such beauty."

And it was true. Lorene wore a long white brocade dress imported from Paris, diamond earrings, and a diamond choker around her neck.

"You are too kind, my dear. Come, everyone is back here."

The singing became louder as they neared the sitting room. The first thing you noticed as you entered the huge place was a mural depicting a bullfight that covered most of the right wall. Spanish-style chandeliers with lighted candles in them hung low from the ceiling, enhancing the earth-colored couches and chairs that lined both sides of the room. Coffee tables made from oak flanked them. A highly polished wooden floor ran the length of the room and ended in front of a fireplace where the Blind Boys, wearing slightly worn black suits, stood singing. Johnny Boy, their attendant and valet, stood nearby. He looked like a young version of King Fish's friend Gus. Malcolm Cage, totally absorbed in the song, stood next to him. Mark, the largest member of the Blind Boys, was leading the song with his very high voice. Next to him was Josh, the showman, who always pretended to wander dangerously close to the end of the stage during a performance. And there was Pete, the junior member by ten years. He was in his mid-twenties. Willa Mae stood in the doorway until the song was over, then called everyone to dinner. Malcolm Cage rushed to shake King Fish's hand and embraced him. He was beaming like a little boy. There was nothing he liked better than colored singing. He, too, complimented Carolyn on how beautiful she looked, and he, too, told King Fish how lucky he was. Lorene directed everyone to the dining room—King Fish and Carolyn first, followed by the Blind

Boys, who formed a line, with a hand on the shoulder of the man in front. Johnny Boy led them. Malcolm Cage was last. Still another chandelier hung over the long dining table fashioned from mahogany that seated twenty-four. A vase of lilacs graced the center and was flanked by a large ham, two roasted chickens with dressing, along with mashed potatoes and greens. Malcolm sat on one end and Lorene sat on the other. King Fish and Carolyn sat across from the Blind Boys. Two servants stood on either side of the room. Malcolm Cage blessed the table with a short prayer before they began to eat. No one spoke much during the meal, only a few scattered conversations and compliments on Willa Mae's cooking. After they had finished eating, King Fish held up his hands.

"Got somethin' ta say. Me and this li'l gal here gittin' married."

Carolyn smiled and showed her ring to Lorene. Congratulations came from everyone.

"You rascal!" Malcolm said. "You never told me."

"Happen yesterday. We ain't even told her father and mother."

Malcolm ordered one of the servants to bring two bottles of champagne from the wine cellar.

"We can also drink to our new deal," Malcolm said. "If you boys like it. Goes like this. I'll be both manager and agent. I'll buy a bus and uniforms and whatever else we need to get started. I'll take care of all bookings and any business. For this I git twenty percent. What ya think?"

"Sounds okay by us," Mark said, speaking for himself and the Blind Boys.

"Deal," King Fish said. "But y'all gotta give me and Carolyn time togetha befo' we git out on the road."

They drank a toast to both the engagement and the deal.

"Have a big beautiful wedding, my dear," Lorene said. "It's something you do only once."

"Yes, I know!" Carolyn said.

She had been thinking just that. Carolyn knew her father would resist a little in the beginning, but in the end she always got her way with him. After all, she was still his little princess. His way of giving her self-esteem had been to tell her stories of her African ancestors and their contributions to the world. He taught her to be proud of her blackness and not to disdain it in favor of the French blood that ran in her veins. He always ended by telling her that she was an African princess.

As King Fish stared at Carolyn, he realized he had never wanted anything or anyone more than he wanted her. He had fallen so quickly, as if his heart had needed to create a love for him to save itself. Sue Ellen was not forgotten, but she receded into some distant place, like a fragrance he was fond of and used to wear. Carolyn Green was the bright new perfume of his existence, if only in anticipation. They were only slightly different, these two women love had brought to him. They were both very bright, and within the fabric of their being a steadfastness and determination was evident. Even Sabria had possessed this quality. But Carolyn Green had something in abundance that overshadowed them all, including himself—class. She was also more articulate, more educated, and more skilled in the social graces. In her presence he regretted not having more schooling. Still, he felt very lucky. Education or not, she had chosen him. He smiled thinking of what his uncle Ed would say: "Sometimes I'd rather be lucky than rich."

Carolyn was talking to Lorene, her voice pitched high with excitement. And there was that quick gentle laughter women produce when speaking about things too confidential for men's ears. In some ways Lorene reminded Carolyn of her mother, although she was sure Lorene had never been that cold. In their style, though, they were alike, had that same lofty bearing that is characteristic of the wealthy. Her mother, having never really been wealthy herself, was through her business in regular contact with women of means. She mimicked them to perfection. Strange how a person can possess all the qulaities one despises in a human being and you still love them. This was her mother. She was pretentious, selfish, inconsiderate, and a racist against Negroes, denying her own black blood. There were times when Carolyn even thought her mother was jealous of her and her father's relationship. Once, when there had been an argument between her mother and father, she had overheard her mother tell him that all he cared about was Carolyn, and that she had needs and feelings herself. If her mother had had her way, Carolyn would have never gone to college, never have lived in Washington, D.C. She would now be married to some well-to-do Creole, someone with light skin and straight hair. As it turned out, her father had demanded she go and live with his oldest sister and attend the school of nursing at Howard. That's where she met Chelsea, her best friend ever. During the two years it took them to complete school, they became like sisters. Chelsea eventually married a white doctor from England and moved to London with him. But before that, she and Chelsea had the City of New York to play in. They both got nursing jobs in the same hospital and they also shared an apartment in Sugar Hill. Chelsea was the gregarious one and the leader of the duo. She was also very pretty. Men flocked to them like bears to honey. There were men standing in line to take them out and they went—to the clubs in Harlem and café society in the Village, where they saw Billie Holiday. There was also a pact between her and Chelsea. They would not engage in sex before marriage. It was never broken. This is not to say Carolyn did not come close to losing both her virginity and her heart. She came very close. His name was Eddy Sacks, a black nationalist who owned a barbershop in Harlem. He had brought his cousin into the ER one evening complaining of chest pains. It proved to be only gas, because his cousin had consumed too many beans. She and Eddy had both gotten a laugh over that. He told her she had wonderful laughter in her eyes. He also praised her for having achieved this status in her life. "The race needs strong black women," he said, and she was reminded of her father. If she wanted, he would take her to a poetry reading where black people's most important historian would speak. He sounded more like one person doing another a favor than a man making advances to a woman. Something else about him impressed her. He was the only man, other than her father, who used the word "black" instead of "colored" with such ease when referring to Negroes. He gave her his card. Then he explained that his combination barber-and-beauty shop was responsible for the hairstyles featured in *Smoke* magazine that were the rave of Harlem.

Carolyn told Chelsea about him, how tall and good-looking he was, and that his cousin wasn't bad either. Chelsea insisted they go to the shop. Besides, she wanted her hair short for the summer.

Eddy was all smiles when they walked in. It was a slow day and he had to finish only one customer before he began with Chelsea. Carolyn waited for the outcome. They both loved the cut and Carolyn got the exact same one for herself. Saturday evening Carolyn went with Eddy Sacks to the poetry reading, which was just as Eddy had said, and much more. It was a gathering of black people who were concerned with the education of the race about its history. J. A. Rogers was the speaker. The very first person he talked about was Jan Ernest Matzelinger, a Dutch Negro who had lived in Lynn, Massachusetts. He invented the first machine for sewing the soles of shoes. Carolyn couldn't wait to write and tell her father. Around the same time Chelsea met and fell in love with her Englishman. Three weeks later Carolyn fell out of her infatuation with Eddy Sacks when he told her he was married and had intentions of making her part of a polygamous relationship. "Like back home in Africa," he said. "No, like back home in New Orleans," she replied. "That's where I'm going." And she went. A two-week notice to the hospital and then the first train to New Orleans. She hadn't been home in four years. Her parents had visited her back east three times, twice in D.C., and once in New York, but she missed New Orleans. Now she had come home a grown woman. She and Chelsea wrote to each other on a regular basis. Then came the beautiful wedding pictures. A year later there were more pictures, this time featuring a newborn baby boy. They exchanged three letters the following year and then none. Maybe they outgrew each other.

Carolyn looked at Lorene. "I do want a beautiful wedding."

"Tell me soon, darling. I'll have to have a new dress," Lorene said.

King Fish smiled to himself. He knew his mother and father would have loved Carolyn and been proud of him. Carolyn's parents, on the other hand, didn't think he was good enough for her. The thought was beginning to disturb him and he intended to prove them wrong. He couldn't change the color of his skin, or his age; but they could do much worse for a son-in-law. He was the pastor of three congregations, if you counted the one from the barn that had followed him to his church in New Orleans. He collected substantial tithes and offerings from the two churches and the jubilee had done very well. The Greens' daughter would never have to work again.

Just then Malcolm Cage smiled over at him. Clearly he was enjoying his conversation with the Blind Boys, learning how they had come together at the behest of an elderly colored lady, now deceased, who insisted that they rise above their handicap. She had been manager, adviser, and sometimes their eyes. Johnny Boy had not been able to fill her shoes; still, he had been what they needed most at the time, a true friend who could see. Now they needed someone to speak up for them, manage their affairs, and get them bookings.

Lorene directed everyone back to the sitting room, where drinks were served. Now it was her and Carolyn's turn to hear the Blind Boys' story. As they told it, Malcolm led King Fish into the study.

"Remember?" Malcolm said. "First night we met. I was a little crazy then. Least you thought so."

King Fish smiled.

"Well, maybe you was right. God changed all that, though. Took some of you and changed me with it. Took some of me and changed you. God's blessed us, Reverend Cook, just like I told you. Never felt about a man like I feel about you, not even Walter Stone. God done that. Took everything outta me but joy! I'm a happy man. You happy?"

King Fish nodded. "I guess I am. Yeah, I guess I'm pretty happy."

They began to laugh.

King Fish and Carolyn were on their way to her house when she asked him how many children he wanted. Something happened that delighted her, made her love him that much more. For a split second she saw him blush like a little boy. He hadn't expected her to speak of children or make any reference to sex. He placed her somehow above all the women he had ever known. In spite of her intelligence, he sensed in her a certain innocence, a kind of underlying purity.

"You so different," he said.

"And when I'm old, will you still feel the same way about me?"

"I ain't gonna change, baby."

"What about her? Do you still think about her?"

"Who?"

"You know who I'm talking about. The girl you were in love with."

"I don't even remember her."

And it was almost true. Thoughts of Sue Ellen had taken a backseat to Carolyn Green. She smiled cheerfully as if something had been resolved and they drove into the night with a feeling of wonderful anticipation.

Carolyn lay awake most of the night wrestling with her decision. She knew what she felt, needed to express it, but there was no one to talk to. She got out of bed and wrote Chelsea a letter that she didn't intend to mail. Then she fell asleep in the chair.

Saturday at noon King Fish was back at her door not knowing what to expect, fearing the worst. Carolyn's smile was reassuring. They both drew strength from each other. She took his hand and led him inside. It was the time her parents took off for lunch from their respective businesses, which were within walking distance of their home. Carolyn called for her parents then stood very still next to King Fish. Her mother, who came in first, paused when she saw them standing there. She knew instantly what was coming.

She screamed, "No, Carolyn!"

Then her father appeared. Carolyn braced herself, and before King Fish could speak, she said, almost defiantly, "Reverend Cook and I are going to be married."

Her father's eyes bulged and reddened. A large vein appeared in his temple. He roared, "Girl, you crazy? You don't even know this man!"

He snatched her by the arm, pulling her away from King Fish. "Now, you git outta my house before I kill ya!"

"No, Daddy!"

Carolyn tried desperately to free herself. King Fish knew this man was serious, that he probably had a gun. At first, he was angry; he had a gun, too, not with him, but at his home in Gator Creek, and the thought that he should go home and get it flashed across his mind. Then logic replaced emotion and he knew there was no other choice. He took one last pleading look at Carolyn and walked out, the sound of her screams in his ears. He was numb. How could this happen? He had lost her just like that. He got into his car and drove, with no destination in mind. He felt she loved him but she loved her father and mother, too, and she had been with them all of her life. Compared to them, he was only a stranger.

People were out in droves, encouraged by a seductive sun, happy faces set with summer smiles. What a beautiful day to have the blues. After a while King Fish found himself in front of his old hotel. He sat there for a moment trying to decide what to do. He knew only that he wanted to be alone. An hour passed before he emerged from the car. His legs seemed heavy when he climbed the stairs, like his body, which was weighed down by the over-whelming disappointment he carried. The man who rented him the room was new. King Fish was thankful for that. He didn't want to have a conversation. The man stared at King Fish's collar and so did a girl on her way down the stairs. This was not a place a preacher was usually found. King Fish had asked for and gotten his old room. Below him the street life unfolded like a motion picture. Hookers like predators strutting their stuff, dope fiends in a panic for a fix, and an old man called Bags selling poorboy sandwiches from a pushcart. King Fish sat there all day trying to chart every moment of his existence, trying to learn where he had gone wrong. Life had been good to him but only in short stretches. Then something always went sour. It seemed he had spent his entire life recovering from life. Darkness came slowly that day, covering the streets, and his room, like a big thick blanket. He didn't bother to turn on the light. Maybe darkness would blot out the pain.

The next day was Sunday. He preached a sermon at his church in New Orleans. He took his text from Ecclesiastes that morning: "I have seen all the works that are done under the sun; and, behold, all is vanity and vexation of spirit."

When he looked up from the Bible, Carolyn was standing in the back of the church, with Malcolm Cage and Lorene behind her. At the sight of them, King Fish lost his voice. While Lorene seated herself, Malcolm Cage and Carolyn walked side by side down the aisle like father and daughter in a wedding ceremony. The congregation shifted uneasily in their seats. Carolyn wore a long powder-blue dress. In her hands she carried a single red rose. She stopped in front of the pulpit and Malcolm Cage went directly to King Fish. A murmur rose from the congregation. Malcolm Cage motioned to King Fish, who stepped aside.

"Brothers and sisters. I'm here to unite Reverend Cook and Carolyn Green in holy matrimony."

A smile spread over King Fish's face, but he didn't move.

"I'm waiting," Carolyn said.

The congregation, catching on, began to laugh. Within moments King Fish was standing beside her, inhaling her beauty, caressing her with his eyes, feeling her spirit quietly embracing his. The vows were repeated without his awareness, as if they were some distant echo from another time. Only she existed for him. No words, no sound, only her. Then it was over. A kiss signaled its ending, a warm and moist kiss that he carried through the well-wishers as they made their way to the car. Inside, they smiled at each other. Soon there was distance between them and the world outside, and a slightly uneasy silence. Theirs was not a perfect world and they both knew it, but the problems of tomorrow were allowed only a brief encroachment. She laid her head on his shoulder and repeated her new name. Like a little girl now, she was quiet and serene. King Fish wrapped his arm around her. It felt good to be responsible for her, to protect this angel, walk with her through life's discords. He felt a new strength, coupled with a sweet vulnerability. So this is what life is, he thought, a big ol' play, sometimes making you laugh and sometimes making you cry.

At the house King Fish carried her across the threshold. Inside, he kissed her again. She fit nicely in his arms and the feel of her body fired his imagination. He hugged her close to him and carried her to the bedroom. When he laid her down she whispered, "Be easy with me." King Fish nodded his head. When his trembling hands removed her dress she lay very still before him, her body glowing golden without benefit of sunshine or firelight, her eyes searched his face, questioning like a child. Ever so slightly her body began to shake, then his mouth touched her breast, and when he entered her she bit down on her lip. Then she began to weep. He was alarmed at first and started to remove himself, but she held him fast. She was not wild in her lovemaking, but slow and smooth, with sighs and whispers. In a final challenge where everyone wins, she lifted her body to meet his. Oh, Chelsea, she thought to herself. When it was over she would not let him move. Her arms locked around his back.

"Did I hurt you?"

She managed a slight smile. "A little, but it's okay."

"I made you cry."

"No, it's just that I'm not my father's little girl anymore."

He stroked her hair. "Baby, can I ask you something?"

"Anything, my love."

"Why you smell like cinnamon?"

She laughed. "That's my mother's doing. She has this cream she made herself. Thinks it's going to make her rich one day. Anyway, cinnamon is its base. She even has a drink to make your mouth smell like cinnamon."

"Baby, what happened with your ol' man?"

She went silent and a pained expression crossed her face. "He said if I left to come to you, I could not come back for any reason except to pick up my things. I was so hurt when he said that to me, I just went upstairs, changed my clothes, and left the house. I got a cab and cried all the way to Reverend Cage and Lorene's house. I told them the whole story and I asked him to marry us."

King Fish smiled. "What yo' mother say?"

"She told me to listen to my father. When you get right down to it she goes along with what he says."

She smiled sadly. "I guess you were right. I got thrown out."

They made love again until they fell asleep in each other's arms.

It was evening when her kisses awoke him. There was a tray with food. A ham sandwich, potatoes, and fruit.

"Mrs. Cook!" he said.

"Sounds nice. You know I was almost named Teresa, Teresa Juliana. La Santa Negrita!"

"Who?"

"Isn't that beautiful? That's what the Spanish called her. It means the black saint. My father wanted to name me after her."

"Wait a minute, baby. Who is La whatcha-call-it?"

Carolyn smiled. "She was a Negro girl from Guinea, West Africa. She went to Spain and became a leading religious figure. She was said to have had miraculous powers."

Carolyn danced her hands in front of King Fish's face. "You think I have any powers, honey?"

"Sho' do." He looked down at his crotch. "You can make me git big and small whenever you git ready."

"James!" She pounded him playfully. "That's so vulgar."

"So, why ain't you named after the Black Saint?"

"My mother, of course. She didn't want me named after an African. She wanted me to have a French name. She and my father fought like cats and dogs over a silly name. Well, they settled on Carolyn. Know what the funny thing is? Teresa Juliana isn't even African. It's obviously Spanish. My mother is so afraid to be associated with Africa."

"A lotta colored people that way. Don't wants ta be called a jungle bunny."

"That's the problem with colored people, they are ignorant of their history. If they knew about men like Abraham Hannible and Khufu, they wouldn't refer to them as jungle bunnies."

King Fish stared at her for a moment. "Okay, baby, who's Abraham Hannible and whatcha-call-it?"

She smiled. "Thought you'd never ask." She kissed him. "Honey, I don't want you to be angry with me for being forward. It's just that you are much too smart not to know about—"

"You ain't got ta tell me all that, Carolyn. Who is the two nigguhs?"

"James!"

"Okay, tell me."

"You really want to hear it?"

"I said it."

"Okay, Abraham Hannible was a black slave boy adopted by Peter the Great and raised as his son."

"Peter the Great?"

"The czar of Russia, honey. He taught military tactics to his adopted son, who grew up to become head of the Russian army. Interesting story?"

King Fish nodded.

"Now, Khufu was different. He was a black pharaoh who built one of the Great Pyramids."

"Baby, how you know he was colored?"

"I know what you're thinking. Egyptians look white. Actually before Egypt was Egypt, it was Memphis, an all-black city named after Menes, an Ethiopian king. Hundreds of years of miscegenation and conquest made Egypt the way you see it today. Besides, Khufu's nephew built a sphinx with his image carved on it, showing he was black."

Suddenly a depression seemed to settle over her. Her eyes filled up with tears.

"I don't understand. He taught me freedom. Now he wants to take mine away. I miss my father, James. He should have been there to see me get married. He should have given me away."

King Fish put the tray aside and took her in his arms. Again they called on love.

She was watching him when he awoke in the morning. Twinkling eyes and a mischievous smile hovered over him.

"Will you have me before breakfast or after?" she asked.

Then she pulled back the covers and placed her naked self on top of him. Afterward, they shared the bathroom for the first time, standing in the tub, washing each other's body. One examining the other like two children. At breakfast she made him eat all of the food she cooked, almost force-fed the last of it to him. Soon it was time to go to New Orleans to her father's house and get her belongings. This task was very troubling to King Fish. He didn't want to have to kill her father. Yet he felt he had been abused at their last meeting, that his masculine standing had been somewhat reduced in front of his now wife. He didn't intend to let that happen again. Without her knowledge he retrieved his gun from under the clothes in his chest and stuck it in his pants under his suit coat.

They drove in silence, but his eyes spoke volumes to her. This side of him she had never seen, eyes fixed, set in a cold deadly stare. She almost told him to turn around. If she had known about the gun she would have. But Carolyn had confidence in her and her father's love for each other. She was also a little saddened by the hurt she knew he would feel when he learned about her marriage. Dealing with that was her main concern. As for King Fish, there was nothing he had to consider, nothing he had to think about. The moment he had picked up the gun he couldn't escape a certain knowledge. This could end with someone's death. Now his actions depended upon her father's. Any hint of aggression and King Fish would kill him. His brain wouldn't be laced with whiskey this time. When they walked up to the house Carolyn squeezed his arm. Her smile was quick, but it was followed by a troubled expression. It was her mother who opened the door. Hostile eyes preceded a voice that hissed with disdain and disrespect.

"What's *he* doing here?"

"I don't want to fight with you, Mama. I came to pick up my things."

Her mother glared, then shaking her head, she quickly left the room. Carolyn intentionally hadn't said she was married. She felt it was her and her husband's place to tell her father.

"Go git yo' stuff," King Fish told her.

Her eyes questioned.

"It's up to me," he said. "I'll tell 'um. It'll be okay, you go."

She moved rapidly up the stairs. King Fish stood tall just inside the door, his hands crossed in front of him, one touching his gun. Time passed slowly and a strange silence reigned. The only sound in his consciousness was the click of the large grandfather clock that stood next to the wall. Suddenly his mouth was dry. He began to perspire. As tiny beads of sweat appeared on his forehead, her father walked in. Her mother was close behind in the line of fire. King Fish's body tensed to alert. Both gazes met across the room, his and her father's settling in each other's eyes. Neither blinking. The promise of death slowly covered the room like the shadow of a giant hand. In one blink her father's eyes looked at King Fish's hands then locked more fiercely with his eyes.

"Thought I told you to leave my house!" His voice was heavy with menace.

King Fish was stoic. "Can't do that till my wife come down."

The words struck her father like an iceberg, froze him in place. Only his eyes showed any life, struggling to regain their focus, fighting to hold back the tears. Then they were overtaken by that pitiful bewildered look. His body trembled and he began to break down, as if in stages, like the collapse of a tall building. He slumped to one knee. Carolyn's mother rushed to his side. She shot one hot look at King Fish then led this broken man with tears streaming down his cheeks out of the room. King Fish remained standing in the same spot. Soon Carolyn, struggling with several suitcases, appeared at the top of the stairs. After helping her downstairs, King Fish explained what had happened. That's when he saw the resemblance between his wife and her father. Both faces registered pain identically, by squinting the eyes and tightening the mouth. Carolyn rushed to the back of the house. King Fish could hear her pounding on the door, crying, begging to be let in.

On their way home she was sad. Her father had not spoken to

her. Neither he nor her mother would open the door. She tried to see his side of things, but she was blinded by the wonderful happiness she felt with a special man. She felt her father should be happy, too. Instead he had broken his promise and her heart. She would always be his princess, he had told her. Nothing would ever come between them.

Each day with him as a child had been special. Each trip to Lincoln Park, each ride on the merry-go-round, the fresh smell of his aftershave when he hugged her. Fishing together or churning homemade ice cream on the back porch. Helping him in his shop or hearing his praise when she brought home high marks from school. Most of all she had loved the stories he told, stories of black greatness. Above all else she had wanted to please him. He was the reason she had given up her dream of becoming a dancer and gone to nursing school. It was for him she endured the boring classes, the hours of study, and the mandatory hospital work—the verbal abuse of doctors who flaunted their superiority. What else did he want from her? What else must she do for love?

King Fish and Carolyn arrived home, where a shiny new black Ford was parked in front of their house. When they stopped, Malcolm Cage and Lorene emerged from the car smiling.

"How you like her?" Malcolm asked.

"Pretty sharp," King Fish said.

"And you, Mrs. Cook? What do you think?"

"I think it's just beautiful, Reverend Cage!"

"Here, then." Malcolm held out his hand with the keys in them. "Wedding present," he said.

Carolyn's face stretched with disbelief. Lorene beamed. Carolyn looked at King Fish. He nodded.

"A pastor of two churches needs a proper automobile, don't you think?"

"Can't argue with that, Reven Cage."

King Fish embraced Malcolm Cage. Carolyn did the same with Lorene. It was that unpromised and unexpected gesture, and its spontaneity, that finally cemented completely King Fish's friendship with Malcolm Cage. This, he understood, was an act of pure love. And Lorene, with that wonderful unselfishness, had supported him in this.

"Darling, let's go and leave these newlyweds to themselves," she said to Malcolm.

King Fish and Carolyn smiled at each other and King Fish removed her suitcases from the car. Malcolm asked for the keys to Sam's car, saying he would have Sam drive him and Lorene home. Then there was another round of embraces.

"Honeeeee, time to eat!" Carolyn called. Then she was all over him, covering his face with kisses and gently tickling him.

"Come on, big bear, wake up, time to come out of hibernation, time for breakfast, Mr. Bear."

He hugged her with one arm, and before he could enclose her with his other she broke away, playfully, and pointed to his erection.

"Ohooooo, Mr. Bear, now look at you, you better take a cold bath!"

Then she was off, calling over her shoulder, "Hurry up. Your food's getting cold!"

He always loved the sound of her voice. He had remembered it from that first time in the hospital. It had a full earthy sound and yet her enunciation was sharp and crisp, like the vowels of the English, sometimes bubbly and lyrical like the French. She had taken the best from all worlds, integrated them into her own, and rendered them forth more beautifully than when she had received them. She was music and rhythm, like a melody set to motion, and she was a good wife.

In the three months they had been married she had taught him many new ways of looking at life. He was never to be a man of high moral conscience, but she had managed to instill in him a sense of self and of racial pride that he had never known. She introduced him to the arts, and they attended every function where Negroes were allowed. At church affairs she was the perfect host-ess. At first he resisted, but again, to a con man, knowledge has a certain lure and he began to devour her lessons with a passion. On some hot nights they would sit on the porch and she would tell him stories she had learned of their African ancestors. He was there when Hannibal, with his army of elephants, crossed the Alps and defeated the Roman armies, and he could see the magnificent city of Timbuktu and the tradesmen from the world over traveling there in search of knowledge. The ancient city of Cush was where civilization had begun and these were people of their own color, she told him. It was the black race who had introduced bronze to the early farmers, who had used only wood before. It was also people of color who performed the first brain surgery.

Carolyn was delightful and childlike with that bouncy carefree, innocence that was sometimes hers when they walked through the grass. She bid him come play with her and he was willingly reduced to a child. She took him on hikes and they waded barefoot through shallow streams and chased frogs and butterflies. In the meadows they laid down blankets and ate from picnic baskets, took naps on the cool grass, and when the sudden summer rains came she did not run for cover; instead, she greeted the raindrops laughing, with outstretched arms.

He sometimes thought of Sue Ellen and how different these two women were. Yet, he thought, if their lives had been the same, how similar they might have become. Carolyn was actually living Sue Ellen's dreams; indeed, the dreams of most women. She was a professional woman with a husband who was respected in the community. She was the envy of all the women in her circle, but, because of her natural charm, still adored by them.

King Fish had been happy to be led through her world as a child leads some great beast that follows passively because it loves the company and adores the child. With Sue Ellen it had been different. He had resisted her at every turn, even to the point of driving her away. Was it that Carolyn was a teacher, where Sue Ellen had only been a student, was that what made the difference? Or had it been his resisting even the very thought of a change in himself? Was Carolyn the personification of a Negro woman's dream of what she could be, and, also, what the Negro man expected her to be? He admitted to himself, now, that he had loved Sue Ellen more than any woman in his life, except, of course, his mother. He would never heed love's call again in so extreme and all-consuming a manner, he believed. He loved Carolyn Green, it was true, but his love for her was more fascination than physical allure, more dependence than passion. She knew precisely the art of making oneself indispensable to another. There was nothing about her he didn't like.

During breakfast they talked about the coming tour of Reverend Cook and the Three Blind Boys, who had been making a name for themselves locally. Carolyn had retired from nursing in order to manage the affairs of her husband's ministry, which included both churches. King Fish recognized that distant stare that always signaled her displeasure. A darkness passed briefly across her face and dimmed the luster in her eyes. She began to cry. She even trembled.

"What is it, girl?" He reached over to her.

She shook her head and turned away from him. He moved around the table and faced her.

"What's wrong?"

"You'll laugh at me."

"No I won't, baby. Now what's wrong?"

She looked up into his eyes. "I had a dream. It was so real. I know it sounds silly. I know you think I'm a big baby, but I'm not!"

"What was it? What you dream?"

"I dreamed we were moving away, going away on a ship. We were all packed and everything. They let you on first, and when I tried to board they held me back. Then, when you tried to get off they held you too. Then the ship pulled away and I was screaming and you were holding out your arms and we couldn't reach each other and then you were gone and I was alone, all alone."

He pulled her close. "It was just a dream, girl."

She clung to him tightly; her words were muffled in his chest. "I feel like something bad's going to happen. I can feel it, James!"

A day later she was ecstatic. She had driven their new car to her parents' house and caught them off guard. They were coming home for lunch when she pulled up in front of their house. Quickly she stepped out of the car and ran to her father. She clung desperately to him, refusing to release him when he resisted. She began to sob. Slowly her father's arms enclosed her.

"It's okay, little princess. It's okay."

Even her mother broke down and the three of them embraced there on the street. They both took off from work and spent the remainder of the day with Carolyn. They reminisced, looked at old photographs, and her father cooked one of his New York dishes. They talked about everything but never mentioned her new car or King Fish. She left promising to see them at least once a week. She arrived back in Gator Creek with a fixed smile on her face. "You know what? I'm going to redecorate this whole house!" She spun around, fanning her arms, and fell into King Fish's embrace.

It was bound to happen. That's the way life writes its story. Everything must be in its proper place, all characters accounted for. Life makes sense of itself that way.

Five years had passed since she walked out of the house that night, five years of such hurried successes that it seemed only a fortnight. King Fish and the Blind Boys were now at the top of the gospel ladder and were playing to a packed house in Atlanta, Georgia.

While shaking hands and exchanging niceties, after the concert was over, he spotted her through a thinned-out crowd. A tall pleasant-looking man wearing glasses sat next to her along with two young children. She was looking at him, too, in much the same way she had done in Gator Creek fifteen years ago. He relived that moment for an instant.

She had changed, but it was for the better. She was sophisticated now and she was beautiful. Her hair was carefully marcelled and parted smartly at the side, and she was smiling that smile of hers.

King Fish nodded, and after a quick exchange with the man seated next to her, who glanced briefly in King Fish's direction, she was on her way. King Fish shook the last hand and there she stood, in a shapely tailored black silk suit, with a ruffled white satin blouse. There was a strained moment and then he politely shook her hand.

"Good evening," he said, never losing his composure. "Good to see you again." He spoke in his best voice.

"Reverend James Cook!" she exclaimed with a smile.

Her voice had a gentle mocking tone. The crowd, perhaps sensing a closeness between the two that excluded them, moved to the Blind Boys, who were signing autographs and shaking hands.

"Is there a place we can have a few words?" she asked.

He looked in the direction of the man.

"It's okay!" she said quickly.

He led her to the dressing room. "Did you get the dog too?" he asked after they were inside.

She smiled. "Yes, I got the dog too."

King Fish noticed her voice was slightly higher and her diction perfect.

"I would have never believed this, King Fish."

"Me being a preacher?"

"Not in a million years," she replied.

He wanted to tell her it was all a hoax, that he had just made it big with another game, but he sensed something, a kind of pride she felt for him having changed his life. Strangely enough he now was concerned with pleasing her. For the same reason he failed to mention he had married as well.

"I guess we all gotta change sometime," he said.

"And what about you? What did you change to, 'Little Sue Ellen'?"

She smiled when he referred to her that way. "I teach elementary school and Robert, my husband, teaches the older children."

King Fish was a little jealous, but mostly he was happy for her. Seeing her standing there, all grown up and quite the proper lady, made him feel good, and he felt lucky to realize that that once-in-a-lifetime thing had happened to him twice.

"Anyway," she said, "I just wanted to say . . . well . . ." Her eyes clouded. "Thank you for helping me grow up."

She kissed him on the mouth and then was quickly out of the

door and, again, out of his life. He knew, somehow, it was the last time he would see her.

The Reverend James Cook and the Blind Boys had suffered all the usual insults on the road—the denials of food and lodging, the evil stares and words. Malcolm Cage had done his best to see that they were treated sanely, but even his efforts were overpowered by the unchecked racism that prevailed throughout the land. As a result, they had spent the majority of their time on the bus. Malcolm Cage stayed with them. There were times, of course, quite a few of them, when the members of some church's congregation, after hearing them sing, would open up their homes. During these times Malcolm Cage would take a hotel room downtown. There were good times too. All the shows were big successes and on the bus they did what they loved, told humorous stories about their past and sang. They even allowed Malcolm to get into the act, and his efforts produced uncontrollable laughter. They had been gone thirty days. Now King Fish was going home.

It was one of those wonderful warm Southern nights when Johnny Boy pulled the bus into Malcolm Cage's plantation. Everyone was tired. Malcolm had insisted that Carolyn stay with Lorene while they were away. King Fish had agreed. He saw her from the bus before they came to a stop. On the front porch under the moonlight she and Lorene stood, both looking lovely. They rushed to the bus.

Carolyn met King Fish first just as he stepped down, wrapped her arms around his neck, kissed him, and whispered, "I love you" in his ear, and then said, "We're going to have a baby." King Fish lifted her high in the air. They had been trying to have a child for two years. That night at home she wrote Chelsea a six-page letter, one she intended to mail this time. As for King Fish, he went through all the changes of a first-time father. He was excited, proud, and sometimes downright scared. Most of all he was the happiest man alive. His awareness of this new creation prompted still another change in him. He became less hurried, quieter, even serene. The jubilant laughter from that past life now existed only in his memory—like the hustling of waves on some distant shore.

It seemed she had been there always, this woman who had brought him a different happiness, who carried a new promise. King Fish had come to be what he never thought he could be—a devoted husband and provider; a joyful expectant father. It was as if he were consciously avoiding the errors of his past. And, although this foreign lifestyle at times provoked a kind of fear and could be unsettling, he gave himself over to it, and released his mind completely from the past. They were wonderfully happy. In the mornings, he planted kisses on her naked belly, and said "hello" to his baby. He cooked breakfast, and some evenings she pretended to be the ballerina she had dreamed of becoming and danced for him. Other times they were cozy with her head on his chest, listening to the radio. Never did they tire of each other.

Lorene often spoke of that adorable glow they exuded during those frequent Saturday dinners they all enjoyed at the plantation. Malcolm smiled on them like a future grandfather, and fussed over their yet-to-be-born baby. When describing this child he was certain would be a boy, words like "healthy," "smart," and "the ministry" rushed confidently from his lips. In their completeness, these four issued a lesson to the world—a song of hope that penetrated beyond all the lines. But the world was not there to hear it; only a few ears whose voices had no impact. In just six days, in an instant, it was all shattered. Somewhere on a highway near Houston, a blown tire sent Malcolm and Lorene crashing head-on into a truck and to their deaths. The radio said only the truck driver escaped with his life.

Carolyn and King Fish didn't speak a word, such was their shock. They stared at the radio as if it were some distant, foreign object delivering them some outrageous lie. Their friendship with Malcolm and Lorene had transcended race, custom, public opinion, and yes, even King Fish's own greed. Suddenly King Fish broke down. He buried his head in Carolyn's breast, and for the first time since he was a child, he cried.

On Sunday King Fish conducted a special service in remembrance of the man and woman who had built the church. He preached from the Book of Ezekiel, where he and Malcolm had begun. Then he and the Blind Boys sang a series of Malcolm and Lorene's favorite songs. It was a solemn service. The congregation shared King Fish's great loss, indeed a loss to all colored people. For Malcolm and Lorene were fast becoming their champions. To King Fish, the thought of a world without the likes of a man and woman such as Malcolm Cage and his wife seemed somehow less inspiring. The world is better served by people of some vision and flexibility, by those who dare even to contradict the status quo for the common good. King Fish, in his earthy style, was able to articulate this to the church. He went home feeling better for having done so.

That evening a great sadness came down on him, something beyond his loss, a threat, or a warning, it seemed, of some impending disaster. He became restless around the house and paced. He was unable to eat the dinner Carolyn prepared. She could say nothing to soothe his anxiety. When he went to bed sleep would not come easy. Only short naps, from which he would awaken to find Carolyn's concerned eyes caressing his face, were possible for him. Today, when he awoke, her hand was gently stroking him.

They stood huddled together outside the huge church. King Fish, Carolyn, and half of the plantation workers, Willa Mae Bean and Nettie among them. They had come to New Orleans to pay their last respects to a couple who showed them compassion and treated them with dignity, but they were not permitted inside. This humiliation only added to the overwhelming sorrow of King Fish and Carolyn Cook. If Malcolm and Lorene could have requested anyone's presence, it would have been theirs. But the members of Malcolm's congregation, filing slowly into the church, acknowledged these intruders with only a blink of the eye, denying those days and months when separate worlds had once come together with such beauty. Carolyn wept openly, but King Fish shed his tears in silence. An hour later the two bronze caskets were brought outside and carefully walked down the steps. Separate hearses took them away. Someone shouted, "Oh, my Lawd," and a part of each person departed with the coffins.

It was difficult for King Fish to imagine a world without Malcolm and Lorene, or remember a life before them. A feeling of abandonment was clear in the faces of Willa Mae and Nettie. Malcolm and Lorene would live forever in these two lives. Even the money King Fish gave this proud mother and daughter to tide them over was somehow a tribute to the Cages.

A month passed as if in a flash, but still the vacancy remained. And they remembered. When a young couple was married, or the Blind Boys sang, even while driving in their automobile, they remembered. Carolyn smiled. She was showing slightly now. In just six months a baby would arrive, and it would carry one of the Cages' names.

To some of the "good ol' boys" it was just plain fun. They were just hanging around the store chewing the fat and drinking beer, waiting for John Morton, the owner, to return so they could invite him on a hunting trip. Big Jim and Davey, the young man who was supposed to be watching the store, were roughhousing in front, thinking of ways to blow off steam. Two men were leaning on the old banister and two others were seated at a table playing checkers when Carolyn Cook drove up in her new car.

"Here come that preacher's wife," Davey said. "She's a looker too."

"I can see that fo' ma'self," Big Jim replied.

Carolyn got out of the car, passed them with a slight nod, and walked into the store. Davey and Big Jim were right behind her.

Davey called out, "John ain't hea, what can I git fo' you?"

"Oh, I see. I'll have a bag of flour, a dozen eggs, and some saddle soap for my car."

Big Jim was staring at her. "You sure a good-lookin' gal, smell good too."

She thanked him but avoided turning around. Beginning to feel uneasy, she put her money on the counter, trying to hurry the transaction along. Big Jim was right behind her now and she could feel his foul breath on the back of her neck. Suddenly he wrapped his arm around her and his hand found her crotch. Carolyn screamed in terror and tried frantically to free herself, but to no avail. The other men outside came in and closed the door behind them. Big Jim was kissing her on the neck and rubbing her crotch. Red, one of the men from outside, got excited and showed her his erect penis.

"You gals seen plenty of these," he said.

Big Jim tore the front of her dress just as John Morton walked in.

"What the hell you boys doin'?" he demanded.

Big Jim released her and she ran crying out the door. Nobody was actually going to rape her was what they explained to John Morton. They admitted they had kept her from leaving but were only trying to scare her a little. Red admitted, too, that he had got a little nasty and showed her his pecker to prove it was big like a nigger's.

"Everybody knows them gals see a lot of peckers, what difference would one more make?"

They all laughed.

She drove home blinded by her own tears and her own rage. She could kill all white men! Carolyn tried to compose herself before she reached the house. She didn't want to upset her husband. After all, there was little he could do. When she entered the house she rushed past him, hardly speaking, her head slightly bowed, as she headed for the bathroom. Once in the bathtub, she scrubbed herself, frantically, in an attempt to wash the memory of those grubby hands from her mind. She had not been raped, but the idea of any man, other than King Fish, touching her, was utterly degrading. God, she could still smell the man's rotten breath, hot and laced with the odor of chewing tobacco and stale beer, when he had tried to kiss her.

When King Fish walked in she was bent forward, sponging her body and weeping quietly. At first she ignored his question, but he became enraged and he frightened her. She blurted out the whole story and leaped into his arms, wet body and all. Then his rage became focused and controlled and she saw a look in his eyes even she had never before seen. Carolyn knew instantly what he was about to do and she screamed, "NO! " She begged and pleaded, but it was like he was possessed. He walked to the bedroom and pulled the gun from the drawer, then dragged her, clinging to his shoulders, to the door. Then he pried her fingers loose and looked straight into her eyes. "Pack some things and go over to where Gus is," he ordered, and then he was gone.

In the car, King Fish's rage consumed him. He thought of his mother and those dirty hands on her. They won't get away with it this time, he thought to himself.

They should have heard the car, even expected him, but arrogance would not let them. He walked casually into the grocery store that was filled with white men and asked for Big Jim by name. A sudden hush fell and the patrons braced themselves against this intruder. Big Jim stepped forward, wearing a cocky smile and looking back at his friends. He asked, "What you want, boy? I'm Big Jim." King Fish said nothing. He just pulled the gun from his belt, pointed it at Big Jim, and pulled the trigger. It barked its violence, then jumped back three times as its deadly message of spiraling lead bored into Big Jim's body, sending him backward into crates and boxes that crashed with him to the floor. The man clawed at his chest as if to remove the bullets with his fingers. Each attempt he made to breathe caused blood to cascade from his nose and mouth onto his neck and chest. He jerked frantically, and then went suddenly still, his eyes frozen in a sightless stare. King Fish surveyed the grocery store, defiantly, looking for any resistance, hoping for it, but the other men only cringed in terror and moved closer to the wall, wondering what this crazed nigger would do next. King Fish laughed big and loud, fired his gun into the ceiling, and walked casually outside and got into his car. As he drove away he whispered to himself, "I did it, Daddy, I laid my heavy hand on 'um."

He knew his life was over, but somehow it didn't matter. Nobody lived forever, and if you had to die prematurely, let it be for something. He was not sorry he had killed the white man, instead he was proud, even happy. And he felt a sense of freedom and a new strength. In killing this man, he had sent a powerful message to every red-necked sheriff who ever raped or molested a colored woman and to every crackuh who had ever lynched a Negro boy: there just might be another nigguh, like himself, who would defend his family and would not hesitate to forfeit his own life by taking theirs.

He felt the Klan would be out in full force, with burning crosses and rebel yells, to strike fear in the hearts of innocent people; there would be fear, but in secret the people would be glad. One of their own had stood up. They would whisper his name with pride, and their children, in later years, would tell the story of how the white man had put his dirty hands on the preacher's wife and the Reverend James Cook had shot him dead.

Carolyn, who had pleaded with him not to go, would be hurt, and maybe she would blame herself, but in time she would realize he had been protecting his manhood and her honor. She would remember him for all time with love and respect. Her father would surely respect him now.

Sue Ellen, would she be sad for him? What a strange thought. There was one thing he was sure of—the Cook family had been avenged. He had stood tall like his father, but unlike his father, he had made them pay the big price. These were his thoughts as he drove to New Orleans and to Congressman Walter Stone's office.

Lightning cracked in the far distance and thunder roared angrily just over his head. The electric rain came down in torrents and clouded the windshield. The sky grew dark and eerie and there existed about the heavens a foreboding air, as in the last hours of Christ. It was strange to King Fish to realize he was having these thoughts. Somewhere in the distant haze of his mind the implacable face of Malcolm Cage appeared. He remembered the last time he had seen him and Lorene, and what Malcolm had said to him: "Reven Cook, meeting Lorene and you the best thing ever happened in my life." That had been the day after he and Malcolm had returned from the gospel concert in Atlanta, where Malcolm had been the guest speaker. That night King Fish had introduced the Reverend Malcolm Cage as his mentor and the single person, next to God, responsible for his success. Now he was gone, leaving behind an unfulfilled legacy, and a true friend. King Fish knew Malcolm would stand at his side if he were alive. "Fuck it!" he whispered to himself. If they caught him before he reached New Orleans, he would take as many of them with him as he could.

He glanced at the two bullets remaining in the gun. Then he spotted them in his rearview mirror. They were coming up fast and reckless, two carloads, swerving from side to side. Suddenly the urge to live gripped him hard and knotted his stomach. A hint of fear registered briefly across his brow and then disappeared in the wave of adrenaline that surged through his body. He floored the gas pedal. The car skidded to one side and then lunged forward. He took the approaching curve full throttle and the tires screamed and struggled for balance, almost lifting one side of the car off the ground. Then, coming out of the curve, he hit a puddle and spun a complete circle, fanning water in all directions, coming to a dead stop, resting horizontally across the road. King Fish tried frantically to start the motor. No luck! Then he heard the squeal of brakes. He saw the first car coming out of the blind curve, tilted on its wheels, and then tumbling over and landing on its side. In an instant the second car roared into view, plunging head-on into the first car, knocking it within a few feet of him. King Fish opened fire immediately. The men, bloody and disoriented, scrambled for cover, in and out of their cars. King Fish tried the motor again and it came to life. He quickly made his escape.

Not long after, the rain stopped, leaving only a quiet mist to float through the falling twilight like waves of stardust that were captured briefly by the headlights of the car. Only the constant roar of the engine challenged the solitude, and King Fish, the car, and the elements seemed to move, en masse, yet remain suspended and frozen in time, somewhere beyond a world of reality and retribution. Then he thought of Carolyn and he knew her pain; her pain became his pain and he could not stop the tears. He could feel her head in his chest and the tremor that shook her body, and at that moment, though they were apart, they were closer than they had ever been.

How had he come to this place where, in an instant, the dreams of life were exploded into tiny bits of nothingness, to a world where past accomplishments existed only as shadowy ghosts? Was life a cruel joke? Didn't you win when you played the game well? His uncle Ed had likened life to a crap game: "Make sho' you ain't gettin' cheated and the odds is in yo' favor and you come out a winner, same way in life." King Fish had followed the rule to the letter. The odds had always been in his favor, both in gambling and in life; one had reinforced the other. Then he realized he had been cheated; he had been born *black*! He had been dealt a hand from the bottom of the deck. For the second time the course of his life had taken a tragic turn because of his blackness. He felt himself becoming angry and he encouraged this anger. He nourished it. He needed his anger now! It made him strong. King Fish outwitted his pursuers easily. He drove down the first deserted road he saw, abandoned the car, and walked through the cane fields until dusk turned into dark. He came up on a group of men finishing their days work. Four trucks stood by, three filled with sugarcane destined for a refinery in the city. They were only three miles from the New Orleans city limits. King Fish knew the white men would be looking for him, maybe even have a roadblock. So he simply hitched a ride on the back of one truck with the men. As soon as they were under way, three carloads of white men came from the direction in which the truck was heading. King Fish tensed, wished he had thought to bring more bullets for his now empty gun, but the cars just roared by, their passengers never looking his way, and he rolled undetected into New Orleans. When the truck slowed to turn into the city proper, King Fish dropped quickly to the ground and darted out of the sight of men too tired to be concerned with his destination. He ditched the gun and made it back to a farm he had spotted just on the outskirts of town and hid in the hayloft of the barn, fifty yards from the main house. It began to rain. "The same ol' rain," he murmured to himself. It had always been there, in his love, in his pain, and now it was part of his impending doom.

Surprisingly, he slept well that night, mostly due to his exhaustion. The next morning, before the crack of dawn, he was up and out of the barn. King Fish ran along the road, hiding in the fields when a car passed by. Finally, in the city proper he caught a streetcar that let him off near the Charity Hospital. It was almost daylight now. He walked into the hospital and sat in the waiting room with several other people. Soon two policemen came in, and King Fish tensed, but they both looked past him to an old man in a wheelchair who was coughing uncontrollably. King Fish actually dozed off while sitting there. When he awoke it was time to call Congressman Stone. There were phones in the lobby, he remembered, and hurried to one.

Congressman Walter Stone received the "life or death" call, as King Fish referred to it, through his secretary, just as he walked into his office.

"Reverend Cook?" he asked, taking the phone. "They're looking for you everywhere."

"I know, suh, I got myself a big problem. I just killed a white man."

There was a pause on the congressman's end. He wanted to know where King Fish was. King Fish told him and said he would wait, as the congressman suggested, but at the restaurant around the corner where he had first taken Carolyn. Suddenly King Fish felt hungry. He made his way to the restaurant hoping some patrol car cruising the colored neighborhood wouldn't pick him up before his meeting. When he was inside, the owner remembered him with a big smile and inquired about Carolyn. Twenty minutes later Congressman Walter Stone walked through the door. King Fish offered to buy him breakfast. Surprisingly, he said he hadn't eaten and accepted. Congressman Stone suggested they talk about the problem when they had finished their meal. After a large serving of fluffy hotcakes, with ham and eggs, Walter listened intently as King Fish related the events of the last twenty-four hours. When

King Fish had finished, Walter lit a cigarette, sipped his coffee, and considered the situation. He was a white man who believed in the Southern way, but he also considered himself a man of honor who believed in the sanctity of the family. In truth, had it been his wife or one of his daughters in Carolyn's shoes, he might well have done the same thing as King Fish. Still, no black man had the right to kill a white man in cold blood. However, he had volunteered his friendship. It was he who had promised Malcolm Cage that he would heed any distress call that King Fish made. He had given his word and Walter Stone was a man of his word. The death of Malcolm Cage made it only stronger. King Fish guessed his thoughts, and, as usual, delivered the compelling line.

"I ain't no killer, suh. I got mo' love in my heart than I got hate. But I got mo' love in my heart for my wife than I got fear of dying. And that's all a real man got."

He paused and looked the congressman in the eyes. "Ain't it, suh?"

"I guess it is," Walter admitted softly.

If King Fish had been a white man or if he had killed another black man, Walter could have gotten him off scot-free. In this case he could only save his life, maybe. He motioned for King Fish to get up. King Fish obeyed. All eyes were on them as he followed this important-looking white man to his waiting limousine. People peered out the window of the restaurant, and a small crowd began to gather outside. The chauffeur held the door open.

"Reverend Cook will ride in the front with you, Charles."

When they were in the car the congressman spoke just one phrase: "To the jail!"

They rode the rest of the way in silence, but King Fish, somehow, knew that Walter Stone would honor his word.

There was no trial. A deal was struck; Walter Stone had arranged for King Fish to enter a plea of guilty before a judge he knew in New Orleans. The "hearing," such as it was, was held on a Saturday so it would not interfere with the judge's regular schedule. It was in the afternoon and the courtroom was empty of spectators, with the exception of the necessary court officials, and Carolyn. She stood frozen and alone, her hands glued to her sides, as if it were she who was about to be sentenced. King Fish stood with his head slightly bowed as the red-faced judge shuffled through his papers. Someone coughed and the *tick-tick-tick* of the clock on the wall was loud in King Fish's ears.

The heat seemed to invade every pore of his body and his shirt clung wet to his back. Strangely enough, he was not afraid. He was sorry for his wife and the suffering she must endure, but King Fish had resigned himself to his fate; to do otherwise would compromise his resolve and to compromise his resolve would surely destroy him. There was no turning back, not even in his mind.

He could feel Carolyn's eyes on his back and he raised his head and stood proud for her. He faced the judge, who looked down at him over his glasses. He uttered words that seemed to echo from some other time and space.

"For the rest of your natural life."

King Fish heard him say this and then there was a scream of anguish from Carolyn. It vibrated in his brain and he turned to look at his wife, whose arm was extended in a helpless gesture. Her eyes pleaded with him as if he could do the impossible and give them back their lives. He would have given his life, willingly, to have spared her this moment; the pain that was reflected in his eyes told her this. His thoughts spoke, "I love you!" but he could not manage to utter the words. They led him away in silence, away from all that had been left for him in this world.

It is true what they say, some things *are* worse than death. Some things force our minds to escape beyond this world into a void where ordinary men become more than themselves and momentarily shed their mortality as a useless encumbrance. But then these men return, however reluctantly, to face some horror of ordinary reality, and so it was with King Fish.

Only his body was present when they beat and kicked him into unconsciousness while he was still handcuffed. He lay in a heap on the hard, cold cement, without food or drink, until the following day—bloody and soiled in his own urine. The breaking dawn was not his friend. It was like some crawling thing that eased through the windows to blur his vision and expose his pitiful state.

The police laughed when they returned that morning. They told him his wife would lay with another man before the week was out. And they joked about his ministry and the fancy car he would never drive again. Then they took him outside and shoved him into the back of a truck with three other prisoners and a guard, who watched him with murder in his eyes. The guard's hand patted the .44 Smith & Wesson in his holster and his look dared King Fish to jump from the truck and make a run for it. He then planted his foot in King Fish's stomach, pinning him in the corner of the truck, pressing harder whenever King Fish attempted to shift his body to find relief from the shackles that were biting into his flesh. The anger rose in King Fish's chest and burned in his eyes. If his hands were only free he would have made this crackuh kill him. He would have given anything for one square punch in the man's ugly face. Fear silenced the other men, a cold distant fear that the unknown produces. King Fish knew that death was his only friend, but hesitated to call on him because of Carolyn. He had to give her time, time to hope and time to prepare herself for a life without him. But these animals would rob him of even this noble sentiment.

The guard leaned his head over the sideboard and spat tobacco juice into the wind, which sent it hurtling back to splatter on the truck. He wiped the stain from his mouth with the back of his hand and began to tell horror stories of the prison farm camp where they were headed.

"They gon' whup you boys good. Then they gonna salt you down like cows."

Two hours later they pulled up to the gate of Camp H, one of ten such camps enclosed in eighteen thousand acres. Gun towers with sharpshooters inside were staggered throughout the camp. On the truck driver's orders, a very tall inmate with a holstered pistol on his side opened the gate. This insane idea of using prisoners to guard their fellows had been instituted by the previous warden to save money. Not including the men in the gun towers, there were only twelve "bosses" to oversee all ten camps; each boss having ten or fifteen of the shotgun-carrying convicts they called trustees assigned to his command. Then there was the captain, who had his own house inside of Camp H. King Fish saw him standing just inside the gate wearing a straw hat and riding boots.

"This 'un hea tha Preacher Man," the guard in the back informed the captain, pointing to King Fish. The captain eyed the new inmate from top to bottom when the three state police pulled him and the others off the back of the truck. A parade of black men, stripped to the waist, walked by, their ebony bodies gleaming in the sun, their legs chained and shackled. They were trailed by a group of bloodhounds on leashes, and their guards, carrying shotguns, ordered them onto the back of an open truck that soon disappeared down a dusty road. All of them, King Fish noticed, wore hats with red paint on them.

"Boy, you 'spose to be dead," were the captain's first words to King Fish.

Then he looked at an old colored inmate who was cleaning the outside windows of the dingy shack that served as his office. "Ain't that right, Rufus?"

"Yes, suh, Cap'n. He sho' 'spose ta be dead." The captain walked threateningly close. "You gonna wish you was fo' we through with you." He turned to the three guards who had transferred King Fish.

"You boys can go now. We'll take care of this 'un."

King Fish didn't show any emotion, but the thought of making them kill him right then crossed his mind.

"Two thangs," the captain warned. "Ain't no gettin' away from hea and ain't no back talk."

King Fish glanced briefly at the tall trustee with the pistol on his hip, then back to the captain. Suddenly he heard an explosion in his ear and a jolt to his head that caused colors to quickly dance across his eyes. He looked up from the ground in dismay.

"Don' know how ta say yes, suh and no, suh?" the trustee taunted as if he was about to hit him again.

"You from down hea boy and ain't learnt how ta talk?" the captain asked.

King Fish thought of Carolyn again and his decision was clear. "Yes, suh, Cap'n, I sho' know how ta talk, suh."

The captain looked at the trustee. "Take this ol' thang wit' the rest and git him dressed in."

King Fish got up slowly. The trustee motioned for the men to walk ahead of him, pointing to a long two-story building. Behind it were a series of bunkhouses. King Fish, for an instant, glanced at the gun on the trustee's hip.

"Know what ya thinkin'. Don't try. I shoots ya dead fo' you can touch me. Now git walking fo' dat big house."

Inmates wearing thick cotton white uniforms with long black stripes were busy coming and going. They only glanced briefly in King Fish's direction. The three of them walked ahead of the trustee until they reached the building.

"You nigguhs g'won inside," the trustee ordered.

It was a laundry room where several inmates were working. Prison uniforms hanging up to dry covered half the room. A giant tub filled with boiling water and clothes was being stirred with a stick by one inmate. Next to him was another tub for rinsing, where a man was wringing clothes and hanging them up.

"Okay, outta yo' clothes!" the trustee shouted. "Shoes too!"

King Fish removed his street clothes and shoes and took them to another inmate as directed. He received a striped shirt and pants with a pair of cheap leather shoes close to his size. The others got the same. After they were all dressed in their stripes, the trustee ordered them out the door and pointed to the far end of the building. This is where they walked, to join the other new arrivals who were waiting in the kitchen. The captain walked in shortly after they were seated.

"Let me tell y'all right now. Y'all dun made a big mistake comin' hea. Now, sence y'all dun got hea, y'all better had done set yo' mind ta weckin'. Hea we wecks from can to cain't from when the sun start till it quit. I'm the cap'n and you got bosses. Now, ya wanta hea' this good. We don' take no back talk and no back sassin' or else you gits the strap. Anybody don't lak weckin', they gits the strap. Now, we got the red-hat cell fo' the real tough 'uns. Ya ain't gonna wanta go there. Now today's Sunday, a free day, make the best of it. Come early Monday mornin' ya gonna be weckin'. That's all now."

The captain walked out. The trustee shouted from the corner where he had been standing.

"You boys what come in hea wit' me, c'mon. We goin' ta' yo' house!"

He ordered them to file out and march to the right. They passed a compound within the compound which encircled a large and foreboding-looking building housing a gun tower with an armed guard inside.

"Dat where them red hats is. Y'all ol' thangs don' wanta git in there."

They walked fifty yards and came upon another small building.

"Okay, this hea yo' house. You's on yo' own now."

The first thing that hit King Fish was the rotten smell, a combination of sweaty feet and unwashed bodies. Even with the men being permitted a shower once a week, each Saturday, which was yesterday, the odor remained. It clung to the wall and the dingy floors like a living organism. The wooden two-decked beds were close together, with mattresses so thin and old you could read a newspaper through them.

"Fish!"

The voice came from the end of this long crowded room. Tree Top Slim and another man were coming in his direction.

"Fish, when you git hea?"

"Just drove up."

"This nigguh's so mean white folks scared to kill 'um," Slim told his friend.

They all laughed.

"King Fish, meet Tracey. Tracey's my bitch. Ain't you, ho."

"You know I am, Daddy."

Tracey was full of muscles but as feminine as a debutante.

"Okay, ho, stop standing there wit' yo' mouth open. Go wash my clothes."

"Okay, Daddy."

With muscles rippling in his arms, Tracey swished away. Slim was a thief who was always in and out of jail.

"C'mon, git you a top bunk, that way the rats won't mess wit' ya."

The men who came with King Fish did the best they could, meaning they took the first available bunk.

"Hey, y'all, this my man King Fish!" Then, with a lowered voice: "Killed a crackuh dead."

Several men came over to shake King Fish's hand. Others, King Fish noticed, stayed away. They reasoned that the boss would have it in for him. They didn't want to draw undue attention to themselves through association. Well, at least there was someone from New Orleans he knew. Most of the other inmates were from small farm towns. Some had committed only minor offenses and, up north, would have received probation. But the South made money off the slave labor provided by these poor souls. This was especially true in the state of Louisiana. Slim was not actually a friend; an acquaintance would be closer to the truth. From time to time he and King Fish played Kotch at the same table, but no more than that. King Fish did know that Slim was a dangerous man with a knife, but this was true of so many of the crowd who lived in the Bottoms. There was a man sitting on a bunk actually reading a book, King Fish noticed, a tall husky inmate with a young face. King Fish nodded in his direction.

"Raymond White," Slim said. "We call him mouthpiece. He real smart. Even went ta college fo' ta be a lawyah. Got three nigguhs cut loose. Wrote som'in' ta dem courts and they dun turn Clyde and 'um loose."

The trustee came in.

"Can't trust them trustees. They's worser than them bosses. Sometimes acts like they thinks they's even white. Nigguhs is sum'in' sometimes, man. Tomorrow gonna be tough fo' ya, but ya can't quit. Gotta keep going else you gits the strap and you lose yo' visit next mont'."

King Fish could see Tracey sitting with his legs crossed, wearing what looked to be women's panties. He was staring at Slim in what appeared to be anger because Slim wasn't paying attention to him.

"Okay, man, talk ta ya tomorrow, this ho wants me to kill her."

Shortly afterward, just before he went to sleep, King Fish could hear Tracey's whimpers of pleasure. Before dawn King Fish was awakened.

"Big line!" the trustee shouted. "You ol' thangs git humpin'. We goin' git Cap'n's cane dis mornin'."

In an instant the entire bunkhouse came to life. Everyone, as usual, slept fully dressed and had only to put on their shoes.

"We gotta go, Fish!" Slim shouted.

Slim headed for the door with the rest of the crowd. Tracey and King Fish followed close behind. A hundred men were assembled at a side gate to the camp. Several trustees with shotguns stood waiting, along with a giant white man.

"Git a little rock fo' the bucket," Slim told King Fish.

"What fo'?"

"That's how Boss John keep track of everyone goin' and comin'. He can't count. When we come back you takes a rock out."

"Tell him what Sonny done, Daddy," Tracey said.

Slim laughed. "This ol' boy Sonny one time put two rocks in the bucket. When we come back Boss John had the whole camp shut down lookin' fo' somebody he thought dun run."

King Fish's burst of laughter caught the attention of Boss John.

"Shut y'all's mouth. Better git weckin' on yo' mine!"

His face was big like his horse's, which was tied to the fence. His arms were large and hairy and he was missing two front teeth. He took one sweeping look over the crowd.

"Let's go! Pit it in da bucket!"

Each man through the gate dropped his rock and broke into a light trot. Five trustees with their shotguns ran with them. They spread themselves out over the hundred men.

"Ten miles," Slim whispered.

Very quickly Slim, Tracey, and King Fish were also running. From the beginning King Fish's muscles reacted to this unfamiliar strain. His chest did, too, with pain. Boss John, on his horse, passed them. This is what they had to follow, a horse. They were running with a damn horse. It was crazy. His lungs were bursting now. He could barely catch his breath. After two miles he wanted just to flop to the ground. He didn't give a damn what they did. But it was the thought of his wife that saved him. He had to have his visit. It was worth dying to see her. He had to press on. Another mile and he was still standing, still running. The pain in his chest and legs was unbearable. If he could only make just one more mile. He pretended he was riding a bicycle. For two miles his make-believe bicycle held him up. He was halfway there. He listened to the sound of feet like drums. He lost himself in that rhythm. The pain grew even more intense. He hadn't thought that possible. He could see Boss John's horse, the movement of its tail, the muscles in its flanks. The dawn broke. He pushed himself still harder. His legs obeyed. The pain subsided. He got a second wind, then he seemed to float. It happened almost suddenly. King Fish felt the crowd slowing down. There was a clearing and a truck just up ahead. He had made it. Everyone slumped to the ground.

"Take five!" a trustee shouted.

"You okay, Fish?" Slim asked.

King Fish nodded slowly. It was the quickest five minutes in his life.

"Cane time!"

Standing by the truck was a trustee. Each man received a cane knife from the back of the truck. There was one exception. One of the new men who had arrived with King Fish still lay on the ground complaining of a twisted ankle. Boss John was off his horse in an instant. In his hand he held a heavy three-pronged leather strap attached to a handle. He demanded that the man remove his shirt. Hesitantly, the man obeyed. He stretched out his arm in a plea. The first blow sounded out across the cane fields along with his scream. Boss John was without mercy. He beat the screaming man until the inmate constricted into a fetal position, until he begged to be permitted to work. With that request, Boss John stopped.

"Okay, let's go, hea! You ol' thangs gimmie some high tops and low bottoms. Pit some nigger in it!"

King Fish didn't know if he could handle being beaten like that. Maybe he would have made them kill him the way King Fish had heard they sometimes did. The beaten inmate's back was like a red-striped tiger, but he was quick to move off to the fields. The work was hard. With backs bent they reached high, cutting the top of the plants, then low, chopping the stalks, nonstop. Pain shot across King Fish's back and down his legs. His arms felt like lead, but he had to keep going. Twenty-nine more days and he could see her. He kept repeating it and he kept chopping. It was nine A.M. before they got a break. They had been working three hours straight. Quickly the men formed another line by the truck. This time there were tin plates with food, corn pone, and blackstrap molasses, all you wanted. Slim, Tracey, and King Fish sat on the ground in a circle by themselves. The trustees and guards, King Fish noticed, had hard-boiled eggs to add to their meal. Tracey twisted over to the large coffeepot and brought back three cups of what the inmates called "black death." King Fish forced the food down and frowned when he drank the coffee. Tracey's talk about his figure and how he had to watch it began to irritate him.

"Sit down, ho, so me and this man can talk."

"Okay, Daddy." Tracey shut up immediately.

King Fish shook his head. "Don' get no better 'an this?"

"Beans and greens later on. Meat once a month."

"What they give ya, Slim?"

"A dime this time, but you only do half here. Got fo' mo' ta go. What 'bout you?"

"They gimme all day. Lucky they didn't take my win."

Slim shook his head. "Tracey in hea for murder, but it wudden no crackuh," he pointed out. "Gave her fifteen. She be out in six."

"I didn't do it, Daddy!"

"Shut up, ho!" Slim looked at King Fish. "Stabbed a trick eight times. Still didn't git no money."

Tracey started to speak. Slim shot him a mean look.

"What that red-hat shit 'bout, Slim?"

"Treats a nigguh real bad over there. Locked up most the time. In a place so small ya can't turn 'round. Food like slop, leftovers. Bring it to you in wheelbarrows. Most nigguhs in there crazy already or fixin' ta be. Spent one week there."

King Fish finished his plate. He didn't like it but he knew he was going to need all of his strength.

"Big line, let's go!" Boss John called.

"Where them white boys at, Slim?"

"Camp B. They don't work in the fields much. Got them easy jobs."

They broke two more times to eat during that first long day. They quit at dusk. King Fish could hardly walk. Still, there was the ten-mile run back to the camp.

"Big line. Hit it!" Boss John called.

Each boss in turn across the acres of cane fields echoed his words. Each man dropped his cane knife in the back of the truck and began the run. King Fish pushed himself at first, past the pain in his arms, back, and legs. His chest was on fire. But he ran on. When they had gone half the way he knew he could make it no farther. His heart beat so loud it seemed to have moved into his ear. Then something happened. His mind left his body. Left it running down a road alone. He was in New Orleans at Jack Stacey's, listening to the cool, soothing sounds of a saxophone. Hearing Pop Creole's laughter. Looking deep into Carolyn's eyes. The time rushed by like giant waves. When they reached the camp it had turned completely dark. King Fish may have been able to run even farther. Boss John stood at the gate with his bucket. The trustees with their shotguns and bloodhounds stood by. King Fish and every other inmate picked a rock from the bucket and made it to the bunkhouse. Then it hit him, the long day, all the hard labor and the twenty miles of running. He barely made it to the top bunk. Fully clothed, he blacked out. No thoughts. No dreams. A kind of deathlike oblivion. It seemed he had been asleep only five minutes when he heard the sound!

"Big line!"

He couldn't move. He was too sore, too tired. Slim shook him.

"C'mon, Fish, we gotta go!"

The thought of the coming visit with Carolyn forced him from the bunk. Seeing her again had become his sole reason for existing. And the baby, he musn't forget about the baby. Maybe it would be a son to make him proud, do all the things he had never done, play baseball, be a famous blues singer, or even attend a university like his mother had. It all came to life before him now as he was running. What might have been. Such a wonderful what-might-have-been. He was there with her and a new baby boy, a strong voice, eyes like his mother's, crying for attention. His beautiful wife smiling proudly up at him. He was there when his son took his first steps and clearly cried out, "Daddy." When he made his mother smile. They would grow old together, he and Carolyn. And they would watch their children—and there would be several—marry and have children of their own. And as they walked arm in arm through the years, a lifetime of special memories would be theirs. The complete scene played over and over for him. He became so much a part of it that he ceased to belong in the here and now. He had put himself in a semitrance where his body alone responded. He worked the fields like a machine, but still, he was not there. He had to be told twice when it was time to quit. During these days he distanced himself from Slim and Tracey lest he be distracted from his trancelike state. Only on Saturday evening did he return to this awful present. Saturday, to appease the bosses, required only a half day in the fields. Saturday evening the men let loose. They put their pennies together and purchased home brew made from sugarcane from the inmates who worked in the kitchen. There was singing, dancing, and storytelling. Later, things went sour. There were fights where some of the strong inmates raped the weaker ones. The bosses were not around and the trustees turned their backs. No inmate dared approach King Fish. Everyone knew he was a killer. King Fish promised himself no matter what, he would never become like them.

The days rushed by and the weeks. Soon there were three that had passed and another Saturday night, a week before Carolyn. King Fish lay very still and quiet in the black nothingness of the overcrowded room. He was almost oblivious to the smell of un-washed bodies, the suffocating heat, that was overpowering, and the muffled sounds of pagan sex as men forced themselves on other men. Yes, he could endure the nightly pricks of insects that crawled over his body and drank his blood, and the constant rambling of rats, and the roaches who went hurriedly about their business un-der the cover of darkness. This, too, was King Fish's time. The night belonged to him. King Fish had, again, discovered the other side of adversity. If you have the will to endure and that certain something that sets winners apart from losers, life's brighter side will reveal itself to you. In King Fish's case he managed to turn cold facts into a hazy semireality. In the three weeks of his intern-ment he had learned to master the senses. His mind had created a never-ending string of vignettes that was his life "story." This night, as usual, his mind was filled with the magic that was Carolyn Cook. Her passion came rushing through, blocking out all that was unpleasant and hostile. She consumed his total being. His nostrils flared as the husky smell of cinnamon that had graced her aroused body invaded his memory. Her eyes, deep and searching, tracking his own, recording his inner thoughts, her touch that brought with it the promise of eternity, all were his tonight.

Sunday, for the first time since he had suffered this tragedy, he felt like singing. And he sang. Sang the Gospel better than he had ever sung it. With all his heart and soul he sang the praises of a God he had claimed not to believe in. He drew a crowd. The trustees came in. They went and got Boss John. He sent for the captain. King Fish kept singing. He saw the faces, the admiration, how they were touched, moved almost to tears, and the hatred in the captain's face, how quickly it vanished. When he was through singing he said a prayer. He didn't know why. He just did. The place went silent; not one sound was uttered. Each man remem-bering his teaching of the Holy Word. The spirit of goodness that he had sometimes embraced as a child. Upon reflection, that Sun-day stood out in King Fish's mind as the day the beast was tamed. Although this resemblance to a truce only lasted for a day, it gave him great pleasure over the next week. Strangely, because of it, and because he would soon see Carolyn, he enjoyed a degree of happiness. However, the days before the next Sunday did begin to slow. Finally thirty days had passed. He had taken a shower, put on a clean black-striped prison outfit, and it was time. He was filled with excitement and was a little nervous walking to the visiting compound. It was a large bare room with wooden benches on either side of a linked screen that ran its length. There was a trustee posted at the far end facing the door. Carolyn was sitting near the entrance on the other side of the screen. So were many other visitors. Only a few inmates had arrived. He had been among the first to be called. She was smiling and she seemed more beautiful, if that was possible, than before. Maybe it was that angelic glow that women sometimes take on when they are with child. Maybe it was because the thirty days, although they sped by, again seemed to him like thirty months. For a few seconds they inhaled the sight of each other, placed their hands on the screen, tried to touch.

"How are you, honey!"

Her eyes squinted the way he remembered when something pained or troubled her.

"Are you okay?" she asked.

All of her love was contained in that one question. He wanted to scream *No!* He wanted to say, I'm dying in here without you, but he forced himself to say "I'm okay."

"I'm not okay, honey. I'll stay strong for you but I'm not going to be okay until you are home."

He gave her a look of appreciation.

"I mean it, honey. I've decided, I'm not going to let my husband be separated from me and my baby the rest of our lives."

"I love you, baby," he said.

"I know, but listen," she whispered. "I talked to both congregations and both assistant pastors. Everyone has signed a petition to go to the governor for a pardon. I even wrote him a letter. Told him I was pregnant. And I told him the whole story. So you see, I'm not giving up. By the way, Gus, the Blind Boys, and the entire congregation, both of them . . . well, they all wanted to come. They love you, honey. I told them you could have only one visit a month.

Oh, guess what? You won't believe this. My father says he's sorry you're in here."

"That right?"

"Sure is. He meant it too. I know him. Now, do you know what kind of baby you want yet?"

He smiled.

"Come on, boy or girl? Not that I can change anything."

"I'll take what you give me, baby," and he thought, A girl wouldn't be so bad either.

"Are you going to become like my father if it's a girl?"

"Ain't nobody can be like your father."

"You just wait. You don't know. I sorta hope it's a girl. Then both of you might understand each other better."

"You mean me understand him, not him understand me."

She smiled. "Maybe. Honey there's something I've been wanting to ask you for a long time. Will you tell me the truth if I ask you now?"

"Don't know. If it's about one a' them gals trying to steal me from you, I'm lying my head off."

She laughed. "You are so crazy and I just know no woman's ever thought they could steal you from me. I got the magic, remember?"

That made him laugh.

"Tell me this, Mr. Thick Skin. Tell me you weren't jealous of Eddy Sacks when I told you about him."

"I ain't thought about it. You the one that almost wore the grass skirt."

"James! No, I wasn't! Anyway, African women don't wear grass skirts."

"Okay, a bone in your nose. You was goin' back to Africa wit that niggah, wasn't ya?"

She began to laugh. "I was not. I know you were jealous, now. I've been knowing you too long, honey. Trying to shift the subject to me gave you away."

They both went suddenly quiet. Her eyes squinted. They both

fingered the screen. She tried to say things to give him hope. He tried to keep her from worrying. The time cheated them. The seconds and minutes passed too quickly. Both hearts begged but time would not slow. The words that told them it was over were loud and harsh, without pity or concern. He left the screen with her face in pain, his stomach in knots, her promising to write every day. It had not been much, that little time. But it had been every-thing to him. He was in a way sad and he also felt recharged. Should he dare to hope, think the impossible? Was there a chance? No, he wouldn't think it. He wouldn't set himself up. His dreams were enough. He knew he could depend on them. Now he would enjoy the remainder of his free day like the rest of the inmates walking with him. All visits were terminated at the same time. All inmates on their own walked to their bunkhouses. No one broke the rules. The loss of visiting privileges was a most devastating thing in prison. Other inmates were busy relating stories visitors had brought from the outside world. King Fish said nothing. He kept his thoughts to himself.

When he got back to the bunkhouse, Raymond White, the smart youngster Slim had told King Fish about, was standing at the door as if he had been waiting for him. Raymond introduced himself. He was a large young man with graceful moves who seemed very self-assured.

"I think it's about time we met. Could we walk around the com-pound?"

King Fish agreed with a nod.

"We have somewhat the same job, you and I. What I mean is, we are both in the business of uplifting people. I'm a teacher and you're a minister. You're even able to soothe the spirit with that wonderful voice."

"I ain't preachin' no mo'. I got all day ta do, man."

"I know, and I understand. That's the reason you're respected, even feared, around here. Not because of your sentence, but be-cause of the reason you got it."

"Ain't nobody scared a' me. Ain't got no reason ta be."

"You lifted your sword up against the oppressor. There are a lot of vicious men here, men who would slit a throat in an instant. But not one had the courage to kill a white man."

He looked much older, this young man, more mature, even wise. "That is what it boils down to isn't it? Courage?" Raymond said.

"Ain't som'thin' I wanta talk 'bout. It's dun now."

"Maybe what I really want to say . . . Well, you need someone to talk to in here. Someone who hasn't passed his limit. Someone to keep reminding you you're a human being." He paused briefly. " 'Let death come quickly to me in the heat of battle so that those who speak of courage will remember my name.' I wrote that after I had been here a year. I had become one of them. A beast living in an eternal rage with no concern for the future. No link to the past."

"Scared a' white folks, though," King Fish pointed out.

"Yeah, afraid of white folks. Just colored gladiators who dueled among ourselves. Warriors without an army or a cause."

"Raymond, ain't nobody ever stood up to these crackahs?"

"There was one. Jo Jo Jamaica, we called him, because he was from the West Indies. Had a real thick accent. Jo Jo was defiant from the beginning. Wouldn't bow his head. Wouldn't show fear. One day Boss John tried to whip him. Jo Jo wasn't very large, but he took the strap from Boss John and was actually getting the better of him."

Raymond stopped talking. His eyes even seemed to cloud. King Fish looked at him intently.

"A trustee blew Jo Jo's brains out, right over there by the fence. The one who works for the captain now. The tall one you saw when you came in. That's how he got his job. You see, Reverend, you are the only person anybody knows who has killed a white man and is still alive."

"How'd you git in hea, Raymond?"

"They say I burglarized a store. I was in the area. I was wearing a pair of slacks and a sweater from the store. That was the evidence they needed to convict me."

"The people that sold 'um ta ya don't remember?"

"I didn't buy them."

"You stole 'em."

"I didn't steal them. They were bought for me by a white girl. Someone with a very important father."

King Fish understood. That situation would have been even more disastrous than the burglary charge.

"I had almost completed law school. Anyway, after Jo Jo was killed, I decided to fight with my knowledge of the law. When a writ I had filed got the first inmate released, I was thrown in the red-hat cell. I continued to file. I guess the big boys in Baton Rouge told them to leave me alone. I don't even work the fields anymore. I do a lot of paperwork for the warden now, undercover of course. Can't make the white inmates angry."

"Wanta ask you som'thin'. What's the chance of gittin' a pardon?"

"That's not a situation where percentages count. Not when that's almost your only recourse."

"How many people you git out?"

"Three, but I can't seem to help myself."

King Fish liked him. Raymond was right. They both needed someone to talk to.

King Fish went to bed early that night. He had a lot of dreaming to do. This time it was Storyville and Hattie Briggs that took center stage in his mind. Even Sabria was there, young and beautiful again, but not with him. There was someone else but he could not see her face. Suddenly he was in the Bucket-of-Blood laughing with Society Red and Big O.

It was still dark when he awoke before his time. He lay there thinking of Carolyn and his yet-to-be-born child. Not too long after, he was running to the cane fields with the others. Then chopping, chopping, chopping. At break time the captain showed up riding a spotted horse with a dirty white color. Not a pinto; this was a huge animal. He was a big man, but robust, as was evident in the spring with which he dismounted. In his hand he carried a large bullwhip. And, of course, he wore riding boots. His eyes found King Fish.

"Singin' preacher, wanta show you som'thin'."

He motioned for a trustee, who came to him carrying his shot-gun. The captain handed the man a strip of paper which had been folded several times to make it thick. The trustee put one end of the paper in his mouth and clenched it with his teeth. The captain stepped back a few paces. Suddenly there were two loud pops as he cracked the whip over his head and down by his side. The next crack cut the tip off the paper in the trustee's mouth. There was another, and still another, and on until the paper was only a stub in the man's face. The trustee had flinched each time, but he never moved. The captain waved the man away and walked over to King Fish smiling.

"What ya think?"

King Fish shook his head in true amazement. "Ain't nevuh saw nothin' like it, suh."

"Been foolin' with whips since I was a boy. Worked for a circus five years, before I got married. Ain't so much as touched a body with a whip if I didn't want to. Come ta talk ta yah about the big dinner Warden Tomson givin' next month. Lot of important peo-ple gonna be here: mayor, chief of police, maybe even the gover-nor. You'll wanta sing at that 'un. Plenty of good leftovers and ya get two days off from the fields, maybe three, if they like ya."

He started back to his horse.

"Okay, show's over. You ol' thangs git my cane!"

King Fish now had somethin' else to look forward to. He had learned the secret of doing time. Time had to be done in incre-ments, interspersed with some kind of reward, ever so small to the free public, but important to an inmate: Saturday evening, a visit, mail, even the meat served once a month, now maybe a chance to sing for the governor, whatever help that could give him. He al-lowed himself to dream the impossible. What if the governor liked his voice so well he pardoned him.

He talked to Raymond White about his upcoming singing en-gagement and was given more hope. Raymond told him the story of the popular blues singer Leadbelly, who sang for an outgoing governor and was pardoned from Huntsville, a penitentiary in Texas. They talked in whispers late into the night.

King Fish found him to be a brilliant young man, someone even he could learn from. Raymond believed that illiteracy was the major problem facing Negroes, if you took away racism, which was impossible. He had taught several inmates to read and write. Even a boss had secretly come to him for help.

Raymond had been there two and a half years. A ten-year sentence had been imposed because the people who owned the store he had been accused of stealing from lived in an apartment over it. This made the offense burglary of an inhabited dwelling in the nighttime, the prosecutor argued. A crime punishable by death in South Carolina.

That talk was on Friday night. King Fish barely made it through the next half day's work. He was met with another surprise that evening. He received four letters from Carolyn. No contact had been allowed in the first thirty days. She was permitted to write only after her first visit. He could feel her through her letters, the warmth of her body, taste her mouth, hear her laughter. She spoke of a love that had grown even stronger in his absence. And she told him to pray as she did. Carolyn devoted one whole letter to their unborn child and its future. She had even dreamed the same dreams of the three of them together, as he had. Her third was a letter to keep his hope alive. The fourth contained a little gossip. One of the ministers was caught cheating on his wife, but mostly this one contained words from well-wishers; and there were many. Something stuck in his mind concerning one letter. The way she had put quotes around the word "pray." Although she had always attended services, he had never known her to be a particularly religious person.

Just then a woman's scream, or so it sounded, startled him.

"Please don't hit me, Daddy!"

Tracey was cowering in the corner on the floor. Slim stood over him. This caused King Fish to smile. Tracey was a powerfully built muscle-bound man who could easily overpower Slim.

The next day was Sunday. Just three more weeks before he would see her again. He sang again. It was the same as it was the first time. He drew a crowd. Only the captain didn't show up this time. A few of the other inmates joined in, made it more fun.

Nothing changed in the camp. The hard, dull routine continued, reducing men's lives to an unrelentingly predictable pattern. King Fish refused to allow his thoughts to wander to the hopelessness of his situation. He had given way to the belief that somehow, someway, he would be free again. Carolyn had willed it so and he believed her, because he wanted to. King Fish began even to make plans. He would rejoin the Blind Boys. Of course they would need a new manager, but that was not a difficult feat. They had earned recognition already. He would buy a larger house too. He and Carolyn needed a bigger place. These thoughts made him happy, made the nights a complete joy. The days rushed by. The weeks. It was time. A trustee came and said the words dear to every inmate.

"You got a visit."

King Fish stepped quickly to the visiting room, smiling as he walked, exchanging pleasantries with the other inmates going his way. He was a little boy again, filled with the special excitement of Christmas. The room was crowded today. He searched for her face through the screen. Then there was shock, followed by terror. A face he hadn't seen in more than three years stared at him, a face heavy with sadness.

"She's okay," Carolyn's father managed. "But there's some bad news."

King Fish felt that desperate, sinking feeling. A knotted stomach came with it. Outwardly King Fish held his composure. But her father's face began to come apart.

He said, "She lost the baby! Our baby's gone!"

Then there was silence. The reality crept through King Fish's consciousness like poison, contaminating all hope, murdering his dream. He could not speak. Her father did not try to hide his tears. Tears shed not only for a lost baby. Maybe he could have kept his composure if it were not for his great shame. Words were difficult for him.

"Lost it last night. All she could talk about was you. Worried about how you would take it. She wanted to come. I told her I would."

King Fish still didn't speak. It was as if this man was far away, as if his words were echoes.

"I'm sorry!" King Fish heard him say. "You gave up your life for my little girl. It's a long time comin' but I'm sorry. I didn't know how much man you was."

King Fish showed no expression.

"You ain't scared of 'um, are you."

It was a statement.

"You really a Garveyite in your heart, one of us."

What could King Fish say to this man who was now so sorry? It was too late. Everything was too late. There was still no sound from King Fish. He wasn't being vengeful. He was merely at a loss for words. Carolyn's father's eyes pleaded with him.

"She's my little girl, Revern. I didn't know how to give her to another man."

Something stirred inside King Fish. Because of his loss, he began, little by little, to understand. His child could have been a girl too. He could have watched her grow up, protected her, loved her. He looked at this man, broken before him for the second time now, a proud fearless man whose eyes spoke his shame.

"I know!" King Fish whispered, almost to himself.

Maybe King Fish should have talked to Raymond, but he couldn't. It was not in his nature. He had found it easy to talk to only two people in his life about really personal issues, his uncle Ed and Lorene Cage. Both always responded in a nonjudgmental way. He wished he could talk to them now. He was too full of pain. The weight of it was riding him like a horse. There was no escape, no floating above it on tomorrow's fantasies. Everything, he realized, had been riding on a child who had not made it to this world. This child had been his guarantee of freedom. At least a part of himself would have been with his wife. He became bitter. He blamed God, who he had told himself he didn't believe in. He was defiant, cursing men and God. The work was challenging now, but he fought it with a rage befitting a great warrior. The night that once was his friend entered into a conspiracy with the day. His dreams began to betray him. They set themselves up in menacing colors, dark reds, and blacks, with horrible themes.

In one, Carolyn was pregnant again, but by another man. He could hear Boss John's incessant laughter echoing in his brain. Once Malcolm Cage walked him down golden steps to hell. Sometimes he bolted awake at midnight, escaping from Bill Black, who was filling his body with hot lead. There were times when he found himself alone in a pitch-black room.

Such was his anger, King Fish avoided everyone over the next two weeks. Raymond included. He was given a wide berth. The desperateness in his face signaled only one thing to the other inmates, a man about to blow. His mind began to come back to him only a few days before the warden's dinner. The con man in him appealed to his reason the way it always had. There was still a small chance for freedom! Freedom was the only key. Freedom could fix everything. Now he must talk to Raymond. He had to pull himself together, call on the best of himself. King Fish saw him Friday evening, two days before the dinner. Raymond was stretched out on his bunk reading a book when they came in from the fields. King Fish walked over to him.

"What's the song ol' Leadbelly sung?"

Raymond looked up.

"They say he made up one just for the governor. You don't know what you're going to sing?"

King Fish shook his head.

"Let me suggest the perfect song for your voice. And the perfect song to sing to a Southern governor. Everyone knows and loves 'Ol' Man River.' " You know it?"

King Fish's eyes brightened. He had sung it before. He nodded his head. He had learned it by listening to Paul Robeson sing it on the radio. He smiled and nudged Raymond with his fist. Tonight was the first time in almost three weeks that life offered hope, and the promise of peaceful sleep.

Saturday afternoon after work he received two sad letters from Carolyn, both apologizing for losing the baby. He had written her several letters which he thought would lift her spirits. Maybe she had felt his overwhelming pain through them. He needed to see her now that there was hope again.

It had all come too quickly, so quick it was frightening. He was perspiring in the back of the truck. Maybe more than the others, it seemed; but then he had more at stake. By rights, he should have been filled with confidence. The day before they had all applauded him enthusiastically, Raymond too. There were three trucks with five inmates and one trustee in the back, talented men from different camps picked by their captain. Two bosses rode in the front. They were also selected by a vote of captains. Boss John was not among them.

The warden's mansion was ten miles from the nearest camp. It was beautiful, an old plantation house clinging to the grandeur that belonged to the South before the war. The guests played their part, too, with frilly colorful dresses and the men in tails and black bow ties. There was also a band for dancing. An unused wine cellar was where King Fish and the other inmates were stored until it was their time to perform. They could see nothing of the festivities from where they were housed. But they had glimpsed them on the way. The affair was held outside. A long banquet table supplied loads of food. People sat at tables and chairs arranged in a semi-circle and a kind of courtyard served as the dancing area. The warden, chief of police, mayor, and the governor all sat on the front porch at a special table with their wives. From where King Fish was, applause and music could be heard. They also heard the crack of a whip, then more applause. Down there the conversations were scattered and forced. The men did not know each other. King Fish would have liked to have seen each man perform. At least he would have known what he was up against, who he had to outshine. They called him third. A trustee he didn't know carrying a shotgun called for Reven Cook and stood a distance away from King Fish. He didn't point his gun, only walked a safe space behind, giving King Fish directions. The plantation reminded King Fish of Malcolm Cage and Lorene, of their quiet wealth. Not that there was any similarity between this much smaller place and the vast acres of the Cages' farm, except maybe a kind of serenity common to most plantations that camouflaged a past during which some of the most brutal crimes against humanity had been committed. A gentle breeze cooled his face and armpits already damp with sweat. From a short distance away he could see the white faces. The smiles of amusement when he entered the courtyard. He heard the announcement. A man read from a paper. "Now, ladies and gentlemen! A special treat, I'm told. Reverend Cook will sing for us." The applause was polite. The man nodded. King Fish felt his stomach grip. He opened his mouth but nothing came out. He could not sing. Panic set in. People were waiting. He saw their brows knit, saw them look at each other. His eyes closed, in a gesture of hopelessness. It was no use. Let them do with him whatever they would. It was all lost now anyway. Then a face appeared, one from long ago. His mother's face, no expression, just staring. King Fish's mind raced backward. There was a nightmare and a terrible fear of the darkness, his mother's face, standing guard in the night, giving him courage. He opened his eyes. He could do it now. There was no fear. The notes rolled off his tongue like thunder. His body became free and he moved with each lyric, talked to them in song, begged for his freedom.

 " *'Colored folks work on the Mississippi. Colored folks work while the white folks play, pullin' dose boats from de dawn to sunset, gittin' no rest till de judgment day.'* "

A hush fell over the plantation. And this was only the introduction to the song. By the time the words "Ol' Man River" reached his lips, King Fish was facing the man he knew to be the governor. All the emotion trapped inside of him escaped into his song, burned its way into the hearts of men and women who had never before been concerned with the suffering of these lesser people. King Fish's tears, too, made a bid for freedom and streaked their way down his face. He finished on his knees, singing directly to this man who held freedom in his hands. " '*An dat ol' man river, he just keep rollin' along.*' " They rose up smiling with their applause, every man and woman of them. For a full minute they gave their ovation. King Fish took bows all around. When he turned back to the warden's table, the governor was waving for him to come forward, a smile as big as all outdoors on his face. King Fish returned his smile, and walked to the table.

"You have quite a voice there, Reverend."

"Thank you, suh."

"How long you in here for?"

"Life, suh."

"Too bad. You have a real talent."

"My wife, suh, she wrote you 'bout me."

"Your complete name is?"

"James Cook, suh."

"Okay, James, I'll look into it. Just keep singing. For now I'm going to ask Warden Tomson to give you a week off. You've been very entertaining. You can go back now. You'll be hearing from me."

King Fish felt like dancing on the way back to the wine cellar. He had done it! He couldn't wait to tell Carolyn.

The men in the cellar had heard the applause and the questions came. What did he do? He told them. Although he was bursting to tell the whole story, King Fish kept quiet. This was not the place.

When the entertainment was over and the last performer called, the warden and guests retired to the house for cocktails. The inmates were then permitted to come out and eat the leftovers. They were also supplied with paper bags to carry what they couldn't eat home. The inmates gorged themselves and then proceeded to clean up the place. King Fish couldn't eat. His spirits were too high. He did, however, fill one bag with ribs, turkey, ham, chicken, and potato salad. The other bag was lightly stuffed with pastries. After they cleaned the tables and the yard, they were ushered back to the trucks. Even the bosses nodded their approval to King Fish.

King Fish scarcely remembered the ride back to his camp. The cool sounds of that saxophone playing "Mellow," his uncle Ed's favorite tune, carried him back in time, to the evenings at Jack Stacey's with his uncle, and later with Sabria. He had been some hustler then, young and cocky, fast with the girls. Everyone knew his name. The old gamblers and con men bragged about him. Their approval had made him proudest. He even thought about Buddy Bolden and about Storyville, the fun he had there, the music. He should have been more forceful, had more confidence in his voice. Now he knew for sure he could have made it with the Bolden band.

The truck made its fourth stop. It was his turn to climb down. "One chicken for the coop!" a boss shouted at the gate. It was opened by the tall trustee with the pistol on his side, the one who had knocked him down, the one Raymond told him had killed Jo Jo Jamaica. "Let's go," were his only words. A guard watched from the gun tower as he escorted King Fish back to his house. King Fish hoped he would see him on the outside, this nigguh who was so quick to kill his own kind to get a little closer to the white boss.

Everyone was asleep inside. King Fish tiptoed over to Raymond and lightly shook him.

"Here," King Fish whispered, handing Raymond the two bags. "Give some to Slim and that whatchamacallit."

"Thanks. How'd it go?"

King Fish made a fist and jerked it back to his chest. "Tell you 'bout it in the morning."

Tomorrow he would write to Carolyn, when it was light.

She came floating to him through a thin mist, her sheer garments flowing behind her. Some distant place uninhabited by mortal beings was theirs. They met in a dream of his dream, high on a cloud, to create a heavenly child. Time did not exist, only eternity.

When King Fish awoke that morning he was wet with the passion that had spewed forth in the night and he was smiling. He would see her in six days. He would share his joy, fill her up with it. "Big line, all 'cept'n the reven!" the trustee shouted. The warden hadn't sent for Raymond, so he was off as well. He handed Slim and Tracey some meat and pastries and told them it came from King Fish. Most likely they would have to eat it on the run, which they did. After the bunkhouse was cleared, King Fish and Raymond smiled at each other. He walked over to Raymond, still smiling, and held out his hand, palm up. Raymond slapped it with affection. "I knocked 'um dead," King Fish said, and went on to tell Raymond the whole story, double-stating the governor's words: "You be hearing from me." King Fish's mind, he felt, was now free. Only his body was lagging behind. They celebrated his good fortune with food and laughter. Even so, King Fish saw the caution in Raymond's eyes, just a hint of skepticism that he avoided. King Fish would not allude to any other possibility lest he spoil his chances. Only he had seen the governor's eyes, felt his admiration. Raymond was very bright, he knew; but Raymond had not been there when he had moved them all. Nothing could slow him now. He himself had witnessed the awesome power of a man's will. It was he who controlled his destiny, his mind. He had seen it even on that second day he had come to this place. He could even speed up time and he did.

Carolyn was there before him as if he had summoned her. There had been no waiting, no anxiety, only him turning day into night, night into day until a week had passed. She had gotten his letter. He knew it by the look on her face. Her hands were on the screen when he walked in. He could feel her joy. See it riding on her electric smile. She had painted her lips the color of molten steel. She was very sexy. Carolyn was letting her hair grow out too. He didn't like that but lied and said he did. "I wanta hear everything about the dinner. What the governor said, everything!" He told it all again, leaving out not the slightest detail. Her eyes followed his every word. When he had finished, her expression brightened even more. "Everything is true. It's really happening!" As he watched the woman he loved bursting with happiness, something occurred to him. He was not like his uncle. He was not a ladies' man. He had really never been. During the three-plus years he had been married to Carolyn, he had never once thought of another woman.

Even Sue Ellen, who he now remembered with a kind of distant warmth, had enjoyed his total monogamy for at least nine years. What he wanted now was simple. He wanted his wife, a child, and he wanted to sing.

"Honey, I haven't told you before; I didn't want to upset you. I'm living with my parents now. Gus is staying at the house. You aren't angry, are you?" she pleaded.

He shook his head.

"There's something else, honey."

His expression changed.

"Don't be alarmed; it's nothing to worry about."

He stared at her.

"Don't look at me that way. I told you it was nothing. I just joined the NAACP."

"*No!* It's too dangerous. I can't look out fo' ya, baby. Don't do it!"

"I have already done it, honey. A lot of colored women have. Even a few whites. Don't worry, I have to be brave like my husband."

He reluctantly accepted it. What could he do? He even admired the fight in her. They talked about small things, silly things, how she had liked him from the very first time they had spoken in the hospital. How jealous of Sue Ellen she had later become. How she had intended to play hard with him but had failed miserably. King Fish even admitted to a little jealousy over Eddy Sacks. Then they laughed and laughed and that was how they left each other.

King Fish became invincible. The daily run became a delight to him. The work like child's play. The reasons for this were twofold. His body had conditioned itself and mentally he had risen above his physical state. He abandoned his body for long stretches of time. Only his monthly visits, Raymond, and the letters kept him grounded at all. The letter that would catapult him to freedom had not yet come. Six months passed, then a year. Both King Fish and Carolyn realized the awful truth, but they never spoke it. They had to have something to hold on to, something to hope for. She came without fail the first Sunday of every month. She was always smartly dressed and full of optimism. Her hair was down to her shoulders by now, and by now, King Fish had learned to like it. This Sunday she had a surprise for him.

"I met someone who wants to help," she said. "A lawyer who just joined the NAACP. He said we should petition the next governor who comes into office and raise the race question, the inequities the Negro faces under this justice system. If that doesn't work, we should appeal to the president."

"Sounds good, baby."

But somehow none of it sounded good to him. He could not continue to dismiss a cold reality. He was never getting out. If he hadn't been caught up in his and Carolyn's dream, he would have realized it from the start. Raymond had wanted to tell him. Even the other inmates knew it. He had killed a white man. The governor couldn't have pardoned him even if he had wanted to. It would have been political suicide. Strangely enough, he felt a sense of relief. As if a great weight had been lifted from somewhere. He smiled and played the game for her.

Raymond left that year. He had finally won one for himself. He and King Fish took one last turn around the bunkhouse.

"I learned something from you, Fish. How to really be a man. I may be educated but I learned that from you. It all comes down to how well you handle adversity. I won't forget you, man."

"You dun helped a lot of folks. That's what ya do. That's yo' life. Live it, man. Lotsa folks won't fo'git you either. 'Specially me."

Raymond was crying openly that Sunday. The entire bunkhouse walked him as far as the trustee would permit. They cheered him the rest of the way.

For two full years she was a faithful and dedicated **13** wife. In the spring of the third year he noticed a change. He sensed a new kind of freedom in her spirit, ever so slight, as it was, but nothing had altered their situation to warrant it. There were other signs. Her hair, which was always impeccably styled, had on more than one occasion looked rushed. But the most telling sign was her eyes. Although they still smiled, they were not engaging as before; in fact, they avoided his and that was when he was sure she had been with another man. He quickly camouflaged his pain by recalling to mind a moment of humor, a time when she had been angry with him and had intentionally cooked the worst meal of his life. She responded with laughter that was forced. Now he realized the end was drawing near. In that same year, after struggling with her conscience, steeped in guilt for months at a time, she came to him. It was in her walk, strong and reaffirmed, like one who has made peace with her new direction. He was not being noble, but there was only one course left to him. He must salvage what he could of his pride and character, lest he give up both in total despair. He released her before she had a chance to free herself. His eyes bored into hers.

"Girl, you listen and get it good. Don't say nothin' till I git through. What you gotta look at in life is what's true and what ain't. What's true is, I'm a dead man and I ain't never gonna raise."

She started to speak but he held up his hand.

"Git yo'self a life, girl. Git you a good man and have some babies. Just think 'bout ol' James every now and then. Now gaw on. Ain't no mo'."

Still, he had grown accustomed to her presence and was missing her even as he spoke, but he had one thing in his favor, his mind. He could still control his mind.

She felt a sense of freedom when she walked through the gate for what she knew would be the last time. It was as if she were waking up from a nightmare, experiencing a new birth or shedding an old habit. She hated the guards with their hungry eyes that undressed her at every turn, and the inmates, who she knew included her in their nightly fantasies, the stench, the ignorance, the foul language, all of it made her deathly sick now. Still, Carolyn was a little confused. King Fish had taken her line and set her free without so much as a struggle. He had let her go and King Fish was a known fighter. Had she meant so little to him? Suddenly she realized that no one walks away from any relationship completely unscathed. She had been wounded too.

Fate had not been kind.

BOOK TWO

Jimmie Lamar

1944

I have to tell my story. I have to for my mother and Masaya, and for all of those who believed in me, even for those who didn't. To clarify the record on how I came to be who I am, I tell it, but maybe, most of all, because I have a need to keep the memory of King Fish alive. The truth is, without his and Masaya's influence, my life would have been no more than ordinary.

My name is Jimmie Lamar and I knew King Fish less than nine months, yet I knew him better than anyone. You see, we were both members of that small society known to only a few as grifters, and grifters understand things squares can never figure, or they wouldn't be squares, at least that was my thinking before I met Mom Myrtle.

It was a mild February day in New Orleans when I pulled into the gas station. The Cadillac had lived up to its reputation as the best automobile in America. I had made it from New York with record-breaking speed, in time for the Mardi Gras. "Fill her up, sport," I told the red-faced attendant who stood staring in amazement. I tossed him my keys and hurried in the direction of where I thought a bathroom should be. "The one what says colored," the attendant cautioned. My temper ran hot and I slowed down. I was young then, in my twenties, and arrogant, but I checked myself. I was no fool. I had heard about the South. Mississippi, Arkansas, and Alabama were places to stay away from, I was told. No such advice was given to me about New Orleans. All I had heard about this city were stories of fine Creole women, good food, and a party that went on for days called Mardi Gras. I had come to believe this to be a different South; or you can bet I would have never come in this direction. Still, I was cautious. That's what "the game" teaches.

When I returned from the "colored" restroom my car was surrounded by three ofays, the attendant and two of his friends. I knew what those hicks must have been thinking about me, a cat wearing a Brooks Brothers dark blue suit, the same color as his Cadillac. The attendant was studying the license plate.

"Y'all from up thar in New Yark City, huh, boy?"

His eyes darted back and forth between the two men for support; satisfied, he became bolder.

"Sho' is a mighty fine automobile fo' a Nigra."

He began rubbing the hood. This was a situation easy to grasp. They were looking for trouble. I called on "the game."

"Ain't my car; belongs to my boss, Mr. White. I'm just a chauffeur. And he don't like nobody puttin' fingerprints on his car."

The man hadn't expected this. I decided to teach them a New York lesson.

"How much I owe?"

I slipped a fifty-dollar bill and a single from my bankroll.

"Two dollars and fifty cents," the attendant said, his eyes focusing on the fifty-dollar bill.

"Damn, thought I had some change." I reached in my pocket and peeled off two more fifties. "Nope. Can you change a fifty?"

"Can't change no fifty hea, boy."

I searched myself again and this time I pulled a deck of playing cards from my inside suit pocket.

"Whatcha got there, boy? You one of them slicksters from up thar in New Yark?"

"No, suh, me and my boss just play high card sometimes."

I chuckled to myself.

"One time he won my pay for two weeks." I paused. "You guys don't play high card, do you? I mean, I'll give you the dollar I have and we can play high card for the dollar-fifty."

I began to shuffle the cards with the bottom card facing them, making sure the ace was always visible and always on the bottom. Then after removing one for myself, I spread the cards on the hood of the car and placed the fifty-dollar bill beside it.

"Pick a card from anywhere in the deck."

The three men smiled at each other.

"Okay, boy, you got it."

The attendant pulled the ace from the bottom and turned it over. I had the four of clubs.

"Now you owe me three dollars, boy. We still ain't got no change."

I began shuffling the cards again. This time a king was visible on the bottom. I spread the cards and left the fifty-dollar bill on the hood.

"Can we play the whole three dollars?"

"You got it, boy!" the attendant exclaimed, nudging the man to his right.

"You can pick first, this time," I said.

The attendant turned over the king of hearts. I pulled the jack of diamonds. The three men broke into laughter. I didn't respond. Slowly I picked up the cards and began to shuffle. The three men looked at each other and smiled. The routine was repeated with the queen showing at the bottom.

"I wanna bet the six," I said. "I gotta win one."

The attendant looked to his friends, who shook their heads.

"Shuffle them cards, boy, till I say stop."

"Okay," I said, shuffling until a king could be seen by the men.

"That's enough," the attendant said. "I'll bet the whole six."

I looked at the attendant then covered my mouth to keep them from seeing my smile.

"Ya still ain't got no change and I feel lucky this time. Tell ya what, I'll bet my change if you gentlemen can cover it."

"What ya say, Bob? Will?"

"I'm in," Will said.

"Okay," Bob agreed.

They reached into their pockets until their grubby hands produced enough to cover the forty-four-dollar balance; then they laid the money on the hood. I set the deck facedown beside it. I ran my middle finger and thumb quickly along the sides, smoothly removing a card. Then I spread the deck. The attendant quickly slid the bottom card from the deck and turned it over. The king of spades stared me in the face. I couldn't resist being clever.

"That's a good card, boss."

The men's eyes lit up.

"But it don't win."

I laid the ace of spades on top of it. I left them in dismay and drove a few blocks before stopping a group of white soldiers and asking them where the colored section was. They had been there the night before and had heard some real jazz, they told me. The Cadillac made them think I was a famous musician. I left them that way. Then I thought of those three hicks. I laughed all the way to the ninth ward. This had been one of the first card swindles Mr. Williams had taught me. The cards had been what hustlers called "drags." One simply removed an ace from a deck and then sanded the remaining cards. Any expert cardplayer could locate the slightly larger ace anywhere in the deck and remove it without detection. The bar I pulled in front of read LUCKY GENTS. Sounded like me. Checking out the scenes in New Orleans. The mental rhyme made me smile to myself. The Lucky Gents was a joke. It was a dive. I was greeted by the smell of greasy hamburgers, loud music, and an overweight patron who insisted I was the finest man she had ever seen. She reeked of alcohol and cheap perfume. She pulled me stumbling to the dance floor and then crushed me against her overly large breasts. The music was slow and sexy now, with lots of saxophone, and she moved her hips in a continual grind and snapped her fingers in time to the beat. Her name was JanElla Good.

"And it's good," she told me, pressing her body even closer to mine and breathing hard in my ear.

The floor was crowded and hot, the air thin and filled with smoke. I had to get away. I am not a man who feels that I'm better than any other person because they drink and I'm careful of others' feelings. New York hadn't changed that about me. Besides, she was an older woman and you had to respect your elders. This rule had been taught in the town where I was raised. So I offered to buy her a drink. It worked. But first she wanted one of her girlfriends to meet the "fine young thing," as she called me. Her friend's name was Carmen, and, of course, she was my style. She was a Creole who had never been out of New Orleans, I learned, after JanElla had introduced me as her property and then invited her along for a drink. JanElla, in a loud voice, called the bartender by name and ordered three drinks, then turned and asked me and Carmen what we wanted. We smiled at each other and made our order. Carmen was a pretty girl, around my age, with smoky gray eyes and dimples. She spoke with an accent in language that alternated between broken English and broken French. She repeatedly brushed her hair back from her face with her forefinger, and chewed gum constantly while she talked. The bartender returned and I peeled a bill from my bankroll and paid him.

"Bring us another round and keep the change, sport," I told him.

"You a rich nigga, too, huh, baby?" JanElla said.

"Gimme five dollars."

I handed her a five-dollar bill and she tucked it between her breasts, downed her drink in one gulp, breathed a heavy sigh, started to speak, and passed out on the table.

"I can't drink like that girl, no," Carmen said, in her heavy Creole accent.

"They say the girls down here are real friendly."

"Where you from?"

"New York. Wanta show me around?"

"I ain't never been to New York, no. Matter of fact, I ain't never been no place but New Orleans."

"Tell you what, show me around New Orleans and maybe one day I'll show you around New York."

"Okay," she said quickly.

I held out my hand.

"Where we goin'?"

"Wherever you take me," I said.

She smiled and we headed for the door, both glancing back to see JanElla asleep. Outside, I wrapped my arm around Carmen's shoulder and walked her to my car. She was really surprised. That's when they appeared.

"Okay, let this gal go back in the bar. You come with us."

Again, I called on "the game." In my best professional voice I addressed the situation.

"What seems to be the problem, Officer? I was simply having a drink—"

"Shut up, nigger! Git in the back of this car!" I was shocked.

"The game" made these ofays mad. I did what they told me and one of them got in the backseat with me. Now I'm nervous. I had an idea what it was all about, but I didn't say anything.

"Steal that fancy car, too, boy?" the one in the back asked.

"Ain't stole nothin'," I said.

The one in the front said, "Think y'all can come down hea from New York and take us hicks, do ya?"

"Man, I ain't tryin' to take nobody."

"Next time I tell you to shut up, nigger, I'm gonna put my fist in yo' mouth!"

That ended the conversation. I was even scared to ask about my car when they pulled away from the curb; most of my money, about five grand, was hidden in my spare tire in the trunk.

As soon as we reached the station I was told that I had been arrested for grand-theft person. The gas station attendant's friends said they had seen me pick his pocket. The attendant had claimed a loss of one hundred dollars, which the officer promptly removed from my bankroll to return to the man. That left nine hundred and twenty-two dollars that I had access to. After the mug shots and fingerprints, I was put into a crowded cell, so filthy I was afraid to sit down. It was a large holding cell with twenty or more people ranging in age from fifteen to seventy. There was vomit on the floor and the smell of urine was so strong it brought tears to my eyes. What had I gotten myself into? These country bumpkins looked at me like I was from Mars. I could tell there was not one hustler in the bunch. I didn't talk to them and they had nothing to say to me. I stood in a corner for what seemed like hours. What else could I do? Some pretty rough-looking cats lay sleeping on the few benches. The rest were on the floor, except for an old man who was walking around the cell. In one corner a junkie, doubled over like a folding chair, was kicking cold turkey. In another corner a young kid began to cry.

"Shut up that motherfuckin' noise, punk, so a nigguh can git some sleep!" one giant of a man shouted, rising up from a bench.

He looked around the cell until his bloodshot eyes met mine. Now, let me tell you, I ain't never been no punk. I even used to pug a little, way back when, but this big motherfuckuh scared the shit outta me. I didn't have a weapon, so I prepared my body and spirit for the worse ass-kickin' of my life. As the adrenaline rushed to my brain, my fear subsided. I knew I had to land the first punch and it had to be to his nuts. My gift is reading the language of eyes; when his alerted me, I would attack him without hesitation. Then he smiled.

"You sho' one clean nigguh. Where you from?" he asked, sitting upright.

"New York," I said.

"New York! Knowed it all the time. Got me a cousin in New York. You know Willie Charles Tate? They call him Radio 'cuz he talk so much."

I shook my head. "The city's a big place. Where does he live?"

"Don' know. Well, he told me, but I dun forgot. He was down here last year, though. Nigguhs down hea is lame, he said. I'm goin' up there wit' 'im. I dun made up my mind! Soon I git out this mess."

He walked over and shook my hand.

"They call me Big City."

"Jimmie Lamar. What they got you for?" I asked.

"I kilt a nigguh last week." He said it with no expression and no feeling, as if he had been caught shoplifting.

He also told me this was his second killing, that his lawyer had gotten him off scot-free on the first one. Then he invited me to share his bench. At that moment sitting down was the next best thing to being free. Just as I begun to feel hunger a turnkey shouted, "Slop time, boys!" He opened the door and a colored trustee with sharp streetwise eyes begun passing out tin plates with an unidentifiable substance the color of mud on it, topped with a piece of stale bread. Big City read my expression.

"Got some change, you can eat what the guards eat," he said.

"How much?"

He told me fifty cents would get a plate and a cup of milk, but I'd have to give the trustee a quarter for doing it. The trustee would buy the food from the cook. They had only allowed me to keep twenty-two dollars. The nine hundred was booked into my property along with my watch and ring. I gave Big City two dollars and told him to work with that for us. Not long after, we—me and Big City—were eating hamburgers and french fries with a slice of apple pie. The rest ate their "slop" and wished they were us.

At midnight they called us out: me, Big City, and the young kid, to go to another cell. At least we would have a bed to sleep on now. I had been lucky. Some stay in the holding cell for as long as twelve hours before they are called out. The three of us followed a turnkey down a long hall to an elevator that seemed would never make it the three floors it had to climb. No one spoke a word. I didn't know it then, but that was the rule when people in custody were being transported. The elevator jumped and made a loud noise when it reached its destination, as if it had decided on its own to go further. When the doors opened to this hall there were cells next to each other, all the way down and on both sides. The first one was unlocked and we were told to go inside. There was one man snoring and three empty bunks. Big City wanted a bottom bunk. I didn't care. I was beat. I climbed into the top bunk over him. The kid did the same on the other side. There were no blankets. I laid down on the hard springs the paper-thin mattress didn't cushion and tried to sleep. Big City had no trouble. After only a few words he was gone. Not the same for me. I looked over at the kid who was very still and I felt sorry for him. I wondered what he had done to land him in this place. I wanted to say something to him, but I didn't, probably because I didn't want Big City to think I was weak. I just sat there staring into the darkness, still unable to sleep, questioning the life I had led. Then her words came to me sharp and clear as if she were sitting beside me. My eyes filled up the way they always did when she said them.

"Bet you gonna forget all about me when I'm gone!"

"No, Mama!" I would say, trying to convince her she was wrong. "I ain't never gonna forget you."

The very thought of her dying was almost more than I could take. She was the prettiest woman in the small Ohio town where I was born. Her eyes were the lightest brown I have ever seen, her skin the color of caramel, and her long hair as black as the night. But there were no roses in her story. My father had deserted us soon after I was born, breaking her heart beyond repair, robbing her of her dreams. Young and alone, my mother searched for an escape from her desperateness and found it in a bottle. All of her young life she fought to gain the respect of others, but every attempt she made met with failure. She was pregnant at fifteen, married to the wrong man at sixteen, alone and homeless at seventeen. By twenty-one she had become an alcoholic. Sometimes she would "take heart" and go on the wagon for several weeks. She was beautiful then; but even her beauty had worked against her. In a small town, acceptance into the church is where respectability is born; but she was not well received there. She intimidated the sisters with her great looks, and reminded the deacons they were not as holy as they would have others believe. Even though her life was plagued with losses, she taught me to be a winner. "Never give up on anything. Whatever you can dream you can do," she told me, but she couldn't take her own advice. Maybe she had asked God to forgo her happiness in favor of mine. This I do know, she loved me with a love so complete it was close to worship. I loved her, too, unconditionally, even when her drunkenness embarrassed me. Times were hardest for us before the Depression when she had a baby to care for, no skills, and no husband. We were literally outdoors at one point. Thank God for Old Lady Kane, a kind woman who took a liking to me and my mother and took us in. My mother then found work as a domestic for a very nice white family who paid her a fair wage. They also became fond of her and gave us food, sometimes clothing the missus was tired of, and things her son had outgrown. Mama also took in washing and ironing. Her drinking was not bad then, mostly on weekends. Old Lady Kane, who was actually standing in as my mother's mother, didn't approve. Mama told her she needed something in her life since she didn't have a man. Both of us loved this woman and she us. I can remember her making a special bread pudding that I loved. She also invented numerous games for us to play while Mama was at work. I still to this day can't duplicate the shadow figures her hands made on the wall. I was seven or eight when she died. Me and Mama both took it very hard. Old Lady Kane had no relatives and she left Mama some money and the house. I don't know how much money, but Mama stopped going out to work and stayed home with me. We never wanted for anything the next few years. Mama did continue to take in washing and ironing twice a week, something she taught me. The better I learned to iron, the more she began to drink. I was doing at least half the work. I didn't mind really, it made me feel grown up. Today I can iron as well as any woman and better than most. When she was convinced I was old enough, she began to go out. Sometimes I would surprise her and show up at the Supper Club, her favorite bar, unexpectedly. If she was wearing that closed-mouth smile that told me she had had too much to drink, I would demand she come home. She always obeyed. When I walked her stumbling down the street, giggling like a little girl, the neighbors would shake their heads and whisper, "What a shame!" But the shame was theirs for not caring. At home I would remove her dress and shoes, leaving her slip and underwear, and put her to bed. The next day I would wake her at noon with a peanut-butter sandwich and a glass of warm milk. She would tell me I was her only man and make me so proud! Only two things really mattered to me in my young life, protecting her and keeping her from drinking her life away. It was a losing battle. Strangely enough, it was her words that kept me trying, and try I did. I hid her gin, cried, even threw small fits. Sometimes I would refuse to speak to her for a whole day, but she would grab me and hold so tight, and soak my shirt with her tears until our roles reversed and I was consoling her. But there were fun times—playing catch in the backyard, or the footraces she always let me win. I played hopscotch with her and jumped rope like Big Jake, the town's fighter. She even tried to teach me to box after my first black eye. As the years passed, her drinking grew worse and I was desperate. But there was no one to help me. I said a lot of prayers, even went to church without her. These were the years I learned to fend for myself and for her. I cooked the food, washed the clothes, and still maintained better than a B average in school. To tell the truth, if I had worked at my studies I would have done even better. The fact is, school was easy for me, like football, basketball, and table tennis. My sophomore year in high school I was "all state" in both football and basketball. Already there was talk of me receiving a scholarship to Ohio State.

I met Shirley in the last of my glory years, a twenty-four-year-old woman to my sixteen. She, too, had grown up in Portsmouth, but when I was very young had gone away to college on a music scholarship—it was said with hopes of eventually singing with the Metropolitan Opera. She did treat our junior-high-school class to her talents one summer, and we were all elated with the beauty of her voice. This time she had come back home to fill the vacancy at Jefferson Community Center. We met the second Friday she worked there. The Friday prior to that, which was her first, our team had been in Mansfield, Ohio, taking a sound thrashing from "Big Red," the number-one team in the league. This night we had regained some of our loss status by defeating a very tough Middletown, Ohio. I was in high spirits, having scored the winning touchdown. Me, Bo, and two other players walked into the Center, a small one-story building with a long dance floor that doubled as a Ping-Pong and shuffleboard recreation room when it wasn't Friday night. Bo was our talented fullback who had thrown the key block that had freed me up for the score. He was also Shirley's cousin. The place was crowded, as usual, cast in a blue light, with chairs that no one sat in lined up on either side of the room. And balloons, lots of balloons clinging to the ceiling like living things. I spotted her at the end of the room wearing a formfitting red wool dress. She was tall and personable, and clearly in charge. She was delighted to see Bo, but embraced him with reserve, as Bo was not the mushy type. He introduced me and her extended hand in mine sent a sensation up my arm and warmed my face. Strangely enough, her sophistication failed to mask the little girl in her smile. It was her smile that gave me incentive, told me she was not completely out of my reach. Let's face it, she was a grown woman and I a mere teenager. From her perspective, any relationship with me other than what the city of Portsmouth had intended when they hired her, could be disastrous. It would surely cost her her job. I understood all of this. But I was simply fascinated by her. No one knows what draws one person, like a magnet, to another. I sure didn't. Was it the color of her skin, that soft shade of brown that actually glowed in the blue hue, that enchanted me, or the rich fragrance that coated the air around her. It may have been the long wave of her hair which covered the right side of her face, or the contour of her slightly full figure that almost invited sex. I knew only one thing. My chances to escape her allure were very slim. In most scenarios of this kind, the young man would have trouble with girls. That was certainly not the case with me. There were plenty girls. My athletic prowess saw to that. For that matter, small-town sportswriters even made celebrities of us. Most people, young and old, acknowledged me as a football and basketball star. But this "woman" never mentioned sports once during the small talk. In fact, she asked me a question I thought was strange.

"I know Bo hasn't, but have you ever seen a play, Jimmie?"

I told her I hadn't.

"The reason I was asking . . . I think, well, I'm sure I can get a sponsor to send a group of kids from the center to Columbus to see a live play."

Bo responded for me and him. "Shirley, don't nobody wanta see no play."

"Speak for yourself, Bo," she said, then looked at me. "What about you, Jimmie?"

I heard myself say yes. Her eyes sparkled when I looked into them, and at that moment I would have gone anywhere with her. She smiled.

"Fine! Bo, you ought to think about it. There are other things in the world besides football. Will you guys excuse me for a moment?"

She had spotted a shy timid kid named Pat standing alone, as he always did, next to the jukebox. Because of his beautiful curly hair, flawless skin, and easy manner, we named him Patty Cake. To us, he looked and acted like a sissy, an observation, I for one, have regretted all of my life. I could have saved Pat from a tragic end. I truly believe this. I was so popular it would have cost me nothing to befriend him, to let him feel a small part of our teenage years. Our last year in high school Pat shocked the whole town and took his own life. The newspaper said he put the barrel of his father's shotgun in his mouth and pulled the trigger. At times that image still disturbs my sleep.

This night I took Shirley's leaving as rejection. But why should I have? She had no way of knowing what I was thinking. This was my sensitivity where she was concerned. I was still a teen and I did what teens do, tried to make a woman jealous who hardly knew my name. I left Bo standing there and headed straight for Fanny Burns, the "Grinding Queen" as we called her, because of the sensuous way she slow danced. Fanny's full breasts and tight skirt proved she had the best shape in town. She was also the best dancer. She was not pretty but had a grown-up way about her, as if she knew things we boys didn't. She gave me a sultry look when she took my hand, like an invitation to much more than a dance. It was a slow tune and I could feel the complete outline of her body, feel her heat. And Fanny Burns did to me what she did to every boy who danced with her, caused the front of my pants to protrude.

"See what you just did?" I whispered.

"Mm-hmm," she cooed.

"What you gonna do about it?" I asked.

Her arm tightened around my back and she thrust herself hard against me. Her body from the stomach down began a rolling motion that increased her breathing, along with mine. When the song ended she smiled up at me and, before I could speak, rushed laughing over to a group of girls. Now my ego was suffering from my second rejection. More than a few boys had bragged about how good her trim was and they didn't even play football. I wanted her more than any girl in school, not to love, but to have sex with. That's the way I viewed females, in two categories: promiscuous or nice. Shirley was nice, therefore she deserved love. Fanny Burns got what she deserved—a big dick. Like I said, I was young then. I eased out the door and tried to hide my embarrassment with my hand. It was cold out there on the porch, but I didn't want to go back inside. I began to walk. I tried to be tough-minded with women, like James Cagney or Humphrey Bogart would be, but the thought of Shirley melted my fortitude like candle wax. Before I realized it, I had walked the seven blocks to my small two-bedroom house. Mama wasn't home. Instead of going to the Supper Club, I lay down across my bed and fell asleep fully dressed, listening to the radio.

The next day, I woke my mother with lots of kisses all over her face.

"Boy, if you don't stop! Honey, I'm trying to sleep."

"Okay," I threatened, "if you don't want to hear the news."

She rose up in bed. I knew that would get her.

"Okay, Jimmie, what?"

"I'm in love!" I told her.

"Oh Jimmie! With what little girl this time?"

"It's a woman this time, Mama."

"A woman! What woman wanta mess with you?"

"I ain't said she was in love—I said I was. That's what I want
to talk to you about."

"Okay, talk. Who is this she?"

"Shirley."

"Shirley?"

"She runs the center now."

"You talkin' 'bout Shirley Hunter—the one that sings."

I shook my head.

"Boy, she's old as me."

"Naw she ain't, Mom."

"Well, she's at least ten years older than you."

"That don't make no difference to me, Mama."

She looked up at the sky and breathed a heavy sigh. "How long
you been talkin' to Shirley?"

"Just last night."

"Boy, if you don't get outta my face. I know you crazy now."

Before I could respond someone knocked on the door. It was
Bo. He was a big kid, better than two hundred pounds, who always
moved slow until he got on the football field. Then he was like a
speeding runaway train. I opened the door and he came inside.

"Shirley's making pizza. She told us to come over."

"She told you to bring me?"

"If you want to come."

"That's cool," I said.

Bo didn't see me smile at Mama, who shook her head.

Me and Bo walked to Shirley's house on Fourteenth Street, but
we took the long way around, over to Twelfth Street, where a fat
pimp by the name of Two Ton Brown ran a cathouse. Two Ton
smoked a big cigar and drove a fairly new Buick. On his finger sat
a large diamond ring and he would sometimes toss change in the
air for young kids to scramble for. We hoped to see one of the
girls walking to Sam Quickies, the all-purpose store on the corner.
Two Ton's girls were young and sometimes very pretty, which
drew him a mostly white clientele from downtown. A few blocks
down the street ol' man Jim Moran ran a clip joint filled with
rowdy men and treacherous females who were usually too loud and

too big to appeal to me and Bo. Even the boldest white men shied away from that place. Two Ton Brown's big shiny car sat in front of his place, but in front of his car was parked a late-model pea-green Buick owned by no one other than Play-Boy's father. He was emerging from the side door just as we walked past the house. Maybe he was getting today's number bets from the girls, but we preferred to believe he was getting something else. Now we had something to tease our friend Play-Boy about. In our hearts we wished we could trade places with his father.

One summer when me and Bo were younger and dark had fallen, we came as close as we could get. After feeding Two Ton's bad dog scraps every day for a month through the linked fence that surrounded his backyard, we decided this was the evening, since the last few times the dog had been so happy to see us. We climbed the fence carrying two ham bones with lots of fat that the butcher from Sam Quickies had given us. That big black dog just wagged its tail and went to those bones. At the back window we took turns looking through a hole in the shade. We saw everything. It was the best secret in the world and the major event of our lives until we got our first piece.

I was very hungry when we got to Shirley's house. When she opened the door the aroma of hot pizza hit me in the face. A miniature apron around her waist was the only other evidence she had worked in the kitchen at all. She was wearing a pair of brown tailored slacks, brown heels, and a yellow satin blouse.

"You guys are right on time."

She ushered us inside and we followed her to the kitchen. We sat down at a table with a red-checkered plastic cloth while Shirley went to the stove. She spoke with her back turned to us.

"Bo, did you get a culture attack overnight and change your mind about going to the play?"

I laughed.

Bo said, "Give all that culture stuff to them sissies. Give me the football."

She screamed. I thought that was a pretty strong response. Then I saw her shaking her fingers and blowing on them. I rushed over to her and put her hand under cold running water in the sink, the way my mother had treated my burns. For a moment she looked into my eyes and I was tempted to kiss her. There was a quick silence and looks that almost spoke words. She recovered and served our pizza with Coca-Cola.

Surprising enough, it was Shirley who brought up the subject of football. She wanted to know if I was going to college. I didn't know. That seemed to disappoint her. We followed her into the living room and she put on a Latin jazz record. Then she taught me the basic steps of the mambo. Bo, who could not dance at all, was bored stiff. Next, it was the cha-cha. Attitude gave it all the Latin flavor. Throwing back her head and kicking up her heels behind her reminded me of a matador. That picture remained in my mind all week long, at school and even after school on the football field. Thinking about Shirley, I threw two interceptions during our interteam practice game.

Friday night came again quickly, but first there was the game with Springfield that we barely won, where I failed to shine. The coach chewed us out and asked me where I was. "You sure wasn't at that game," he said. But the players made me feel better. We were that way as a team. We were solid. Even the difference in our race was not a factor when it came to winning football games. I used to think about that sometimes, how white folks seemed to love you if you could win for them. And the white players on the team would not hesitate to come to the aid of another teammate, colored or white, even if it meant fighting. We showered together and talked about our favorite subject—pussy. We all lied about how much we had gotten. When we dressed, we were proud to wear the word "Trojans," the name of our team, across the back of our lettered jackets. We were proud of our team, our school, and our city. But we did not really live together. The boundaries that divided us were not articulated, only etched in our minds. As soon as school was out or the game was over, we went our separate ways as if we had only known each other in passing. Three other boys hung with me and Bo: Speedy, a small wisecracking kid who got his name because of the rapid way he talked. Spike was our team's tall tight end, with the second-best reception record in the league, who was an even better player on the basketball court. He got his nickname by leaping high and stuffing the basketball into the net. And there was Play-Boy, who never started a game, a kid spoiled rotten, who was on the team only because his father, the town's numbers bookie, demanded it of him. He got his name because he dressed like a playboy. It was his new Ford convertible we rode in. The first thing he said when we left the stadium pissed me off.

"Hey, Bo!" he called over his shoulder to the backseat. "You sho' got a fine cousin."

"You got a fine mama!" Bo cut back.

We all laughed.

"See? I ain't playin' no dozens wit' you, Bo. I ain't said nothin' 'bout your mother," Play-Boy whined.

Bo started again. "I ain't gonna talk 'bout yo' mama, Play-Boy, but me and Jimmie seen yo' daddy comin' outta Two Ton Brown's with his dick in his hand."

We cracked up for five minutes.

"C'mon Bo!" Play-Boy pleaded.

"Then git off me 'bout my cousin, nigguh."

Speedy couldn't resist a comment. "I ain't got nothin' ta do wit' it, Bo, but he sho' right."

"Fuck you, Speedy!"

But that's as far as it went. Nobody, not even Bo, wanted to play the dozens with Speedy. He had been known to make some boys cry talking about their parents. Speedy had rapid-fire quips like: "yo' mama so ugly she'd made a stick horse throw her," or, "yo' daddy so greasy you can't catch him with a pair of ice hooks." Suddenly everybody wanted to get hamburgers. I didn't have any money, but as usual, Play-Boy paid for me. Even then, I was aware what it meant for him to run with me. Maybe the only difference between Play-Boy and Patty Cake was that Play-Boy's father had money, which in a way bought Play-Boy popularity. I sure hoped we didn't see my mother. The Supper Club was only across the street and a few doors down from where we were going. I hated for my friends to see her drunk. There was only one thing on the mind of a sixteen-year-old and I didn't want my mother, in her vulnerability, to be the object of their lust. Bo, as usual, wanted to ride past Two Ton Brown's, which again was out of the way. Everyone agreed. In the summer the girls would often sit on the porch and we would drive by and ask them for a blow job; then we would speed away, laughing. I don't know what we expected to see on a cold January night. Maybe the thought of what went on inside of Two Ton Brown's excited us. Anything can spark the sexual imagination of teenage boys.

When we got to Twelfth Street three white men got out of a car and walked toward Two Ton's place. Speedy told Play-Boy to slow down. "Y'all gon' yodel in the canyon?" he shouted. That's what oral sex by a man was called. The men turned around, and like always, we sped away, laughing. No colored man or boy would admit to giving a woman "head." We pretended that only white men did that. I laughed louder than everyone to divert any suspicion from myself, because I was guilty as hell. Her name was Cynthia Prichard and she had transferred from junior high school in Baltimore, Maryland, to our all-colored junior high school. We were only integrated when we reached Portsmouth High School. It was the night of our prom and Cynthia was beautiful in a silver-blue dress nicely complemented by the white corsage I had given her. Mama thought so too. We double-dated with Play-Boy and his girl, whose name I forget. It was after the dance, in the backseat of the car, which was parked on the side of a seldom-traveled road, that I was compelled by some unknown force inside of me to put my head underneath all those ruffles. Luckily, Play-Boy was busy in the front seat with his date. What a chance I had taken. For the exact same act Josh Hamilton had almost been ostracized from our community. Sonya told everyone who would listen how Josh "yodeled" in her canyon and you would have thought he had the plague. Mothers would pull their children close when he came near and no one would even shake Josh's hand. I was saved, I'm sure, by Cynthia's moving back to Baltimore. Until this day I can still smell and taste "Mum," the underarm deodorant she had applied between her legs. I have often wondered what drove me to take such a risk in that small town. The conclusion I come to is always the same. I could never resist a dare. It was the same reason I climbed to the top of the reservoir, boxed with Big Jake, or tried for admittance at the segregated swimming pool. All of these things were done on a dare. With Cynthia Prichard, I suppose I dared my own self.

We stopped at Lucille's, a greasy spoon with no name on the window, and got our hamburgers. "No onions on mine," I told Lucille, a heavyset woman who smiled all the time and openly flirted with all the football players. After we had swallowed our burgers almost whole, we piled back into the car headed for the center. Bo wanted to drive back past Two Ton's, but we booed him and went to the dance. We parked right in front and walked cool and slow, like gangsters in the movies, showing off our lettered jackets that only the heros of Friday-night sports were permitted to wear. We were the only kids to arrive in a late-model car; in fact, there were only two other colored kids in the town who owned a car: Ronnie Washington, a great basketball player, who attended St. Mary's Catholic School, and Johnny Simms, who shined shoes downtown; but both were old cars. Ronnie was the only colored boy at St. Mary's. One mixed girl went there but didn't live in our community. Ronnie was a big star at St. Mary's and we kinda envied him because the prettiest white girl at his school was his, in secret, of course, but not to us. She was bold enough to come to the center one Friday night and upstage the colored girls with her blond hair. Because white girls were forbidden fruit, we all wanted to experience one. Ronnie kept us wide-eyed with stories about him and her petting in the backseat of his car. I really don't know if he ever went all the way with her; at least he never told us. The first person we saw was Ronnie, wearing St. Mary's colors of blue and yellow. He was talking to several players from Springfield, who wore jackets of purple and white. On the dance floor Fanny Burns was dancing close to the flashy halfback on their team. The place seemed even more crowded tonight, but I still managed to glimpse Shirley looking away. The guys fanned out in the direction of their favorite girl. I made it to the far end, where Shirley stood close to the jukebox. The song was almost over and I put in a bid for the next one. She accepted. Now I hoped it was a slow tune. They usually played two fast and two slow. I got my wish and she was in my arms—not too close and not too far away. I could feel her breasts firm against my body and her minted breath on my neck.

"I heard you all won tonight?"

I shook my head like a donkey. I knew she was trying to make conversation, but my tongue froze in my mouth. She pulled back her head and looked up at me. I was six-one at sixteen.

"You are a good dancer, Jimmie!"

"You too," I managed feebly.

Then there was nothing until the record was over. She thanked me and I walked her back to where she had been standing. Before I had a chance to redeem myself, a girl came over and pulled her away on woman's business. I knew those whispers by now. I made it to the other end of the floor, speaking to a couple of the girls I knew had eyes for me. Feeling very stupid and looking for something to do, I anticipated the next record and had Fanny's hand as soon as the first note was played. I wanted to show off. I guess she did, too, for the two Springfield guys who were standing around her. We made a hip dance team and this time we drew a crowd. I had learned a showstopping move from a dancer I had seen in one of those colored movies. I spun completely around, did the splits, and pretended to pull myself up by the back of my collar. I spotted Shirley clapping enthusiastically, with a big smile on her face. When it was over everyone yelled their approval. Shirley stood waiting for me to come her way.

"You are just full of talent, Jimmie! What else can you do?"

I found my confidence and my voice. "I ain't trying to brag, Shirley, but I can do anything I want. My mom taught me that."

She was pleasantly surprised and very much impressed.

"That's something I want to get across to young colored kids," she said.

She slowly and silently nodded her head a couple of times, then said, "Yes! I like that, Jimmie." A slow tune began to play, and before I could finish nodding my head she was in my arms. I could feel her closer to me this time. She even seemed to be responding to my gentle embrace. I swear I could feel her arm tighten around my back, but I still couldn't believe it. She was so much more than me in my mind: a grown woman, a brain, and the director of the center. She was also well thought of, not only by the community, but in the town too. There was no logical reason I could think of for her to be interested in me the way I was interested in her. I knew I was a football star and the girls thought I was nice looking, but again, she was a grown woman and the other was teenage stuff. We danced on in silence. My heart beat like a snare drum. I tried to think about the plays I would call against Hamilton next week to avoid the embarrassing erection I was experiencing. When the song ended I thought I saw on her face a flicker of a smile. Then she told me to ask Bo if he was still walking her home. I was quick to volunteer my services. She smiled again and thanked me and again her smile was like that of a little girl. I hung around her the rest of the evening, dancing with her on every third song so as not to seem too forward.

When the dance was over, I told the boys I was staying to help Shirley clean up. They all gave me looks. I also told Bo I would walk her home. Cleaning up consisted of folding a few chairs, wiping a table, and push-brooming the floor. After that she locked up and we were on our way. It was cold but I didn't mind. Even the snow flurries added something to the night. We walked all the way in silence, but I could feel something I wasn't sure of from her, something I still couldn't bring myself to trust. It was not a long walk, maybe ten short small-town blocks. She smiled at me once and I did the same. When we arrived at her house I could almost swear she hesitated long enough for me to kiss her. She smiled again and told me she would see me on Friday. I hastened to say that I would walk her home every night, except on the Fridays when we played out of town. She thought that was nice, smiled again, and went inside.

When I got home Mama had a big surprise for me, or a shock. Big, because of the man towering over her and me like a street lamp. She stood there like a little girl who was waiting for her father's approval. She began talking fast.

"This is Mr. Henry. He's my boyfriend and he don't drink and he don't smoke, and he's a Pullman porter."

Then she looked at me with pleading eyes. "I like him, Jimmie."

I heard something almost desperate in her voice that touched me very deeply. This is my chance for happiness, she was telling me and that made me want to give the man a chance.

"I'm Jimmie."

I held out my hand and made myself smile.

"You can call me Grady John, everybody does."

My mother rushed into my arms. "Thank you!" she whispered.

I went to bed that night trying not to be possessive about Mama.

The next morning the three of us had breakfast and Mama did the cooking. She didn't eat much but Grady John and I stuffed ourselves. She just drank tomato juice and smiled a lot.

"Your mother tells me you play the heck outta football and basketball. I'd like to come and see you play."

"We go to Hamilton next week, then there's the homecoming game and only four more."

"Grady John used to play professional baseball; tell him, Grady John," my mother said.

"Oh, it wasn't all that. I tried out for a team in the National Negro League when they first started."

I asked him what happened.

"I got a pitching job with the Blue Jays. It didn't pay too much. We was all just startin' out and everything. Then this job came along with the railroad."

"You took a job with the railroad?"

"Yep, same one I got now."

"Why? You could be rich!"

He smiled. "I couldn't gamble. I had a new baby to take care of."

"You got a baby?"

"That was a long time ago. He's your age now, lives in St. Louis with his mother."

"He play football?"

"No, but he's smart in school."

Mama was pleased we were talking. She was hoping I would impress him. He was trying to impress me. He was a nice man, I had to admit that, with friendly eyes and a pleasant smile. He wasn't handsome like the picture I had of my father, but nice. The most important thing was, he made my mother happy. When he was not on the road, and at home with us, they spent every minute together, mostly in the bedroom. She would come out blushing always when she saw me. The rooms were small and the walls very thin. She knew I could hear them, but I pretended I couldn't. I must admit, I was uneasy about it at first, maybe even a little angry. No, mad is a better word. If there is one thing in this world a manchild doesn't like, it's the thought of his mother having sex with a strange man. That was my feeling, at least. But like I said, seeing her really happy for the first time changed all of that. Seeing her completely sober drew me to this man. He liked me too. I could tell by the support he gave me, the way he stressed the importance of me going to college. My mother would smile during these times and wrap her arms around his. On his insistence, they both came to my homecoming game. I was really excited. It was like having both a father and a mother. We won the game, but I could have played better. Still, life was fine for me. Shirley and I had become even more friendly. I had become even more in love. Bo thought I was crazy. "You just a kid to her," he told me. I knew he hadn't talked to her about me. He wasn't that way. Anyway, what did he know? He didn't even have a girl. I continued to walk her home on the Friday nights we played in town, inhaling her perfume, watching the stars, listening to the sound of her heels against the pavement. Always the words I had rehearsed remained silent and unborn, only to be conceived again and again then aborted at a later date. There were still the Saturday evenings with her and Bo. The gin-rummy games we played. The pennies I won went into her bank. She played the piano and sang Broadway tunes to us, and read poetry. Sometimes we just listened to rhythm-and-blues songs on the radio. The thoughts that ran through my mind when Bo would leave and we were alone. Should I dare? This was crazy! Maybe there was a chance. Her eyes would never leave mine when she sang a love song. Still the fear of her rejection would not let me kiss her.

It happened in November, when icicles hung like sparkling daggers from glazed treetops, when mounds of fresh snow hid the ground beneath it. The air was cool and winter clean. That was when I told her I loved her. The words had come without warning, like a whisper echoing softly through the night, catching us both by surprise. She stopped and studied my face. Then she turned away. I knew I had lost her, maybe even her friendship. Then I heard her words, far away, speaking from some distant place inside of her.

"I love you too," she confessed. "I don't know how or why, but I love you too," she repeated softly.

We walked to her house in silence.

The news of our affair hadn't sent shock waves throughout the community as one would have expected. Shirley was held in such high regard she hadn't been reproached, even questioned. There was talk, of course, but most looked on it as a charming courtship, chiefly because of my maturity and because of who I was. Still, out of respect for small-town morality we could not flaunt our relationship. This is the hypocrisy of small towns. Everything is said in whispers, nothing straightforward. We were forced to play the game called "the secret everybody knows." To me and Shirley it was more than just a simple affair. We were, in spite of our age difference, very serious. All logic said we were mad. My mother shook her head and joked about it. Grady John agreed; even Pam, Shirley's closest friend, spoke against it. But we were undaunted. It was the happiest time of my life. This time I had everything. Mama was sober and smiling, her amber eyes twinkling, and I had captured the classiest woman in town.

When basketball season had arrived my jumpshot was working

perfectly. We even defeated East Tech, last year's state champions, in our second game. Grady John and Mama were there. I was inspired and scored twenty-one points. That night after the dance, I walked Shirley home. And that night we made love for the first time. She taught me how to control my passion, to be in sync with her. And she taught me patience. I emerged from her house that next morning with a new confidence, a man who had proven himself. What a night it had been! I had satisfied a real woman.

At home I made Mama laugh, bragging about my sexual prowess. She did not mind Shirley. I could sense she was pleased that Shirley Hunter was interested in me. We had fun that day. I helped her cook this big meal for Grady John, who had taken on extra work and would be coming in that evening. She looked younger somehow, more alive than I had ever seen her, even prettier. That evening the three of us had dinner like one happy family. Three days later the letter came. Grady John was back on the road. When I got home from school she was sitting in her room, wearing only a slip, sobbing her heart out. A half-empty bottle of gin sat on the nightstand next to an empty glass. Beside the glass was the opened letter. She hadn't bothered to lift up her head when I walked into the room. I guess the weight of the alcohol wouldn't let her. I picked up the letter.

I'm writing to tell you Mama died. We buried her last week. You should know she never forgave you for running off with my husband-to-be. Neither did I.

Bessy

I could feel the hate. She didn't even address my mother. She could have given her a little respect, said "Dear Mae" or "Dear Sister." I didn't like this aunt named "Bessy."

"Now you can hate me too." Her voice slurred while her head bobbed up and down.

She still didn't look up.

"I ain't never gonna hate you, Mama. This is why you never wanted to talk about your family? You could have told me, Mama."

"Explain to a kid how I stole his father from my sister? Well, she doesn't know it, but she got the best end of the deal."

She reached for the glass. A sudden rage overtook me. I knocked the gin bottle off the table into the wall. It didn't even break.

"How could you do this, Mama, to me, and to Grady John!" I screamed.

Now she raised her head. A quick pitiful laugh escaped her lips.

"Do this to you, and Grady John? What about me, huh? What about *me*?" she screamed back.

I had to leave the house. I didn't want her to see me cry. While I was walking, the tears came. I headed for Waller Street, a road without sidewalks, mostly traveled by car.

It was small-town quiet. I let it all out then, all the pain, all the anger. I cleansed myself with tears. It was my first real lesson on life, a lesson I would learn over and over again. Happiness and sorrow follow each other. I walked under the viaduct into the white neighborhood. People passing waved at me. I was Friday's hero, but no more. What a strange town, where people touched your heart with their admiration, but wouldn't sit at a dinner table with you or swim in the same pool.

When I returned home Mama was asleep. That made me angry. She could sleep after all that had happened, after throwing it all away? Grady John would not stay with her. I knew that. I could sense the kind of man he was. Life to him was uncomplicated. You learned what the right thing was and you just did it. If you gave your word, you just kept it. He had given up the chance to shine with a professional team in favor of a sure, steady job. That told everything about this proud man. I knew I could never be like him, but I had great admiration for the simple way he approached life, for the strength he had to live it his way. As it turned out, I was right about it all. He came home on the weekend and Mama was smashed. He didn't say a word, but the look on his face told everything. The hurt, the betrayal, the loss of confidence, all were contained in that look. Mama added insult to great injury.

"What you lookin' at me like that for? Never seen a lady take a drink. Oh, I know, you're too good. Well, why don't you take your too good ass outta my house and leave me alone?"

Grady John did just that. He packed his things and left. At the door he told me he was sorry. She never saw him again. I learned something about Mama that day. She never expected to be happy. She didn't think she deserved it, like some people who can't take success. Failure and loneliness are welcome companions.

Her drinking became worse, along with her crying. She pulled me down with her. It began for the first time to affect everything in my life—basketball, my studies, even my relationship with Shirley. Maybe it was because I really believed, for the first time, she had gotten over her problem. Even the five scholarship offers hadn't lifted my spirits. I did graduate that year, but Mama wasn't there. Shirley came, but it wasn't enough. My heart was so sad it made Shirley cry. Her efforts to make me feel better succeeded, but only for a while, only during the intensity of our lovemaking. Afterward she held me against her breasts.

"You have to let her go, Jimmie. Live your own life, be your own man."

She didn't understand. Me and my mother had a special bond. We had gone through every adversity together.

"Deserting my mother won't make me a man, Shirley."

"Every young man sooner or later deserts his mother. That's the way life is."

"This ain't the same, Shirley. She's in trouble."

"There's nothing you can do, Jimmie. I know how you must feel, believe me. Please listen to me!"

She held my face in her hands. Her eyes burned into mine. Very plainly she repeated, "There's nothing you can do!" I didn't say any more. There was no use. We were missing each other. I had learned something too. There are situations you can never abandon, even if all the evidence says you should. I had to leave. The crack in our relationship would only widen if I stayed. I tried to smooth it over with a kiss, but her teeth stood firm behind her lips. There was no response when I walked to the door. But I knew she didn't want me to go. I had learned something about women from my mother and her. Sometimes they gave misleading signals. My mother had done this with Grady John. Her cry of pain had come out as an insult.

The night was warm and peaceful the way small-town summer nights are. I would walk to the Supper Club. It was Thursday, my graduation night, time to celebrate. Every year Danny, the club's owner, would permit the graduates inside for one night only. Walking along, I was still troubled that Shirley saw me as an adolescent clinging to his mother's apron strings. The truth is, I was growing into my manhood, and determined to protect and defend her no matter what. My mother had done the same for me all of my life. I hoped Shirley wasn't trying to make me choose between her and Mama. The thought made me uneasy. I'm not saying Shirley had no claim on me. This was not the case. Promises had been made, commitments as strong as marriage as soon as I completed my second year in college. Then we would be sure, we had agreed. She had stood by me in those months when the weight of the world was too much. It was her loving embrace and words of confidence that gave me the strength to hold on. Still, I could feel myself losing ground. Maybe Shirley was right. Maybe that's what made me angry. I didn't want her to be right. Where is it written that one must draw the line even where someone you love is concerned? And if it is written, who determines when it is time? Is it the first disappointment they hand you, the second, third, or tenth? Maybe it was one of the mysteries life tosses at you, something you have to feel your way through. One thing for sure, I was learning about the concentrated power of true femininity.

Although our courtship remained in the shadows, the desire to be in each other's presence overpowered our caution. Like I said, there existed in our town a strange hypocrisy. We were permitted this secret love that everybody knew about, but could not openly flaunt it. Shirley managed to make every game I played in and out of town. This was done at the risk of her job, with her girlfriend Pam standing in for her. There were dances and parties she volunteered to chaperon because I would be there. We arrived separately and left the same way. We fooled no one. The stolen looks, the quick smiles, did not go unnoticed by suspicious eyes. Neither did the one dance we dared.

At the center, time had increased our boldness. It was as if the blue lights made us invisible. No more did we settle for just a few dances together or scattered moments of conversation. We defied the town's gossipers. And when I walked her home, the night was ours until the next morning. Some Saturdays we took the ninety-mile train ride to Columbus. We were free then, free to be in love, free to live! I saw my first play with Shirley—*Porgy and Bess*. I loved it. She was surprised, because it was a light opera. In Portsmouth most people listened to rhythm and blues. Secretly, I liked opera too. It was something in the way opera singers could control their voice, and the drama, that impressed me. I could feel it even without understanding the words. I also saw *Show Boat*, and *Othello*, a play by William Shakespeare, that Shirley said every colored person should see. One day, I promised myself I would learn the words from the final scene and recite them for Shirley. Maybe I would even become an actor. I imagined me on a stage dressed like Othello, and found myself in front of the Supper Club. I walked inside past Danny, who gave me a knowing smile. I'm sure all the older men couldn't see what a woman of Shirley's stature saw in a kid like me. The club was a small place, as clubs go, with a bandstand, dance floor, and tables and chairs. A bar ran half the length of the right wall when you walked in. Reesey, a redbone with a toothy smile, was the barmaid. She was also Danny's girl. A jukebox supplied the music. Very rarely was there a band. Through the lowered lights I could clearly see Bo, Play-Boy, and Spike standing at the bar, beer in hand, trying to look grown-up. They were surprised to see me.

My time had been spent mostly with Shirley these past several months. Speedy told me what the joke behind my back had been. He told me right after graduation, before leaving for Cleveland with his father. My "other mother" wouldn't let me "come out and play," the guys said. Even Bo had been part of the laughter. That taught me the do's and don'ts of friendship. Another lesson I learned during my development as a man. Friendship should never take a backseat to camaraderie. Bo and I were never as close again. He lacked one of the essentials of true friendship. I waved at them but walked to the corner where Mama inconspicuously sat with her two drinking buddies, Bill Ford and his longtime girlfriend, Lizzy. Nice people, both of them. If only they hadn't been drinkers. They did look after Mama, though, especially Bill Ford, who called her "Little Sis." He was from New York, or at least had lived there. The stories he told made me feel like I'd been there, too. Bill Ford had been a member of the all-colored Fifteenth Regiment of New York's National Guard, which was part of the 369th Infantry Regiment. Under fire, their valor was legendary. Over six months unbroken in the trenches. They had been referred to by the French as "Hell Fighters" and awarded the Croix de Guerre. He loved to tell about their coming-home parade through Manhattan. Bill "Bojangles" Robinson was the regimental drum major. Sergeant Henry Johnson rode in an open car. He had been the first American to win the Croix de Guerre with star and palm. After running out of ammunition, he killed four Germans with a bolo knife and took twenty-five prisoners. It was a grand parade attended by thousands—one only New York could host. Among the society people cheering were Mr. and Mrs. William Randolph Hearst, Mrs. Vincent Astor, and many more. Bill Ford told his stories of trench battles and the march from Manhattan to Harlem so many times I knew them by heart. But I never grew tired of hearing them. Afterward his eyes would fill up. "We never got credit. Never got our right as human beings either." Talking to him let me know the true extent of racism. Even dying for your country didn't change it. Sometimes I became very bitter. Mama was wearing that smile. I spoke to Bill Ford and Lizzy, then held out my hand for her. "Jimmieeee?" I shook my head. She took my hand, as always, smiled at her friends, and came with me.

On my way out the door I nodded at Bo and the boys. I walked tall. I had made up my mind not to be ashamed of her ever again. It felt good to walk her home. Like a little girl, her head rested against my shoulder. This night I knew for sure I could never leave her. No football, basketball, and no college. I was all she had. She began to sing "Straighten Up and Fly Right." I joined in. We sang it loud all the way home. When we got inside she wanted to talk. I wanted her to go to sleep. She flopped down heavily on the sofa and pulled me down beside her. Then she began to cry.

"I didn't mean no harm. I was just a young little girl who fell in love. Every boyfriend my sister ever had wanted me. I wouldn't talk to any of them. Mama knew that. Even Bessy knew it. They shouldn't hate a little girl forever."

She broke down again.

"It's okay, Mama."

I held her. Through her tears she managed to smile up at me.

"My strong, handsome man. Tomorrow I get to see my baby graduate."

I didn't have the heart to tell her then. She fell asleep in my arms. After I had laid her back on the sofa, I went to my room. Then this thought came to me. I had had it before, but tonight it was overpowering, almost vocal, this feeling that greatness awaited me. In my dreams I could hear thousands cheering my name, "Jim-mieee! Jimmieee! Jimmieee!"

"Jimmie, Jimmie."

I opened my eyes.

"You have to git up, baby. You gotta get ready!"

She was wearing a cool white summer dress. Her hair fell soft and beautifully to her shoulders from under a smart little hat, but her face was hard and determined. She had recaptured her parentage.

"Mama?"

"C'mon, boy, talk when you git up."

I jumped up and grabbed her by the shoulders. "Mama, it was yesterday."

"What do you mean, today's Friday."

I saw a look of horror creep into her eyes.

"I know, Mama, but we graduated yesterday."

Suddenly there was silence. Like Grady John, she didn't say a word. But it was there, in the way those expressive eyes went blank, the way her face dropped. She walked slowly into her room and sat on the side of her bed. I didn't know anything to say. This was to be her jumping-off point, where she would launch her campaign of redemption. I could say nothing. Words from me would only make it worse. I left my mother sitting there to face herself alone. I knew she would get drunk. It was a mistake. I walked over to Thirteenth Street, where Big Jake the boxer lived. I needed to work out, to punch something, maybe to fight somebody. I didn't care if they were big either. Let the boys dare me now. I took all dares. Ever since I was twelve years old I had taken all dares. I had been the first one to the top of the reservoir on a dare when Billy Reilly was almost killed. He had climbed up after me and lost his footing. Miraculously he landed on the catwalk around its perimeter. The possible consequences of our actions sank in only after it was all over. My next dare no one believed I would take. It was a hot day and me and the boys were in the park, with our shorts on, pitching horseshoes, then running through the sprinklers trying to get cool. The town's swimming pool was restricted to whites, leaving only the muddy Ohio River for us to swim in. No colored person had ever tried for admittance in the all-white pool. They dared me to try. It was more of a joke than any serious challenge; just words uttered for lack of something to talk about. I was scared to death, but I accepted. The boys were too afraid to walk with me and see if I really took the dare. It was as if my going would somehow affect them because they, too, were in the area. As I came within sight of the gate that guarded the pool, I began to perspire, a bad sign. White people already believed colored folks produced too much sweat. They could refuse me for this reason alone. What I was so terrified of, I don't know. I didn't really believe they would kill me, but still, my legs were heavy. My heart was pounding when I reached the gate. A muscle-bound blond-haired boy much older than myself met me with questioning blue eyes.

"Uh, uh, I come to swim," I finally managed.

"Oh," he said. "You'll have to fill out a form."

He stepped inside the small office and quickly returned with the paper.

"Take this home with you, fill it out, and mail it back."

I was as relieved as I now know he must have been when I left. When I met the boys standing near the park, I had the proof. They stared at me in disbelief. I can't describe the feeling that gave me. The fear was worth it. I loved being looked up to that way. The act was enough to make me a small hero around town. People smiled their approval. I became even bolder with my next dare. I entered a Battle Royal with fourteen- and fifteen-year-olds. The word was out that young boys interested in boxing could earn up to five dollars for one bout. All of us boys went to the Elks Club downtown: Play-Boy, Speedy, Spike, and Billy. Bo's mother had him on punishment. When we arrived at the club we were met by a friendly white man.

"You boys here for the fight?"

We all nodded, and he led us into the club's dance-and-floor-show area now converted into a gym. It was filled with drinking white men, talking loud and smoking cigars. Except for us and four older boys, Jake was the only colored person around.

"You boys ever been in a Battle Royal?"

"We came ta box for the five dollars," I said.

He laughed. "You're gonna box, but in a Battle Royal. Five of you have to box each other. The last one in the ring wins. We got a space open for one more boy."

We stared at the four boys shadowboxing and dancing around like professional fighters.

"Them boys too big for us," Speedy said.

"Yeah," Play-Boy agreed.

"What if you don't win?" I asked.

"You still make the five dollars?"

"Everybody makes something. This is the way it works. The last one standing stays in the ring. People throw money in. He gits all of it. After he leaves, the other boys git back in the ring and they throw money in for them. Put on a good show, the more money you make."

I looked at the faces of my friends. They were not about to fight with these high-school boys. Two were even on the football team.

I had to maintain my status as "Mr. Fearless." I didn't want to lose my spotlight.

"I'll fight 'um," I stated strongly.

I was tall and lanky then, but my heart was big. I looked at my friends. Their expressions told me I was still their champion. I took off my shirt and the man put a pair of boxing gloves on my hands.

"Go git 'um, tiger," he said.

"Okay, we're ready!" he called.

I walked to the ring, scared to death again. When I climbed in, Tom, the largest boy, sneered at me.

"What you gonna do, chicken chest?"

I didn't say a word, but I knew I was gonna punch him first. He wasn't so much anyway. He was only second string on the football team. We all took our places in the ring, one to each corner and Tom in the center. There were no seats in the gym and the amused faces peered at us around the ring. The nice man called up to us.

"Anybody knocked down is eliminated. When the bell rings, you boys start."

There was a long silence, it seemed. I focused my attention on Tom and decided to right-hand him with all my might. The bell rang. The melee broke out, everyone swinging at everyone. I rushed over to Tom, sidestepping a wild swing on my way. He was busy with another boy and didn't notice me. I smashed my fist to the side of his head and felt it all along my arm. His head snapped to the side and he staggered, but he didn't fall. I thought I heard cheering. I smiled inside. I saw the glove flying toward me a split second before I heard the thud and saw the lights. After that came the pain, and the ceiling lights which I saw from the floor. For a second I wondered how I had gotten there. Then it occurred to me that I had been ambushed. Rage took over. I jumped up to get my revenge, but the friendly white man was holding me.

"You did good, kid. You got heart."

The glances from the men around the ring were approving. Jake's face had a wide grin. I made $2.75 that day, and retained my reputation as a boy without fear, even increased it. Tom was the last one standing, which also increased my status. I had come closer than anyone to eliminating him. That day was when Big Jake took me under his wing.

Jake opened the door with that big smile.

"Hi ya doin', young blood, c'mon in."

"Hi ya doing, ugly?" I joked.

He laughed. "I wanta say, yo mama, but she too fine."

He punched me playfully. "Heard you graduated yesterday."

"You heard right. Now I can kick yo' ass mentally and physically."

He laughed double hard. "You still gotta learn ta git away from this left hook," he said, and faked like he was gonna throw it.

I danced, bobbed and weaved, and stuck out my jab the way he had taught me. He had trained me for four summers. He began right after he suffered the eye injury that stopped his career. Margie, Jake's wife, had said no more. One week before he was to make his first appearance in the Garden, it had happened. In training, for that matter. The doctors said there was a chance he might lose his eyesight if he fought again. All Jake had left after that were photographs of his bouts, and me.

"Got any grub, Jake? I'm starved."

"Gotta fix it yourself, blood. I ain't gonna be your cook and trainer too. Next you'll want me to do your fuckin' for ya."

"Your dick might not be big enough to do my fuckin'."

That really made him laugh. The only problem with cooking in Jake's house was, you had to leave the kitchen spotless the way you found it. Margie was that way, a clean freak. She made all of Jake's friends go downstairs in the basement when they came over. This is where me and Jake trained. To work out he had a speed bag and a heavy bag. Downstairs is also where he made his cabinets and coffee tables. Jake was good with his hands. He did a lot of wood paneling around town and all through his house. Margie was good with numbers and was the only colored person who wasn't a cleanup lady, the only one to work in an office downtown. After I cooked myself ham and eggs, I made sure the kitchen was the way I found it. Then me and Jack went downstairs. I removed my sweater and we worked out on both bags.

"You got good power," he told me. "Fast reflexes. You could be a contender."

I smiled at him.

"I mean it. It's just one thing about you, you think you're too cute to git hit."

That embarrassed me a little and I laughed to hide it. He held up his hand.

"It's okay not to git hit. You're supposed to protect yourself against it. But you can't be scared to take a punch. You gonna git some, that's for sure. Think about it like this. Your body is a fighting machine. It acts on reflexes alone to protect itself. But it has no fear. Its real aim is to destroy. No emotion, no feeling. Just systematic destruction. That's what's known as the killer instinct. Now, let's spar a few rounds."

We traded hard punches that day. He hit me harder than he ever had. Strangely, it almost felt good, made me feel like a man, like a contender.

I jogged home, shadowboxing on the way. I thought about becoming a fighter, like Joe Louis. Maybe in a different weight class, though. I didn't want to fight the Brown Bomber. Nobody could beat him. I already weighed a hundred and seventy pounds. I was fast becoming a heavyweight. I turned the corner onto my street, then I saw the flashing lights. My stomach flipped. It appeared that the ambulance was pulling away from where I lived. The sirens were screaming now as it sped up the street. As fast as I could I ran, not letting up until I reached my house. I rushed by the people standing outside straight through the front door.

"Mama!"

I ran into her bedroom. She wasn't there. My heart quickened.

"Mama!"

I looked in my room, then the kitchen. I saw the blood smears on the wall phone, a trail on the floor leading to the bathroom. I pushed open the door, and I screamed. Blood was everywhere, in the bathtub, in the sink, and on the floor. I ran from the sight through the house and out the front door.

"They took her to the hospital."

Someone shouted. The words followed me. I didn't break stride. Mercy Hospital was fifteen blocks away. I knew my mama wasn't dead. My mother couldn't be dead. The tears came and I ran on. I began to feel guilty. I shouldn't have left her like that. I saw her hurt. I should have stayed. It suddenly occurred to me that I may have been punishing her for getting drunk and missing my graduation.

"Oh Mama!" I cried.

I couldn't take that thought. I tried to run faster. A car blew its horn, almost hitting me as I crossed an intersection. I turned the corner. I could see the hospital now. I was only a few blocks away. I ran even faster, until my lungs were bursting, until I was there, up a slight grade into the emergency room, right up to the nurse. I couldn't catch my breath, couldn't speak.

"My mother!" I managed. "They brought my mother in here!"

"Calm down, I understand. What is your mother's name?"

"Lillie Mae Lamar."

"Please have a seat over there. I'll be right back."

I took a chair by the wall and watched the doors she went through. Other people were there, but my mind would not acknowledge them. My stare was fixed in one direction. Soon the nurse came back through the doors, taking long controlled steps, confident in her nursing abilities. I couldn't read her face, but her manner was very professional. I stood up to meet her.

"Your mother's going to be just fine. The doctor's in with her now."

"What happened?" I asked.

She hesitated a moment. "How old are you?"

"I just turned seventeen."

"I think she will have to explain it to you. You should be able to see her soon."

I had an idea all the time what had happened. When I saw her lying there with an IV running and both wrists taped, I knew for sure. Her eyes were sad.

"Why, Mama?!" I whispered before leaning over to kiss her.

"Because I was ruining your life."

"No, Mama." I took her hand.

"I wasn't even good at that. Couldn't even keep my word to myself."

She looked up into my eyes.

"When I thought about leaving you I couldn't go through with it. It was me who called the ambulance. Do I look awful? I do, don't I?"

"No, Mama."

"I bet my hair's a mess. Remember, Jimmie, when you were a little boy and used to fix my hair?"

I smiled.

"I wore it that way too. You were good at that like everything else."

"Mama, don't do this no more."

"I won't, baby, I promise."

I stayed with her most of the evening, went with her to the room they assigned. When she fell asleep I left. The nurse had told me she would be kept for a twenty-hour-hour observation. Maybe it would have been longer if she hadn't called the ambulance herself. I couldn't go home. I couldn't face my mother's blood again. I walked to the center. It was now dark outside. It struck me before I got halfway that my mother had tried to kill herself. That's when I began to shake. Cold tremors went through my body in waves. I couldn't stop them.

Shirley spotted me as soon as I walked through the door and rushed over to where I stood. Everyone else, seeing my face and not knowing what to say, kept their distance.

"You okay?"

I managed a slight nod but I was still shaken. She wrapped her arm around mine and led me to the far end of the room. She was not concerned with what people would say. She directed me to a seat and pulled up a chair next to me, took both my hands in hers. I still couldn't stop them from shaking. I kept seeing my mother in a casket, lying still and cold like an image of stone.

"I'm here with you, Jimmie. I'm right here."

"I can't go home. There's blood everywhere. Mama's blood's all over the place."

"I'll clean it up tomorrow," she assured me. "You stay with me tonight."

That night I slept soundly, like a little boy, wrapped in Shirley's arms. When I awoke the next morning the shakes were gone and so was Shirley. I fell asleep again. Shirley kept her word and cleaned the blood while I slept.

Three days later Mama came home. She had changed. She seemed to have a different focus, a determination missing in recent years. It was as if nothing had happened. The first thing she did was give the house a general cleaning. Next she cooked dinner, never mentioning the incident and never taking a drink. We sat across from each other.

"I need to talk to you," she said. "I'll never take another drink. I didn't quit for you or anybody else. I quit for myself. I don't even care who believes me as long as I know."

She was so confident I could feel her power.

"We make our own choices, Jimmie. You have chosen to be a winner all of your life. I chose to lose. I should have learned from you. Now you're trying to teach me how to be a loser. I'm an expert on that, baby."

"What do you mean, Mama?"

"You say you're not going to college, you don't want an even chance like white boys your age. You wanta start off losing."

I started to speak; she held up her hand.

"Not wanting to leave me is no excuse anymore."

I believed her, not because I wanted to; I didn't. That kind of disappointment was too painful. I believed her because what I witnessed that day compelled me to do so.

Two days later I was to meet the woman responsible for my mother's positive attitude. She entered our lives easily, with no regard for the difference in race or social standing. Her hello was bright and friendly like her dancing eyes that seemed to question even when she made her first statement. I was looking at her short hair, tailored like the mane of a prize stallion, so black it seemed unnatural.

"You're Jimmie," she said, standing in the doorway. I nodded. Quickly, she continued.

"Born in Covington, Kentucky, because your mother and father happened to be there. Football star, basketball star, five scholarship offers, one from Ohio State. Your favorite music is rhythm and blues."

She smiled at my mother sitting on the sofa.

"C'mon in, Paris," my mother said.

"Paris Vernazos," she said, holding out her hand to me.

"Conceived in France by an Italian father and an American mother who loved the City of Lights so much she named me after it. I suppose I should consider myself lucky they weren't in Brussels, or worse, Copenhagen."

We all smiled.

"Well, as it happened, I was born in Columbus, attended Sarah Lawrence, in New York, where I received my degree in sociology. My favorite music is jazz."

"Have a seat, Paris," my mother said.

I sat on the sofa next to Mama and Paris took a seat directly across from us.

"Jimmie, I especially want to talk to you and your mother together. You are a family. I believe all problems a family incurs together have to be addressed the same way."

Mama looked at me and smiled with a confidence I hadn't seen before.

"It's all quite simple, really," Paris said. "Together you identify the problem, then concentrate totally on the solution."

She talked about Mama seeing herself as a victim, about her guilt and unwillingness to take responsibility for her own actions. It was she who had been assigned to Mama during those three crucial days of her hospital stay. She was one of those rare individuals whose mere presence instills confidence. I learned, from Paris, lessons that would influence me the rest of my life. She would eventually become the yardstick by which I judged all white people. My life seemed to pick up speed after that day. The events of change struck me in rapid succession. I was confident Mama was well enough for me to go to college, but not so confident about my intended marriage to Shirley.

Five weeks had passed since my mother's accident. I call it an accident because the truth is too painful. Shirley called it by its rightful name, maybe unconsciously, to get back at me. I was now spending weekends with Mama, who had taken a job as a house-keeper for Paris's mother. She had the weekends off and insisted on spending the time with me. Paris had told me this might happen, for me to encourage it. My mother, she said, needed new friends who didn't drink. Well, besides Paris, who had become very close to Mama, I was her only sober friend. Mama, too, needed to make up for the quality time she believed her alcoholism had stolen from us. I loved her like this. She, in a way, became the sister I never had. I switched roles from son to big brother and began to stand guard against those who would violate this still-beautiful woman. No need for me to worry on this score; Mama was too busy enjoying her freedom from the addiction and her new bonding with me for just any man to hold her interest. Maybe I should explain myself. I wouldn't have minded if she found a nice man, like Grady John, who didn't drink and wanted to marry her. I just didn't want anybody using her. In some ways the situation was appropriate for the both of us. I needed new friends too. All of the old gang had suddenly disappeared. Bo left early for Wilberforce on a football scholarship. Speedy joined the army in Cleveland, never coming back to Portsmouth. Spike didn't accept his scholarship in basketball, but instead got married, moved to Youngstown, Ohio, and took the job his uncle had gotten him in the steel mill. Play-Boy went to school at Miami of Ohio. As difficult as it was for me, it was even harder on Mama. Not that she was so lonely, she had me and Paris. It was having to break with old friendships. I saw tears in her eyes when she turned Bill Ford and his girlfriend away from our door. It made me sad, too, but the rules to staying sober had to be obeyed. Like I said, we became like brother and sister. Sometimes we attended church together, movies, even had a horseshoe-pitching contest in the park. I won, of course, but she actually beat me in badminton. I pretended to have let her win. She laughed loud at my embarrassment. On the Sundays we didn't go to church, we took a bus to Ironton, another small town forty miles away, where a swimming pool was available for colored folks. I taught Mama to swim there. I also knocked a guy down for what I considered disrespect to my mother. She had just swam across the pool in the shallow end to show me she could. As she was climbing out, a boy of eighteen or nineteen rushed over and kissed her flush on the mouth. I was around the pool in an instant. He never knew what hit him. Mama had to pull me away.

In the bus on our way back home she laughed about it, said I acted like a jealous husband. In a way I think she enjoyed the attention. She told Paris about it when we got back. They whispered something and laughed. I still didn't see what was so funny.

By the time August rolled around, Mama had been sober for almost two months and was still going strong. She had found life's comfortable niche and an eternal friend in Paris. Such was Paris's influence, Mama talked about going back to school. As for me, on the other hand, two major changes were about to occur. Shirley and I would go our separate ways and I would enter Ohio State University. Maybe it was my fault, the breakup between us. And again, maybe there was no fault to be found. I had to stay close to Mama at this crucial time and Shirley needed to fill the void my devotion to my mother had left. It all exploded quietly one Friday night in a series of the most tormented and painful facial and body expressions I had ever witnessed. She and I planned to drive to Columbus and catch the Nicholas Brothers' show. I had been exuberant. I had learned all of my fancy dance steps watching the Nicholas Brothers in the movies. That Friday morning before Mama went to work, she excitedly told me of her plans for us to go to Newport, Kentucky, and attend the Saturday Night Dance. It had been her and my father's favorite place. Nearby was Covington, where I was born. I sensed it was therapeutic on her part. She needed to dismiss the demons, free herself from still another addiction—the addiction of living in the past. I believe Mama intended somehow to close the door on yesterday by revisiting it. Before I had a chance to tell Mama about my and Shirley's plans, she had told me hers. I could not explain this to Shirley. The moment I told her I couldn't go, she drew away from me as if I had contracted some dreaded disease. She spoke no words in anger, just simply held up her hand in disgust and walked away.

A week later Paris and Mama drove me downtown to the bus station to see me off to college. Mama cried as if she would never see me again. I almost cried too. The thought to remain there with her crossed my mind. Paris picked it up.

"She will be just fine, Jimmie. She may even join you next semester."

Mama smiled and nodded her head. When she looked up at me the light caught those amber eyes just right and they glittered. That picture stayed with me all the way to Columbus.

College was not really that special place most students speak about. The racism hit me the first day of summer practice on the football field. The players lined up according to the positions they played. I lined up with the quarterbacks. The coach called to me.

"Lamar, over here."

"I'm a quarterback, coach."

"Not here you ain't. Here you play halfback."

I started to quit right then. It was the same old bullshit I had endured back in high school. I was a quarterback there but couldn't take a snap from the center. White folks in town couldn't bear to see a colored kid as the team's field general. I did call all the plays, but from a halfback position. They even had two homecoming queens because I was captain, one colored and one white. They made sure I didn't kiss the white one.

The coach pulled me to one side.

"Look, I know you can play quarterback. I know you can read defenses. I've even seen you throw accurately many times on the run. But look around you, son. You see any colored quarterbacks in any major colleges? Do you see even one in the pros?"

I had to shake my head, but I didn't like it.

"Son, you're a good player, maybe even great. This could be your ticket to success, grab it."

I agreed to what I believed amounted to coercion, but only because of my mother. She wanted this so much for me. My reward was to become the only freshman on the varsity, a reward that left a bitter taste in my mouth. Our first game I played second string and still scored the only touchdown in the rout we suffered. The next day I was on the starting lineup, proving the reward had been the coach's, too, and not necessarily mine alone. The coach was not a bad man, I knew that. He did not really call the shots. Still, I was waiting for one of these good guys to stand up for right. I wondered how Jesse Owens felt when he went to school here, how they really treated him. Well, I had a feeling that playing football was not what I would do the rest of my life. But I didn't see how I could take four years of this! Not that learning was ever difficult for me; it wasn't and I liked it. The structure is what I had grown tired of, the boring approach most of the professors had to education, the hypocrisy. You could never challenge them on really controversial issues like religion, or racism, for example. Bring up race and they would stammer and stutter, trying not to offend, but accomplishing just that by evading the truth. I'm sure they didn't care much for me and the reverse was true. It is very difficult for me to justify or even explain my feelings at that time. I believe being homesick was a major part of them. But there existed in me a deadly mix, a combination of forces and emotions that twisted through my very being with devastating consequences. My mother's accident somehow kept surfacing in my dreams and in my mind. Also, everything seemed unfair for a colored man in this world. And if all this wasn't enough, I had no idea where I was headed. It all resulted in me going through a period of rage that aided me only on the football field. This is where I shone brightly, where they cheered me. Outside the stadium I didn't have a single friend. No one could get close to me. There was no party going for me that first semester, no dances, no socializing, not even one girl. The off-campus bookstore that employed me and the library is where I spent most of my time, reading about great men: religious leaders, kings, and conquerors. These were the only times I felt settled inside, except when I received a letter from Mama. The last time she wrote she and Paris were looking forward to me coming home for Christmas. It never came for Mama.

The emergency call came December the ninth in the morning. Paris's voice was heavy with emotion.

"Jimmie? Jimmie, listen. I have to talk to you."

A wave of fear struck me in the stomach and doubled me over.

"I don't wanta talk," I said.

"You have to listen, Jimmie."

"No!"

"Jimmie, you have to come home. Your mother died last night."

I stood there with the receiver in my hand. Maybe I had heard her wrong, but I knew I hadn't. I slid down the wall and let the receiver fall free. Clutching my stomach, I began to rock very fast. I thought I heard Paris still on the line, but I couldn't pick up the receiver. Then I suddenly went numb.

I took my first drink ever that day. I gathered myself up and walked. Avoiding the eyes that looked my way, I walked off the campus and into that vociferous world of traffic and city sounds. I walked for an hour, with the pain following close behind. Sometimes hovering over my head, threatening to envelope me as soon as I admitted this tragedy into my consciousness. I found a state liquor store and stood outside until I could convince some man I needed a bottle to make out with my girl. I stood erect, trying to look normal, trying to hide the desperateness in my face. Most turned me down but finally one complied.

"Got a hot little gal, huh, boy?"

I nodded and forced a smile. No time for pride now. I ordered gin just like Mama. When he returned with the bag, I took it without saying thanks. Instead I unscrewed the top and hit it hard right there in front of him. I wanted him to know he had been suckered, that it wasn't no gal as he said. He shot me a look of contempt and walked away as my distorted face, reflecting the burning in my chest, returned to normal. I coughed a few times, took another swig, and walked to the bus station. I stuck the bottle in my back pocket the way I had seen winos in Portsmouth do.

By the time I reached the station, my tongue was thick with intoxication. At the ticket counter my words were slurred. Now I understood Mama better, how she had avoided pain, retreated from it, demanded it come back another day. I had found her secret. I managed a smile and a warm sensation spread across my face. I'm clever too, I thought. I should be overwhelmed with sadness and with pain. I wasn't. I managed to call Paris.

The bus driver called out "Portsmouth!" It was now two P.M. Four hours later, I ducked my head and emptied the bottle, staggered off the bus, and walked directly into Paris. She embraced me, then quickly pulled back. Her eyes met mine. I avoided her gaze.

"Jimmie, you've been drinking."

"I know," I said, my tongue thick and full in my mouth.

She slapped me hard across the face. The sound echoed loudly in my ears, drew even more attention to us.

"You could disrespect your mother this day? How could you, Jimmie?"

I dropped my head. This time when she looked at me, her eyes were filled with tears.

"Oh Jimmie, I'm sorry. It's not your fault."

She embraced me again.

"Come on, I'll take you home."

The bus station was ten minutes from my house. I was asleep before we got there.

When I awoke it was dark both inside and outside. I was in my own bed, clad only in my shorts. My head was throbbing and foggy, but my heart pounded with excitement. It had all been a dream—college, my mother dying, everything. One awful nightmare. God sure has his way of getting your attention. I would do better now. I rushed into Mama's room to tell her how much I loved her, to let her know how proud I was going to make her. She lay quietly, the way she always did, curled up in one spot facing the wall.

"Mama, Mama, wake up!"

Paris rolled over to face me.

"She's gone, Jimmie."

"Oh no! *Oh no!*"

I screamed and fell to my knees beside the bed. A sound I couldn't identify escaped my lips, hung in the air. Nothing to hide behind now. The truth that I had refused to accept, couldn't accept, was undeniable. Mama was dead, dead, dead, dead. The sound of my pulse drummed out the word in my temples. Beat me down to the floor. A great sob shook my body. The tears were uncontrollable. Paris knelt down on the floor beside me, pulled me to her, stroked my head, and muffled my sobs in her breast. I looked up once into her face and saw Mama in her eyes. Then I went to sleep.

When the dawn peeped in I awoke with Paris still holding me. She was crying silently, gazing at some distant place.

"How did Mama die?"

She remained still. "Pneumonia. She died in her sleep."

There was a long silence. I started to move but she held on.

"She was the most beautiful woman in the world," Paris said. "I loved her as much as any person could possibly love another human being. One day you will understand what that means."

I was a grown man before I ever did.

I went with Paris to the funeral home to make the arrangements. It was still as foreboding as it was when me, Bo, and Speedy came to view Pat's body. The same strange smell greeted us. We were fascinated with death, all three of us. We had come to see up close the hand of death at work. We also came to see if the holes from the shotgun blast were still visible. Now Mama would be here. My knees grew weak. I tried without success to fight back the tears. I told the funeral director and Paris to stop here, that I could take no part in the process. Selecting clothes and a casket for Mama was too painful for me. Paris assured me she would take care of everything. The director also was understanding. His eyes even seemed a little misty, maybe because of my youth, or because I reminded him of a tragedy that had occurred in his life. To this day I'm sure his concern was genuine. I felt better knowing my mother would be in his care. My head ached now and I began to feel nauseous. Then I realized I hadn't eaten for almost two days. Paris solved that problem. After we left, she took me to dinner. We sat across from each other sharing sorrow, filled with love for the same person. Sometimes crying together, sometimes giving each other strength. We ignored the stares that came our way, the questions we heard in the people's minds. As we sat there it occurred to me how much I cared for this woman. She should be my kin, my mother's sister, instead of Bessy. Just when I had decided not to like white people, a white woman had become the dearest person in my life.

The service was held in the funeral chapel, not in the church, where she wasn't good enough for acceptance. Still the church people came, out of curiosity, I guess. Bill Ford and his girlfriend came for Mama and there were some who came for me. I remember, especially Jake and Fanny Burns. I recall how afraid I was to walk up to the casket. What would I do when I saw Mama like that; an artifact with no trace of a human being left in its structure. The casket was rose-colored. I trembled standing before it. She was as beautiful in death as she had been in life, with just the hint of a smile on her face. In her hand she held three red roses. I kissed the lips that would never speak to me again and broke down. I screamed for her. I didn't want to let go. It was Paris who came to take me back to my seat. I remained there uneasily. The funeral director had a few kind words to say, but it was Paris who delivered the compelling eulogy. She talked from her heart and from love, spoke of Mama's courage and tenderness. She spoke of my mother's love for me. When she had finished, her focus shifted, caused me to turn around. He stood like a giant shadow in the aisle. Grady John had come to pay his last respects. I rushed back to him. In his hand he held an opened letter. I embraced this man I almost had for a father.

"She wrote me a letter. I came as soon as I could, but I came too late."

I never learned what the letter said.

I stayed in Portsmouth five more months trying to drink myself to death, lying on the floor with Mama's pictures around me. Paris tried with all her heart to save me, but I was beyond saving. She did put the house on the market for me. She thought it would be better if I lived away from the memories. I never saw her much after that. I had found a small policy of Mama's that kept me in food and drinking money. There was nobody now. Even Shirley had gone. She had left as soon as I went to college and was now living in Cleveland, married to a doctor almost twice her age, rumor said. I didn't care. Better to die alone. I was just eighteen. My birthday in January had come and gone somewhere in my darkest depression.

Maybe it was Fanny Burns—the Grinding Queen—who in a weird suggestive way unwittingly shamed me back to my senses. She came to my house one hot muggy evening in May, wearing shorts and a blouse tied in front revealing her midriff.

"Thought you was hibernating in here," she said, when I opened the door.

"Peeeew! Stinks in here. Why don't you take a bath?"

I was surprised and also pleased, but I didn't show it.

"I did, last month," I replied. "Anyway, what do you care? You wouldn't give me any."

She laughed. "You believed it too? Jimmie, I never gave nobody any. Those boys!" She shook her head. "They used me to prove to each other they knew what it was about."

"You mean you . . ."

"Until graduation night," she said.

"With who?"

"Skipper."

"You gave Skipper some!"

"One time. I used to like you but I knew all you wanted was that. Anyway, you was in love with Shirley."

"Shirley ain't here now."

"Like I told you, you stink."

"You wait here," I told her. "Be right back."

I dashed to the bathroom and into the tub. I hadn't been with a woman in nine months. I bathed as fast as I could. After I finished I dried off, put on my robe, my smile, and walked into the room. She was gone.

The next morning I poured myself a drink as soon as I awoke. I also got into the tub. It had felt good being clean again. At noon Fanny Burns came back.

"You lie," I said as soon as she walked in.

"At least I got you to take a bath. You look good now."

"Why'd you come here, Fanny? Still teasin', huh?"

She grabbed me suddenly, and stuck her hot tongue in my mouth. Then she unzipped her skirt and stepped out of it. And Fanny Burns, the Grinding Queen, made me feel human again. I knew I had been with a mature woman, once more. There in my room with the sun streaking through the blinds. She spoke the only words of logic I had been able to digest since Mama died.

"Jimmie, stop foolin' yourself. You don't wanta die. You just wanta stay drunk to have an excuse for not being successful in life. Don't be scared, Jimmie. I know you can make it."

When she left I cried until my temples throbbed, until my very soul threatened to escape my body, rising up in resistance at the last moment to silence my swan song. She was right. I was a coward hiding behind my mother's death. Mama would not be proud. I was not an alcoholic. My only addiction was to self-pity. But in spite of it all I realized I had been born for better things. No, I was not an alcoholic. I pushed the bottle aside along with my grief, picked myself up to rejoin the living. I had to leave this place now. My future was waiting. The words of Paris came ringing home. "Concentrate on the solution. Take the initiative."

The next day she showed up at my door. She smiled when she saw me.

"You have a buyer for the house."

It was one of those hot, sticky, Manhattan summers when I stepped off the train. The heat seemed to shimmer off the buildings, almost visible, dancing above the hordes of people who made their way frantically through the crowds they helped to create.

New York was a foreboding place, a city of strange sounds, unfamiliar odors, and streets almost too wide to cross. Giant colorless buildings stood like stone icons directing the affairs of little people. New York made you feel small and insignificant, and crowded at the same time. It drew you in like a magnet, tested the fiber of your being, and challenged, even dared you to reach for your dreams. It was also an unforgiving city. Bill Ford had told me this. New York had no sympathy for losers and discarded them like bits of garbage to rot in some obscure corner until the end of time. Immediately I sensed this about New York and was filled with a kind of nervous excitement and I welcomed the new adventure.

In my pocket I carried five ones and three five-dollar bills. The remainder of the money from the sale of the house was hidden under the clothes in a single suitcase I carried. I knew there was only one place in New York for a colored boy and that was Harlem. After a few directions I walked into a subway entrance, down a flight of stairs, and boarded a crowded train headed uptown. The stations flashed by in a blur. I gripped my seat to steady myself, but my stomach didn't obey; it danced, flipped, and fluttered like a butterfly and thrilled me like a child at a state fair. I transferred to the "A" train and realized that in New York I had become invisible. In New York there were no friendly smiles or nods of reassurance, only a cold and distant preoccupation with time and speed, and also there was fear.

The train stopped at 125th Street. I climbed the stairs of the subway and stepped into the world that was Harlem. Never had I seen this many of my own people in one place. They were everywhere. In hat shops and clothing stores. They crowded the streets. Some sold merchandise on the corners. Others wore dark shades and strolled, slow and easy, past the store windows to catch their cool reflections in the glass. Even the streetwalkers were different here. In Portsmouth, they were slow, shadowy creatures who hid in the doorway of Jim Moran's beer joint, or did a sixty-forty deal at Two Ton Brown's place. In Harlem they were visible and bold, as if they were proud of their profession. They wore pastel-colored cheerful dresses that clung to their bodies like running water. They greeted you with bright lipsticked smiles and exaggerated laughter. There was an urgency to test the wares. The idea of possessing a woman who openly advertised herself was arousing. The one I chose called herself Passion but did not fit the image of the whores that the boys and I had joked about back home. She was tall and slender and her long black wig brought out her perfectly shaped oval face. Her slightly slanted eyes gave her an exotic look. She was not "hot and sexy" with her walk, like most hookers, but smooth and fluid like a dancer.

"You wanta sport?" she asked when she caught me looking at her. I nodded.

"Come on," she told me.

I followed her to a building with a front door held open by a large brick. We climbed a flight of stairs and she led me to a dingy room that was bare, except for a bed, a chair, and a sink with a wet towel strewn across it.

"You live here?"

"I work here."

She told me it would be five and one. I didn't understand.

"Five for me and one for the room," she explained impatiently.

She seemed younger than me but I was the nervous one. After I paid her she began to undress quickly.

"First time in the City?" she asked, rolling her stockings down her long chocolate legs. "Come on honey, git outta your clothes. Let's get this show on the road," she said before I could answer.

I sat my suitcase down and undressed. She told me I was cute, as if I were a little boy. It was all very professional and over in a few moments. She gave me a standing invitation then rushed me out of the room. I felt strange when I left, as if somehow I had been taken. In reality, my ego had been slightly damaged. The truth of the matter was I had not made an impression on her. She did not know I had been a high-school basketball and football star. Now I realized she wouldn't have cared in any case. As far as my looks were concerned, well, Harlem was the Mecca of handsome black men.

I crossed 134th Street and entered the first store that sold those cool dark shades. The salesman was helpful and friendly and he also thought I was "cute." He told me where to find reasonable apartments, gave me the glasses free, and then invited me over to his place after work. I smiled at him and left.

Five blocks away I took a one-room apartment with a community bath down the hall. The manager, a fat and greasy dark-skinned man, was rude, slow, and needed a bath. The room he showed me was not much different than Passion's place. There was a chair, a table, and a clean towel across the sink. The bed was lumpy and covered with a spread old enough to vote. I studied myself in the cracked mirror and decided I looked more foolish with the shades than cool, more like a small-town hick trying to be hip. Quickly I unpacked my suitcase, tossed the glasses aside, removed a pair of black gabardine slacks, which I placed between the box spring and mattress to press, hung my plaid sport coat in the small closet, and rushed down the hall to the bathroom. The water was refreshing, cool against my skin, and the Ivory soap that washed away the dirt from the train ride reminded me of my childhood and my mother. For a moment I was sad and homesick, and I thought, maybe, I was misplaced in New York, that Cleveland or Columbus would have been better for me. Then a strange thing happened. I thought about Passion and got an erection. She sure was fine. I could still feel me inside of her, feel her movement. A loud pounding on the door startled me.

"Hey, you, in there! An elephant don't get that dirty! Give somebody else a fuckin' break!"

Just like I said, New York people were rude and always in a hurry. I dried off quickly, wrapped a towel around myself, grabbed my clothes, and hurried down the hall to my room. Now I felt like a nap and lay down across the bed. I remember the room being very warm and that's all.

Seven hours later I awoke full of energy and dressed for the streets. I wore a black shirt, my black slacks, a gray tie, and my sport coat. I walked to the first large street I saw. I was happy just to mingle with the people. As in my life, my evening stroll had yet to find a destination. Harlem exploded into a celebration of colors, a parade of fancy automobiles that moved slowly down Lenox Avenue and ended in a fashion show of slick hats and low-cut gowns. The people moved in adagio to the rhythm of an inner beat; even their voices made music. I was proud to be one of their color, even if I was not yet one of them. As I made my way through the streets, unnoticed, visiting one club after another, I knew things would be different. One day all Harlem would know the name Jimmie Lamar!

The following day I saw Harlem more completely, without the makeup that the night had provided, without the eyes of a small-town boy. This time I saw the poverty through the lens of a true observer. People leaning out tall, overcrowded buildings to escape the heat compressed in their rooms. Clotheslines hung high, completely full, stretched from one building to the next. On the sidewalk, derelicts, drunks, and dope fiends mixed with half-clothed children. Some played in the street under a powerful flow of water the fire hydrants produced. I was on my way to the bank. An old

man sitting on a stoop in front of my building directed me to
Lenox Avenue a few blocks away. The smell of poverty was strong
in the air, like some houses I had visited in Portsmouth with too
many unwashed children in them. Nonetheless, I was excited to be
in New York. I made it to Lenox Avenue and opened an account
in the large bank. I kept twenty dollars in my pocket for spending
money. As I was leaving, a very dark-skinned man with big teeth
and an even bigger smile approached.

"You from the Windy City," he told me.

He grabbed my hand and shook it. Before I could speak, he
shooed me to silence. Looking around as if he were being followed,
he pulled me aside.

"This your lucky day, man. I noticed you ain't wearing a watch,
right?"

I nodded.

"Great!"

He looked around again. Satisfied, he opened his coat. From the
inside pocket he produced a gold watch still in the case. A tag with
the price of $37.50 hung on it.

"Solid gold," he assured me, looking around again. "Dig this,
I'm selling it for ten bucks, but since you and me both from Chi-
cago, you can gimme a five spot, but you got to do it in a hurry."

Sensing the urgency, I pushed a five-dollar bill in his hand as
quick as I could and he was gone. I looked around too. Then put
my gold watch on with a smile. Play-Boy's father back in Portsmouth didn't have a watch like this, I bet. I continued up Lenox
Avenue, looking back to make sure I wasn't being followed. I felt
good. I had twenty-four hundred dollars in the bank, rent paid for
a month, money in my pocket, and a new gold watch. I could live
for at least a year before being forced to go to work. The sign in
the window of the first restaurant I came to pulled me in. NEW
YORK STEAK DINNER 49¢. The waitress reminded me of Fanny
Burns, but she was married. Still, her smile invited me before I
left. But I didn't come all the way to New York to lose my life
because of some unfaithful wife. I wasn't that dumb. A block away,
coming through an outside speaker in front of a combination rec-

ord and bookstore, I heard an excellent jazz-piano solo. I followed the sound to the door.

"Ease on in," a cool voice invited.

He wore dark shades and a tam. Instantly, you knew he was hip.

"Who's that playing?" I asked.

"Art Tatum, my man, Art Tatum. You got him?"

"I don't have a record player."

"You gotta git a sound box, 'Cool Breeze.' How can a cat live without Art Tatum and Lester Young. What they call you, 'Breeze'?"

"Jimmie Lamar."

"Bobby Christian."

He touched my hand lightly with his fingertips.

"Where you from?"

"Ohio!"

"Cleveland? I knew a cat from Cleveland once, played trumpet. He's an ol' man now."

I let him think I was from Cleveland, at least he'd heard of it.

The sound of drums and trumpets outside drowned Art Tatum out. We both walked to the door. It was a parade coming up Lenox Avenue. First a full band in blue uniforms, next a fleet of expensive automobiles draped with banners proclaiming FATHER DIVINE IS GOD ALMIGHTY.

"Who's Father Divine?"

"He's the Sweet Man."

"Sweet Man?"

"You know, a sweet man lives off women. Papa Divine lives off men and women."

I didn't understand, but didn't want to appear square and I let it drop. They kept coming. Now there was a line of men and women dressed in white as far as you could see, some with banners telling the world to join his holy realm. Father Divine was next, a small man, no more than five-foot-two, sitting in the back of a convertible Duesenberg. He was dressed in a white suit with hat to match. The deity did not look impressive to me. Still more marchers came after he had passed.

"How long you been in the City, Jimmie?"

"This is my second day."

"You ain't even got your feet wet, Breeze. Dig, I know two fine ofay chicks from Queens. They both love jazz. One wants to meet a colored cat."

"What about the other one?"

"She already did." He pointed to himself and smiled. "Want me to set it up? They got a car. They'll come down here."

"Okay, when!"

"Tonight. Dig, Jimmie, you got any bread?"

"In the bank."

"Don't git me wrong, Breeze, but you gotta git New York hip. These chicks are classy. Dig. Go to the jug, git fifty bucks, come back here, and I'll take you over to Fat Charles's store. Git you a front and a pair of Staceys."

I did what Bobby asked and he did what he said. I left the store with a pin-striped suit and a pair of black Stacey Adam shoes, gray silk tie, white shirt, and gray hat; all for forty-eight dollars. I gave Fat Charles a fifty and told him to keep the change. Bobby liked that.

"You gonna be all right Jimmie. I dug you right away."

On our way back to his store, on the opposite side of the street, two of the blackest and prettiest women I had ever seen walked out of a door. My mouth must have hung open because Bobby laughed.

"Lot of them come outa there. That's the Satin Doll, choicess beauty salon in Harlem. Chicks go in there so fine they make you dizzy. I swear, Jimmie. If I didn't have my shop I'd go to beauty school and git me a gig in there. C'mon, I'll introduce you to Mason, the owner; that way we can peek inside."

The elegance leaped out at you in a black-and-silver decor. Huge chandeliers like crystal spiders hung from above. The walls were mirrors flanked by giant plants that stood in silver planters. No less than ten operators were busy working. And five customers sat in the waiting room. Bobby walked over to a medium-sized man with a thin mustache sitting behind a desk. The man rose up with a quick smile when he noticed Bobby.

"I want you to meet a friend of mine. Mason, this is Jimmie Lamar, all the way from Cleveland, Ohio."

I flinched.

"Been here not even two days."

Mason smiled at me.

"Jimmie, this is the fabulous Mason Alexander, the creator and owner of the Satin Doll!"

Mason actually blushed. "Oh, go on, Bobby," he replied with a quick hand wave.

He shook my hand warmly and held it maybe a second too long.

"You interested in being a hairstylist, Jimmie? We have a school, you know."

"I get to work here?"

"If you're good enough when you graduate, darling."

"I'm good at everything I do!"

"Whoo! Now, that's something good to know."

This time I blushed. Bobby laughed.

"We gotta dash, Mason," Bobby said.

"Whoo-ee, must be a hot one. I see you took Jimmie to see Fat Charles. Jimmie, you come on back if you wanta try beauty school. It's only a six-month course."

We raised our hand and left.

On our way to the record shop Bobby asked me what I thought of Mason.

"Kinda feminine," I said.

Bobby laughed. "He's got peaches in his back pockets," he said.

"What's that mean?"

"You know, he likes men."

"I thought so."

"It's New York, baby. Everything happens in the City."

Bobby arranged for the girls to meet us back at his shop at nine P.M. In the meantime I took my clothes home, lay down, and took a nap. I dreamed I was working at the Satin Doll, with hundreds of beautiful girls waiting in line for me to style their hair. When I awoke I laid there for almost an hour, pondering my future. I could get a job at the post office, something steady, a choice Grady John would make. But I was not Grady John. I had to reach higher. It was for sure I didn't want four years of any college. Then I realized, without knowing it, I had already decided on beauty school. The idea grew more attractive by the minute. There were even visions of owning a salon like the Satin Doll, maybe a chain of them.

It was late afternoon now and I was hungry again. I had dinner at a small café around the corner, then came back home, took a bath, and dressed for my date. My image in the mirror reflected a total transformation. I looked like a New Yorker. I picked up the extra fifty-dollar bill I had taken out of the bank for tonight, wrapped it around the singles for effect, and walked out. I have to admit, I adopted a new walk, even a strut. It may have been my imagination but people seemed to be looking at me differently. I made it to Bobby's shop by eight-fifteen. The brown suit contrasted nicely with his beige tam.

"That's the look I'm talking about, Jimmie!"

He held his palm faceup and I touched it lightly with the tips of my fingers the way I had seen him do.

"I called over to Smalls Paradise. Man, they got a show to-night—Earl Fatha Hines and Billy Eckstine."

"You know, Bobby, I've been thinking about that beauty-school thing."

He smiled. "That's a good thing, man. You getting in the groove now. That's what I did when I first come here, attacked the City."

"I thought you were born here?"

"Naw, St. Louis. I left when I graduated from high school. Kinda like you. Guess that's the reason I dug you. I saw me when you walked in. It was hard when I got here, though, a depression, no jobs. I stayed with my aunt. Every day in the rain, cold, whatever, I was in the garment district begging for a gig. Finally I got to talk to Saul Goldstein. 'Mr. Goldstein, I said, I know times are hard, but that's when people should do favors for each other. I'm ready to do you one.' 'What can you do for me?' he said. 'For half the pay I would normally git, I'll work harder than any employee you have.' 'And my favor to you?' he asked. 'A job,' I said. I worked for Mr. Goldstein five years. He did raise my pay when things got better. But I learned something more valuable than money from Jewish people. Something every colored person should know. Jewish people love Jewish people. That's one of the keys to their success. They spend their money with each other and they support each other. Colored people need to learn that. The other difference between us and them is, we teach our children to prepare to get a good job and they prepare their children to own the job."

"What made you leave?"

"After five years of saving everything I could, I did what they do, bet on myself. I won. Business might be a little slow through the week, but I make it up on the weekend. I've done okay for myself. I haven't stopped yet, Jimmie. In two more years I'm going to open up the choicess jazz club in Harlem."

I could see Bobby visualizing his dream club, talking with his hands.

"The finest food, Jimmie. The best jazz bands in the country. Man, I'm gonna get the right chick, marry her, dress her in fine rags, and we're gonna greet them when they walk through the door."

"What about the ofay chick. Ain't she the right one?"

"She has the class, all right. I could even see her there, but, man, those chicks come from rich families. They can't marry no colored cat. They'd get disowned. Anyway, they're just trying out a new experience on their break from college. In five years they'll both be married to some rich ofay cat, have two kids, and be pretending to their snobbish friends the only colored person they ever knew was their maid."

I had to laugh. "You're telling me to watch my step. Don't lose my head or my heart."

"Not if it ain't the right one, man."

Three customers walked in, two young girls and a large man wearing an expensive suit. There was a diamond stickpin in his tie and an even bigger diamond on his pinkie. The three of them were filled with laughter. The man told the girls to pick as many records as they wanted. While Bobby was waiting on them, I had a little time for reflection. Already I had learned some important lessons on my sojourn. From Mama I learned to love completely and unconditionally. She gave me self-confidence and, by example, taught me how not to deal with adversity. Paris taught me how. She also taught me the depth of love, that it crosses all boundaries and even encompasses the offspring of those you love. From Big Jake, I learned self-defense; steadfastness and honor from Grady John. And racial pride from the war stories of Bill Ford. Now, during me and Bobby's short acquaintance, I had learned a simple lesson on Negro unity. I also learned where to apply the word "tenacity." You simply selected a single goal and didn't detour from it no matter what.

When the trio left, with the girls carrying a small stack of records, I could see Bobby was impressed. There was a different tone in his voice.

"That was Nate Holden, big numbers man, in with them guineas downtown. That cat spends more bread on women than I make."

I saw the car drive up first.

"Bobby, I think they're here."

He looked. "That's them," he confirmed.

Two women got out of a new sedan, tossed their hair, and walked quickly to the door. Bobby was right. The word "aristocrat" was written all over them in spite of their obvious attempt to appear ordinary. The first one through the door was Bobby's girl, a stunning redhead, self-confident, fearless, and aggressive. Her friend was more laid-back. She was a cute petite blonde with large questioning green eyes who stole glances at me. The redhead embraced Bobby and kissed him before turning her gaze on me.

"Jimmie, this is Constance. Constance, Jimmie."

Her outstretched hand was like a floating swan. I took it, and at once was aware of the great contrast in colors.

"My pleasure, Jimmie. This is my friend Daphne."

I turned to her.

"Hi," she said stiffly, her hands fastened on her purse.

"Any glasses?" Constance asked, producing a silver flask.

"Paper," Bobby said.

"Paper's fine," Constance said.

After Bobby turned his sign around and closed the blinds, he went to the back and returned with four paper cups. I was hesitant but didn't show it. You might have known, the flask contained gin. There was only one seat in the place, a stool that sat behind the counter. We stood in the front, and toasted "peace" because there were rumblings of war on the horizon.

"Where do you girls go to school?" I asked.

"I go to Sarah Lawrence and Daphne goes to Ol' Miss," Constance answered, frowning at Daphne's school.

"It's not that bad," Daphne said. "Constance is just a snob."

"Darling, you don't have to be a snob to not want to associate with those uncivilized people."

Daphne shook her head. "Don't you all believe her. There are some really nice people in the South."

"I have a friend who went to Sarah Lawrence," I offered.

"Really," Constance said.

"When?"

"I guess it was a long time ago. She was mostly a friend of my mother. I go to Ohio State, myself."

"Your major is?"

"Football," I replied cleverly, trying to impress.

"You said the wrong thing, man," Bobby said. "They don't like sports."

"It's not that we dislike them so much, it's just that intelligent people place too much importance on them." Daphne said.

Constance was straightforward. "I believe that participation in sports is an adolescent behavior by adult men resisting the natural process of male maturity. Let's face it, nothing profound ever really occurred by two men intentionally running into each other on a football field. I mean, they didn't paint the *Blue Boy*, find a cure for smallpox, or invent jazz, now did they?"

How was I to recover from that?

Quickly I said, "I won a spelling bee once."

Everyone broke into laughter. One more small drink and Bobby announced we should be leaving. Constance put away her flask and we walked to the car. I sat in the back with Daphne.

"You're a good sport, Jimmie," she said, and touched my hand.

I could tell the drinks had broken down barriers.

"Why Ol' Miss?" I asked.

"My older sister went there. Came back and convinced my mother that seeing the South would be educational for me. Also my sister could keep an eye on me there."

"What would they say if they saw you now?"

"Don't ask. I don't want to think about it."

"Why go out with a colored guy?"

"Probably because everyone says it's the wrong thing to do. I just can't see what's so wrong about it."

In spite of Bobby's warning, I liked Daphne. There was something very honest about her.

All eyes were on us when we entered Smalls Paradise. Constance loved the attention. Daphne stayed close to me. It seemed crowded for a weeknight, and we were not the only mixed couples there. I ordered fruit punch for both Daphne and myself on her request. I knew she and I were not really drinkers. Bobby and Constance seemed unaffected by the amount they had already consumed. When Billy Eckstine took the stage the girls went wild, Constance included.

"He really is a very handsome man," Daphne said. "You are too," she added.

That took me by surprise. I hadn't expected to be compared to Billy Eckstine. He sang several songs, and when he did "Sophisticated Lady," I was reminded somehow of Paris, maybe because she was alone. Bobby and Constance were wrapped up in each other completely now, inches apart, talking with their eyes, expressing their desires. Another band was grooving and Daphne's eyes were dancing. I was enchanted.

"What do you study at Ol' Miss to make your eyes do that?"

"What are they doing?"

"They're talking."

"And what are they saying?"

"That I'm the coolest colored cat they've ever met, excluding Bobby, of course."

"You are."

"Let's change that to ever seen."

"Now you're in competition with Billy Eckstine."

"Wait a minute, let's go back to ever met. I think I can win there."

She laughed. "You are so funny, Jimmie. I think you're very nice."

"Nice enough to hold hands with?"

She placed her hand in mine on top of the table.

"How does this daring experience feel?" I asked.

She closed her eyes. "Mmmmm, feels like, let me see. Feels something like holding hands with a colored cat."

We both laughed.

"You've been out with lots of white girls, I bet."

"I wouldn't say lots."

"Well, a few."

I shook my head. She laughed.

"You mean . . . ?"

I nodded my head. She began to laugh.

"You *are* funny, Jimmie."

"Well, I could have lied."

She was so very personable, so seemingly unaffected by our differences. And she was insightful. She believed that racism was as rampant in the North as the South. Her own father was her chief reference. Like I said, I found her to be honest and almost noble. She had the courage to stare the truth straight in the face and speak to it. To add to that, she believed as Bobby and I did that jazz was a wonderful expression of freedom and worthy of national recognition.

We all went to Bobby's brownstone in Sugar Hill, one in a row of handsome houses, in the most affluent section of Harlem. Constance knew the way. She drove up a hill to a handsome five-room house. The inside reflected Bobby's bachelor status. There were no bright colors except for an array of small lights that decorated the left wall ceiling. Pictures of jazz musicians hung beneath them. On a far wall a painting of a half-clothed woman stared directly at you. His house reminded you more of the nightclubs Bobby loved to frequent than a home. He turned on the music for Daphne and me, then with his arm around Constance, they disappeared into the bedroom. Daphne relaxed back into the sofa with closed eyes, listening to the music. Louis Armstrong's trumpet took us on a journey of highs and lows.

It was early morning before we left. Constance had obviously loved Bobby to sleep. She emerged from the bedroom wearing a sly smile of victory.

"How did you two birds pass the night?" she asked with a suspicious smile.

"Talking," I said. "I think Daphne is one of the most honest people I've ever met."

"That doesn't sound too good, Daff. Spend a whole night with a man and honest is the word he uses to describe you."

"Constance, will you stop?" Daphne replied. "We should be getting home now," she said.

"How will I see you again?" I asked.

"Now that's better," Constance said.

"I'll call Bobby, okay?" Daphne answered.

"Come on, Romeo, I'll drop you unless you want to stay here," Constance said.

"And watch Bobby sleep?"

I had them drop me in front of the first decent building closest to the dump I lived in. Before I got out of the car, Daphne promised she would call soon. I walked home. The next day I woke up late at four o'clock, had dinner, and made it over to Bobby's. He was smiling when I walked through the door.

"She's already called, man."

"Daphne?"

"Who else, they're gonna meet us again, tonight. They wanta go jitterbugging at the Crystal Ballroom."

"What happened to you last night, lover boy?" I asked.

Bobby laughed. "The chick is too much, man. You won't believe it."

"Say, man, I've never been with a white girl. They any different?"

"Sure. But not better or worse than a colored girl. Just different, like maybe the difference between Billy Eckstine's voice and Frank Sinatra's. Both great but different, dig?"

I nodded.

"Daphne likes you man. Constance told me."

"Daphne told me too. Know what, Bobby? I like her too."

Bobby took me back to Fat Charles's store. This time I purchased two pairs of slacks, two shirts, and another pair of shoes. Fat Charles was an excellent salesman, a large man who looked always to be on the verge of smiling. When he did, deep dimples appeared in his jaws. The cologne he wore was a lady catcher. I managed to beg him out of his personal bottle. The only one left in the store. Daphne's first words to me that evening were a compliment on the way I smelled. My 'postulating with Charles had been worthwhile. We all had a drink, which Constance provided, and converged on the ballroom. It was surprising but these two rich ofay chicks could really dance. Of course, it was my time to shine. I stole the show by releasing Daphne's hand, spinning a complete circle, dropping to the floor into the splits, and back up in time with the beat. We were both damp with perspiration when it was over. Constance and Bobby were smiling approvingly at me when we all returned to the table. Everyone was having fun and I couldn't resist one little dig at Constance.

"You looked good out there, Constance. I know you didn't discover a cure for TB, but you sure had fun."

She didn't like being checkmated that way, but had to force herself to be a good sport and join in our laughter. Bobby was surprised at my sharpness. Nobody knew it but I was still only eighteen years old. I glanced down at my gold watch, and to my surprise, it was beginning to turn green. I later learned I had been the victim of what's called the "Slum Jewelry Game." I quickly

took off my watch and slipped it into my pocket. The next tune
the orchestra played I danced with Constance to smooth over any
rough feelings.

After that night the four of us made all the spots in Harlem.
Mitton's Playhouse, the Club Black and Tan, and Smalls Paradise.
Bobby and I even convinced them to attend a Harlem Globetrot-
ters performance. They enjoyed it thoroughly.

One evening in July, Daphne gave herself to me. All four of us
were at Bobby's place. Constance and Bobby were in one bedroom
as usual. Me and Daphne were dancing close. I could feel her heart
beating against me. After the song ended, neither of us spoke. We
simply walked holding each other into the other bedroom. That
special moment was marred only by her fear of becoming pregnant.
Constance, on the other hand, seemed to have no such fear. Over
the next month Daphne and I were inseparable. There was almost
a desperateness in our being together. A haunting thought that this
was not to last. Still her fear limited our physical affection for each
other. She left me for good in late August. We both knew she had
struggled with that decision.

"Maybe in another lifetime," she said that evening, forcing a
smile.

After our last kiss, she clung tightly to me. Finally she looked
up into my eyes. She was crying.

"I could have loved you, Jimmie Lamar; maybe I do."

She broke away quickly and ran out the door of Bobby's house
into the car where Constance was waiting. I watched them drive
down the hill. When Bobby returned, he was filled with excitement.

"She said yes, man! As soon as the school year's over!"

"You sure she's sure, man. You know what you told me?"

"I was wrong, Jimmie. We don't need her folks' money. She
knows that."

But he wasn't. He didn't hear from her for thirty days. The letter
he received was postmarked Los Angeles, California, with no return address. Constance explained she had told her father about
their plans. His response was to take her out of school in New

York and move to their summer home in California. Bobby never heard from her again. After that he wasn't the same. There was no more laughter in his eyes.

I decided to attend the Satin Doll Beauty School. Mason himself taught some of the classes. Again, I impressed someone with my natural ability. This time it was hairstyling. I learned to work on every texture of hair: straight hair, nappy, curly, coarse, and fine. We learned it all. That was Mason's way of teaching. I moved in with Bobby that month. It was good for him. Somehow, even though I missed Daphne, her leaving hadn't the same effect on me as Constance's had on him. I began to date other girls, but Bobby wasn't interested. He never spoke again about his dream, never mentioned Constance. Just worked endlessly and listened to his music.

The next year in April I graduated from beauty school. A month later I was working at the Satin Doll. Then, in just seven months, the world changed. It was December 7, 1941. We were at war. Negroes volunteered in droves, me and Bobby included. We went down together, right after Bobby sold his business to a West Indian lady and arranged to rent out his house. We went because we thought it the right thing to do for our country and for our race. I was rejected because of fallen arches. Can you believe that, a football and basketball star rejected for having flat feet! I told Bobby I would rent his house and saw him off to boot camp. That was the last I saw of him. I returned to work at the Satin Doll and the world opened up for me. I began to make money. My clientele increased daily. I was just twenty years old, but had identification that said twenty-five.

There's one advantage in staying home during wartime—women, lots and lots of women. Of course, I felt guilty, my best friend was over there. Then I thought about Bill Ford and the men of the 369th, who were never granted equality in life or even in death. After thinking about them, I didn't feel so guilty.

Then one chilly winter evening she walked in. She stood briefly in the doorway. Mysteriously beautiful like my mother. Only much lighter in complexion. If she hadn't been in Harlem, she could have passed at least for a dark Italian. But she could never have fooled us colored folks. We know our own. Her long black hair rested on the shoulders of a full-length mink coat, and her eyes were painted with that same shade of brown Mama wore. She was larger, but they both stood alike, carried a proud head. She looked directly at me and smiled.

"I want that pretty boy to do my hair," she told the receptionist loud enough for me to hear.

She removed her mink coat and handed it to the girl, who carried it to the back room. Gingerly she moved over to my chair with a confident, bouncing walk. She was not fat but she had big bones, one of those types who would look less attractive with a smaller frame. From her expensive tan dress to her alligator shoes, she was a fashion plate. She descended into my chair and crossed her legs.

"Trim my ends, shampoo, and a warm curl, okay?"

She looked up at me and smiled.

"I'm Masaya."

"I'm Jimmie."

Her name sounded biblical. She had Shirley's self-assuredness and sophistication.

"You're new here."

"Almost a year," I said.

I draped her.

"You must have come just before I left town."

I leaned her back in the shampoo bowl. "Probably. Close you eyes."

As I lathered her hair with her eyes closed, I studied the soft lines in such a strong face, her lips full and ripe like fresh cherries. She was older than me, but I couldn't tell how much. Here I go again, I thought. I rinsed her hair, wrapped it in a towel, and sat her up. Then I gave her a wet trim the way Mason had taught me. She didn't talk much then, just a few simple questions: where was I born; how long had I been in New York. She asked me if I had children, to which I replied, "No babies, no wife." Afterward, she had no more to say. Her hair was shoulder length and naturally curly. When she came out from under the dryer, I used warm curlers to give her a smoother look. After a part, I swept the main body of her hair to one side. Her smile gave me the answer.

"You're talented to be so young."

"What's 'so young' mean?"

She traced her upper teeth with her tongue in thought. "Okay, I'll put it this way. I'm twenty-six. Bet you're not that old."

"Thought women didn't like to tell their age?"

"If the package is unraveling, I don't blame them."

Her eyes looked straight up at me.

"No, I'm not," I said.

"No, you're not going to have dinner with me? I haven't asked you. At least you should know I'm buying before you say no, Jimmie."

"I was talking about the question on my age."

She slowly shook her head. "You'll have to catch up, Jimmie. We left that subject a while ago."

That made me smile. "You're something else, Ma . . . saya. Is that right?"

She nodded slowly. "See what I mean, you're doing it again, changing the subject. We were talking about me taking you to dinner."

I laughed. "Okay, when?" I asked.

"Tonight, handsome. When do you get off?"

"You're the last one."

"Pick you up in an hour and a half. I'm starved. What's your address?" she asked.

I wrote it down and handed it to her. She began to laugh.

"You live right around the corner from me!"

Now I was surprised.

"Okay, see you in an hour and a half. Oh, where we're going requires a tie."

She paid me, gave me a tip, got her coat from the receptionist, and strolled out the door. When she left, three female operators rushed me, trying to explain who Masaya was, but they didn't actually know. The nearest to any truth they came was that she was involved with the Mob.

She was knocking on my door at nine sharp. Around her shoulders was draped a silver-fox stole and her shapely frame added life to a long satin dress. I was dressed, too, at least fifteen minutes before she arrived.

"Do I come in, or do you come out?"

I held up my hands and walked out my door. "Don't shoot, I'll come out."

She nodded her head and smiled.

She drove me in her yellow sports car to a posh downtown restaurant where the waiters were snobs and pranced around like mechanical men wearing tuxedos. A colored man in black-tie attire sat stiffly in a corner at a piano playing classical music no one seemed to be listening to. He was the only other Negro that we saw in the place. The sounds of casual conversation rose above the music and went suddenly quiet as the maître d', who was well acquainted with Masaya, led us to our table. I could feel eyes on my back, piercing eyes, that questioned our presence in their space, yet curious about the livelihood of these Negroes who could afford to eat here. The waiter had no such concern. He was concerned only with giving the best service possible to ensure the biggest tip. "Madam" and "sir" were his favorite words. We dined on lobster and steak, and of course, the finest champagne. "Nineteen twenty-five," the waiter said, holding the bottle wrapped in a towel and presenting it to me. I sipped the sample he poured and nodded my approval. "Thank you," the waiter said, and was gone. We drank a toast to the "good life" and I wondered what her intentions were. I was not in her class; even my male ego wouldn't let me deny that. On the other hand, I knew I was a sharp-looking "cat"; at least, that's what the girls who came in the Satin Doll told me. I was just about to say something clever when I noticed the couple seated at the table next to us. The man, a dark, young Italian, expensively attired, and seated with a dyed blonde, was staring at Masaya. She looked up to catch the man's gaze and they smiled at each other. The man leaned over and whispered something to his companion, causing her to look in my direction and smile. Then I became uncomfortably silent, prompting Masaya to explain.

"His father is a friend of mine. He owns the place."

She looked at me and smiled. "Having a good time?"

"I like the food and the company," I replied, touching her hand.

"Let's go back to 'our town,' where the patrons like us, okay?" she asked.

"Okay," I said.

She tipped both maître d' and waiter.

Thirty minutes later we were back in Harlem, sitting at a front-row table in the Club Black and Tan, watching two comedians called Pot and Skillet and laughing our heads off. When the first show was over the Who's Who of the Black underworld came to our table, most of whom were policy writers and grifters, but no pimps. Masaya didn't care for pimps . . . she respected them as men, but they demanded too much control over their women and she wouldn't be controlled by any man, not to that extent, she told me. I sat back in my seat and my chest expanded when I saw the attention and respect she was getting. They also inquired about "Folks."

"That's my brother," she explained afterward. "They call him White Folks, his name is Sidney. You'll meet him."

At the beginning of the second show they spotlighted her and gave her a celebrity-status introduction. I didn't know it then, but that's the way top players were treated in the clubs, mostly because they were the big spenders. We left after the second show and she drove me to her brownstone in Sugar Hill. It was a plush affair with stained-glass dividers that slid open and closed, sectioning off the lavish house, introducing me to a world of European crystal and expensive Persian rugs. She strolled to a softly lit glass bar and mixed us her special drink. I declined the "reefer" she offered me as a bonus. Her quick smile made me feel slightly uncomfortable, but I had never smoked a reefer. It just wasn't my style. She lit up a joint and, with a drink in her hand, led me to a long winding sofa in front of a brick fireplace, and pulled me down beside her.

"Where you from, Jimmie, and where are you going?"

"I'm from Ohio and I'm going to the top."

"Where's the top?"

"I don't know right now, but it's waiting for me."

She looked into my eyes and knew I was serious. She almost said, I'll help you. Instead, she sipped her drink and took a long draw on the joint, which fogged our space with thin smoke when she exhaled. She leaned back and looked at me.

"You got a woman?"

"Not really."

"You have a woman who's not really a woman or you don't really have a woman?"

I gave her the old up-and-down with my eyes.

"I don't really know!" I said.

She smiled, excused herself, and disappeared into the bedroom. I leaned back on the sofa and closed my eyes. I thought about my hometown and how far I had come from there, and I smiled. Ten minutes later she appeared in the doorway like magic. Her long sheer gown was bright red; it reflected her mood, hot and seductive. When she moved to the phonograph the scent of perfume followed behind her in waves, circling my head, pulling my senses into her. A glass record case sat beneath an oil painting of Paris. She selected a jazz record by Charlie Christian, a favorite artist of Bobby's. The pleading sounds of his guitar electrified the night, creating the mood she wanted. Like a king's favorite, she pranced across the floor and stood wide-legged before me. I could see clearly the nipples of her ample bosom pressing against the fabric of her gown and the softly feathered nest of black that divided her shapely legs.

"Anything I can give you?" she asked in a hoarse whisper.

"Anything?" I asked for reassurance.

"Anything!" she replied, without hesitation.

Then, like some magnificent bird of prey, she descended slowly toward me, her eyes luminous and hypnotic, fixed on my own, unblinking as she came, until I could almost smell her passion. I tasted her lipstick and felt her tongue, warm and wild, in my mouth. I pulled her gown away. She was undressing me, first my coat, then unbuttoning my pants while she planted hurried kisses all over my naked chest. Now I was kissing her, too, brushing her hair and her ears with my lips. I lifted her head and kissed her mouth. Then I kissed her neck and breasts. We rolled over and landed lightly on the floor with me kissing her still, moving slowly down her body. My tongue found her navel and darted inside, then raced downward and heated the inside of her thigh. I blew my breath slowly on her and I felt her hands gently on my head, pressing it down, harder, as my tongue flickered. Her body stiffened and she moaned softly when I found the spot where her passion lay. She tried to move but my strong young hands locked her legs. She grabbed at her hair and slammed her hands on the floor beside her, clawing the carpet like some beautiful wild animal. Her body arched just before a shrill scream that began and ended on one note. Taunt and strained, she slowly relaxed. Then she touched my face lightly with the tips of her fingers. Now she was ready for the entry that would keep us locked in love's embrace until dawn.

At noon we awoke still hungry for more and she giggled delightfully when I pulled her to me. We never left each other that week, night or day, no work for me, no business for her. Passion was our only guest and we found it in every conceivable way.

Some nights we spent quietly at my house and exchanged stories about our youth. I told her about Shirley; she told me about her folks. She had been the offspring of mixed parentage, her mother being a dark-haired Sicilian and her father an okay Negro jazz musician who traveled around the country with a small band that never got a break. He had loved her mother and the child born out of wedlock, but would not forgo his dream of musical fame in favor of a normal family life. Her mother, for this reason, refused to marry him. Masaya had been two years old when they finally split up. Two years later her mother met and married a successful blond-haired Irishman who accepted her as his own. She had not been confused by these two important men of different color in her life. Instead, she was delighted to have two fathers. The times she went to Harlem to visit her natural father, after he returned from playing on the road, were very exciting. Anything she desired was hers. The band pretended she was an actual member and engaged her when she played her toy horn. She had been a cheerful, precocious child who immediately loved the half brother her stepfather and mother produced. In school she was voted Most Likely to Succeed and was a member of the homecoming queen's court. The kids wrote "Miss Ambition" in her yearbook.

She suddenly became quiet, even misty-eyed.

"And then?" I asked.

"My father died," she said softly. "They found him lying on the floor clutching his horn like it was all he had in the world. After that, I changed. Maybe I grew up. That's when I met Vinnie."

She looked straight at me. "You wanna year this?"

I nodded.

It was the same old story of a girl's first love, but this one had a twist. Vinnie was twenty-nine, a mobster and married. She had backed into him one evening at Macy's department store while shopping for a Mother's Day gift. She was just seventeen years old, and impressed by everything: the way he dressed, his new automobile, and the fancy apartment he kept in Manhattan. Her virginity was quickly lost. After that, she saw him wherever and whenever she could. Her parents objected, of course, even before they ever met Vinnie. But she was her own woman and there was little they could do. When they finally met him she was eighteen and it was already too late, too late to be firm and too late to stop her from moving in with him, or moving into the apartment he got for her.

She earned the reputation of being a smart dame very fast. At the Mob nightclubs she met all the right people at the right time and was included in some major schemes. She sold fake diamonds to greedy businessmen, steered high-rollers to rigged gambling dens, and participated in bank frauds. She made loads of money, but she was always in touch with her younger brother and she always spent time with him when she visited her parents' home on Long Island. She took him to plays and movies, bought him expensive gifts, and in the summer they went to Coney Island. When

Sidney graduated from high school, she was there. His freshman year in college she threw him a big off-campus party on his eighteenth birthday. When he gave his valedictorian address at Dartmouth, she sat in the front row with her mother and stepfather.

Three days later Vinnie was killed in a Mob war and she was on her own. She had loved Vinnie very much, like a young girl would love the first man who had introduced her to the world.

The club's bosses and the wealthy patrons flocked to her after Vinnie's death, offering proposals of marriage or handsome, lucrative arrangements, but she was neither a kept woman nor a gangsters' "moll." Because she involved herself with no one, she earned the respect of everyone and utilized her well-cemented connections. She worked herself into a secure financial position. It was then that her need to experience her own blackness drew her to Harlem. Within a year Sidney had quit his job at a bank and moved to Harlem with the sister he idolized. He told her he was terrified of leading a structured life, a humdrum existence like his father. His brilliant mind and executive appearance made him the perfect partner for her and they quickly became known throughout the subculture of the underworld as the most effective confidence team in New York. I had never heard anything like it, didn't even understand it all, but I kept quiet so as not to appear too much like a hick. That was the reason I began to smoke reefer with her. Sometimes we would laugh at everything and at nothing.

Falling in love with her was divine, it was giddy and delightfully insane. Who was this woman who had consumed me so completely in such a short time? Who was this woman who anticipated my thoughts and serviced my needs before I expressed them? This was happening too fast. I needed room to collect my thoughts and I told her it was time for me to return to work. She was livid. No man of hers was going to be any woman's flunky. She would teach me the "game" first, teach me to play "con." This was how I first met her brother, Sidney.

I hadn't liked this tall, blond, handsome man at first. In spite of his quick smile and pleasant manners, he was just an ofay cat who I couldn't fathom as Masaya's brother. He was older than me maybe by three or four years. I had to admit he was a jazzy dresser for an ofay cat who wasn't in the Mob. There was also a smoothness about him. My instant dislike of him was mostly a result of my past experience with white males. I had never had a white male friend, although I had interacted with them all through high school. Why should I trust this man Masaya had called her brother? In addition to my distrust, my woman accepting her own biracialism instead of declaring herself as simply Negro the way the white world viewed her, was very upsetting to me. If we in our race were to divide ourselves at this late date, according to the amount of white blood in our veins, we would self-destruct. We would begin by losing a man like Frederick Douglass, whose father was white. Of course, I had not considered Masaya's position. She had grown up in a white world. Sidney had no knowledge of my feelings. He had come over because his sister had asked him.

"Sidney, this is Jimmie. Jimmie, my brother, Sidney."

"Hi ya doin' sport?" he said, reaching out his hand. "Seems like I already know you."

"I was telling Jimmie he didn't have to work at the Satin Doll. If he connected with us he could buy the place."

Sidney laughed. "You know what I always say," he responded. "Two principal objects stand in the way of making money—too little knowledge, or too little courage. The facts indicate the knowledge is in this very room."

He looked at me and smiled. Curiosity did kill the cat, or in my case, made him money. Masaya left the room. She knew I was ripe. It was man-to-man now.

"Jimmie, a very funny man named W. C. Fields once said something very simple and very profound. 'You can't cheat an honest man.'"

He stated that the best target for the game is someone looking for an illegal or unprincipled advantage over the other person, like a wealthy landlord who subjects his poverty-stricken tenants to less-than-human conditions. A greedy unfeeling person of this kind is very susceptible to the game.

"You may really appreciate this, Jimmie. Masaya and I stung a redneck in Mississippi who thought he was cheating poor colored folks out of thousands of acres of prime real estate they didn't know they owned. Now, as for the banking institutions, insurance companies, and other big business concerns, well, they are the true leeches of society."

"What do you need me for?"

"We don't need you, sport. My sister just doesn't want her man to be a lame. Look, man, she felt the same way about me."

My mind was operating rapidly, trying to find a reason not to join in their lifestyle. I could find none. The possibility of going to jail never was a concern. I never even thought about it.

"Okay, when you want me to start?"

"Today. There's a mark we can take on the weekend. All you have to do is pretend to be an African who doesn't speak much English. You have to speak with an accent."

"I don't know if I can do that."

"Sure you can, it's easy."

He taught me to omit certain words in a sentence, like the contraction "I'm," in the sentence "I'm going to the store." I also learned to place greater emphasis on the wrong words. My eyes had to rove suspiciously around as if I were in fear for my life. Well, I wasn't playing Othello, but I managed to produce the desired effect. Only when I had achieved it did Sidney call for his sister. She seemed detached from me when she came in, didn't speak a word. As Sidney and I repeated the routine we had worked out, she sat silently, watching with sharp eyes. When it was over she called her brother to the side and whispered something to him, then left the room again. I was puzzled.

"I want you to be less articulate even with the accent. I should have to explain to the mark what you say," Sidney said.

"Why didn't she tell me? What's wrong with her?"

"Stay with it, man. She doesn't want to be her man's boss. That's why she called me."

One more time he called her in and the routine was played again. This time her eyes smiled. That's when Sidney shook my hand and kissed his sister on the cheek good-bye. She made a transformation immediately.

"You ready for dinner now, baby?"

"Maybe I'm ready for more than that!"

She smiled and came into my arms.

Although Sidney had impressed me that first day, there still was not a total trust. It was not easy to dismiss the lessons I had learned in Portsmouth. But of course this was not Portsmouth, not even Ohio. This was Harlem and Harlem was not representative of any place in the country. There was mixing of the races openly in Harlem. Everything of importance that was black was showcased in Harlem—politics, art, and music. Harlem had style, some borrowed, for sure, but "jive" was born there and with it a new language, a different way of talking, of singing and dancing, and a cool way to "strut." Harlem was magic glazed in black, and people from all over the world, who made it to America, had to visit the "Black Capital." Harlem meant the Cotton Club, which featured some of the most beautiful women and the best talent in the country. Harlem introduced to the world Charlie Parker, Duke Ellington, Billie Holliday, and Lena Horne, to name a few. Langston Hughes and Richard Wright protested oppression and inequality with their pens. Paul Robeson used the spoken word and he had delighted and moved the world from the stage. This, too, was Harlem. It was in vogue to have an affair with Harlem and sometimes with its people. Understanding this, and that the sister Sidney loved so much was colored like me, made me warm up to him. Besides, Harlem was light-years away from Portsmouth.

Every day Sidney came by, Masaya would leave us to each other. It was he who initiated the delicate conversations about race. He talked openly to me about the problems of the Negroes and the problems of the whites as well. The blame should be placed with the institutions of this country and big business, the schools that taught lessons of inferiority, the church that turned its face from the slave trade, the shipping industry, the cotton mills, and the plantation owners, all of whom profited from it, and every president who did nothing to stop it. Sidney was never patronizing and he didn't apologize for being white. He just stated the facts and let me know he understood. We talked for hours about many subjects—his family, my hometown, Masaya, and sports. Sidney thought his sister represented the best in all women. I agreed, completely. Maybe it was inevitable that I be drawn to him. The relationship that Sidney had with his sister and the people of Harlem proved that love and friendship were his only colors. The cold reality was that in spite of past and present mistreatment of blacks by whites, the Negro's primary objective was to be accepted and loved by their former slave masters. Of course, I would never openly admit this, most colored people wouldn't; but love brings with it no shame. To love is godlike! Sidney understood even this.

That Saturday my life would undergo its most major change ever. A shady jeweler friend of Masaya's furnished the stones along with the phony duplicates, for twenty percent of the action. I was to be the African who had smuggled a bag of fine cut diamonds into the country. Sidney played the go-between who would collect twenty percent if he arranged the transaction. Masaya was the Cuban woman who brought the African to Sidney. The mark was an upstate businessman who owned a huge used-car lot and dealt in stolen merchandise. He came to the City regularly to gamble and chase women. He also loved to play the horses. The mark had been fingered for Sidney a week earlier by a racetrack touter dubbed Long Shot Harry, in a Manhattan bar. Sidney engaged the man in conversation and after a few drinks let drop the story of the African and the diamonds. The mark bought it hook, line, and sinker, and begged Sidney to cut him in on the deal.

The meeting was arranged at night in a secluded part of an Italian restaurant in the Village owned by some of Masaya's friends who pretended not to know either Masaya or Sidney. I was wearing a multicolored dashiki and sandals when Masaya led me into the restaurant. Sidney was already there with the mark, a sweaty heavyset man with suspicious eyes who had brought along his jeweler friend. I carried an attaché case covered in leopard skin. When

Masaya saw the jeweler she went into her act, a convincing Spanish accent.

"What this you do, bring the *policía*?"

I followed suit. "Pyleese? Where pyleese?" I shouted.

Sidney jumped up. "No police! No police! This man jeweler. He examine stones. No police. Please sit down!" he pleaded.

Pretending skepticism, I sat down next to Sidney, who sat across from the two men.

"I stan', hide de looking eyes," Masaya said.

"Okay, let's see them," the jeweler said.

I looked at Masaya; she nodded. I opened the attaché case. The diamonds were brilliant under the lights. The jeweler took a loupe from his pocket and thoroughly examined every stone. He whispered something in the mark's ear.

"Okay," the mark said. "I'm prepared to pay twenty-five thousand cash for everything."

I stood up and slammed the case close. "I go now. White man want cheat black man. Now I no sell you, bawanna."

"Okay! Okay! Final offer, thirty-five thousand."

I again looked at Masaya. She nodded. I pretended to be considering the offer.

Finally I said, "Okay, you pay money. I give diamonds."

I opened the case again. The mark produced the money all in one-hundred-dollar bills. Representing the amount he was prepared to pay for over a hundred thousand dollars' worth of diamonds. I flipped through the stacks as I had been told to do, to make sure the serial numbers were different and there was no "mish," meaning a phony bankroll. Satisfied, I began handing him the stones. He wanted the attaché case.

"No, my wife give for me present. Like juju."

"He's saying his wife gave it to him for luck," Sidney explained.

The man relented and put the diamonds in his coat pocket. I placed the money in the case and closed it. Masaya and I left. Sidney followed, talking about his twenty percent. Sidney turned right when we were outside. Masaya and I hurried around the corner and got into her car.

"Now you're a grifter, baby."

She smiled over at me, started the engine, and zoomed off. I was lost for words. How could it be that easy to make thirty-five thousand dollars? I was hooked. We stopped first at the jeweler's home. He and Masaya gave each other a knowing smile when he answered the door. He was an old man who moved slow, but had dark alert eyes. I gave Masaya the attaché case, which she opened and lifted the thick leather cover revealing the authentic stones. The case had been custom-made with a duplicate hidden tray that dropped from the top of the case when it was closed and pressure applied to the sides. This scam had been worked over and over, according to the jeweler. It had never once failed. Masaya counted the money. Every cent was there. We all laughed. She gave the jeweler seven thousand dollars and we left. Sidney was waiting at the house when we got there.

"You're a natural, Jimmie," he said, wearing a big smile.

"What did I tell you?" Masaya said.

"My baby picked the police line up right after me."

Sidney laughed.

" 'Pyleese! Where pyleese!' " Sidney mimicked. "That was great, man."

Masaya laid the attaché case on the table.

"Okay," she began. "We kicked Marty seven grand. We have twenty-eight here. That's nine grand a piece. We have to give Mike over at the restaurant fifteen hundred and Long Shot five hundred. New man pays for the party. That's you, baby." She smiled at me.

The first thing I thought of when she handed me my share was, I had made enough money in less than an hour to buy three houses in Portsmouth, then I remembered the "solid gold" watch I had bought for five dollars, a watch I would always keep to remind me how lame I had once been. I laughed out loud.

"What's so funny, Jimmie?" Sidney asked.

I shook my head. "Private joke, man!"

True to the tradition of the "grifter's code," a party was thrown to celebrate the entrance of a new member into an old lodge. Every top grifter and card swindler in Harlem was in attendance, and a few more, at the Club Black and Tan. Masaya was proud to present her newly acquired man to them; there was Double Dollar, who boasted of making one hundred dollars a day short-changing in stores. I didn't believe it. Masaya assured me it was true, that it was not silver money he was talking about, but a way of using a ten- or twenty-dollar bill to cheat a store owner out of nine dollars whenever he made a transaction. There was Murphy Joe, who Masaya said sold more imaginary women to prospective johns than actual procurers. Big Chink was a colored grifter who looked Asian, and Society Red, who had caught a rich ofay chick and was considered, maybe, the best one-pocket pool shooter in the country. I had stepped into yet another world and I loved it. Everybody seemed to be having a wonderful time. We had plenty of food, also a free bar. Some of the people smoked reefer in the bathrooms. And Sidney, well, he was trying to prove that what they say about the Irish is true. This cat was rocking on his feet, balanced on the shoulder of a cute Puerto Rican girl. Masaya was in her element, the true Queen of Harlem, and even though I was not yet a king, I was part of the royal family. I never returned to the Satin Doll.

"No, I won't leave you alone, Jimmie. It's just wasting money!"

"I told you, Masaya, I'm keeping the place for Bobby!"

"Bobby's dead, Jimmie. He went to war. People get killed in war."

"You don't know that, do you? You don't know everything, Masaya."

"There you go again! Sometimes you make me so mad!"

She actually stomped on the floor.

"Why do you do this to me? I've never tried to make you feel less than me," she shouted.

"That's what you say, but that's not what your actions show. You do it to your brother too."

She shook her head.

"Look at me!" I said. "I know I'm only twenty-one, but I should at least be able to go shopping on my own."

"That's not it, baby. I just love picking out nice things for you."

"Well, I don't like it."

She threw up her hands. "Okay, I won't go shopping with you and and you can stay in that fuckin' house. Move all your shit out of here, over there. I don't care!"

She stormed into the bedroom. It was spring and instead of acting like new lovers, we were like an old married couple.

The two months had been wonderful for us. We were very much in love; Sidney and I had become best friends and every scam we attempted was a walk, although one caused me and Masaya's very first fight. We played the drop on a little old lady and this compromised my conscience. I had to give the money back. Sidney had not been involved but in principle agreed with Masaya, if principle can be applied here. Grifters never retreated from their actions, no more than soldiers are compromised by killing other soldiers. As far as I was concerned, my feelings about the whole matter was the important thing. I stood strong on them. Masaya relented. In a strange way, because of my stance, both Sidney and Masaya seemed to have acquired a different respect for me. Masaya began to even smother me with love and, in so doing, became obsessed. Her obsession caused her to use her considerable knowledge in a backdoor way to maintain control over her brother and me. She had even gotten angry with Sidney on a few occasions when he and I went to clubs without her, accusing him of setting me up with other women. I must admit, we were both a little rebellious having this female lord over us, and as a result, caused her some anguish by pretending interest, openly, in different women in several clubs. I did love Masaya, even wanted to marry her. But I knew marriage would destroy any chance of me coming out from under her cloak, which I was determined to do. Fate had not intended for me to be subservient to anyone. There were other times when we held heaven in our hands, when the whole world danced to our music, when our world was one of candlelights and soft music, bubbly champagne and caviar. We made love on the bearskin rug in front of our bedroom fireplace and slept there all night. We saw every major production on Broadway and every new act at the Club Black and Tan.

This day I was trying to retain a certain independence, and keep my word to my friend just in case what I hoped against wasn't true turned out to be true. She would be angry for a while, but that's the way women sometimes are. They resort to underhanded means to have their way. I wouldn't starve to death if she stayed in the bedroom, but she knew I loved her cooking. I wish I had learned how to stay angry for long periods of time, but I hadn't. My mother had seen to that. The truth is, I can't stand being in the same house with someone and not speak to them. Just when I decided to really fix her and go to my place, someone was at the door. Sidney's expression spoke before he did. Something was terribly wrong. He handed me the letter in his hand. The first word was "Greetings."

"I've been drafted," he said.

Masaya came out of the bedroom. She embraced her brother lovingly. There were some uncomfortable moments; then, as if on cue, we rallied our spirits and the three of us went out on the town. What else could we do?

Sidney took his basic training at Fort Dix, New Jersey, not too far from New York, but was allowed no contact with the outside world during this time. Learning how to kill must be very private business. After his training was complete, which took about six weeks, he was permitted a short furlough before he shipped out. Sidney spent his with his mother and father. Masaya and I drove there to see him off to war. Going to meet her family for the first time was uncomfortable. Maybe because I was going to be forced into lying and knew it. The question "And what do you do for a living?" was on the lips of every parent. I could hardly tell them I was a grifter like their son and daughter. Parents will accept lies from their children that are told to protect their parents. But lies from strangers are, they understand, told only to protect strangers. Then there was always the ugly question of race, ever-present in the mind of a colored man. Would her mother look on me with disdain because of her unsuccessful relationship with Masaya's natural father? Would Sidney's father really accept me in his home? Had he only extended himself to Masaya because the love he had for her mother forced him to? There existed no such incentive where I was concerned. Masaya was amused by my fears and enjoyed laughter at the expense of them. At one point, when we had driven halfway to Long Island, she said with a serious face, "Baby, maybe that suit is a little too flamboyant for my parents." When I responded by agreeing, she broke into laughter. "You see," she said, "you're not so tough after all."

Her parents' home was a handsome red brick affair surrounded by flowers in a quiet neighborhood with magnificent lawns. Sidney looked good in his uniform standing next to his dad, being fussed over by his mother. This cat's a natural chameleon, I thought. Harlem would not believe this. "Not Folks," the guys would say.

We all sat around a dining table and had coffee from the old country that their mother made. Our conversation was mostly about the war. In the Pacific we were suffering defeat after defeat, and the Germans had overrun Europe. But there we were, Irish, Italian, colored, white, male, females, hustlers, and squares, all differences aside, united in support of our country, confident that victory would be ours. A big part of me wished I were going with Sidney. I felt we could overcome anything together, that he would be safe this way. Although we all felt cause for concern at the table, Sidney showed no fear, only a fierce determination to defend his country. We rode to the ship on a wave of patriotism.

16 It was cold standing there on the docks that Monday morning watching the ship sail away to war. It was cold, lonely, and sad for the four of us. We had watched Sidney climb the gangplank with boys not yet old enough to vote, or buy beer, boys only old enough to die. The real fear is one of not knowing, or the thought of some impending disaster. That is the worst part of fear. Maybe his smile of encouragement and final wave would be the last we would see of Sidney. Maybe he would be captured and held in some prison camp until who knows when, and then there was the possibility of him being killed outright.

Masaya's mother made no attempt at a show of bravery, or strength, but released her fears in a flood of tears against Sidney's father's chest. Masaya rushed to her side with words of comfort and encouragement that had no basis in reality. I stood vacant and still, like some deserted monument, unsure of the correct response, afraid to show my true feelings. They may have had an adverse affect on Sidney. I had waved and smiled too. I had not told him I loved him like a brother. He had not told me. Because we were men and men were supposed to be strong in times like these, we had put on our brave fronts and denied ourselves a last comforting truth.

He was gone but his absence was present in all that we did, in every scam, in every club we went to. His image was clear in our minds, his name on the lips of everyone we met. Even our fights, absent a referee and a sounding board, seemed much longer and more redundant. There were the quiet moments when we smiled, recalling something funny he said or something crazy he had done. I got my first taste of jail soon after Sidney had gone. The old diamond switch went bad when a previously well-played mark with a great memory recognized me in a men's store and tipped off the cop. But in New York, big money and a fast mouthpiece equals certain freedom. I walked with a smile.

It was thirty days before our first letter came, and although it didn't say so, it was probably written from the ship. Sidney and the rest of the men were in good spirits, prepared and eager to defeat the Japs. He joked about the food and wished for a cold beer. With a promise to write more and with his love, he closed. After assuring Masaya and me that he was okay, the letter actually eased the tension between us, which had been building feverishly as I developed as a man, and a grifter. So hostile had we become to each other, we were forced to confront our situation. Although the love was strong, our relationship was falling apart and neither one of us wanted that. We approached the problem with open minds, promising to actually listen to the other person. I inserted the knowledge I had gotten from Paris. "We have to agree to concentrate on the solution not the problem," I told her. She agreed and was pleasantly surprised.

We created a romantic mood to have our conversation in—wine, fruit, and soft music. Also we agreed to use the words "I love you" as much as we could. We kissed and I began. I told her she had to let me be my own man, that she couldn't control me.

She listened intently, and then in her most sincere voice, she said, "As your friend, I tell you this. Equality is never freely given. It is always won. It is not for me to step down from my womanhood, but rather for you to step up to your manhood."

Her eyes spoke to the staunchness of her position. Mine reflected a quiet hostility that her statement had invoked. For a moment we sat there in silence, the space between us charged with conflicting opinions threatening to erupt.

"I love you, Masaya, but your statement suggests that I'm less than a man, maybe just a boy. As your friend, I must tell you that pissed me the fuck off."

"I love you, Jimmie. I'm sorry if you feel insulted. That was not my intention. I'm simply saying you are even more of a man than you realize you are. I love you, Jimmie. I want to have babies with you. Jimmie, I want to be your wife, but you haven't asked me."

"I understand," I said.

I knew inside that was part of the problem, but I couldn't give up what I thought was the last vestige of my freedom. I kissed her and for the moment we buried that question beneath our passion.

Things, however, did get better for us, mostly due to the extraordinary woman Masaya was. She let go of her dream of marriage and children and began to find ways to cement our relationship. Only a week later she came bursting through the door with this wonderful news.

"Guess what, baby?" Her eyes lit up with her smile. "Mason wants to sell the Satin Doll!"

"Why?"

"He's in love, baby. Met a man when he was in Paris and they plan to open this fabulous salon when he goes back. He only came back here to sell the Satin Doll."

"What'd you tell him?"

She looked at me in the most questioning way. "That I had to talk to you," she said matter-of-factly.

My heart filled to overflowing. She had done it for me, everything, the way she had refused to make a decision without consulting me. I had to give her something back.

"What do you think?" I asked.

"I say let's go and get it."

We did buy the Satin Doll and I made the deal. My first legitimate business venture. I was proud of myself. We had paid less than I expected, due to my smooth bargaining, I like to think. When the deal was done we threw a small party to acquaint the patrons with the new owners. Masaya's parents were there. I had also sent an invitation to Paris. Everyone seemed happy, but still the question loomed. When were we getting married? I asked her right there in front of everyone, and it didn't hurt one bit. It was the first time I had ever seen her indecisive. She really didn't know whether to cry or laugh. She did a little of both, and even forgot to say yes. When I whispered in her ear, she shouted, "YES!" Her mother and her father's politeness turned now to true warmth. The four of us stood together in front of the salon like a family and were photographed. It was a very good feeling.

I bought her a ring the next day—three carats—from Marty. He was as happy as her father. "A good wife is the best thing that can happen to a man next to children," he said. We drank a toast to wives and children and I left.

Masaya was sitting on the sofa with a photograph of her and Sidney on the coffee table when I walked in. One month had passed and not a word. There had been four letters the second time we heard from him. We only knew he was in the South Pacific.

"Sidney's okay, baby. We would have heard something otherwise. He's smart, you know that."

But I wasn't nearly as sure as I sounded.

"He is, isn't he." She forced a sad smile.

"I am too. I played the choicest chick in Harlem into a marriage commitment. She even has to wear this ring."

"Jimmie! " She knocked me over. "Jimmie, I love you," she whispered.

I was pinned to the sofa. She was kissing me all over my face.

"Baby," she said.

"Yeah?"

"Baby, don't think I'm crazy but I want my brother to be at my wedding."

"So do I, baby."

The next thing I purchased was a 1941 Cadillac from a private owner. I read the ad in the paper and went and got it. I paid cash. Masaya loved it. We took long rides through the New England states, like before, ate steamed clams and drank cold beer. Two wonderful weeks of going everywhere and nowhere. One night we parked on the first beach we came to. We stood near the water, close to the stars, and listened to the quiet, distant rustling of the waves, watched them turn into a white foam before expiring on the shore. I thought about what Marty had said and I held tightly to this dream woman named Masaya. I gave my thanks to God in a silent prayer for the happiness. I only wished my mother were alive to meet her.

Masaya's and my lifestyle slowly changed. We retreated from that fast-paced existence of street hustlers, at least she did. Masaya fell in love with the Satin Doll and became an on-the-scene proprietor. I, who had no such passion, took to gambling. I began to spend hours at Mustache's on a 135th Street. The high rollers crowded into this dingy, smoke-filled joint and wagered thousands of dollars. I won my respect as a big bettor the first week, in less than two hours. I came home and tossed thirty-seven hundred dollars on the bed. I expected Masaya to share my joy, but she was less than ecstatic. She inhaled deeply before she spoke.

"Baby, this is something you don't know about."

That made me angry.

"What are you talking about? Can't you see this money? I won, Masaya. I won!"

"Baby, please don't get upset with me. I'm your woman. I'm glad you won. It's just that you're a professional grifter, not a gambler. Some of the slickest players in the City go into Mustache's place."

"Maybe they're not as slick as you think. Jimmie Lamar left there with almost four grand of their money."

She let it go but I glimpsed an expression of exasperation before she turned away. It hadn't all fallen on deaf ears, what she told me. It's just that, maybe, I felt a little put down hearing it from my woman, and had this need to prove her wrong. I went back the next day. I was hailed when I walked through the door.

"Here comes Big Time!" someone called out. "You nigguhs and ofays gonna git some action now fo' sho'."

The little man they called Mr. Williams, who I had given a double sawbuck yesterday, had something different to say.

"Walk slow, son," he whispered.

I thought he meant not to bet too fast. I couldn't get to the table quick enough. When I pulled out my roll I could hear the silent whoooooos.

"Five hundred I hit!" I said, tossing five one-hundred-dollar bills on the table, money enough to buy a new Ford.

Several men attempted to put their money together to cover the bet. I looked down the table and Smitty, a player from Jersey, was staring at me, unblinking, with no expression on his face.

He nodded. "You faded, young blood," Mustache said.

I picked up the dice. Smitty motioned to Mustache.

"Hold it!" Mustache shouted. "Smitty wants to check the dice."

I reached them to Mustache and he passed the dice to Smitty. Smitty blew on them, then rolled them between both hands. A quick sensation passed through my brain, like a warning. I ignored it. Smitty tossed the dice back to me. I glanced at Mr. Williams. I thought there was a faint movement of his head. I let the dice fly and felt the quick bittersweet rush only gamblers know.

"Deucy ball. Too low to call!" I heard Mustache say.

The dice had settled on snake eyes. I couldn't believe it.

"Fill your hole up, Big Time," someone said.

Smitty still didn't speak. The sarcasm made me mad.

"I'll shoot a grand!" I said.

Again, Smitty nodded. This time the dice landed on three, another loser. After that it was downhill all the way. It all happened so fast, the shouting, the big bets, Smitty's eyes staring through the thin smoke, the sweat, the pounding of my heart. The next thing I realized I was at home, playing the game over and over and over again. . . . I had lost the thirty-seven hundred dollars I had won, plus six thousand dollars of my money. I had run like a prime mark between the bank and the gambling joint, always hoping to catch up, like a man in a trance. I didn't tell Masaya. But she knew.

As the days passed I agonized about the money I had lost, had nightmares about it. I began to make a mental list of the different things I could have done with it. Even the Satin Doll had cost only slightly more than ten thousand dollars. I began to shun Masaya. Maybe she had been right and for that reason I didn't want her near me, gloating over her advice which had proven to be correct. One night after we had gone to bed and I had gotten back up and was standing in the window gazing out into the distance, she eased close to me.

"Let it go, baby."

"What?"

"The whole town knows, baby. It's only money and we're not broke."

She hugged me to her. I was so ashamed, but tried not to show it.

"You know how much money?" I asked.

She nodded. "I don't care," she whispered. "I don't care."

I let the money go and held on to my woman.

On Friday I received a letter from Paris. She would be in New York for two days in July, after the fourth. She had a surprise, she said. It was now the last of June. The following day we received three high-spirited letters from Sidney. The boys were fighting their butts off and he had won a battlefield commission. All in all, the month of June had turned out very well. Especially when I considered the ass-kicking Admiral Nimitz had given the Japs at Midway, an ass-kicking that was now turning the war in our favor. But I couldn't help but think about Bobby. I knew he didn't make it.

Since I lost my money I hadn't returned to Mustache's place; so running into Mr. Williams was purely by chance. I was somewhat embarrassed being caught coming out of a drugstore carrying that box with no name on it women sometimes send their men for.

"Young blood!"

The voice startled me. It was Mr. Williams.

"Young blood, can you stand a fin?"

I reached into my pocket and peeled a five spot off my bankroll.

"Now, young blood, you come and go with me."

"I don't have time now, Mr. Williams—"

"Wanta know how you got beat, don't you?"

I stopped in my tracks. "What you mean?" I asked, feeling my anger rise.

"You a grifter, you know what I mean. They played you like a slide trombone. I tried to tell you, but you's too hot with that sucka fame to pay me any mine. You come on with me, now."

He lived just two blocks away in a little first-floor studio.

"Ain't nobody ever been here but you. I wanta keep it that way."

He halted me at the door and studied me a moment.

"What I'm 'bout to show you is for our eyes only and our lips only. It ain't for you ta get all mad like a sucka and talk 'bout killin' somebody, you hea' me?"

I nodded. My curiosity was about to explode. What did this old man know? I asked myself. When he opened the door I saw nothing, except a beat-up old sofa, a chair, and two tables, one with a vise on the side, some sandpaper, and several pairs of dice. A deck of playing cards lay next to the dice. The second table was empty except for a green felt top. He motioned for me to follow him to the table with the dice on them. He picked up a black pair and stuck them into his mouth. Then he picked up a white pair, blew on them, and rubbed them between both hands. When he opened his palms the white pair had turned black. He spit the white pair out of his mouth. I couldn't believe my eyes. I was watching it, but still didn't see the switch.

"That's how they beat you, young blood."

"They? They who?"

"You don't think Mustache let somebody beat a nigguh in his joint and not be up on it?"

"But still, how—"

"The dice was weighted. Two dead aces and one dead deuce. They supposed to throw two aces or three, both losers for the shooter."

I stayed there with Mr. Williams for five hours, watched him place the dice in a vise, drill a hole in one end, and fill the hole with lead. Then, leaving the dice to dry and settle, Mr. Williams moved to the cards. With a toothpick he opened a brand-new deck from the bottom, removed the cards from the plastic, leaving it intact. He then took a razor blade and carefully, without damaging the seal, removed it. He marked each card with a thin brush, returned them to the box, glued the seal, and slid the deck back into the plastic. He then resealed the plastic at the bottom. Next he used the green felt to test the working of the leaded dice. It was Mr. Williams who supplied crooked dice to Mustache and some of the other gambling dens. But, as brilliant as Mr. Williams was about gambling, he had one flaw. He loved to play the horses. They kept him broke. After that revelation, I made it to Mr. Williams's house every day, after the racetrack closed, for three weeks. I learned to switch dice, palm cards, deal from the bottom, move the second card, to cold-deck and pull drags. Then it was practice, practice, practice. I drove Masaya crazy. Always with the cards and dice, day and night. I was determined to master these skills.

It was a New York Sunday, and we were in our shorts. Masaya had talked me into washing the cars with her, but the intended labor had turned into horseplay, erupting into a battle of soapsuds. She had sponged my hair and was running, circling the Cadillac screaming, with me following close behind. We hardly noticed the taxi slowing to a halt in front of the house. I caught Masaya on a turn and was sponging her hair just as a female in an army uniform stepped out of the taxi.

"Paris!" I shouted, and rushed to greet her.

I took her bags and, keeping my wet distance, kissed her cheek. I shook my head.

"Paris, you're in the army!"

"Looks that way, huh."

We walked to where Masaya stood. When I made the introduction I saw Paris's eyes react.

"I know just what you're thinking," I said.

"Incredible," she replied.

"Look at her eyes, just like Mama's."

"I think we're making Masaya uncomfortable, Jimmie."

"No, I'm flattered, really," Masaya said. "Just a little embarrassed meeting you looking like this."

"I understand," Paris said.

I led everyone inside, took Paris's bags into the guest bedroom, returned, and fixed us both a drink. Masaya rushed to the shower. Paris gave me a look. I smiled.

"It's just social. I quit drinking before I left Portsmouth."

She smiled at me for a moment. "You've grown up on me, Jimmie. I guess I came here expecting still to see the young boy with the sparkling eyes."

She touched the side of my face. "The eyes are still there, but the boy has gone."

There was a trace of sadness in her discovery, coupled with the pride a parent would feel. When I was near Paris I felt my mother's presence, her smile, beaming on us from some distant place. If she wasn't, it was what I wanted to believe.

"If she could see you now, Jimmie."

"And what about you, an officer in the United States Army?"

"That's right, Lieutenant Vernazos, on her way to the South Pacific."

"When, Paris?"

"Two days. I leave with the medical corps. I guess the doctors need more females to boss around. I was a nurse before I went into sociology, you know."

"They turned me down, Paris. My friend made it but they turned me down."

Suddenly I was very sad.

"I think they killed Bobby."

That was the first time I had really admitted to myself that Bobby was dead. She kissed my cheek and rubbed my head. Then she embraced me. She again had found the little boy she thought had flown out of her reach. I was happy for this, happy to learn that even with the certainty of change, some things can forever remain the same.

"You're too young to have experienced so much death," I heard her say.

But I had moved past my moment of sorrow into a celebration of my good fortune. It occurred to me how lucky I had been for four of the most wonderful women in the world to have shared a part of my life.

Masaya came in wearing her bathrobe and a towel around her head. I motioned her over and embraced these two special women.

The three of us decided to take a tourist tour of the City. We began with the Statue of Liberty, then the Empire State Building. We watched a clever magician in Central Park, and afterward took a buggy ride through it. At Scoffield's we had oysters on the half shell and giant Alaskan crab. That evening we went to Harlem to hear a young alto saxophonist named Charlie Parker play at Shelly's Inn. Paris was hypnotized. We came home intoxicated, all three of us.

The next day Paris took a taxi. She didn't want us to say lengthy sad good-byes, just a quick so-long. She had told me everybody couldn't be a warrior, and I bought war bonds the way she suggested. Two days later Masaya shocked me with the question of a lifetime. It came unexpectedly, from pure curiosity, with no slander intended. We were lying in bed.

"Baby, I want to ask you something that may be delicate."

"What is it?"

She hesitated. "Baby, did you know Paris was a lesbian?"

The question caught me so completely off guard. I couldn't give an immediate response.

"Why do you say that?"

"I'm a woman, baby, and I've been around."

"Did she tell you?"

"In a way she did by telling me what she was not interested in. I didn't mean to upset you, baby, I just wondered if you knew."

The truth was, I wasn't upset, although something kept telling me I should be. I couldn't picture Paris and my mother together that way, but then I couldn't picture my mother with a man that way either, not even Grady John. Then I wasn't sure my mother had known, and finally, I didn't care. It didn't diminish my love for Paris. How could it? I watched Masaya looking at me and felt her approval.

"You're one hell of a man, baby."

It could be said of us what was said in the book *A Tale of Two Cities.* Where we were concerned, it couldn't have been more true. The next two years proved it so. "They were the best of times and the worst of times." The financial success the two years brought us made them the best of times. I had recouped more than half of my losses and now had my own gambling joint. Mr. Williams was happy and so were the people who ran the racetrack. Masaya had scored big with this new product that lightened the skin. She had shrewdly invested in this idea a young graduate from Howard had presented one day at the Satin Doll. They now had a small factory producing a bleaching cream in jars. The money was rolling in. The worst of times was the failure in our personal lives. It was not standing up to the test of time. We hadn't worked together in a year and a half, not one sting. There was no need to. Our lives had taken different paths. She believed too much of my time was invested away from home. I believed too much of her time was spent with her young business partner. We became competitive, then suspicious, and then, sadly, jealous. It all came to a head one afternoon without warning. That volatile moment took us to a point where we had never ventured, and beyond. It was Valentine's Day, but I hadn't remembered. She pranced around the house ignoring me, but demanding my attention with the slamming of doors and pots and pans. She suddenly gave me the stare that could kill.

"You know, Jimmie, you could have given me something. If not a gift, at least a goddamned card! Did you give your other bitch one! Did you at least do that?"

"Why don't you shut that trap? You don't get paid for talking anymore. And maybe I do need somebody. Somebody who can keep quiet for about five minutes."

"You already have her, Jimmie. You can't fool me!"

"Wish I did. I might get some peace."

"Well, mister, I hope you get peace and you know what kind I mean!" she screamed, and ran into the bedroom, shaking the house with the vicious slam she gave the door.

But that wasn't enough. She opened it again.

"Don't forget to tell the bitch who made you. Tell her you were a little nobody, a lame who bought solid-gold watches for five dollars before you met me. And you can tell her I taught you how to eat pussy!"

She slammed the door. I rushed into the bedroom. She threw up her hands.

"Don't you hit me, Jimmie."

I was tempted. She had gone too far. What would she say or do next? I knew it wouldn't get better. I said nothing. I got my suitcases and began to pack. She stood in the doorway watching me. When I had finished, I forced my way past her. I knew her eyes were on me when I walked to the car. I couldn't turn around now. My pride made me stick to my decision. I thought about New Orleans. I had always wanted to see the Mardi Gras.

Big City woke everybody up screaming. He ran full front into the bars. "Git it out. New York! Git it out!" He pinned himself against the steel, facing us like a man being crucified, his eyes wide with horror. A small mouse, even more frightened, scurried past him.

"Did you see that rat, New York? You see that rat?"

"I saw him, big man."

"They all gone?" he asked, looking hesitantly at the floor.

"Ain't no more, big man."

"Damn thangs'll run up yo' pants leg and bite yo' dick off!"

I had to laugh. The kid and the other man were afraid to.

"I'm serious, New York, happen ta my cousin when he was a boy. That's the reason I tie my pants at the bottom with my shoe-strings."

I looked at his pants and almost fell off my bunk laughing. I saw him getting angry and changed the subject.

"Hey, man, why don't you put me in touch with your mouth-piece?"

"Mr. Gayton?" Okay, New York, I'll git 'um word."

I looked at the kid sitting silently on the top bunk. "What's your name?"

"Jerry," he answered.

"What they got you for?"

"Say I stole a bike but I didn't."

I could hear tears in his voice. "How old?" I asked.

"I don't know, I didn't take it."

"Not the bike, you."

"Fifteen."

"City. You think your Mr. Gayton can help the kid out if I grease him a little?"

"Sho' do, New York. I 'spose ta see him anyway today."

A new turnkey came around with breakfast—corn pone, grits, and blackstrap molasses. A different trustee was with him.

"Hey, sport," I called.

"There's four of us in here. I got two bucks. Do something for us on this grub."

"I need another dollar," he said.

"That's all I can stand. I gotta pay the shyster," I told him.

"Okay, I do what I can."

I gave him the money and he was gone. I looked down at the man no one knew.

"What's your name, sport? I don't eat with strangers."

"Moses."

"Jimmie Lamar."

Moses was a sleepy-eyed little man with a shaved head that needed a shave.

"Took this gal from Detroit to New York one time when I was in the army," Moses said. "Neva got use ta them trains running so fas' underground," he added.

That got Big City's attention.

"You know Radio?"

Moses shook his head. After a while the trustee brought the food, scrambled eggs and thick slices of bacon. He slid the trays under the bars. After removing the grits we slid him back the trays containing the first breakfast. Everybody thanked me.

Before noon a turnkey came and got Big City for an attorney visit. When he returned smiling the turnkey took me. We rode that same jumpy elevator down to the floor I came in on and I was led to an unoccupied cell. I could see the processing of the new residents the sheriffs brought in, the fingerprinting and the photographing. Most were colored. Soon a serious-looking white man wearing glasses was let into the cell with me.

"I'm Mr. Gayton."

He didn't bother to shake my hand, just handed me a business card that read WILLIAM GAYTON, ATTORNEY-AT-LAW.

"I'm Jimmie Lamar."

"Okay Jimmie, let's see what we can work out here."

"Sounds good to me, William."

He shot me a quick look. "You know, son, you could have saved yourself a lot of trouble if you hadn't brought that New York dipsy-doo down here trying to slick our boys."

I lost it right there.

"I don't know about no dipsy-doo, but I know your boys down here are some goddamn liars!"

"Wait a minute, don't go gittin' all uppity with me. I'm here to try and help you."

Right away I realized the foolishness of my error. The game hadn't taught me that. A quick temper was something for marks.

"I didn't mean nothing against you, Mr. Gayton. I'm just a little upset. My wife left me, you know, that's why I came down here, to try and find her."

He eyed me suspiciously.

"What kinda work you do, Jimmie?"

"I own a beauty shop."

His eyes narrowed. "You ain't one of those queers, are you?"

I shook my head. I told him I was married to a very pretty girl who was from New Orleans. She had left me for fooling around. I had to find her and beg her back. He seemed to like that story. It probably rang a bell somewhere in his life. We worked out a price for both me and the kid. That part I thought was fair. I knew I wasn't gonna get away without doing some time, but no more than thirty days. I made arrangements for him to put my car in storage. I hoped they wouldn't go through it and find my money. But what else could I do?

Maybe one of the drawbacks of being a grifter is we sometimes underestimate other people. That would prove a costly error with William Gayton. I should have known by the vinegar smile he gave me before I left. I carried the image all the way back to my cell.

Big City was in good spirits. Mr. Gayton wanted City to do some carpentry work on his house as payment for legal fees. Big City knew now for sure he would be getting out. We all had another lunch together that I sported. Three days later I was in the back of a truck headed for the state prison. There were five of us, all young men, all colored, except the grim-faced deputy holding the high-powered rifle. It was raining, but I was too angry to care. All I could think about was William Gayton, who had taken my money and sold me down the river. And that fuckin' judge. It was not justice he was concerned with. His major concern was keeping a nigguh in his place. The funny thing was, he appeared to be a fair man, at first. Even friendly, the way he laughed and joked with the bailiff and court reporter. That was before he focused on me and read the guilty plea William Gayton had advised me to sign. After I repeated it again in open court, the judge tore into me. His words seared in my brain now, despite the rain.

"You got off on the wrong foot here, boy. The sheriff put in a call on you to New York. You been in trouble back there for some kind of flimflam. They might let you boys git away with that sort of thang up there, but we don't tolerate it down here. Three years' hard labor!"

He banged his gavel on the table. William Gayton looked at me and shrugged his shoulders. There had been no deal as he had promised if I pled guilty, no floater, no probation, no fine. The judge had agreed to nothing. He was actually intimidated by me. With my erect posture, expensive clothes, and big automobile, I was a threat to the Southern way.

The rain hadn't stopped when we arrived at the prison farm camp, which gave us a hazy view of the surroundings. We did see a white man wearing a hat and slicker directing colored men with shotguns who in turn were ordering around inmates wearing white clothes with large black stripes. We were told to descend the truck one at a time. Then line up in single file. We learned the white man with the hat and slicker was the captain. He pranced around us in his jackboots making inspection while we stood in the rain. Coiled in his hand was a large bullwhip. I remembered a war was on and we were winning. Everybody wanted to be a soldier. We were forced to march everywhere, to the laundry for prison uniforms, to the mess hall for the captain's short orientation, and finally to the bunkhouse. As soon as I walked through the door, someone whistled at me. I looked his way and, smiling, walked toward him. He was bare from the waist up with menacing muscles that rippled in his chest and arms. I quickly planted my right foot the way Jake had taught me. I looked down at his feet. He looked down and I smashed a left hook to the side of his head that jarred my arm up to my shoulder. He hesitated, then fell slowly to the floor, landing hard on the wood. I kicked him in the face before I knew he was out. His eyes rolled back in his head and he let out a loud groan.

"Anybody else think I'm a bitch? Anybody else want some of me?"

The man groaned again. I kicked him hard in the stomach and he puked on the floor.

"Ain't this nigguh got no friends. I'll kill this faggot."

Everyone stood frozen, mouths agape.

"Don't kill 'um, young blood. He's got enough."

The voice was firm but still understanding of my situation. If you failed to react swiftly and with violence when another man made a pass at you in prison, it was a sure bet you'd be turned into a woman. The voice came from a man in his fifties, who looked to be in good condition. He walked toward me.

"Told the niggah he's gonna mess wit' the wrong person one day."

The man on the floor was coming around. After his head cleared, he grabbed the side of his face and scooted away from me.

"Where you from, young blood? Not the Bottoms, I know."

"New York," I said proudly.

"Come on down ta my roost. There's a empty bunk."

He kept talking as we walked to the far end of the room. The other inmates watched us.

"Had a homie up in New York," he told me.

"Good player. Society Red was his monicker."

"Ol' man Red? You know Society Red?"

I was excited to find any connection to New York here, even if it was via a friendship between this old man and one I knew back there.

"Know him? We sold slum jewelry together thirty years ago. Wasn't no niggahs around with heart enough to beat a crackuh but me and Red. What's ol' Red doin' now?"

"Red don't do nothing. He's got a rich ofay chick. Red just comes in the joints talking trash. Talking about he's got enough money to burn up a wet elephant."

That made the old man laugh. He shook his head.

"That's Red, all right. He's a player too!"

"Yeah, he can play," I agreed.

"I saw him cold-deck on one of them guinea gangsters in a poker game. The guinea was a hit man for the Mob too. Red didn't give a fuck. The old man's got plenty heart. He's so smooth he made the switch right in their faces, the guinea and his henchmen. Beat him for a grand."

"They call me King Fish, young blood. What's yo' name?"

"Jimmie Lamar."

We touched hands lightly.

"You know the game, don't ya, Jimmie?"

"I know it all," I bragged. "From the pigeon drop to the uncut-diamond game."

I didn't stop there. Young players have to try and impress the older ones. But King Fish impressed me much more than I could have ever impressed him.

"I play cards too," I said. "I can move the second, and swing. I can cold-deck too."

He was pleased to have another player there with him. Somebody to really talk to.

"You play the light, Jimmie?"

He knew I didn't. He knew I would have included it in my list of accomplishments. The light was something only a master card cheat could negotiate in a game. A tiny mirror under the nail of a finger moved in and out of a breast pocket with a handkerchief. I conceded his superiority with a smile.

"What about the Mitt?" he asked.

I immediately thought about Father Divine, and I thought about Bobby.

"Naw, I ain't up on preaching."

"It ain't 'bout preachin'. It's 'bout what suckahs want ta believe, like they can own the Brooklyn Bridge. Like niggahs gon' be equal ta whites one day. Playin' the Mitt is helpin' them believe what they already do."

"That's what you're in here for?"

He told me why he was there and what his sentence had been.

It was Saturday and we stayed up late, both glad to relate our life stories to each other. He talked about his two churches and the women who had been in his life. The more he related his story, the more respect I gained for him. Strangely enough, as soon as I learned he could play the light, I knew he was going to be one of the most important teachers in my life.

Sunday King Fish sang. They all crowded around him making requests, everyone except the man I had knocked out. King Fish told me his name was Snooky and he had gotten himself a transfer to another bunkhouse. When night came King Fish told me how they had had to run to the cane fields, but now rode to work in large trucks. For some reason I slept well my first night in prison.

18 The truck pulled away from the bunkhouse on its way to the river bottomland, bouncing over the rocky roads and kicking up bits of gravel along with clouds of dust that mingled fiercely with the thick rolling fog of the breaking dawn. In the back, a trustee holding a shotgun rode with us prisoners. And in the early-morning silence the pathetic faces of men, beaten, both physically and in spirit, stood frozen, like figures of bronze touched by the genius of Rodan.

It was a long way from Harlem, I thought, a whole world away. I vowed never to become one of these lost souls, men without direction or hope. I would die first. I was from the City. Cats from the South let ofays do them any kind of way. Of course, this was a myth, a kind of one-upmanship, born from the Negro's need to feel superior to someone, even if that someone was his own people. I fell into that same trap. The truth is, the culture of America has always been one of hypocrisy and racism, and in the main, geography has little to do with it.

The rich bass voice of King Fish broke the silence. The others joined in a rendition of an old spiritual tune. I didn't understand. These spooks were singing on their way to the white man's "slave." I could croon a little, too, but singing was the last thing on my mind. Again, the point had been missed by me. Music may have been the most important factor in bringing the Negro race through slavery.

The truck stopped and a red-necked guard, wearing a beaten straw hat, jumped down from the front. He waved the shotgun he was carrying and shouted his command. "Okay, ol' thangs, clear them swamps!" We leaped to the ground, one at a time, and were handed a machete by the inmate trustee. He was a mammoth man with massive chest and beady eyes that rolled recklessly in his ebony face. Eyes that gave off a hint of determination that lay somewhere between ignorance and madness. The most brutal inmates were the ones selected as trustees, I learned. They were given shotguns and warned that if any prisoners they guarded escaped, the remainder of that prisoner's sentence would be attached to their own. As a result, murder came easy to them and they committed it often with impunity. The few real prison guards who supervised them encouraged their brutality, even enjoyed it. There would always be these kinds of men, I thought. Big, hulking brutes who threw their weight around and hid their cowardice behind uncontested acts of violence. They convinced themselves that this was the way of superior men. I knew them well. In the City I had watched them back down from real men, sometimes begging for their lives. I smiled at this lesser man, then took the machete and followed King Fish and the others into the swamp.

There were three straight hours of backbreaking work, of chopping, of lifting and clearing before there was a lunch break. I was exhausted.

"What we doing out here in a swamp, man?" I asked, walking over to King Fish.

"Building a road to nowhere."

He wiped the sweat from his forehead with his sleeve and planted the machete into the ground with a swing.

"What's that supposed to mean?"

"Just what I said, workin' fo' nothin', 'cuz they want us to."

The guard's voice, with its off-key whine, tried my nerves and crawled along my flesh like a many-legged insect.

"Okay, ol' thangs, git them grits."

Everyone rushed to the pot. Afterward me and King Fish sat down with our food.

"Anybody ever get away from here? They ain't got no chains on us."

I was already considering escape.

"Don' need 'um. Ol' man swamp the best guard in the worl'. Out there a man good fo' three days if he lucky."

A wave of despair caused me momentarily to bow my head. But not for long. I was young and recklessly strong-willed. The tears welling up in my eyes became more tears of rage than sadness. I felt my jaw tighten. I had already had my fill of it: crazy crackuhs, stupid spooks, dog shit, horse shit, and insects. I was through hearing "Yes, suh, boss" and "No, suh, boss" and I was tired of being called "old thang." In fact, I was ready to die. It happens to you that way sometimes, when nothing matters, when consciousness is lost and reason and fear are replaced by a black void. When I raised my head, anger so distorted my face that even King Fish was startled. I would have probably lost control in any case, but spotting the alligator slithering into the stagnant waters in the distance caused me to explode.

"What the fuck *is* this, man! " I shouted, jumping to my feet. "A motherfuckin' jungle?"

"Sit yo' black ass down, boy, and shut yo' mouth!" the guard commanded, walking in my direction.

I screamed at the top of my lungs. "You want us to get ate up by a fuckin' *alligator*?"

A fist smashed into my jaw and sent me sprawling. King Fish had knocked me down and was on top of me before I could recover, his hands fastened around my neck.

"Freeze, blood. These crackuhs'll kill ya. You're a player," he whispered.

Then he spoke out loud. "Don't ever talk to the boss that way, boy! You make it hard on everybody."

I recovered quickly; maybe the punch jarred me back to reality. The will to survive returned as quickly as it had gone. My unchecked rage transformed itself into a quiet and sober cunning. I looked up at the guard standing over me. I bowed my head and buried my pride, because I was a player. The words were bitter in my mouth but I still managed to mimic the other inmates.

"Sorry, boss, ol' gator got the best of this ol' thang."

The guard looked at King Fish.

"He be all right now, boss," King Fish assured him. Then he looked at the trustee.

"Want me to teach 'um, boss?" the trustee asked, with clenched fists that had turned into steel hammers.

"I think he taught enough, boss," King Fish said.

"When I put these on 'um."

King Fish continued showing his fists. "They sho'nuff taught." I didn't move, not even to touch my throbbing jaw, not even to keep from wetting myself, like I did. The warm liquid spread over the front of my crotch, settling in a puddle around me. The loud laughter of King Fish could be heard, it seemed, by every living thing in the swamp. The jubilant roar created movement and little noises in its wake; like rodents and lizards, escaping. King Fish knew laughter was contagious and he prolonged his own until he could see the cold threatening face of the guard crack, along with the trustees'.

"Look there, boss," King Fish said, pointing and still laughing. "We dun scared the piss outta that ol' thang."

And they all had their laugh. King Fish took out a bag of tobacco and began to roll a cigarette, another ploy, he later told me, he sometimes used to deter the guard from evil business.

"Roll me one, too, ol' thang, but don't lick it," the guard said.

Then he took the cigarette King Fish handed him and licked it himself. He spit a wad of tobacco near my feet.

"Git outta this 'un, ya won't be comin' down har' no mo'. Will ya, ol' thang?"

"Not down here no mo', boss," I replied, forcing my voice to crack. The guard struck a match on the seat of his bibbed overalls, lit his cigarette, and spoke to me as he began to walk away.

"Mind yo' manners, boy; by God, ya almost got her that time."

The ground was littered with both mine and King Fish's breakfast, but it didn't matter, we had no appetite now. Something of my pride had been damaged, maybe forever, and King Fish spoke softly to my pain.

"Son, you can't pull the lion's tongue with yo' head in his mouth."

"I'm not a 'Tom,' Fish. I'm a man!" I stated. "I'm not scared!" I added, reinforcing my declaration.

"They don't bury the scared, son. They bury the dead. You gotta reach back and git all yo' game if you wanta stay alive in here!"

He reached out his hand and pulled me to my feet.

"Young blood, you a good grifter, I can see that. I seen 'um come and I seen 'um go, the slickest, the ones who thought they could really play 'con.' They's little more than suckuhs theyselves, but it's wrote on yo' face, son. You's one in a hun'ard. The fix you in now is asking fo' some game, not no suckuh move. Ain't but two ways to go here on in, young blood. You either a 'Tom' or you play the 'Jeff Davis.' "

"I told you I'm not a Tom, man, and I'm not hip to no Jeff Davis," I protested.

"Git this, son. A Tom's a niggah what thinks white folks is bet- terin' him and lets 'um know it. The Jeff Davis is when a niggah makes white folks think he thinks they betterin' him but knows it ain't so."

I learned that day that courage and cowardice were interchange- able. Both catered to different spaces and different times. I learned that there is no factoring in emotion in any equation because emo- tion was capricious. In a more familiar setting I would have met any challenge, even if my life was hanging in the balance. Death has no sting where honor and glory prevail; and brave deeds are more frequently performed when someone is there to record them.

The next day we were loaned out to the state as a road crew to begin the building of a highway. We were chained together with our legs shackled. We sang of our misery as we put pick to ground in the burning sun. The captain beat a path toward us on the back of his white horse. When he reached the clearing, the beast blew and snorted to a prancing halt. He hopped down with the spring of a man much younger than his fifty-odd years, removed a bull-whip from the saddle, and began a slow menacing walk among the men. They shied away from his pointed stare. The sun's rays had turned the back of his neck beet red and he patted it with a large handkerchief.

"You ol' thangs gonna git my highway built? Gimme some sweat. Put some nigger in it!"

He cracked his whip over his head.

"Y'all heard the cap'n, put some nigger in it," the trustee echoed, kicking the closest man to him. The captain stared at the men working furiously in single file. Satisfied, he patted the trustee's head, walked back to his horse, leaped on its back, and rode away. The captain's mission was accomplished. The pace sped up. I was working behind King Fish, who made a game of hard labor, with wisecracks, work songs, and wagers on speed.

"Damn, Fish, you trying to kill us?" I joked.

King Fish laughed his big laugh. "I been workin' hard for twelve years."

He rolled the pick over in his hand like a baton. "Ain't nothin' you do for twelve years you ain't good at," he said, doin' a little dance that wiggled his rear.

I kept up with him, though.

"Man, twelve years too long to be rich," I countered.

Again, King Fish laughed. These antics and witty exchanges helped us make it through the long days and brought us closer together.

It took three weeks, an attempt on my life by Snooky in which King Fish was wounded, before all the other inmates began talking to me. They had finally decided I was okay, even if I was from back east. It probably would not have been the same without the closeness between King Fish and me. After me and the rest became friendly, I wisecracked them.

"I don't know what you spooks was mad at me for in the first place. Y'all wanted me to let Snooky fuck me?"

Everybody laughed. I held my hand out palms up. Pee Wee slapped it.

"Who's got the lightning. I'm buying for everybody," I announced.

"Hold on," Pee Wee said.

He rushed outside and was back in ten minutes carrying two large jugs filled with moonshine. I paid him and sat the jugs in the middle of the floor.

"Okay, you spooks drink until your dicks get hard."

I filled my and King Fish's tin cup and we went over to our bunks. He had almost a worried look on his face.

"This shit them crackuhs dun ta you, you gotta take it serious," he said. "You gotta play above white folks. See what they dun ta me? You see, I wudden thinkin, got too mad. I shoulda ambushed that crackuh. Found out who he was, took my time, and laid somewhere and ambushed him. Who could tell who dun it?"

He reached in a box under his bunk and handed me a Bible.

"This is how ya play above 'um. I want ya ta read this every chance ya git."

I looked into his eyes and read the love of a father for a son there. That touched me. I had skimmed through the Bible before, but this time I really read it. Every chance I got, at night by the light of the Southern moon, on Saturdays and Sundays, I read. I became obsessed with reading again. The other inmates began to call me "Rev." After three months of reading, I handed King Fish back his Bible. I had finished it. He smiled and placed his hand on my shoulder. It felt like a father's approval. After that he began to teach. He taught me everything Malcolm Cage had taught him and more.

"It's the people what ain't got that makes a Mitt Man so's they can be part of the success they made. That's just what a pimp do."

I thought immediately about what Bobby had said about Father Divine, that he was a pimp who lived off both men and women. Father Divine, a small unimposing man, who owned his own airplane, a fleet of expensive automobiles, and a mansion in New

Jersey. Thousands of followers of all races proclaimed his divinity. I knew I could do at least half that good.

"Playin' the Mitt ain't like no other game," he told me. "Ya gotta stay the person ya say ya is. Gotta stay away from other players, act like a square fo' the rest of yo' life, like you sho'nuff a man of God."

"What about that healing trick?" I asked him.

"Them suckuhs play that trick on theyselves. It's in they mine. If you believe somebody can heal ya, they can. Now, the ones what don't git healed. Them preachers tell 'um they don't believe hard enough."

I laughed.

"That's playing ain't hit, son?"

"Sure is," I agreed.

I won his confidence in my ability three days later while discussing with him my opinions on certain chapters. Even offering an opposing view on one chapter. He saw the Book of Joshua as one of the Bible's great contradictions. "Thou shalt not kill," he said was one of the Commandments, but in the Book of Joshua, murder was ordered by God himself. I saw Joshua as a perfect lesson of man's obedience to God.

"The Book of Samuel talks about the consequences of being disobedient to God," I said.

I also reminded him that whatever it was that God demands of man, man can demand nothing from God. King Fish was ecstatic. He let out that big laugh and slapped me on the back.

"Tell me this, Father Jimmie Lamar. Who was hit said, 'All things under the sun is vexation of the spirit and strivin' after the win'?"

"Solomon," I said quickly.

"What book?"

"Ecclesiastics."

"Who was the 'voice cryin' in the wilderness'?"

"That was John the Baptist," I said.

He smiled at me. "What was hit he said at the river?"

I thought about it a moment. I wanted the phrase to be exact.

" 'I baptize you with water, but there will come one who will baptize you with fire and the Holy Ghost.' "

He nodded favorably. "Remember them good lines. People pay for good lines."

With each passing day he began to live vicariously through me. We daydreamed about my ministry, even decided what I should wear. We selected a white robe trimmed in white velvet.

"Give the women the attention, but don't touch 'um. Use yo' good looks and yo' style to draw 'um in. The men gonna follow," he told me.

We were the perfect match, the brash youngster and the wise old man, the going out and the coming in. Each into each other's sphere.

The Fourth of July came on a Saturday that year. We celebrated with extra food provided by the prison staff after the inmates put on a minstrel show to entertain them. Afterward we drank white lightning. Me and King Fish lay on our bunks across from each other. I expressed concerns about the new game I was learning to play. I had been drawn to the glamour and flash of the hustling life, the easy manner in which hustlers lived, their seeming independence. I had embarked on this lifestyle in a cavalier fashion with no thought given to repercussions. I hadn't been like some of the others who vented their hatred of themselves on society, nor had I been exposed to a life of crime. My involvement had been one of adventure and thrill seeking, but playing the "Mitt Game" was risking God's disfavor. This required some thought and I voiced these feelings in an offhanded manner.

"You know, Fish, sometimes I think I wasn't cut out to be a grifter. I mean . . . I know you ain't supposed to have no feelings for a mark. I know if a mark knew the game, he'd play it on me. . . . I remember, one time, my dame and me caught this old lady, you know. She had just got a settlement from her dead husband. We beat her for seven grand. You know what happened? You ain't gonna believe this! I got to thinking what my mother used to say. She'd say, 'Don't do anybody wrong, because if you do, it can come back on you.' You know what I did? Kicked the money back."

King Fish shook his head in amazement. "That's a suckuh move, boy. You fallin' fo' the game yo'self."

"You don't understand, Fish."

"No! It's you what don't understand. Now you lissen and you lissen good! Ain't but two kinda people in the wurl'. The ones that gives and the ones that takes, and know'n what ya gonna be is the difference between bein' a player or suckuh. Ya understand?"

Still I did not share what seemed to be King Fish's atheism. The evidence against it was too overwhelming. I myself had had my private talks with God and most of my wishes had been granted, like winning a scholarship for my mother, or having her overcome her alcoholism. Above all else, I had sought my mother's approval and her love. This wish, too, had been granted me. As a youth I could not boast of a new car to drive or even afford the latest fad in clothing, but I was easily the most popular boy (*black or white*) in the small Ohio town. Because I was a wizard on the basketball court and the flashy, high-stepping quarterback on the football field, everyone loved me. Every young girl seemed smitten with my good looks and captivating personality. The teachers in school smiled when I passed them in the hallway and old people sitting on their porches nodded their approval when I walked by. Even then, I was aware that God had a hand in my success. Everything came too easy for me. I never really worked that hard at anything. It was just that God had given me the brains and the natural talent to excel, because of my mother's condition, I reasoned.

King Fish had not understood that beneath my slick New York exterior there existed, in part, a small-town boy who still believed there was a God.

19 King Fish sank slowly to the floor gripping his chest and rolling on his back. The three men who had been singing with him stood petrified until I rushed over and ordered them to help move him to his bunk. The rest gathered around, expecting the worst, afraid of death, but still drawn, by some morbid curiosity. Then King Fish smiled and passed gas. "Too many years of eating garbage," he joked, and took a sip of moonshine from a fruit jar that lay on the floor beside his bunk. This was the day the warden announced that the invasion of Normandy had begun. Prisoners had been allowed a small celebration and a decent meal. King Fish did confess to me that he had a bad heart; but the illness changed nothing for him. He continued to drink his moonshine, sing his songs, and work in the fields. He could easily have become a trustee and received some special privileges, maybe even an occasional prostitute. Could I be as much of a man in the face of such adversity? Could I spend the rest of my life in prison without going crazy? I spoke to King Fish about my feelings.

"A man gotta handle the pain of love and lick the fear of dying before he become a real man; and he gotta be just what he say he is," he told me.

But to rid one's self of the fear of death one must first come

face-to-face with death's certainty, lest he appear at death's door
naked and trembling when eternity comes to call. In the days of
one's youth a sense of immortality temporarily frees him from this
fear, but youth is fleeting and death is not.

Rufus died that following week and, since there were no surviving relatives, was buried in the prison graveyard. He was the
prison's oldest inmate.

King Fish remembered this old, toothless, broken man. He had
been present the day of his own arrival. He told me how Rufus
had shuffled and grinned for the captain. He also said Rufus had
committed a few unsavory acts over the twelve years King Fish had
been there, even exchanged information with the guards for favor-
able treatment. But King Fish couldn't hold that against him now.
Rufus had done what he thought he had to do to survive. King
Fish felt compelled to lead the only family Rufus had, in a single
file, walking slowly to mourn him. We walked with our heads
down, singing "Swing Low, Sweet Chariot, Comin' for to Carry
Me Home." We came to pay our respects to one of our own and
in a way to face a convict's major fear, the fear of dying alone and
old in prison. It was not so much the dying we feared, but more
the fear of being robbed of the most poignant moment at life's
end, the visit of friends and loved ones. We brought a jar of moonshine and each man took a small drink after we had circled the
grave. The remainder was poured where Rufus lay. The prayer
King Fish offered was simple. "The Lawd giveth and the Lawd
taketh away." Then something I never expected happened. This
solemn group came to life and began to dance. They sang "When
the Saints Go Marchin' In" up-tempo, all the way back to the
bunkhouse. King Fish called it Second Line, New Orleans's way
of saying good-bye to the dead. What a strange thing, I thought,
a celebration of death. King Fish must have had a premonition of
his own end that evening. He made me promise to put myself down
as his next of kin when I left. When he died, for me to make sure,
wherever I was, to have his body buried in Slidell, Louisiana, with
his family. It was not with sadness he made this request, but with
a feeling of having come full circle in his life. At last we had found

each other, me a father, him a son. He knew I would carry the knowledge he gave me into the free world. That was all he had had to give to make him live on. It was a promise I was to keep sooner than I expected.

There was pain in his eyes. His breath shortened. His body extended itself, trembling slightly. His face broke out in small beads of perspiration, but he showed no fear. He did not try to fight for the life he knew was slipping away. "Life is like some big ol' play," he said, "makin' folks laugh sometimes and sometimes makin' 'um cry." And then he was gone.

There was a strange stillness in the bunkhouse that night; there were no conversations and no songs. The sound of the rain on the rooftop was the music that accompanied my soft weeping. King Fish's death devastated me, almost as much as my mother's, probably because of where I was and because most of the people I had come to love were either dead or separated from me.

I was tempted to write Paris, but too embarrassed. I did bury my pride and write to Masaya. The fight we had that brought me south in the first place seemed insignificant now. The loneliness was overwhelming. The following days were almost unbearable, especially seeing them take King Fish's body away. I kept my word to my "father." I spared no expense. I spent every dime the booking office was holding for me. It wasn't enough, not for what I wanted. My father deserved a marble headstone with his image carved on it. In his belongings were several pictures of a younger King Fish along with pictures of a beautiful woman with the words "To My Loving Husband" written on the backs of them. There were also letters from Raymond White. King Fish had told me wonderful stories about this man, stories that were reinforced by his quick response to my letter. It was Raymond White, professor of law, who paid the balance of the burial arrangements, and oversaw them as well.

I had been in prison almost a year. With my time split in half for good behavior, I would go home in six months. Damn, I sure missed New York! Man, I didn't want to see a movie about the South when I got home.

20 It was Monday morning, the day we usually worked the road. The men had been working for five hours now and I was glad I was no longer one of them. I, too, experienced that feeling of weightlessness the inmates said freedom would bring, especially when the gate closed behind me. The first thing I saw when I walked into the free world was my Cadillac, but the sun reflecting off its chrome temporarily blurred my vision. I took a deep breath and walked straight ahead, afraid to look back. Maybe this, too, was one of the many dreams of freedom I had had. I still didn't know why I had been given an early release. I didn't trust these ofays down here, and hurried to my car. When I opened the door Sidney and Masaya were sitting in the backseat. My heart jumped with excitement. Sidney even looked hip in uniform, except for the dark glasses that reminded me of a blind man. I wanted to embrace him but Masaya held up her hand, then brushed her shoulder, the signal all grifters understand to mean back off.

"Drive, baby," she said.

"Got a kiss for Daddy?"

"Don't be crazy," she warned. "Let's get away from here."

"Still mad at me, huh?" I joked.

"Jimmie, drive please!" she implored.

I put the keys in the ignition and quickly removed them. "Just a minute," I said.

I rushed back to the trunk. It was all there just the way I had left it.

When I told them about the money, Masaya thought it was an indication of my luck changing. Sidney agreed. Grifters are notoriously superstitious. I've known some who would never split a pole or walk under a ladder and would turn and head in the opposite direction if they so much as saw a black cat. King Fish was the exception. Skill was all he believed in. "Luck only helps a nigguh over a ditch if he jumps hard," he would say.

I wouldn't have noticed the change in Sidney so soon if he hadn't removed those glasses. His lackluster eyes betrayed a pasted-on smile with no warmth. A strained air existed in the car. This was not at all the joyful union the three of us together should have inspired. Then I noticed the crutches on the floor.

"Drive, Jimmie—we have to get away from here!" Masaya pleaded.

I got into the car and did as she told me—remaining quiet about what I had seen; but, I had a bad feeling. The silence reinforced it.

"Lost a leg on Saipan," Sidney stated flatly.

My mouth opened, but nothing came out.

"At least I came back. Some of the guys weren't so lucky," he almost whispered. Then, brightly, he said, "There's something here worth recording, sport. A one-leg white soldier with his half-breed sister, who passes, frees colored flimflam man."

"Don't forget the blind part," Masaya added.

"Right! Blind one-leg white soldier," Sidney confirmed.

"I don't get it," I said.

"Me and Sidney played white wounded war hero with his faithful white wife for the judge who sent you."

I began to laugh. "You played the blindman routine, the one we beat that mark in Buffalo with?"

Sidney chuckled. "A soldier blinded in battle who lost a leg to boot. No judge could refuse him a favor," Sidney said.

"Sidney told him you worked for us before he went overseas, that you were the only one of them he trusted," Masaya said.

After that, things began to loosen up and we revisited the past. As I put the distance behind us, and the prison, my anxiety slipped away. The images of guards, trustees, and caged men vanished into the peacefulness of a warm summer afternoon.

We drove through the shantytowns where poor colored folks lived, their children dressed in rags. They waved from broken-down porches and from the roadside when we passed them. We saw women and children plowing and planting, probably share-cropping a land that would never be their own.

When we reached Memphis we were exhausted and found a nice colored hotel. That's when Sidney broke my heart. He refused any help from me or Masaya and, as a result, got a faulty start on his crutches. He ended flat on his face. The most painful part was seeing my teacher and best friend on the ground helpless and em-barrassed with one pant leg pinned up to where his knee should have been. He grew pitifully silent when we helped him up. At the office he wanted his own room. Masaya and I honored his request and rented a separate one for ourselves. I couldn't wait to tell her about King Fish; but when she heard I was going to play the "Mitt," she laughed. I tried very hard to hold back my anger, or maybe I didn't try so hard at all.

"Oh, Jimmie, a preacher?"

"What's wrong with it."

"I just can't imagine you as some jackleg preacher."

Her laughter tormented me.

"Don't laugh at me, Masaya, and don't ever try to make me look small."

"Jimmie, baby, we haven't seen each other in almost a year."

But it was too late. This was something I was doing on my own and she couldn't support me in it?

"Anyway, I'm talking about playing it big like Gandhi, that cat in India," I told her.

"Baby, I was raised up in the church. It doesn't feel right."

"Aren't you the one who didn't wanta kick the money back to the old lady we beat that time? Wasn't that you or am I mistaken?"

"That was then, but it doesn't mean I would feel right playing on those poor old church people."

I shook my head in disbelief. "Those poor old church people, as you call them, were too good to associate with my mother."

"Baby, baby, all church people—"

"Fuck 'em!" I shouted. "It's all a game. They played high society with my mother. Well, her son's gonna be at the top of the high-society church game."

The decision had been made not by weighing the pros and cons or by considering the basic ethics like fairness and honor. The decision was made through obstinacy. I had become a victim of arrogance, born out of a sense of insecurity. The battle began to rage inside of me. Conscience and decency collided with greed and revenge. I thought of King Fish and his lesson about givers and takers. I'm a taker, I thought to myself as Masaya went quietly into the bathroom. I could hear the shower running, imagine her naked body, the black tangled nest between her legs. My anger did not stay my passion. When she came out wrapped in a towel, I took her without ceremony, partially against her will. No tender "I love yous" escaped our lips, no gentle caresses. Desire and hostility was the mixture that fired us, and wild clawing animal lust. That's what we brought to the night.

The next morning we didn't talk much to each other. Maybe she was thinking what I was thinking. It wasn't going to work. Maybe there was too much mistrust between us.

I drove the rest of the way. Sidney sat in front with me. She sat in the back. The conversations were between Sidney and me or her and Sidney. I pushed the car mile after mile, stopping only for gas, the bathroom, and to eat. The war had changed Sidney. I could tell that much. His reflexes seemed to have dulled and he was conspicuously silent for long periods of time. Masaya had grown even more stubborn and so had I. Some parameters should be set in a relationship and there should be someone in charge. The idea of a dual leadership doesn't really make a lot of sense when you think about it. It doesn't exist in any successful union or organization, from an army to a basketball team. Someone has to have the final say. It was this lack of clarity where the role of leader was concerned that was to be our undoing. We could not, either of us, accept this position from the other. The love, however, buried sometimes as it was, by layers of mistrust and arrogance, still survived.

Two days after we left Memphis, we were in New York. It was late at night and we dropped Sidney off at his apartment on Strivers' Row. Again he refused our help. Before the doorman showed him inside he did make one positive gesture toward us.

"Dig you later, sport, sis."

Then he hobbled away. In silence Masaya and I drove to our place in Sugar Hill.

The next morning was spent exactly the same way we had spent the last two days, mimicking the behavior of adolescents who pretended not to care, avoiding each other's eyes, speaking only when necessary.

"You want two eggs?" she asked.

"One."

"Bacon?"

"Two."

It continued like this and she had her thoughts.

"You had no reason to yell at me, Jimmie."

I said nothing.

"All I did was give an opinion," she continued.

"I didn't ask for your opinion. I just told you what I was going to do. Like I told you once before, you don't know everything, Masaya."

"I knew how to get you out of the pen," she replied. "I knew something then! You want two pieces of toast or one?" she said, with that edge in her voice I hated.

"None!" I responded hotly. "You eat the whole fuckin' breakfast yourself! You so fuckin' smart!"

I jumped up from the table, picked up my car keys, and was out the door. In the car I thought, She's doing it again. She even had the nerve to make fun of me, "some jackleg preacher." Now I remembered why I had gone to New Orleans. It was to get away from her. She must have thought I was incapable of making a sound decision. I drove to 134th, where I had first experienced Harlem. Nothing much had changed. The same women in short skirts and painted lips passed by and the same "jive-ass spooks" talked that talk and walked that walk, but they didn't try to hustle me this time. I was a New Yorker now and they knew it. No one hailed the car as it crept along, no hooker motioned to me, and no junkie tried to sell me a gold watch for five bucks. I passed the apartment building where I used to live and stopped the car. The place looked even more run-down than I remembered. I rounded the corner where I had first met Passion. Children now skipped rope and played hopscotch where whores once walked. I wondered what had happened to her. Was she somewhere crouched beneath a naked lightbulb, stained and unwashed, in some filthy bathroom, with a host of lost souls running poison from a secondhand needle into her veins? Maybe she was dead. Maybe she had made it out! That was possible too. At least it was a nice thought.

I pressed my foot on the gas pedal, turned the corner, and went in the opposite direction. I headed for Strivers' Row, where Sidney lived. Elegant two-story brownstones with balconies stood silently along this residential street. There were also rows of trees wearing their summer green. Sidney was in his robe when he opened the door, leaning on his crutches. He seemed glad to see me. His eyes and his questioning expression told me he knew why I had come. We had always bonded together against our mentor. He turned to lead me back to the bedroom, moving confidently. In his home he mastered the crutches. I sensed he needed to show me.

"You're up pretty early, brother-in-law," he said over his shoulder. "Where are you on your way to?"

"No place, Sid. Just had to get out of the house."

"Oh, I see. What did my sister do now?"

"Everything, she's not gonna make no punk outta me, Sid. She doesn't respect me, man. I'm not one of those lames. I'm a player!"

"I don't think she means it like that, it's just . . . Well, man, she's been assuming that mother role, at least all of my life."

"My mother's dead."

"What did she do, Jimmie?"

"Tried to make me look small, even laughed at me."

I explained it all to him. Even the reason I had left when I went to New Orleans.

"I understand. She's wrong talking to you that way. I do agree with her about you becoming a preacher, though."

"Sidney, what are you talking about? I'm gonna play the game. You taught me, remember?"

He looked at me real strange before he spoke. "Being over there taught me something, Jimmie. There is more to life than we understand, more than the game, more than we learned in college, even more than our parents taught us."

"Sidney, where are you going with this?"

He looked at me and his face saddened. He didn't speak for a long time. Suddenly he began to weep. I had never seen that before, and I was paralyzed again.

"No more games, Jimmie! I've done you a grave injustice. We are our brother's keeper. If we don't believe this literally, then we'll kill our brother."

"Sidney, I'm not going to kill anyone, I—"

"You believe in God, Jimmie?"

"Sure I do, I'm not a saint, but I'm not the worst person in the world, either."

"If you believe in the power and glory of God, how can you make a mockery of His Word?"

His eyes were fiery now. I hadn't expected to hear this, not from the man I looked up to. Not from the man who had moved through life as easy as a breeze, without concern or fear. This was a different Sidney. Someone who spoke like a preacher, making me feel guilty. I left him standing in the doorway. I was too confused to say good-bye. Suddenly the world seemed more complicated, even distant, and I seemed more like a spectator racing in a circle, holding on to one theory and then chasing after another, desperately trying to find a place to enter. I felt lost again, like someone with no destination.

I drove past the people filing into the huge church of Father Divine. They stood in line, women dressed in white, resembling nuns, some holding the hands of well-dressed children who were on their best behavior. Some smiled blissfully and chatted with clean-cut Negro men. The procession took up half a block. Clearly, these were people happy in their faith. Then, just as clear as this day, I thought of one word—children. I could help the children. I smiled. "Oh yes," I said out loud. If I became a "Mitt Man" and actually did some good, it would work for me. I could live with myself. I was free now, free of my conscience! I felt hungry and I drove four blocks to the Paradise Café, and luckily found a parking spot in front.

I spotted her walking toward me as soon as I was out of my car. It was like going back in time. Her maturity made her look even better than I remembered. That same painted smile played on her lips when our eyes met.

"Hello, Passion," I said as smooth as I could.

Her expression questioned, briefly. At once she beamed an exaggerated smile.

"Hi, baby, how ya been, sugah?"

A sudden gust of wind made the sky-blue dress cling to her body and caused the excitement to stir again in me, but this was a time for control. I gave her a confident smile and chose my best dominating posture, a wide-legged stance with both hands planted on my hips. My stare was unwavering. It stayed her advance for a second only, but she was a professional who had read a thousand postures, most of them contrived by men to convince her they were more than just tricks anxious to buy her body. I'm sure that's a hooker's expertise.

"You remember Jimmie, don't you?" I asked.

"Sure, sugah," she replied, without a clue as to who I was. "Where ya been, honey?" she asked, slipping her arm inside of mine.

"Looking for you, baby. Let's get some food," I said, placing an arm around her shoulders.

"Sounds good to me."

She glanced over her shoulder at my car as we walked into the café. We took a table beneath a shaded yellow light in a secluded part of the restaurant. The waitress came quickly with pad and pen in hand.

"Same thing, Jimmie?" she asked.

I nodded and looked at Passion. "Steak and eggs?" I asked.

"That's fine. Well-done and over easy," she told the waitress, who made her notation and left.

"What *is* your name?" she asked, tilting her head to one side. "You do look familiar."

"Jimmie Lamar," I replied.

"So, you're Jimmie Lamar!"

I smiled.

"Okay!" she said, barely hiding her enthusiasm.

"You don't know me, do you, baby?" I asked.

"I've heard the name."

"You remember sporting with a young man a few years ago? He had just come to town. Had his suitcase with him?"

She shook her head, then her eyes widened.

"You . . . *No!*"

"Yes," I said.

"How? I mean what happened to you?"

"I grew up. Still think I'm cute?"

She smiled.

"Who's the lucky man in your life?"

"No got no mo'," she stated in clever colloquialism. Her eyes questioned. "What about you?"

"If you heard about me, you know Masaya's my woman."

"So, I don't want no trouble."

I leaned close and looked into her eyes. "We got trouble already, baby. We like each other," I said.

"We do, do we?"

"Yes, we do," I confirmed, with a smile.

The waitress brought the food and told us to enjoy, and was quickly gone. We ate in silence, smiling at each other between bites, each waiting for the other to speak. I was basking in the triumph of the moment as I watched the respect in her eyes grow. I could feel my presence overwhelming her. I could feel my manhood. Perhaps man's biggest enemy is his ego. This giant relentless monster who has followed him throughout history and compromised kings, marched with armies, destroyed friendships, and estranged lovers. In my case, my ego demanded Passion's respect for me as a man, a lover, and a player. I was, after all, JIMMIE LAMAR! The sad thing is, I never once considered Masaya.

"So, what are you saying, Mr. Jimmie Lamar? The way I learned it, a girl is either payin' or gittin' paid."

"I ain't no pimp, baby, and I don't need to trick."

"So you wanna chippie with me?" she asked.

"I want to experience the real you and I want you to experience the real me."

I knew the score where the ladies of the evening were concerned. The fact was, the most ardent professionals, at least in the black subculture, rarely engaged in uncompensated affairs and almost never with a square john. They preferred hustlers, pimps to be exact. Contrary to popular belief, it is the latter that is the more suited to them. They both speak the same language and understand perfectly the society in which they live. On the other hand, outsiders visit this subculture for the thrill of the experience, bringing with them morals steeped in hypocrisy, and quickly condemning that which they have helped to create. Hustling women know them well. They are not true to their code, like players, or uncompromising in their interpretation of what a man should be. In short, hustlers are loyal to the streets and squares sometimes forfeit their loyalty to society by dwelling in their midst. This is what I had learned and Passion had learned it even before me. I paid the bill and wrapped my arm around her as we walked to the car.

"What's your real name?" I asked.

She stared at me.

"Like I said, I wanta know the real you, baby."

She smiled. "Nadine, Nadine Taylor."

"So tell me," I said.

"Tell you what?"

"You know."

"Oh, no! Not you too?"

I smiled. "I am trying to get to know you," I said.

"You really wanta hear this?"

I nodded.

"Okay, when I was fifteen I ran away from home to become a model."

"Where's home?"

"Paterson, New Jersey. When I got here I fell victim to the old I'll-make-you-a-star game, but first you'll have to pose nude. Then it escalated to making a very important person in the business happy. After they were through using me, they just discarded me."

"Then you went on the street?"

"Not right away. I went hungry a couple of days. Then I met this well-dressed man."

"A pimp."

She nodded. "Actually what he told me made sense. Why give my body away for nothing and be hungry when I could do the exact same thing I was doing for free, for money. And waa-laa. Here I am!"

"What happened to the pimp?"

"Fell victim to the mighty heroin."

"You know what, Nadine Taylor?"

"What, Jimmie Lamar?"

"I like you," I said.

She smiled. "You just wanta fuck me."

"That too," I replied, and laughed.

We drove to her flat in the Village, where we spent the rest of the day. This time I was a success. This time all of her loneliness poured out in wave after wave of Passion's passion. She bit down on her lip and moaned. She cried. I even saw the little girl she had forgotten she once was.

I left at dusk with her still on my mind, knowing I had to see her again, but feeling surprisingly guilty. This had been my only affair since Masaya and I had been together. My woman was so sharp, I hoped she wouldn't find me out. Suddenly that became a major concern.

I saw the note on the dresser as soon as I walked into the bed-room.

> *Gone to Mom and Dad's for the night.*
>
>   *I love you, Masaya.*

I felt even more guilty: "I love you" at the end of the note meant reconciliation. I took a hot bath and went to bed.

The next morning her kisses awoke me.

"Still mad?" she asked, smiling.

How could I, of all people, be mad? I pulled her into the bed and we made tender love to each other for the first time since I had come home. When we had spent ourselves she produced four letters Paris had sent while I was away. All were from the South Pacific, praising the boys and sending us her love. The last one was from Hawaii. She intended to move there. I looked at Masaya. She was happy again. That made me feel good, and more guilty.

"Masaya, I love you. You think you could let me be the boss?" I joked.

She almost fell off the bed laughing. She laughed until her eyes ran water.

"Sure, baby. You are now officially the boss."

To my great surprise she meant it. That same day we went together to lease a building for our church. We found an old aban-doned theater in the center of Harlem. I remembered King Fish saying a minister was a performer and the church was his stage. I decided to make my church just that. I called the contractor to come in for a complete remodeling job, theatrical lights included.

During the four months of remodeling, Masaya tended to her thriving skin-cream business. I attended Miss Dailey's Speech School four days a week without fail. On my first day I passed by the gambling joint I had opened before I left town. The doors were barred. Miss Dailey was a refined little lady of grandmother age whose classes were conducted in a building on 125th Street. She taught voice, speech, and elocution lessons to would-be singers and actors. She was always the epitome of elegance and grace. When an error was made, her eyes would look piercingly above the lorgnette that rested on the end of her nose. Her methods were as old as speaking with pebbles in one's mouth and as modern as the most current methods of the time. She simply knew that the effectiveness of the method depended on the person.

"To speak well you must first relax. Then you must have confidence; and to have confidence, you must have command of the language. Then, young man," she said to me, "you must have something to say. Can you sing?"

"Yes."

I wanted to say, I'm great in the bathroom.

"Ah! You see, we have progress already. People who sing understand how to turn words into music. The great ones understand clarity and phrasing."

She taught me to sing a phrase slower and slower until I was speaking and then she taught me to breathe properly, how to bounce syllables off my palate and how to project my voice. I began to choose my words carefully, avoiding colloquialisms and street slang.

"Now, young man, you must command your body to communicate precisely what you intend. For an example, if you would be a king, your carriage must be royal. Your posture must say, 'I am a King.' "

I understood her exactly. Women seemed to be way ahead of men in mastering the language of the body. Each day I left Miss Dailey's school I was smiling and walking properly.

Three weeks had passed since I had seen Passion. I had genuinely exercised my self-control. There was no reason to see her again. I had already reclaimed my lost pride. I didn't love Passion. I loved Masaya and everything was wonderful between her and me. Only one reason and one reason alone compelled me to see Passion—lust. And lust is hardly reason enough to deceive your mate.

It was certainly not enough to risk losing her. In spite of my understanding all of this, I still found myself dialing Passion's number. This is a factor that must be figured into the equation of human emotions. This is the unknown. The voice on the other end was syrupy, low, and sensual, the voice she used for her customers. It worked on me.

Forty-five minutes later I was knocking on her door. Ten minutes after that we were in bed. I could tell she was glad I had come back by the way she had grown so comfortable, snuggled up in my arms.

"You know, baby, I'm going to build an empire," I told her.

"Go ahead, sugah. Build all the empires you want. I'll help you."

"Passion, I mean Nadine, did you ever think about doing something else?"

"No, sugah, like what?"

I chuckled. "There are better ways, you know."

"You mean like your woman, Masaya? I don't commit felonies, Jimmie. I'm not going to risk going to prison. I make good money without taking chances."

"That's not what I'm talking about. I mean something legitimate. You know, where you don't have to do this!"

She raised up in bed and squinted her eyes. "Man, are you judging me?"

"That's not what I'm saying."

"You are. Let me tell you something I thought you knew. I'm a real woman! One way or another, one time or another, all women do what I do. You didn't know that, did you?"

She studied me for a moment.

"You're really a square all dressed up like a player. I've been laying up here free-fuckin' a square!"

"Wait a minute!" I said.

"No, you wait. You've been playin' with me. You're not a real man like I need. You just another niggah with pussy on the brain. Now pay me like a trick's supposed to or get the fuck out of my house!"

What could I say? She was right. I dressed quickly and was out the door. She shouted to me from the doorway.

"And don't call me no fuckin' more!"

The words trailed after me like a swarm of angry bees, stinging me all the way to my car. She had been right. There was no need for me to feel sympathy for her. It was an insult. She wasn't steeped in self-pity or guilt. Her course was direct and unwavering, even more so than mine.

Maybe the months in prison had dulled my senses, but it seemed that Harlem was even more alive that night. It seemed to be moving, unchecked and unaware, toward Gomorrah. The streets hosted a variety of hookers, beckoning from every doorway, sharing drinks on street corners with soldiers, some buying dope from diamond-clad pushers, others strolling and swaying, then disappearing into hotels on the arms of white men. The rich ofays from downtown came also, with smiling faces and shining eyes. Inside, they fluttered throughout the club like butterflies caught in an eclipse. Some laughed too loud and too often, giving away their unease. A jazz band was "cooking" low and easy, setting a groovy mood. As soon as Masaya and I were seated at our front-row table, the master of ceremonies walked to the bandstand.

"Good evening, ladies and gentlemen! Welcome to the Club Black and Tan. It gives me great pleasure to introduce a special lady this evening—Miss Patience Valentine!"

A lovely caramel-colored young woman, with lavender gardenias in her hair, strolled amorously, amidst thunderous applause, to the microphone.

"I would like to dedicate this first song to a couple of friends. One has a birthday today. This is for you, Masaya, happy birthday.

For you, too, Jimmie," and she sang " 'It Could Happen to You.' "

Masaya smiled at me and fingered the diamond heart hanging from her neck. My birthday present to my woman. It was to be our last night together in the Black and Tan, or any other club. All places such as these were off-limits to a minister.

22 The choir I had hired sang beautifully. The robes they wore matched the purple-and-gold decor of the pulpit. The stage lights were dazzling; but only four people saw them. That was the size of the congregation. I remained in my suit clothes. I thanked them for coming. When the choir sang their last song, I ended the service. What had I done wrong? On our way home I posed the question to Masaya. She seemed hesitant to address it. Maybe she didn't want me to think she was trying to take over. She could also have been reluctant to aid me in something she didn't really approve of. In any case, she evaded the question by suggesting next time might turn out better. I cornered her when we got home.

"Why are you going strange on me, Masaya?"

"Jimmie, I don't want to get into an argument with you. That's a promise I made to myself."

"You have something to tell me? We're on the same team, Masaya."

"I'm not falling into that trap," she said.

I grabbed her shoulders and pulled her close. I whispered in her ear.

"I love you, Masaya, I promise whatever you tell me this night will not make me angry."

She waited for what seemed like forever.

"I promise," I reaffirmed.

She looked at me again to be sure. I nodded.

"You need a hook to catch them and you must be more than a jackleg preacher to hold them."

She smiled and I smiled too.

"Seriously, baby. You have to rise above that mentality. You have to become 'Father Lamar,' in fact, and in deed. Jimmie Lamar knows he's a 'Mitt Man,' but it must always be a secret to Father Lamar. Getting them to come will be easy for you. Just remember the game. You need a 'hook.' "

Then she shook her head as if she had done something terribly wrong. My spirits rose with this new understanding and I smiled at this remarkable woman. Like a small boy, the answer walked boldly through my mind.

FREE FOOD FOR THE NEEDY

WITH OUR SUNDAY NIGHT SERVICE

FATHER LAMAR WELCOMES YOU

They came from all over Harlem, the young and the old, the believers, the nonbelievers, the curiosity seekers, and the plain hungry. The church was overflowing with them. Happy, a young blind girl, played my theme song on the organ. The choir swayed back and forth as they hummed the beautiful melody Happy had written. The air was ripe with the smell of incense. The faces of the people were already filled with the Spirit. Happy's voice rang crisp and clear, traveling before me on silver wings as I emerged from the vestry. The white robe and the fez I wore signified the quintessence of purity. I floated to the pulpit and was immediately bathed in a blue light from the balcony. King Fish was with me, every gesture, every movement, I copied from him. Even as I began to speak I could hear his voice in mine, the way it rose with thunderous power, and suddenly dropped to a whisper. I paused and looked at this crowd that had come to see me, and just as I know he had been, I was overcome with a feeling of great importance.

My eyes became transfixed. I felt somehow more than myself, not even of this world. I became some mystical reproduction of what once was "Jimmie Lamar," entering a state of mind that defies articulation. Maybe this is what a great actor does—loses himself in the part, becomes completely what he pretends to be. When I began my "spiel," the choir continued to hum my song of love and peace, creating in the room an air of serenity.

"Isn't it wonderful! Isn't it glorious! God is here *tonight*!"

I held my arms up as if I were reaching for the sky.

"Can't you feel Him? He has come here from India, from Rome, from faraway China, and yes, from Germany. He was there too! Brothers and sisters, God loves you, each and every one of you. Be you Baptist, Catholic, Jew, Hindu, or Buddhist. The same God loves you! Now, isn't that wonderful? Could we talk about God's love, brothers and sisters? Let's talk about it for just a moment. There is no color to God's love. It has no boundaries, no countries, no cities, and no neighborhoods. No matter the language or the color of your skin, God's love is there and He is always listening and ready to give. There have been many prophets and it is fitting that these holy men relate God's idea of truth and love to their races and creeds; this is right and fitting. But now, after a war that would have enslaved the world, we must rise up as one people and our Universal Language must be the language of LOVE! In a world where might is honor, we must build a new world, a world where giving, not taking, is the order of the day. Let us give praise to the givers and not to the conquerors!"

I walked to the organ and placed my arm around Happy's shoulders.

"Let's love our children, not frighten them with hate and war. We must feed our poor and hungry, not cast them from our conscience."

I waved my hand and from the vestry the ushers appeared carrying bags of groceries, which they began passing out among the people. I continued to speak.

"He called me in the midnight hour, on my way to a nightclub."

My voice took on a gospel rhythm. A kind of half-speaking, half-singing way of phrasing, something else I had learned from King Fish.

"It was late one E-V-E-N-I-N-G. . . . I had dancing on my mind. I heard a voice that E-V-E-N-I-N-G . . . it said, 'You got work to do. Come and unite my people. We got work to do.' The voice said, 'J-I-M-M-I-E! You got work to do! J-I-M-M-I-E! You got work to do!' "

I raised my hands and walked to the choir.

"Sing, children," I said.

The choir burst into song.

"Sing, church," I said to the church, and the congregation joined in!

"Isn't it WONDERFUL?"

The choir followed me down the aisle and I shook hands and embraced the elderly.

"We must learn how to give! Thank you for coming. Thank you for letting me love you!"

I walked outside into the street with the choir following behind. The rest of the church began to join us and the people walking the streets became a part of the procession. Traffic slowed and Harlem began to listen to the inspiring words of Father Lamar.

After I had shaken the last hand and the choir had gone, Masaya and I spotted an older woman and a small boy sitting in a corner of the church. The woman's eyes were closed as she rocked back and forth, humming. Masaya and I walked toward them.

"Ma'am—" I started, and she cut me off.

"Ain't never had the Spirit like I had it tonight," she said.

She was a handsome woman who may, in her youth, have been beautiful.

"Thank you, good sister," I replied, sitting down next to her.

The face was careworn with time and her eyes reflected the hardships of past years. Probably the length of time the small boy had been in her charge. Still, there was pride in the way she tilted her head and pushed her bottom lip against the top. Inside her faded breasts beat the fierce heart that protected the life of children and the divinity of the Word. Her strong face said as much. There was a passive power about her that was almost troubling.

"I see God in yo' eyes," she told me, causing a warm feeling to run the length of my body.

I trembled slightly for some unknown reason. I thanked her and asked about the boy, who was watching with big eyes. He was a well-mannered boy with a round face and deep-set dark-brown eyes. His worn clothes had been scrubbed spotless and his beaten shoes freshly polished. Quick and electric was his smile. He reminded me of myself as a boy, so much so, I was drawn closer to him than I realized. I could even read the boy's thoughts (*I want to be like you, when I grow up*).

"This is Paul, Father Lamar. Everybody calls me Mom Myrtle," I heard her say. "His mother died five years ago. He don't know his father," she went on, but I didn't hear the rest.

I felt compelled to embrace him, but instead I introduced Masaya. She said a warm hello, but her mind was on me. I guess she had seen a new side to me, one maybe I myself hadn't known existed.

I stood at my window looking down at the lights in the valley. Such a distant place from Sugar Hill to be so near in mileage. Even with the events of the evening fresh in mind, my heart would not forget that boy. Kids need a chance to realize their full potential. They need a mother and a father. I thought of how my mother had struggled with no man around. I knew even then what I was going to do. I had promised myself and made a pact with God to help the children.

"Jim—mieee."

I walked into the bedroom.

It was a different Harlem I drove through that day, one without laughter that received no pity, one that existed for most of the people, a Harlem of run-down tenements, overflowing garbage cans, and dirty streets, of shattered ideas and lost hopes, of drunks, the homeless, and junkies who would sell even their dreams for a fix. For some reason it was the worst I had ever seen it or smelled it. The kids flocked to the car when I emerged with gifts I had purchased for Paul.

"Wow!"

"Look at that!"

"Hey, mister, you rich, huh?"

"Hey, mister, that yo' car?"

"Mr. Man, take me fo' a ride!"

I handed each boy a dollar bill and they dashed off in different directions like grasshoppers in a vacant lot. Then I bounded up the stairs to Mom Myrtle's apartment. She opened the door on the first knock, as if she had been expecting me. More than likely she had been looking out the window. She looked larger somehow, almost imposing. Her strength resonated like that of a much younger person. She spoke no words that day, but I could feel something I couldn't explain.

Paul was standing behind her. His bright eyes grew brighter when I handed him the boxes. Then I told Mom Myrtle I wanted her to be the "Mother" of my church. The words had just come rushing out, with no plan or thought to them, but it was a decision I had made on my own, I thought. Before she could respond, Paul had embraced my legs and the feeling I got from this little boy hadn't been surpassed by anything in my life.

When I drove away, a rush of piety came over me, along with a certain feeling of power all ministers must feel. The joy of seeing the old woman come to life and Paul's wide smile made me want to do more.

When I arrived home I spoke to Masaya about it. I wished I still had Bobby's place. Mom Myrtle and Paul could stay there. After all, she was going to be the "Mother" of my church I told her.

Masaya smiled. "I was saving this surprise for your next birthday, but it's too far away."

She hugged me. "Baby, we own Bobby's house. I worked it out with the bank while you were away."

I was speechless. I knew what I had to do as soon as possible, what I wanted to do. I asked her and we set our wedding date.

Sidney's condition seemed the only obstacle in the way of our complete happiness. More and more he began to experience extreme mood swings. The nightmares became frightfully real, he would say, and recurring. If I knew anything for sure, it was that Sidney would never be the same again. Then, surprisingly, there were periods of hope, times when he was almost his old self and we had some down-to-earth fun. We drank the best whiskey, played cards, and relived every sting the three of us had taken. He joked about how lame I had once been. One such evening, after too many drinks, we ducked Masaya, who had promised to join us, and he took me for the first time to his new hangout. We drove to Paterson, New Jersey, to a sleazy dim-lit joint called the Dew Drop Inn. It reminded him of every clip joint he had ever been in, even the ones overseas, he said. Down-home, country, and rowdy, the blues was played here. Sidney was the only ofay cat in sight. He liked it that way. No pity, no sympathy, and no quarter was given to him. He'd even had a fight here, and in defeat had given a good account of himself, something he bragged about. And there was the earthy girl who liked him and made that known to me. Of course, Sidney was still a handsome man, but more importantly, he was free with his money. "White Folks" was still the name he went by. Here is where he forgot it all. The war, his missing limb, and his dead friends.

When I finally made it home Masaya was fuming. She said we were both like children, but behind all the anger I could tell a part of her was glad to know her brother had been out in the world. Other times were not so promising, when he sat brooding and quiet, or refused to even open his door.

Masaya and I spent two weeks preparing for our next temple meeting. We had posters placed throughout Harlem stating that Father Lamar, at our next meeting, would give his worldly possessions away to the poor. We also managed to have Mom Myrtle and Paul move into their new residence. I must admit that what little good I had done was also a tremendous boost to my ministry. Making small deeds into noble acts is the key to garnering good publicity.

My next church meeting was designed to exploit this theory. I arrived late at the church with Masaya, Mom Myrtle, Paul, and a man for security. As expected, the place was crowded. My adopted family emerged first. My security man was next, and then me. A camera flash caught me head-on before I made my way through the cheering crowd into the church. It was completely filled, with some people standing. The choir had already begun singing when I stepped onto the pulpit. I raised my arms.

"Brothers and sisters! It's time to LOVE again, time to give. I know some of you are wondering who I am! I have no origin, no race, and my religion is my love of God! I am all men and all men are me. But I am not without sin. I am no saint. I was a liar, a con man, and a cheat, like many of you. But God lifted me up to show His unlimited power. He lifted me up to teach, to glorify His name. Now, isn't that WONDERFUL?"

I raised my hands again. The choir began to hum.

"Bring the last of my worldly possessions that I might give them to the poor!"

The ushers placed two large chests in front of the pulpit. Mom Myrtle, dressed in all white, stood up and began to read a list of the names she had selected to receive these possessions. The poor and most needy people in Harlem marched down the aisle and the ushers gave them, one by one, all of my personal possessions: diamonds rings, authentic gold watches, and my two mink coats. There were suits, shoes, and an array of silk shirts, even silk ties. I borrowed a line from Gibran's *The Prophet* that suggested we give today so the season for giving may be ours and not our inheritors'.' "

I reached out my arms, and to my own surprise, I had tears in my eyes.

"Those of you who can, please look into your hearts and give. Please help me to do God's work. He has blessed me with the power to augment the natural through contact with the supernatural wisdom. It isn't meant for man to suffer here on God's earth. There are no races here, only people of different hues, beautiful people, like the trees and flowers, that attest to His infinite genius. Now, isn't that WONDERFUL!

"I feel wonderful this evening!" I shouted as the usher began to pass the collection plate. "I feel close to God! The only possessions I need are those that help me to do God's work. Now, isn't that wonderful! Give, God's children, but if you can't afford to give, bless the plate to show God your heart."

Happy began to sing. I noticed a young colored woman with a camera taking pictures. I wondered who she might be. Sitting in my gold-leafed chair that evening, I remembered my first day in Harlem, how far I had come, and I thought of King Fish with a faint smile.

The headlines screamed.

THIEF TURNED PROPHET GIVES ALL TO POOR!

An imposing picture of me adorned the front page of the *Harlem News*. More than anyone, I now realized I was on the brink of a great success. My stomach reacted to the challenge and excitement of my "manifest destiny." The world awaited me, yet I moved uneasily toward the future. It happens that way sometimes with men of conscience whose purpose is not totally honorable. The threat of failure haunts them. Even the possibility of incurring God's disfavor.

I had begun to believe in Father Lamar, in his words, his deeds, and in his ministry; but Jimmie Lamar was not a prophet. He had not set out to save the world. He was a hustler playing a safe game, the way King Fish had taught him, but nothing in life is completely what it seems. There are no absolutes. Every pretense brings with it a certain amount of truth, and truth was, there was a war between the good and the greed in my heart.

The headlines in the *Harlem News* marked a new beginning and set in motion the pattern I would use on the path to success. First the deed, then the publicity. I began to use the paper on a regular basis. The fund-raising drive I organized to sponsor a trip to the circus for needy kids was a success—due to me advertising in the *Harlem News*. The gospel shows were next, and the Sunday bake sales that were so successful prompted me to open my first pastry shop in Harlem. This could be attributed to the delicious cooking of Mom Myrtle, who surprised me with her organizational skills as well. She had a way with people—almost a hold on them, it seemed—and her dedication to the ministry was without question.

In the midst of my success there was Sidney, steadily growing worse—hostile, indicting, sometimes leveling charges of blasphemy against me. But he was my friend, and for friends you make allowances. The last time Masaya and I were at his place he was unshaven and filthy—a pathetic skeleton who'd had too much to drink. Once, in an unprompted outburst, he referred to his sister as a "church whore." The next moment he was recalling their youth together and smiling blissfully. We left with Masaya in tears. I'm sure the same thought occurred to us both, but was never spoken (*Sidney was going crazy*). Even her parents avoided the subject. Mental illness in the family was a source of the worse kind of embarrassment—a blemish on the bloodline.

The ministry continued to grow along with Masaya's skin-cream business. The Satin Doll, as always, was *the* hair salon in Harlem. Even though our days were filled with great demands, we managed to set aside Friday nights for ourselves. Gin rummy, hot dogs, and Pepsi-Cola was a delightful trip back to another era. Now I remember them as the happiest of times. The two of us together, fighting over a game of cards, making up, both reeking of onions, frowning with each kiss, then making love on the bearskin rug. Those were the happy times. I could never retain them, these fleeting moments of completeness. Always the challenges of the future invoked a different spirit, took me away in search of something I already had.

They marched through the towns and the cities, helping the sick, the old, and the poverty-stricken—embracing the children. Adorned all in white, they were led by Mary Magdalene carrying fruit in a basket that replenished itself, and fed hundreds. The sky was as bright as I had ever seen it—the air pristine and scented with the breath of flowers.

I awakened to a strange and wonderful melody that I was for-getting—even as I was hearing it. Gently, I shook Masaya. With a smile on her face she turned for my embrace. I kissed her quickly on the forehead, then told her about my dream. She listened in-tently, and after I had finished, a look of admiration appeared on her face.

"Jimmie, I think God just spoke to you. He wants us to be the guardian over His people."

I didn't share her interpretation. Lately she had suggested that more than one incident was a result of "divine intervention"—like the fact that I became a minister at all.

"If I were God, I would have picked you for the job," she said jok-ingly. "Everybody knows the worst sinners make the best prophets."

Another time a similar statement rang with much more sincerity. Sometimes I didn't understand my woman. Was she feeling guilty about all the marks she had played? Not her, not the one who once told me that being fair in an unfair world was disastrous and stupid. In my mind the thought of God choosing me as His spokesman, or showing me visions, was worthy of no more than a hearty laugh. The reason I had made a bargain with Him was to spare myself His wrath, not to enlist Him as an employer.

I appealed directly to the women that Sunday morning, telling them what I had seen in my sleep. The ideal began to completely take shape, even as I was speaking. A group of elite Christians I would name "The Saints" would be formed. Men and women dressed in white traversing the city doing good (*first the deed, and then the publicity*).

"No woman in history has suffered a heavier burden than the one carried by Mary," I said. "No one has lost a son like Jesus. I speak first to you, my sisters, because life begins with you."

I closed my eyes and clasped my hands together and I began to tremble.

"I saw them coming, dressed in white, the 'Sainted Sisters,' led by Mary, marching through the towns and cities—helping people, saving our children."

I opened my eyes and walked over to Masaya, seated at the far end of the pulpit, and motioned for her to rise.

"Will you shine like Mary for God?"

"Yes!" she said softly.

Now I spoke to the people.

"Will you walk with me and this saint of our church? Who will be the first to join us and give all to God and His people? Will you help us tend to the children? Will you walk with God and us through Harlem?"

They came in single file down the aisle, walking slowly as the music began, a parade of poor people, pure in thought and filled with a divine purpose. At the pulpit they knelt. I said a prayer for strength and endurance and a prayer of thanks for the vision.

The next day "The Saints" marched behind me and Masaya down Lenox Avenue. They were an army of handmaidens led by Mary, as in my vision. They were armed only with baskets of fruit and a message that a new "Prophet" had been sent to the people by God. They stood on the corners and passed out fruit and each woman testified to her past transgressions and to her new and full life in Father Lamar's ministry. With their eyes aglow they spoke with pride and passion about their mission to help this righteous prophet unite the world under the banner of "Love and Peace." Their voices were reassuring, their smiles warm, and as constant as the afternoon sun.

The Saints began to appear everywhere at once; they were with the sick and dying and they laid their hands on the foreheads of the unwed mothers. Children sparkled with laughter when they were near and the old people developed a sense of belonging because of them. They went into the jails and prisons and brought comfort and hope to the inmates and to their families.

"A new prophet has been sent by God to spread the word and lift up the people's spirit. Now, isn't that WONDERFUL!" they would say, and then all would bow their heads and praise the Creator's name.

They engaged high-priced lawyers and sometimes convinced them to take cases free of charge, and they cajoled the great white judges into waiving the probable jail terms of fallen youth and paroling these young men and women into their custody.

With every good deed the Saints' popularity increased, as did their ability to raise funds for the ministry. Because of the Saints' humanitarianism, almost every hustler in Harlem owed them a favor, and repaid these favors with money and merchandise. One gangster donated a new automobile. Gamblers considered it good luck to help these angels of the subculture. There were donations from businesses in and out of the City, some from other states. The food, materials, and clothing poured in. I borrowed a line from Shakespeare: "The good that men do lives on after them."

Mostly the change was evident in Masaya's eyes. Beneath that constant smile was always the bright glow of discovery and compassion. Her demeanor was no longer aggressive and challenging like a woman of the world, but warm, engaging, and empathic. In short, she seemed to like helping people much more than fleecing them. We now lived in a thirty-room mansion located in New Jersey, only a stone's throw away from New York, but eons away in sophistication and glamour. The ministry had forced us to live a completely different lifestyle—a kind of subdued existence where wealth delighted, but didn't offend. We selected ten of the most faithful to live with us. Mom Myrtle, Paul, and Happy were among them. In my heart my mother and King Fish were there as well. After all, everything had been for them, my adopted father and Mama. That's how a son pays tribute, shows the most respect. He takes the knowledge from the father then surpasses him, always delighting the mother. I imagined they both were somewhere smiling. It must be true; there has to be more to life than just living and dying. There has to be an existence beyond existence, a place where souls congregate to speak about the living. Here in this life of flesh and pain, I was on my way to the top. Having accomplished what I had in these few years, I turned my attention to Father Divine, Daddy Grace, and Prophet Jones, men who had taken the Mitt Game to astronomical heights. I would be bigger than them all. I would spread my ministry across the country, and maybe further. This fantasy took hold, caused me to feel myself above other people; that my life had more meaning, more importance. This feeling of my own superiority was shared by my followers, most of whom gave all their earnings, their property, and their skills to the ministry. Masaya and I lived like royalty. But Masaya was still changing. She was searching for more than she had had the majority of her life—a clear purpose for her stay on this earth. There were no children in her life, and up until now, no causes. She did not consider herself so special, and became embarrassed and more "common" when other Saints paid homage to her, making them love her all the more. Mom Myrtle became her best friend, Paul like her son. They became the example true believers should live by—always available, always with a smile, quick to give their all to the ministry. Every Saturday they were visiting a hospital or jail, sometimes an old-folks home. Every day they found time to help some child. More and more Masaya began to retreat from her business interests—little by little giving the responsibility over to one of her trusted sisters in the ministry. Every night without fail she said a special prayer for her brother, who was now, after much effort by her mother and stepfather, living back home with them. There was one moment in June, three years after the war was over, when Sidney was more himself than I had seen him since before he went away. It was Masaya's birthday, and maybe he had fought especially hard these demons that plagued and distorted his life, so that he could enjoy it with her. He gave us laughter and hope, referred to me as "sport," a name that over the years had evolved into one of deep affection. It was on this evening, when the family party had ended, that he spoke for the first time about being in battle.

"It's the smell that stays with you—the smell of busted guts, burned flesh, and rotting bodies, mixed with a sulfur stench, all attributed to exploded shells and bombs."

He talked about seeing a row of American heads impaled on stakes along the roadside, like a prelude to a horror show, and the dismembering of a living Japanese prisoner by his own men gone wild. It continued, this nation sanctioned murder and mayhem, until he gave up the thought of living, because he knew he was going to die, until the loss of a limb became a blessing. Then he suddenly said to me, "We're like brothers, aren't we, sport?" I'll never forget the look in his eyes that evening, as if for a moment only, he had recaptured himself.

Three days later we received a call from his mother telling us Sidney had tried to take his own life. His father had pulled him down from a rope, unconscious. Finally, out of fear, he was sent by his family to a private mental institution. Sidney never spoke again.

Our wedding was scheduled the last of October. In August we added a children's wing to the mansion, and I met the Countess in September, a week after I spoke to a large crowd in Central Park.

23 I didn't know it then but she had been in such a state she had even considered suicide; but it didn't show. I watched her from the huge picture window in my living room. She was the Countess Camille Benoit, and she was all grace and class, in a highbrow European way. She emerged from the eggshell-white Rolls-Royce and passed the chauffeur without breaking her stride. Her legs were long, her waist small, and her hair a mild blond. When she was near the door a faint smile of approval momentarily appeared on her face. I had expected her a half hour earlier. Sonni, a young ofay girl and one of the Saints, opened the door before the second ring.

"I am the Countess Camille Benoit. I have an appointment with Father Lamar," I heard her say, in that wonderful French accent.

"Welcome to the House of Peace. Father Lamar is in here." Sonni indicated the way.

I stood up and walked toward her. "I'm Father Lamar."

"I know."

She held out her hand. There was a temptation to kiss it like Charles Boyer would have done in the movies, but I simply shook it lightly. I wasn't that Continental yet. I directed her to my study, a room of large plants, books, and ebony wood. On the shelves were works by Plato, Hermann Hesse, William Shakespeare, Voltaire, Dostoyevsky, and Khalil Gibran. She removed Hermann Hesse and leafed through the pages.

"You know, Father Lamar, Hermann Hesse should have been the conscience of the German people. They should have learned from him before the First World War. Instead, they chose to listen to Hitler."

"Would you like to be seated, Countess? I hope you like tea."

"Thank you. Tea will be fine. I heard you speak in Central Park, Father. You were very inspiring. Like you, before the war, I , too, considered myself a friend to the less advantaged. Not on such a grand scale as you, Father, of course, but a friend nonetheless. For as long as I can remember, I always sided with the underclass, whether in my choice of friends or the stray animals I adopted."

She stopped suddenly and her eyes filled up. She began to speak slowly, as if to herself.

"That was before the war. Before they came."

I stood up and took her hand. "Come and walk with me, good sister."

I led her to an adjoining room that was lined with lighted candles. Pillows were placed around a pool of water with a lighted fountain. On the walls hung pictures of holy men from every religion the world over. I motioned for her to sit, then joined her.

"I come here to meditate. This fountain signifies life, always changing, always moving, yet always here. Look into the water," I whispered.

I let the silence take command of the moment. In silence there does exist a kind of music that can be heard in the minds of two people—even briefly connected. My voice came from deep within.

"Relax your body and let your mind run free until you come face-to-face with the torment that is eating away at your heart. Listen . . . until you can hear the sound of your own heartbeat."

Her eyes were fixed on the fountain, watching the changing colors, the different designs; listening to its melodic sound.

"That's it," I whispered. "Flow with the water. The water is you. You are the water. Tell me your problem, good sister. God is listening."

She began slowly, pain accompanying every word.

"I was there when the Germans came," she whispered. "They assured our family no harm would come to us, that we would be treated decently and fairly."

Suddenly she began to weep.

"Then . . . then the killings began. People . . . women, children, they were shot down in the streets. I saw the hungry faces, children searching garbage cans for food, sickness and death everywhere, except . . . except for the rich and, of course, royalty."

The last word was bitter in her mouth.

"We turned our backs and hid in our 'ivory towers.' When the war was over I tried to make it up. I donated money, worked in hospitals, but I still see the faces of the children, the orphans, the widows, all the suffering I had been no part of."

My voice came out soft and soothing.

"Look around you, my sister, we are surrounded by the images of great and holy men and women. Their spirits are here. This is Peter, he denied knowing Jesus in his last hour, and David, he had a man killed for his wife. There have been others who have faltered, but their lives weren't lost. They went on to become holy in God's eyes. You, my sister, have paid the penalty of living with this. Now you must put it behind you and make tomorrow's deeds good ones. We love you, sister, but most of all we love your sorrow. For your sorrow is but a reflection of the good in you and God loves his fallen sheep more. Now, isn't that WONDER-FUL?"

She looked up and the tears shone in her eyes. "What must I do?" Her voice was pleading.

"Abide with us for seven days and seven nights. God will give you the answer."

For six days the Countess became one of us. She saw the young children learning from the older children and she witnessed the love they had for Father Lamar, the "hero-worship" they bestowed upon me. They delighted her with their songs and endeared themselves to her with their innocence. The old people lifted her spirits with their enthusiasm and unshakable faith. They nourished her soul with the wisdom and words my life's experience had taught me. Mom Myrtle nourished her body with delicious meals. Her third day at the temple she insisted on becoming an honorary Saint and dressed herself as one. She accompanied them on their rounds and was excited with the good they were doing. She returned to the temple, elated, filled with ideas of establishing a similar order all over the world.

On the seventh and final day, a dinner was prepared in her honor to celebrate her freedom from herself.

I told her, "You are free, you know. You will always be one of us."

"I know," she replied, in a whisper.

The dinner turned out to be a feast, presided over by Mom Myrtle, Paul, and Masaya, (*who, for some unknown reason, was overly nice to the Countess on her last day*). Masaya had never been less than cordial before, but she was a female, and females have their ways. The slightly strained air that existed was something both she and the Countess understood. I understood it too. Still, it was never reflected in the conversations, which were light and cheerful and mostly about dreams of a better world and my plans to make those dreams a reality.

We dined on chicken, pheasant, and Maine lobster. The fruits came from as far away as Florida. There was music too. The choir gave three stirring renditions of popular gospel tunes. Happy played a beautiful solo on the organ, and testimonies were also given. Paul was the first to testify. He stood upright and proper, with both hands stiff at his sides.

"Before . . . before, when I was a little boy, before I met 'Father,' I didn't love anyone but Grandma. Now I love everyone and I always tell the truth. Now, isn't that WONDERFUL?"

The room was filled with thunderous applause and cheers. This was my way. Children should always be encouraged and applauded for any good effort or deed. Clara Belle Johnson, a heavyset, dark, older woman, who was second only to Masaya and Mom Myrtle in her devotion to the ministry, rose slowly and her big voice boomed with praise for me.

"I been a member of many churches in my lifetime," she began. "Many churches, dun heard the best preachers preach. They preach good, all right, but after church they's gone in they big car wit' they big smile. But the peoples got troubles, some of 'um hungry, but they's just awatchin', takin' they pride in what the preacher got. But he don' look back, just go on home to his big house. See ya next time when ya got some mo' money, he might as well say. But Father Lamar, he give it all away and when he got mo' he hep the ol' peoples and the churin'. Father Lamar learned me ya gotta help others fo' God bless ya. You ain't really happy till ya do. Now, ain't that WONDERFUL!"

The applause had hardly ceased before Happy rose.

"I wanta testify," she said in a loud and clear voice.

She was a pretty girl of fourteen, light brown and slender, with her hair in a long ponytail. Her stare, behind the dark glasses, was indirect and unfocused. That characteristic, and the movement of her head, told you she was blind. I had named her Happy because of her winning smile. She was also a Saint and the biggest fund-raiser of all.

"Father Lamar has been so good to me. I was full of self-pity. I use to sit alone in my room. Why did I have to be born blind, I'd say to myself. Then my mother told me a new church had opened and they needed an organ player. The day I met Father my life changed. He told me that I must be united with the cosmic forces in the universe, at one with all things living, and at peace with myself. Let me tell you, he gave me a far better sight than I could have been born with. I can see with my heart. Now, isn't that WONDERFUL!"

She sat down to play and the small children began to sing as they marched around the room, passing out flowers that they called love roses. A little boy, with dimples, walked over to the Countess, handed her a rose, and said, "I love you, Miss Countess," his voice filled with sincerity.

"I love you too," she said, and hugged him to her. "I love all of you." Her voice was just above a whisper.

She left that evening with a warm smile and soft good-byes and a promise to return someday. As she was leaving, Paul spoke to Mom Myrtle.

"What's a countess, Grandma?"

"Someone very important," she answered.

Masaya had become more serious about her image as a Saint. Without any suggestions from me she discarded the beautiful wardrobe she owned in favor of the plain white dress worn by them. Even that failed to camouflage her good looks. I couldn't resist teasing her about that. We began to take our Fridays at Masaya's brownstone. We could scream there if we wanted to. I had told the church Masaya and I were married in the eyes of God, that the eyes of man would be satisfied when we determined it was the right time, but there was never any show of intimacy between us. No congregation wants to picture their minister locked in a sensual embrace. That day we were free of the world outside and we exercised that freedom. We drank champagne and walked around nude all day. Made love on the sofa and took a shower together.

"Baby, I'm glad you're the boss now. It's a lot more fun than when I was." And then she laughed.

I laughed too. We had both grown.

She was the happiest woman alive, she told me. There was only one thing. She wanted to see me again after this world. She wanted to be in heaven with me. I didn't know what to say. I no longer believed in the concept of heaven and hell, this threat the Christian church has held for ages over the heads of its subjects. I no longer believed it, but I did believe in something—some law of retribution. I expressed none of this to Masaya.

She was quick into my arms wanting to adopt Paul to ensure there would be a child in her life.

Saturday turned out not to be so happy. It began with a telephone call. Sonni announced it.

"You have a call from the Countess, Father."

"Thank you, Sonni. I'll take it in the study."

Masaya did not like this but she said nothing. She went upstairs to Paul's room.

I called to her before I left and explained I had to go out. She said okay, but I knew she wasn't pleased. I went outside and got into the Rolls the Temple had purchased a week ago for me.

The Countess had said it was important that she see me. I wondered what the urgency was for me to drive to the City. As it turned out, it was a pleasant drive. I passed the Baby Grand on my way, Society Red's old hangout, and I thought of King Fish. I thought of Passion, too. She had impressed me; I had to admit that. I drove downtown on Broadway and turned east on Seventy-ninth Street until I reached Park Avenue. Then I drove to the lower Sixties.

A doorman, posted beneath a large canopy, stood with a puzzled expression on his face as I emerged from the silver Rolls-Royce. I was dressed in my black robe and fez.

"I'm Father Lamar," I said. "The Countess is expecting me."

The doorman hesitated and moved quickly to the phone. He soon turned around with a smile.

"A bellman will escort you to the penthouse, sir."

The doorman motioned to a red-haired, freckle-faced lad, who hurried over.

"Penthouse," the doorman said.

I was led across a large lobby amidst the stares of people, who owned old money, to a glass-enclosed private elevator. The piped-in music was an aria from Verdi's Rigoletto. I remembered it from my childhood. The elevator let me off in front of her door. It opened before I knocked. She wore a lavender duster that contrasted beautifully with the white decor of her apartment. She greeted me with a bright hello and an impetuous smile that told me why I had been invited. We stared at each other briefly. In that instant the desire hidden beneath the facade of my ministry and her call of distress claimed its rightful place in our minds. It was love at second sight, not the kind of lasting and possessive emotion that eternity demands of dreamers, or dreamers demand of eternity. This love carried with it no hope or promise of tomorrow, but it was love nonetheless. Love cannot be defined in terms of time; a moment can be as precious as a decade. This was our moment.

The drinks that she mixed, the small talk, the compliments we gave each other, could not alter or postpone the inevitable. The time had arrived. It was in the sound of our voices, rather than in what we said; even more present in the brief spaces of silence, heated up by our engaging looks and deep breathing. This would be a first for us both. Her first black man and my first countess. Now words failed us and the guards of unfamiliarity vanished into the distant glow of the dim lighting. Raw emotion became king. We moved as if an unseen signal had been given from someplace unknown, desperately embracing, finding each other's lips in a wild and passionate kiss. I walked her, clinging to me, into the bedroom and we sank into a cloud of pillows. We hadn't time to undress, so eager was our desire. We spent ourselves, half-clothed, like schoolkids in the backseat of an automobile. Now she removed her clothes, revealing the young-girl body she had preserved so well. I undressed and she watched me with those lustful eyes. Her body glowed winter white in the light of the moon. I was again filled with desire. This time we both held back and explored the wealth of each other. This time I called her name out loud and she smiled. We drifted slowly back to earth, like feathers from a busted pillow. Somewhere in my mind I heard her voice.

"Tell me you will always remember this evening, whatever you do."

I smiled.

"Say it," she coached. "Say, 'Camille, I will always remember this evening.' "

"Camille, I will always remember this evening," I repeated sincerely.

"I will too," she said, and handed me an envelope from the nightstand.

"This is for the ministry I love."

I opened it and the bold letters on the cashier's check read *One Hundred Thousand Dollars.*

"And this is for you," she added, handing me a solid-gold pocket watch, complete with gold chain.

Again I remembered the phony one I paid five bucks for and I smiled. She explained that she, along with a few friends, who loved seeing their names in print, had donated it, and would it be all right to make an official presentation at the temple? The press would be there, of course, and the publicity would do my ministry even more good.

I have never been able to explain with any satisfaction to myself why the twinge of guilt I felt was so small; it was unworthy of my love for Masaya. Maybe I was also unworthy of her.

It was 1:30 A.M. when I returned home. Masaya was packing. She avoided me completely. Her eyes were glassy; mostly they were filled with pain.

"What are you doing?" I asked.

"I'm packing."

"What's the matter?"

"Oh, nothing's the matter."

I wrapped my arm around her shoulders. She jerked away.

"Don't you touch me, after you've been with her!"

"You're wrong, baby," I said. "What you're thinking is wrong."

"You're a damn liar!" she screamed. "You're a low-lying bastard!"

I slapped her across the face before I thought, and was immediately sorry. I moved to console her.

"Get away from me!" she screamed.

"I'm trying to tell you you're wrong!" I implored.

"You can't tell the truth for one minute. You can't even tell yourself the truth!"

"What are you talking about now?"

"Just what I said. You wouldn't know the truth if it slapped you in the face. Your whole life is a lie, big MITT MAN! You're just a niggah hooked on the crowd, like some junkie, and I'm tired of being your whore, tired of being one of the 'Good Sisters,' tired of your lies and *tired of you!*"

"Okay!" I shouted. I held up my hands in front of her. It occurred to me I might actually lose her. "Please don't leave me, Masaya!"

I wanted to keep lying, but I knew she was too smart. She stood there, staring, trembling, her eyes expressing a feeling beyond hurt.

"Oh God!" she cried, and dropped to her knees.

She wept silently for ten minutes. I didn't know how to console her. Even my apology was weak. I was beginning to think it all so useless. I would never be close to her again. I wondered what I would do without her in my life. She stopped crying suddenly. I heard her speak.

"Thank You, Lord, for the strength. Oh God, please help this man that I love to find his strength and his soul. Help him to be the true instrument of Thy word. Help him to forgive himself for this pain I am suffering."

I could not believe this woman with the saintly name. Was it true? Had she left us mere mortals here on earth and gone to dwell among gods? In that moment, before my very eyes, she had risen to a plateau most only speak about. This was pure, unconditional love. I knelt down beside her, not to pray but to pay homage to this woman who had become what I only pretended to be, and to make her a promise of fidelity I never intended to break. She retained that composure for the rest of the evening, was even at times close to being cheerful. Sometimes, riding on the wings of faith in your pain makes you feel close to God. But the night proved she was only human after all. Endlessly she tossed and turned. Sleep would not come to her. With each movement my opened eyes were forced to witness this agony I could not stop. How stupid and insane if I had destroyed it all. Strangely, I thought about my mother. Was I guilty of what I had observed in her? Had I sabotaged my happiness because I didn't believe I deserved it? The fact was, I hadn't gone to any great lengths to conceal my affair with the Countess. I wished Paris were here to tell me what to do, to talk to Masaya for me.

I could hear my woman muffling her tears, then quietly slip down from the bed to her knees. It even occurred to me to call on

God, to try and make things right with Him; to become truly righteous. But the sacrifices of the righteous were far more than I wanted to make. I kept hearing the words God spoke to Nicodemus: "Go sell all you have and give everything to the poor." There would be no center stage for me, no twisted dream to pursue. Finally Masaya climbed back into bed, and I drifted uncomfortably into a jerky sleep.

The next day we both pretended nothing had stepped in the way of our happiness. Masaya made a gallant effort to cover any trace of her pain, but it was still evident in the quick flash of her eyes. I suggested we take a leave from the responsibilities of the ministry. She agreed. The deal was struck, not verbally, but a mental agreement. We would ride it out the way we always had. We set aside our church wear in favor of common street clothes, and took her sports car. We drove to Manhattan, visited art galleries and a museum, then had lunch at Scofield's—raw clams and wine. We had done it all a hundred times before, but we were attempting to escape from the present by reliving our past. In the Village we stopped at every store, listened to poets in coffeehouses. We made a great show of it, but it didn't work. By the time we made it back to our home, her pain had turned to anger. It exploded as soon as we were inside.

"Just one question, Jimmie. *Why?*"

I couldn't answer.

"Didn't I satisfy you? Weren't we good together?"

I nodded my head, but still couldn't speak. A look of sadness, coupled with a hot rage, darkened her face.

"I can't get past it," she said.

"Masaya . . . ?"

"I can't, Jimmie. I have to go."

There was finality in her voice and in her eyes. For a second the world went dark, as if someone had turned it off. A blackness that carried no sound engulfed me. In an instant, wave after wave of fear invaded my total being. She was really leaving. I could not move. I stood there in the doorway and watched her pack, the way she had watched me. When she finished, she pushed the buzzer for the driver. Now she avoided looking me in the eyes—busying herself with a rush of nothing. The driver came quickly and was quickly out the door loaded down with her luggage. Independently, she struggled with the remaining bags, hesitating for a moment only. "Don't call me, Jimmie," she warned, and then she was gone. These words cut me deep, echoed over and over in my consciousness.

My decline began as soon as she left. First there was that hollow feeling and deafening silence, coupled with a loss of direction. I could hardly remember what I had done with my life before her. And then the pain began, creeping up on me like some crawling monster unleashed. I ran to the bed the way a child would, but there was no sanctuary under the covers—only her scent still faint on the sheets. Her touch was everywhere—in the drapes and matching spread—the cool sky-blue she had ordered the room painted. She had made me love fire places, bearskin rugs, antique lamps, and the music of Charlie Christian. My despair and my shame confined me to a single room in a mansion of thirty. After a day Mom Myrtle sent Sonni to me with a tray. There was no other contact with the world outside, except to phone an assistant minister to stand in for me on Sunday. The pain continued. Always the pain. I couldn't bring myself to call her parents' house, and hear them tell me she didn't want to talk. I couldn't bear that. She was suffering too, I knew. But she held all the cards. She had right on her side, and she could hold on to the strength in her anger. For me there was nothing, no one to blame but Jimmie Lamar. Being wrong can drown you in your own self-pity and guilt. I fought furiously to pull myself out of it, to stay alive, and then maybe I didn't fight at all. Maybe death had claimed my spirit without me knowing it (*"M-a-s-a-y-a!"*). The sound of her name resonated as a whisper in my brain. As time progressed, I found more love for her than for myself. It was my memory of her that was flourishing while my life was fading.

Nine days after she had gone, I became very ill. An excruciating pain settled in my stomach along with a crippling headache that blurred my vision. Nausea and diarrhea were constant companions. I called a physician who was a member of my temple. He could find nothing. "A virus of some kind," he thought, but the pills he gave me failed to assuage the unbearable physical and mental stress the evening brought. I lay in my bed unable to move, lest I increase my suffering. Masaya's image was always with me.

So emaciated was I at twilight, I was forced to make a mental retreat from this overwhelming present. Even a prison farm camp was more appealing to my imagination. I drifted back easily, shedding my pain as I went to reunite with my adopted father.

How frightened I was of the unknown those first few days, but even more frightened to show it. I had quickly been forced into the thick of hard-core prison life, first a fight with an inmate who would take my manhood, then a conflict with a guard who resented my dignity. Now, on my second Sunday, I walked the compound with King Fish. "You gotta look out for Snooky," he told me. "He'll try to steal ya. Don't eva turn yo' back. Hit ain't ova." He paused. "Ya got a woman?" he asked. I told him about Masaya. "Can't do no time thinkin' 'bout no woman, got ta be all hea wit' yo' mine. This yo' home now. Thinkin' 'bout a woman can make ya wanta die 'sted of livin' ta go home. Folks that ain't neva gittin' out gotta play them ol' times ova and ova, 'cause they ain't got nothin' else." He stopped suddenly and pointed to a small sharp-faced fellow standing in the doorway of another bunkhouse. "See that l'il niggah ova there? That's Weasel. Watch out fo' him, too. He one of Snooky's hoes. Snooky might put him up ta do sumthin' ta ya." Damn, I thought, now I have to watch out for two of them. I felt a cold shudder when I thought about dying in prison—so far away from home. "I'm gonna stick wit' cha, young blood," King Fish said to reassure me. I knew he was in my corner then. He was saying he'd put his life on the line for me. We took one last turn, then headed back to our bunkhouse. I heard the single crack of a rifle from the gun tower and immediately saw a man fall off the high fence. Two trustees and a guard rushed over to him. "Somebody dun hit the fence," King Fish stated coolly. "Tried to escape in broad daylight?" I asked. He shook his head. "Not escape, just git out. Anybody hit that fence wit' them sharpshooters in the towers know he gon' leave one way only." We were ordered back inside our bunkhouse by screaming trustees and guards. I saw them dragging the man's lifeless body before we went inside. The killing was all the talk in the bunkhouse. It seems the inmate was a killer himself who had once lived in our house and had fifteen years in on forever. I thought of King Fish, and I was glad I wasn't him.

We walked to our bunks past the cool stares of the men who grunted their hellos to King Fish while ignoring me completely. I hadn't been accepted. "C'mon, young blood. I'm gonna hip ya how to move the 'light' so you an' all-'round player." He produced a tiny piece of mirror and handed it to me.

One Sunday, a week later, while walking the compound, he spoke to me from deep inside himself. "I neva tol' nobody this, young blood, but my wife lef' me fo' another man. I been making excuses fo' her all these hea years. See, I couldn't be mad at her. Where was I gonna go fo' my memories?" This confession was difficult for him, but still, for some reason, he seemed compelled to make it. "Young blood, I dun learned ya how to play the light, even how to play above these crackuhs in hea, but that ain't nothin' when it comes to women. Its them what runs the wurl'. We think we grifters? Huh! Besides them we ain't nothin' but marks." I resisted that theory and asked him why he believed it. He laughed that big laugh. " 'Cause they takes ova a man's hol' life and makes him like hit. Now that's playin'." A sudden blur of an image caught my peripheral vision. A movement so quick my mind failed to grasp its meaning. King Fish was quicker. He caught the blade of Snooky's knife on his forearm, blocking a plunge toward my chest. Before I could react, Snooky had fled. Blood cascaded down King Fish's arm onto the ground. He cursed loudly. I tore off my shirt and wrapped his arm, applying pressure to stop the bleeding. We both walked coolly down to the little shack inhabited by an alcoholic doctor who could find no other work.

After King Fish was bandaged and we were back in the bunkhouse, I got in touch with that kind of anger which allows a man to do murder. I now knew firsthand how an inmate with a relatively light sentence could easily parlay that sentence into the rest of his life. I wanted to kill Snooky. Strangely enough, it was King Fish who talked me out of it. "But the motherfucker tried to kill me, Fish!" "I know, young blood, but ya goin' home soon." "I'm not goin' home at all if I let that punk kill me." "He ain't gonna try no mo'. He think we after him now. Probably gon' git himself put in the red-hat cell."

King Fish was right. That next evening after work, word came to us. Snooky had turned himself in as the assailant and was now in the red-hat cell.

King Fish looked vulnerable, lying on his cot with a bandaged arm in a sling—even weak. The truth was, he was not young anymore. Maybe I saw his age for the first time. He looked sad and alone. Without me there was nothing for him. "My wife lef' me fo' another man," I heard him say again in my mind.

Then I rushed back to the present. The pain was there waiting. But this time sheer terror accompanied me. King Fish's statement had triggered a concern of my own. The thought of Masaya with another man hadn't occurred to me before. Now it loomed large as a possibility. I was forced to call her. But what if she wasn't at her parents' house—what then? How would I keep from going insane? What if she refused to talk? They had to let me speak to her NOW! I'd make them understand how important it was. My heart pounded in my ears as I dialed the number. Masaya was my woman. She was going to be my wife. It rang twice and then I heard a cheerful "Hello." It was her! How could she be cheerful when I was suffering so? Had she been expecting someone? Did he make her happy? Was she giving herself to him? I'd go over there . . . I heard the "Hello?" again, questioning this time.

"Masaya, it's me," I heard myself say.

There was silence.

"I have to see you!" My voice cracked.

Her response was whispered in a voice laced with tears. "I can't, Jimmie!"

Then the phone clicked in my ear. I wouldn't beg her—begging would only make things worse, cause her to lose the little respect for me she had. I was at a dead end. Everything came down on me at once, and with such violence my body became cold. I lay shivering for two hours, freezing in my own sweat, trying to hold my vomit inside. I could find no relief. It brought me to tears. Then I became angry for crying. I had told her I was sorry. She could have forgiven me this one weakness. She wasn't perfect herself. Holding it against me proved that. I was so sick and she didn't give a damn. What if I died? Would she forgive me then? Dying didn't really seem so bad, now that I thought about it. It would mean freedom from this agony and she would be sorry. I needed her to be sorry.

There was a strong knock on the door. It wasn't Sonni. This knock was filled with confidence, a different familiarity. My heart danced. My hopes soared. I struggled to get there. When I opened the door, Mom Myrtle stood motionless, holding two candles—one black and one white. Her eyes spoke a language I had not heard from her—something so foreign and so powerful it altered the shape of her face, made her appear younger somehow, but not young. Without speaking, she suddenly passed me boldly, found two holders, and lit the candles.

"White is for cleansing and for hope," she said. "Black gonna put you in touch with the earth, help you fine the Light in the dark."

I shook my head. I didn't need this hocus-pocus.

"You sit on the bed!" she ordered.

I obeyed silently. I'd let her have her ritual and then maybe she would leave. I felt a heated hand on my forehead. So much heat.

"This is where the sickness is," she said. "I can make you well whenever you're ready."

I started to protest. Her hand became firmer.

"You don't believe me, do you? God gives us all the power to heal ourselves. I'm here to tell you there's another choice. You can choose well over sick."

I remembered something King Fish had said about this. "If you think someone can heal you, they can." Her hand was soothing like my mother's and Paris's. Time passed and in the silence I began to trust her, the way you trust a doctor, priest, or your Sunday-school teacher. I latched on in desperation to these images her touch invoked, and rode to safety. Then came the shock.

"You don't know who I am," she told me. "But I know who you are. I was never took in by all those empty words you speak so good. I was filled with joy the first time I saw you only because I marveled at this God of mine who would pick a sinner like you to turn into a prophet. Yes, I know who you are, but you don't."

I became speechless, not for the obvious reasons, but rather because of a discovery I had just made. It was she who had been instrumental in Masaya's transformation—the prayer meetings together, the good deeds, and the deep friendship. She had become to Masaya what King Fish once was to me. To add to this discovery the pain had vanished.

"Give her time," she said. "A woman like her needs time to heal."

And then she walked out.

I slept well that night. Her last words had given me hope—confidence that Masaya was not doing what I had.

I woke up missing Masaya, as usual, but there was no sickness. I knew I would carry a torch, but no more self-destruction. Sonni knocked on the door. There was a call from the Countess on the temple phone downstairs.

The presentation was a snobbish, self-indulgent affair held at the temple in Harlem which relegated
me to a supporting role. The reporters were more
interested in the socialites than the recipient of the donation.
There was one high note: the young colored reporter from the
Harlem News. Her professionalism made me proud.

"So, we meet at last, Father Lamar," she said.

"It was you who wrote the article on me?"

Her smile was nice, even sincere, and filled with enthusiasm.
"Don't look so surprised. Women are coming up in the world."

I thanked her for the flattering article.

"Our people are in desperate need of a righteous leader, Father
Lamar. I hope you are up to the task."

With those words she left to join the others.

I was photographed receiving the check from the Countess and
a few friends. Her smile revealed to me alone its hidden meaning.
Luckily Masaya wasn't there, I thought. Afterward the other
women to whom I had been introduced earlier wished me well in
my ministry. When the opportunity permitted, the Countess made
a sign with her hand for me to call her. I was tempted. I needed
the warmth of a woman's body next to mine, but I had made a
promise to myself.

Within an hour everyone was gone. A sudden sadness almost broke me again, and I thought about Sidney. I drove straight to Long Island. I had to talk to him. Of course I realized he was less than he had ever been. I knew only a trace of the old Sidney existed, but he was still my friend. The sorrow I felt for him was no longer an excuse for my estrangement. The truth was, my own sorrow for having lost him had played a major role in it all, but no more.

As I drew nearer this warehouse of lost souls, remembering the past joys of our lives made me stronger somehow, gave me a smile to wear.

Cold and gray, these buildings void of character and of art stood like giant defiant stones that had created themselves. Their lack of feeling was matched only by the lack of feeling in the people who ran the institution. More important than Sidney's name was the number they had assigned to it. More important still was the fact I wasn't white. Luckily, they had heard of Father Lamar. There was no hope for Sidney in the conversation an administrator had with me. With the exception of an outburst of laughter and tears on a couple of occasions, Sidney had not spoken. I was led to an elevator that climbed three floors, then down a long hallway to a door with the letter "Z" painted in red on it. The administrator used a heavy key and let me inside. It was a large room painted white with bars on the windows and plastic chairs—some occupied, some empty. The patients were all lost in a world they had created for themselves. Like children, they issued stern orders and responded to questions unasked. One man sang, another danced a slow waltz, alone without music. They all acted out their own little vignette, all except Sidney. He sat at the far end of the room, staring at the wall. I was advised to report any trouble to a huge man who looked like a storm trooper, and stood with his arms folded, to my right. I summoned my smile, just in case, and approached Sidney. Several times I spoke his name softly, but there was nothing—no recognition, no change in his stare. I pulled up a chair beside him and focused on the spot where his stare led me.

Then I forced my mind to connect with his. I sat there for a while until I felt something. Imagined or real, there was something.

"She left me," I said. "It was my fault, Sid. I messed up. Maybe you were right—maybe God makes you pay for the life you live. Maybe all three of us are paying . . ."

I had to laugh.

"But it sure was fun. Remember our first sting together? That car salesman? He deserved it, Sid. And the party you and Masaya made me pay for? You got so drunk man, so drunk!"

I placed my hand on his forehead for a moment, and then I left my friend. When I got into the car this time, I felt better.

Suddenly I missed my home, not New Jersey or New York, but the small town where it all began for me, where birds are not afraid to sing in the morning, and butterflies are more than just a photograph in a child's textbook. Even with this city's magic and allure, I still found something comforting about quiet streets, high-school football games, and couples who stayed married forever. Funny how we keep reaching back to a past that continuously eludes us. The sweetness of my childhood now dangled before me like lush unattainable fruit. And there was Mama—oh, how I missed her now.

I stepped on the gas. Maybe someday I would go back, but today there was only Masaya.

It was dark when I finally made it to Jersey, but the mansion was lit up like a holiday. Inside Mom Myrtle's prayer meeting was just ending. I was greeted by all with a cheerful hello, intended to convey their lasting support. Paul was more direct. He dashed into my arms. Happy and Sonni were among them, ten Saints in all, each with an outside guest, a once-a-month practice Mom Myrtle had begun. I felt almost like an outsider myself in her presence, not actually one of them; and yet, I was still their spiritual leader. I was gracious and personable with the guests, but I had to speak to Mom Myrtle—alone. After squeezing Paul close to me, I sent him along with Happy, who was now teaching him to play the piano, and walked with Mom Myrtle into my study.

I was surprised I had been guilty of such a gross underestimation

of her. Now I realized that only she might hold the key to a reconciliation between me and Masaya.

"Did you talk to her?" I asked hurriedly. "Did she tell you I
called? She wouldn't talk to me."

Mom Myrtle was silent for a moment. "She's trying to save her
soul, Jimmie, keep her faith in her pain."

It was the first time she had referred to me as "Jimmie."

"I just need her with me," I said.

"You still don't understand. God's gonna have His way in all of
this. The only way you ever gonna git close to Masaya again—you
gotta get close to God. You think He done let you rise up the way
He did just so you can suit yourself? He done called you, boy, and
you better hear Him."

She offered me her dreams as proof of what she was saying—
said she saw me in them before she had ever met me. There were
other powers she said I had been blessed with. Like her, I had the
gift to help people heal themselves. All of this was part of the vision
God had given her. Then she showed me how God had worked
His will in my life: the creation of the Saints, building that children's facility onto the mansion, and the plans for the old-folks
home I had made were nothing short of God working through me.
It was something to consider. I really hadn't that far to go to total
salvation. I had always believed in God, and it could be said from
our past relationship, He believed in me. I remembered how He
had stood by me in my childhood. It was true, in spite of all my
troubles, I had lived a blessed life. Now, in the quiet of the room,
I dropped to my knees in prayer as she did. It felt good to purge
myself, to move toward righteousness. I confessed my innermost
thoughts in silence, my greed and my obsession with my own glory.
I even confessed about Passion, as if He didn't know. There were
promises of truth in my ministry made, and a promise to make
Masaya an honest woman if He brought her back to me. Suddenly
the idea of me being a true prophet became appealing, more plau-
sible. Why not me? I may have done some wrong, maybe even
blasphemed a little, as Sidney had suggested. But I never denied
God. I was never as bad as some of the rest. I wished God would

give me a sign. Then I thought maybe He had. Maybe Masaya's and Mom Myrtle's belief in my calling was indeed that sign. Mom Myrtle's smile bespoke her approval. "I told you once I saw God in your eyes; now I see Him all over you," she said.

The next day was Sunday, and in the temple that morning I felt wonderfully different, as if I had made a discovery I had known all my life. How proud Masaya would be. My sermon was on the fiery furnace and Shadrach, Meshach, and Abednego. I preached about trusting God as they had. Mom Myrtle's nod of approval inspired me, as did the frequent shouts of "Amen" from the Saints. My transformation began to grow inside of me like a living thing. I became one with the congregation and they with me. The room filled itself with the Spirit. All inhibitions were cast away and we began to dance in the glory of the Lord. I tasted the sweetness of true salvation, and it caused me to tremble and speak in tongues. My eyes ran wet with tears of joy. There in the temple, with His praise on my lips, God spoke to me. Not in some great resounding voice, but with the breath of a whisper on my cheek, and a thought that I had been given the power to effect a healing. The call I made to the sick came without warning, even without my permission. They came quickly down the aisle and stood in front of the pulpit. One was an old man hampered by arthritic legs. I bent down and grabbed them firmly with both my hands. My hands, too, like Mom Myrtle's, were consumed with heat, as if an ungrounded current had passed through them.

"Do you believe?" I asked.

"Yes!" he replied.

"Do you believe in the power of the true and living God?"

He began to weep. "Yes," he whispered.

I could clearly feel his pulse and hear the pattern of his breathing; so loud and clear they were. I matched my own with them. I squeezed his legs.

"Do you believe God can give you the power to heal yourself?"

"Yes!"

"Do you believe?"

"Yes!"

I freed his legs. "Then walk in God's glory!"

And he did, straight and strong as a young man.

"Oh, my God!" he cried. "Oh, my God!"

So drained was I when I rose up, I stumbled backward, almost falling. Mom Myrtle rushed to the pulpit and guided me to my seat; then she addressed the other sick people and the congregation.

"Father Lamar gave all he can today. God bless you. This service is over."

Besides the obvious, there are other advantages to reaching salvation. Most of all the world slows, enabling you to inhale its beauty—makes you conscious of being alive; the way, perhaps, a near-death experience does. And so it was with me. My life took on a different coloring, a new flavor. My love for Masaya now lost its urgency, settled into a warm peaceful flow that was equally sustaining, permanently etched into the days of our existence. I told myself I had no need to possess her now. This is what I told myself; but still, I was lonely. And there was King Fish. What should I think of him—a man who had openly rejected God? How would his image fare next to my newfound redemption? I was deeply troubled. There is no choice between God and man. The events of King Fish's life story flashed before me and I searched for an answer until my mind was exhausted. It came one morning. It wasn't that he hadn't believed in God, but more that he felt abandoned by God. He had not been an atheist. He, being a child of a great tragedy, had never learned to communicate with Him. I prayed that he not be judged too harshly in the hereafter.

In the following days I looked to Mom Myrtle for guidance. Becoming a prophet is much more difficult than portraying one. It is a person's perception of himself that stands at the center of every decision he makes about others. She conveyed this to me in a pure and direct way. "Now, Father Lamar, you speak for God. Everything you say, everything you do, is done in His name." She warned me how truly responsible I was for the well-being, even the life, of one seeking my advice; that thinking of others over myself had to be my chief concern. This is who I was now. These were the times when Paul and I became closest. Before then, I hadn't given myself time to appreciate his brightness and his charm. At ten years of age he was easily as mature and smart as any fourteen-year-old. He was well-spoken, and even quoted from the Scriptures to make a point. With confidence he informed me that he, too, intended to be a minister. He never talked about Masaya, so I concluded that they had been in regular contact with each other. He never spoke about his natural mother either, and neither did Mom Myrtle. It was obvious that complete silence on the matter was the rule, but she and I had become like mother and son. I told her everything about me, even about Mama and Shirley.

"It's time I told you a story," she said while we were having tea alone in the study one evening. She rose up from the coffee table and began to walk, almost pacing. Clasped hands and a knitted brow spoke of the pain of remembering. Then her story unfolded.

It began as a paradise for two on a Caribbean island. One, a native fisherman, the other a restaurant owner from Harlem on vacation. They fell in love and were married. The woman sold her business in Harlem and opened one in "paradise." A daughter was born to them and, in time, an illegitimate son to the daughter. The daughter loved her father more than anything, almost became the son he had hoped for. Her child loved his grandmother and his grandmother adored him. They had been very happy. On the fishing boat one day, on which the father and daughter, often to the chagrin of others, went together, tragedy struck, and they were lost at sea. Suddenly Mom Myrtle broke down. She couldn't prevent the tears. I rushed over to console her, but she refused. Her anger took over. "There's no paradise on this earth. There's only God. I took my baby and left that island that stole my happiness!" She was reading my face for a response when the phone rang. Mom Myrtle picked it up.

"Hello, Father Lamar's House of Peace . . . This is Mom Myrtle."

There was silence and a very troubled look on her face.

"I'll be there as soon as I can. Tell her."

She hung up the phone. "Masaya took real sick. That was her mother. Masaya wants me to come."

A selfish thought flashed across my mind. Why didn't she ask for me? I went to the door and called for the driver to bring the Rolls around.

"I'll drive you," I said, "even though she didn't ask for me."

"Don't be petty, boy. You know Masaya's got her pride too. Only reason she ain't talked to you because she love you so much, and scared of gittin' hurt again."

"I'm a true man of God now. I would never do that again."

"I believe you, Jimmie, and I told her. I think she needs to see for herself."

The driver brought me the keys. As soon as we were inside the car, Mom Myrtle began to pray. I, on the other hand, was not afraid for Masaya. I knew this was God's way of bringing us back together. Also, between Mom Myrtle and me, the power to effect a healing was awesome.

When we arrived, Masaya's mother's face was frozen with fear. Her father was drawn and quiet, the way a man becomes when he feels helpless. The introductions were made quickly. The focus being mainly on Masaya's room down the hall.

"The doctor just left," her mother informed us. "He gave her something to kill the pain and to make her sleep."

"What did he say?" I asked.

She shook her head. "He has to run tests."

A strange anxiety overtook me as I neared the door—part joy and part apprehension. I entered her room with a painted smile. Mom Myrtle rushed over to her bedside with a big tender embrace. Then Masaya's eyes found mine. She did look weak. All the color and luster was washed from her face. Only her eyes refused to succumb to the illness. Quick and alert, they related her innermost feelings to me. Above all else, the love was still there. I walked over and kissed her softly on the lips, and even in her sickness, she brought my passion to life. I wanted her badly. We simply stared at each other. Mom Myrtle took the hint. "Trust in the Lord, chile," she said. "I'll come back later." She left the room. Masaya's parents followed. Masaya's smile was weak, but constant—void of any anger or cynicism.

"What did the doctor tell you?"

She shook her head. "They don't know, Jimmie. None of them know. I just got weaker and weaker."

"There is someone who knows," I reminded her.

She was delighted. This was her personal proof.

"Let's say a silent prayer together," I said.

She closed her eyes. When we finished I spoke again.

"Listen to what I'm saying. God wants you well."

"You should know I never stopped loving you," she said.

"You wouldn't even talk to me," I replied with a smile.

"Don't joke, Jimmie. I think I might be dying."

For the first time I saw fear in her face.

"No, baby, you're not. God is here with us. You have a choice, honey. You can choose well over sick. With God, I can do anything. I can even heal myself. Say it!" I told her.

She repeated it. I pressed her forehead.

"Say it again and believe it!"

She did as I asked and then she said, "I love you, Jimmie," and was fast asleep. I called my driver and told him to pick up Mom Myrtle. I was not leaving Masaya. When Mom Myrtle and Masaya's parents walked in, I put my finger to my lips. They backed out quickly. All was quiet now. I sat in a chair beside her bed, not moving. Not even aware of my own thoughts—falling into the blackness of a deep sleep.

A terrible scream shattered the night and sent me in a frantic rush to her side. Masaya lay in a fetal position—her mouth half-open, her eyes wide with terror, trembling like a frightened child. Her parents came rushing in.

"We need an ambulance!" I shouted.

Her father complied. Her mother rushed to her bedside. I cradled Masaya's head in my arms. Her mother petted her lightly on the face. Masaya attempted to speak, but another scream, more terrifying than the first, escaped her lips. This one permeated my soul. It took away my breath. The sharp haunting sound lingered on through every attempt I made to comfort my love, through every tender word, and each gentle stroke of my hand, through every tear, until it finally blended with the distant scream of the approaching ambulance.

Somehow I became lost to this present reality. My mind shifted to a place where I was a spectator witnessing a series of dark face-less images, acting out a tragic scene from some play without a name. Still, I was vaguely aware of the emergency lights, the ride in the ambulance, even the shadow of death that hovered over us like some giant apparition. I had to escape, and I did. My mind soared far above all that threatened my sanity. Higher and higher, into another world of time gone by. I could hear the laughter of children there, and my mother's footsteps chasing behind me as I ran through the park. "I'm gonna get you, you little devil," she would promise, quickly catching me and swinging me into the air. There would be warm kisses that covered my face and candy that would suddenly appear in her hand. I could remain there forever in this world of butterflies and mulberry trees, hidden safely beneath the blanket of yesterday. Somewhere among these fuzzy images a doctor's face appeared and the word "cancer" was spoken.

I remember a long air-conditioned corridor with no end and Masaya, her face ashen and still, being rushed through a set of swinging doors. We waited, forever, her parents and I, afraid to move, no words to speak. "God, don't leave me now," I said.

In the morning, when the nurse entered she walked directly over to me. "She's asking for you," she said. She was very professional in her manner, crispy clean in her uniform of white, and she held her head proud, as nurses usually do. I moved in her direction. "Come with me, please," she said, with no hint of what I should expect. I could feel the support of Masaya's parents as if all their hopes depended on me, as if my seeing her could make the difference. I followed the nurse down the corridor and around the corner, where she stopped in front of a private room. "She's very sick and heavily sedated. She may be asleep." Then she turned and walked away.

Quickly, I went to Masaya's bed, careful not to awaken her, but wanting to. I watched her lying before me, beautiful even then, in her illness and her deep sleep, like Mama. The memories that I had resisted crept from their hiding place, one by one—like thieves. They assaulted my senses, invaded every sinew of my body, forcing me to recall each celebration of our love—her misty eyes, the taste of her lipstick, the scent of her perfumed hair, and of course, that very first night when God gave her to me. "Please don't take her away," I whispered. I fell to my knees and rested my head lightly on her breast the way I had sometimes done when I needed strength. The sound of her heartbeat overtook me. I lost my bearings, along with my awareness of time and place. My body shook. "Mama," I whispered. "I'm sick, Mama. Don't leave me!" I felt her hand on my face. Her voice was a weak whisper.

"You are a prophet."

Her lips were gently smiling when I looked up into her face.

"You're going to be fine," I said, and kissed her softly on the mouth. "Just fine," I repeated in a desperate effort to convince myself.

"You owe me a wedding. . . ." she stated weakly.

"I know!" I said quickly.

She winced in pain. Then her eyes began to slowly lose their focus, as if she were entering into a deep meditation, slipping away from this reality, until the light in them disappeared, until death covered her face like a thin sheet of winter ice. I heard myself howl like a beast, a great pitiful sound that brought a doctor and two nurses rushing into the room. I cursed the nurses. I cursed the doctors. I cursed God. They left me with Masaya. The thought to join her was foremost in my mind. God had abandoned me the way He had done King Fish. Now I had to hurry, find a way to be with Masaya. "Wait for me, baby," I whispered, and rushed out the back way down the stairs. For some reason, I couldn't face her parents. Outside the hospital, I decided to walk. I needed time, time to think of a suitable way to die. And then somehow the fear of death crept in, made me ashamed of my cowardice. I walked for two hours until I was exhausted. I cried for Masaya and for myself. Finally I flagged a taxi.

It was during the funeral that I knew I still wanted to live, when I touched that cold, hard shell that used to be Masaya. When the finality of death struck me.

Afterward I went home to Sugar Hill. My memories could better nourish me there. A month passed like a day. I opened the door for no one. This reality was not for me. All that I loved was beneath the earth. I joined them day and night with my mind. Soon the months turned into a year of self-pity. I was responsible to no one—not the temple, not even to myself.

One evening Paul came all alone to my home. This was not the first time. But this time, without Mom Myrtle, he was persistent. He pounded on my door and cried until I let him in. Then a boy of eleven exercised his will over mine, almost demanding I come back to the living and be his father.

Year by year I helped Mom Myrtle to guide his growth, and year by year I felt guilty toward Masaya for finding happiness without her.

Now thirty years have passed. I never got over Masaya and I never preached again. Maybe, in a way, I was getting back at God. I'm sure He understands—I'm still here. Mom Myrtle is too. Paul is now the head minister at the temple. Oh, I still attend service. I just don't preach. There are times when I ask myself what this thing called "life" is all about, and I think maybe King Fish was right in what he said. "Life is like some big ol' play, makin' folks laugh sometimes and sometimes makin' 'um cry."